Jillian Hart grew up on her family's homestead, where she helped raise cattle, rode horses and scribbled stories in her spare time. After earning her English degree from Whitman College, she worked in travel and advertising before selling her first novel. When Jillian isn't working on her next story, she can be found puttering in her rose garden, curled up with a good book or spending quiet evenings at home with her family.

Betsy St. Amant has a heart for three things—chocolate, new shoes and sharing the amazing news of God's grace through her novels. She lives in Louisiana with her adorable story-telling young daughter, a collection of Austen novels and an impressive stash of pickle Pringles. A freelance journalist and fiction author, Betsy is a member of American Christian Fiction Writers. When she's not reading, writing or singing along to a Disney soundtrack with her daughter, Betsy enjoys inspirational speaking and teaching the craft of writing.

Wyoming Sweethearts

Jillian Hart

&

Rodeo Sweetheart

Betsy St. Amant

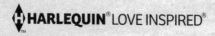
HARLEQUIN® LOVE INSPIRED®

 LOVE INSPIRED BOOKS

Recycling programs for this product may not exist in your area.

ISBN-13: 978-1-335-00662-2

Wyoming Sweethearts and Rodeo Sweetheart

Copyright © 2017 by Harlequin Books S.A.

The publisher acknowledges the copyright holders of the individual works as follows:

Wyoming Sweethearts
Copyright © 2011 by Jill Strickler

Rodeo Sweetheart
Copyright © 2010 by Betsy St. Amant

www.Harlequin.com

Printed in U.S.A.

CONTENTS

WYOMING SWEETHEARTS   7
Jillian Hart

RODEO SWEETHEART   229
Betsy St. Amant

WYOMING SWEETHEARTS

Jillian Hart

To Keneta

I will sing to the Lord,
because He has dealt bountifully with me.
—*Psalms* 13:6

Chapter One

"Do you know what your problem is, Eloise?"

"I didn't know I had a problem, Gran." Eloise Tipple held the diner's heavy glass door for her frail grandmother and resisted the urge to roll her eyes. Her helpful gran had been doling out a lot of advice over the past three months, ever since Eloise returned home to the small town of Wild Horse, Wyoming. "When I look at my life, I see blue skies. No trouble of any kind."

"Then you aren't looking closely enough, my dear." Edie Tipple padded by, the hem of her sensible summer dress fluttering lightly in the wind. "Your life has been derailed. I intend to fix that."

"It wasn't derailed, Gran. I had a car accident, not a train accident," she quipped. She let the diner's door swoosh shut, adjusted her pink metallic cane and followed the sprightly elderly lady toward a gleaming 1963 Ford Falcon. She hoped humor would derail her grandmother because Eloise knew precisely what track Edie was on. "Are you going to stop by the church before you head home?"

"Don't try and change the subject on me." Gran

hauled open her car door. "It wasn't fair the way you lost your career and your fiancé."

"We had only discussed marriage, he hadn't actually proposed to me."

"That's still a big loss. It cost you so much." Gran rolled down the window, cranking away on the old-fashioned handle. "I have a solution in mind."

"A solution?" Oh, boy. She gave her long blond hair a toss. The car accident had ended her ice-dancing career, a career she had desperately loved, and her heart had been broken by a man who left her for someone else. At twenty-four, a girl didn't want to feel as if the best part of her life was behind her. She didn't want to think there were no more dreams left in store. "You don't mean another blind date?"

"There's nothing blind about it. I know the boy's grandmother. He's the one for you, Eloise. I can feel it in my bones." Gran folded herself elegantly behind the wheel, diminutive in stature but great of spirit. Her silver curls fluttered with the brush of the breeze as she clicked her lap belt.

"I don't want to go on another fix-up." Eloise gently closed the heavy car door with a thud. "The last twelve have been complete disasters. I don't want to be tortured anymore."

"How hard can it be to have a nice dinner with a young man?" Gran recovered her car key from behind the visor and plugged it into the ignition. The engine roared to life with a rumble and a big puff of smoke. "His name is George, and he's an up-and-comer. I have it on good authority that he's a hard worker and very tidy. That's important when you're considering a man as marriage material."

"Sure. I'll make a note of it." Eloise, unable to stop herself, rolled her eyes.

"I saw that, young lady." Gran chuckled. "You don't want to work at the inn for the rest of your days, do you?"

"I don't know. I like my job. I'm trying not to look too far ahead. My future may be an endless line of one blind date after another. Scary. Better to live in the moment." She pushed away from the car door. "Thanks for meeting me for lunch, Gran."

"Then I'll tell Madge to tell George it's a date." Gran put the car into reverse. "Friday night at the diner. Don't frown, dear. Hebrews 11:1. Believe."

"I'll try." At this point, she was a skeptic when it came to happily-ever-afters. She was recovering from a broken heart. Love hadn't turned out well for her. Could she endure one more blind date?

She simply would have to find a way. The hot, late May sun chased her as she circled around to her car, slipped behind the steering wheel and dropped onto the vinyl seat. Hot, hot, hot. Eloise rolled down the window and switched on the air conditioner, which sputtered unenthusiastically. She swiped bangs from her forehead and backed out of the space.

Now faith is the substance of things hoped for, the evidence of things not seen. That was the verse Gran had referenced, and it stayed on her mind as she drove down the dusty, one-horse main street. The precise stretch of sidewalk-lined shops, the march of trees from one end of town to the other, hadn't changed much since she was a child.

Way up ahead on the empty street, a pair of ponies plodded into sight, ridden by two little girls heading toward the drive-in. They were probably getting ice cream. Memories welled up, good ones that made her smile as she motored toward the library.

She caught sight of the grill of the sheriff's Jeep peeking around the lilac bush next to the library sign. Sheriff Ford Sherman had his radar set up and was probably reading a Western paperback to pass the time between the span of cars.

She glanced at her speedometer—twenty-four miles an hour. Safe. She waved at the sheriff who looked up from his book and waved back.

Ice cream. That was an idea. There was nothing like the Steer In's soft ice-cream cones. Her mouth watered, clinching her decision. She had plenty of time left on her lunch hour and the temptation was too great to resist.

She hit her signal, crossed over the dotted yellow line and rolled into the drive-in's lot. The girls on their ponies had ridden up to the window in the drive-thru lane and one of the animals looked a little nervously at the approaching car's grill, so she slipped into a slot and parked beneath the shady awning. A brightly lit and yellowed display menu perched above an aging speaker. She rolled her window down the rest of the way and hot, dry air breezed in, no match for the struggling air conditioner.

"Eloise!" A teenager on roller skates gave an awkward wave and almost dropped her loaded tray. "Hi!"

"Hi, Chloe." She unbuckled so she could lean out the window. Chloe Walters still had the exuberant disposition she'd had as a small child, when Eloise had babysat her. "That's right, school is out for the year. Are you a senior now?"

"Yep. One more year and freedom." Chloe nearly

dropped her tray again as she swept forward on choppy strokes of her skates and grabbed the edge of the speaker so she wouldn't crash into the car. "It's so cool you are working at the inn. We went there for dinner for Mom's birthday and it was really fancy."

"It is a nice place to work." The Lord had been looking out for her when she'd landed the job as executive manager at the Lark Song Inn. Good thing she had a business degree to fall back on. "How about you? I didn't know you worked at the drive-in."

"It's new. I really love it. I get all the ice cream I can eat." She grinned, her smile perfect now that her braces were off, and nearly spilled the contents of her tray yet again. "I'd better go deliver this before it melts. Do you know what you want?"

"A small chocolate soft ice-cream cone." The large size was tempting, but she'd never get it eaten before she was back behind the front desk. "Thanks, Chloe."

"I'll get it in just a minute!" The teenager, eager to please, dashed off with a *clump, clump* of her skates.

A big, dark blue pickup rolled to a stop in the space beside her. Tinted windows shielded any glimpse of the driver, but she recognized the look of a ranch truck when she saw it. The haphazard blades of hay caught in the frame of the cab's back window, dust on the mud flaps and the tie-downs marching along the bed were all telltale signs. The heavy duty engine rumbled like a monster as it idled, a testimony to the payload it was capable of hauling.

Chloe, her tray now empty, skated as fast as she could go up to the far side of the pickup. Eloise lost sight of the teenager, but judging by the speed with which she'd crossed the lot, it was someone she knew or wanted to. Remembering what it was like to be a teenager in this town, she smiled. She'd worked part-time in the library after school shelving books and hadn't had the chance to meet too many cute high school boys on the job. A serious downside to being a librarian's assistant.

An electronic jangle caught her attention, and she reached over the gearshift to dig through the outside pocket of her purse for her cell phone. No surprise to see the Lark Song Inn on her caller ID. A manager's job was never done. "Let me guess. The computer system froze up again."

"Good guess." It was her boss and the owner of the inn, Cady Winslow. "But after crashing twice this morning, the computer has given up the fight and has accepted it is going to have to talk with the printer."

"Maybe it's a lover's quarrel. Now they have made up and all is well." Since she was in her purse, she dug out a few dollar bills. "Maybe it will be a happily-ever-after for the two of them."

"It had better be. If their differences of opinion last and they refuse to talk, a breakup may be pending. The printer might have to move out and we'll never see him again." Cady's sunny sense of humor made it easy to work for her. "I know you're on your break, but I'm taking off and I want to make sure you see this text. It's from my little goddaughter and I think it is about the cutest thing I've seen in a while."

"Send it."

"Here it is. I'll see you bright and early for the staff meeting tomorrow?"

"I'll be the one holding the jumbo-sized cup of coffee and yawning."

"Jumbo-sized coffee cups. I'll put that in my to-buy list." Laughing, Cady said goodbye and hung up.

"Here!" Something clattered and clanked, drawing her attention as she scrolled through her phone's list. Chloe held out her hand. "It will be a dollar fifty."

"Keep the change." Eloise handed over the bills and took the ice-cream cone thrust at her. She was trying to scroll through her phone at the same time, so she didn't instantly notice the ice cream was the wrong flavor.

"Hey, Chloe!" She hung out the window, but it was too late. No Chloe in sight. A tall, broad-shouldered shadow crowned by a wide Stetson fell across the pavement. The shadow strolled closer accompanied by the substantial pad of a cowboy's confident gait as he moseyed into view.

Handsome.

"I think there was a mix-up," he said in a deep baritone, layered with warmth and humor. "The little waitress didn't look like she had things together. Is this yours?"

"Uh…" She might be able to answer him *if* she could rip her gaze away from the shaded splendor of his face.

That turned out to be nearly impossible. The strong, lean lines of his cheekbones, the sparkling blue eyes and the chiseled jaw held her captive. He looked vaguely familiar, but her neurons were too stunned to fire.

Wow. That was the only word her beleaguered brain could come up with. Wow. Wow. Wow.

"I think the carhop girl is new at this." He swaggered over with an athletic, masculine gait.

If only his drop-dead gorgeous smile wasn't so amazing, her command of the English language might have a chance of returning. She might be able to agree with him or at least point out that Chloe was simply being Chloe.

"You didn't order a chocolate ice-cream cone?" He was near enough now that she could see the crystal blue sparkles in his irises and the smooth texture of his shaven jaw. The gray T-shirt he wore clung to muscled biceps.

Again, wow. Fortunately, the power of thought returned to her brain and she was able to move her mouth and emit a semblance of an intelligent word or two. "I did. This must be yours."

"Guilty."

"Pink ice cream. Really?" She felt a smile stretch the corners of her mouth. She arched one brow as she held out the paper-wrapped cone.

"Hey, it's strawberry, not pink." His chuckle was brief but it rumbled like dreams. He plucked the cone out of her hand and offered her the chocolate one. "That looks good. I thought about keeping it. Tell me something."

"I'm not sure that I should." She daintily licked the cone before it decided to start dripping.

"Why do you look familiar?" He leaned back against the steel arm holding the speaker and menu. "I've seen you somewhere before."

"I thought the same thing." Looking up at him with the dark Stetson shading his face and bright sunshine framing him in the background, the realization struck her like a falling meteor. She had not only seen him before, she knew him. She remembered a younger version of the handsome cowboy on the back of a horse riding through town years ago before she left town, attending the church service in a suit and tie, and in the back of the Grangers' pickup as they motored away from the diner. "You're Sean, one of Cheyenne's cousins."

"You know Cheyenne?"

"We've been best friends since kindergarten." Long distances could not change true friendship. "I'm the one with the white mare. Cheyenne and I used to always go riding."

"Now I remember." He took a bite of ice cream and nodded, his bright blue gaze traveling over her as he considered the past. "You have a gorgeous horse. Almost as fast as Cheyenne's girl."

"On the right day, sometimes she was faster. She still is." A drip landed on her knuckle, reminding her she was holding ice cream, which was obviously starting to melt. "What are you doing this far south? Don't you live with your family up near Buffalo?"

"Used to, but they tossed me out of the nest. My dad wanted me to get my master's, but I've been begging my uncle Frank for a job for years. He finally gave in."

"That's hard to believe."

"I know, that's what I tell him every day. But I'm determined not to be a disappointment." He winked, his easygoing humor only making him more attractive. He gave off the aura of a man confident of his masculinity so he didn't need to flaunt it.

"I wasn't talking about your work, I was wondering why you turned down the chance for more schooling? Why would you choose to live in Wild Horse?"

"Why not? What's not to like?" Dimples flirted with the corners of his chiseled mouth. "Clean air, more freedom than a guy knows what to do with and I get to ride my horse every day all day. There's nothing better than that."

"You are highlighting only the good parts." Why was she smiling? She simply could not seem to stop. His grin was infectious and, to make matters worse, sweet little bubbles began effervescing in her stomach. "It's an hour drive to see a movie or shop in a mall. Nothing ever happens here. Everyone knows your business."

"I don't mind all that one bit." His baby blues twinkled charmingly and made the pops in her stomach multiply.

She wasn't attracted to the man, was she? Goodness. She shook her head, determined to keep that from happening. "Then you are right where you should be. I'm currently suffering from urban withdrawal, but it's slowly getting better."

"Urban? Where?" He tilted his head a notch, leaning a fraction closer to her as if he were interested in her answer.

"Seattle." She took a swipe of ice cream before it melted and tumbled off the cone. "Where did you go to school?"

"Seattle Christian University." He chuckled. "I can't believe we used to live in the same city. Cheyenne should have mentioned it."

"She's had a lot on her mind going to vet school." Intrigued, Eloise forgot about the tingles in her tummy and the fact that the man's handsomeness pulled at her with all the gravitational force of a black hole. "Where did you live?"

"In an apartment just off Fremont Avenue. How about you?"

"I rented a house with some friends a few blocks off 45th."

"Not far away at all, not really, and we didn't even

know it. How about that?" Sean leaned back, a deliberately casual movement and yet the power of his gaze
remained locked on hers and made the world fade away.
The distant *clomp, clomp* of Chloe's skates, the nicker
from one of the ponies, the sun's heat and the whine
of the car's struggling air conditioning all turned to
silence.

An electronic ring shattered the moment, time rolled
forward and the sounds of the hot May day returned.
Chloe clomped up on her skates. "Oops. I saw you two
across the lot exchanging cones. Did I make a mistake?"

"Don't worry about it," Sean said breezily as he
tugged a cell from his pocket.

The girls on ponies rode leisurely by, licking ice-
cream cones. A diesel truck rumbled along on the street
behind her and a second electronic chime came from
the phone she didn't even remember tossing onto the
passenger seat. Right next to her cane.

Her cane. She stared at the snazzy pink length of
metal—she'd gone for the bright, cheerful color hoping to jazz up the fact of her disability—and the fizz
evaporated from her stomach. The smile died on her
lips. She knew full well Sean Granger hadn't spotted her
cane in her car or he never would have taken the time to
talk with her. This she knew from personal experience.

She glanced at the screen, where the text her boss
had sent her was overlaid by Cheyenne's cell number.
She considered answering it, but then she would wind
up saying where she was and what she was doing, and it
would be impossible not to mention the handsome man
chatting amicably on his phone a few feet away. No, best
to hit the ignore button and get back to her friend later.

"Well, duty calls." Sean pushed away and offered

her a dashing grin, making time stand still. Again. Her neurons forgot how to fire. Again. She sat captivated by the wholesome goodness of the man as he tipped his hat to her. "I'll see you around, Eloise Tipple."

"Bbb—" The closest thing she could manage to goodbye, but he didn't seem to notice her jumbled attempt at speech. He loped away with a relaxed, confident stride and hopped into his truck.

"Do you think he was mad at me?" Chloe spoke up, startling Eloise completely. The phone tumbled out of her grip and hit the floor. The teenager scrunched her face up with worry. "Are you? I couldn't believe I got your ice-cream cone wrong. My manager is right. One order at a time. I'm no good with two."

"It's not a big deal." As the truck motored away and took Sean with it, her neurons began to fire normally. Her vocabulary returned. "Have a good day, Chloe."

"I will, now the lunch rush is nearly over. Bye!"

It wasn't until Eloise had pulled onto the street heading away from town that it struck her. Sean Granger had remembered her name.

Chapter Two

Find homeless horses, Eloise scribbled onto her to-do list. This was her new assignment, added to all the others. Her desk at the inn was tucked a few steps down the hallway from the front desk. Her only window gazed out at the new rose gardens and gave a peek at the new stable. Cady wanted to offer horses for the guests to ride and that meant someone had to find the appropriate animals. That someone was her. Eloise took a sip of bottled water and smiled at the text message shining on her phone's luminous screen.

Aunt Cady, you promised to get your horses from the shelter. You have to save their lives so they can have a home and be loved.

Eloise sighed. Cady's little goddaughter's message was too cute, but how did one go about finding homeless horses? Did the county humane society take them in? There was only one way to find out. She grabbed the yellow pages out of her bottom desk drawer and began leafing through it. *If the phone book doesn't help, then Lord please send a hint or two to guide me.*

The bell above the front door chimed and the tell-tale snap of sandals on the polished hardwood had her rising to her feet. She grabbed her cane and tapped around the corner, expecting to see the Neilsons, who were yet to arrive for their reservation. So when she saw a tall, slender young woman with auburn hair and smiling eyes wearing a Washington State University shirt and denim cutoffs, she let out a surprised squeal. "Cheyenne!"

"It wouldn't have been a surprise if you checked the message I left you." She threw out her arms wide for a welcoming hug then stepped back, squinting. "You look good. Really good. How's the pain level?"

"Better. How does it feel to finally be a vet?" Eloise led the way toward the comfortable sitting area near the front desk.

"I start working for Nate next Monday, and I still can't believe this is really happening. You would have thought graduation might have made it clear to me." She shook her head, bouncing along, full of exuberance. "I'm jazzed. I can't wait to start."

"When did you get back in town?"

"Last night much later than I'd meant to. What are you doing after work?"

"Nothing exciting."

"Want to grab dinner at Clem's?"

The phone rang before she could answer, so Eloise grabbed it at the front desk. The Neilsons had landed at the airport one town away and wanted to verify their directions. Simple enough to make sure they were heading the right way. Eloise got their cell number in case they didn't show up in an hour, kept the cordless phone with her and leaned on her cane. "Want an iced latte?"

"Do you have to ask?"

They changed directions and headed for the dining room, which was nearly empty. The lunch crowd had gone and the early diners wouldn't start showing up for a few hours. Pleasant clinks and clanks from the kitchen rang like discordant music.

"So, is that yes for dinner at Clem's?" Cheyenne chose a table near a sunny window. "Or is the diner too common for you, now that you work in such a fancy place?"

"Are you kidding? I'm a diner gal through and through."

"Me, too. I'm way underdressed for this dining room." Cheyenne plucked at the collar of her T-shirt. "It's a good thing I have an in with the manager."

"Exactly, or we would toss your kind out." It was fun to banter. A great perk to being home was seeing old friends. She leaned her cane against the window sill and settled into the cushioned chair.

"You look good. How is the physical therapy coming along?"

"It's done. My leg has come as far as it can." She shrugged one shoulder, as if that wasn't a big deal. As if she didn't feel torn apart every time she said it. Life dealt you hard blows and you had to deal and keep moving forward. That's what she decided in the ambulance when she was being rushed to the trauma center. She'd known before the firemen had cut her out of the car that life would never be the same. The paralysis had improved but not disappeared, which was amazing enough. "I can ride my horse. That's the good news. I can't complain. Now, down to business. Are you ever going to tell me what really happened with Edward?"

"I told you, he thought I was getting too serious so he broke things off." Cheyenne rolled her eyes and turned her attention to Sierra, who bounded over in her black-and-white uniform. Cheyenne lit up. "Hey, I heard a rumor you're marrying my brother. Nice engagement ring."

"Shocking, but true. When he asked, I accepted." Sierra radiated happiness. "I don't know what came over me."

"I can't imagine," Cheyenne agreed. After they ordered and Sierra disappeared into the kitchen, she propped both elbows on the table and rested her chin on her hands. "So, what's new with you?"

"With me? I'm not buying the innocent look. I know exactly what you're doing."

"What am I doing? I'm just sitting here."

Eloise wished she could make her friend's pain disappear. Anyone looking at Cheyenne wouldn't guess she was nursing a broken heart. "You and Edward broke up on Valentine's Day. That's three months ago. You aren't over it, I can tell."

"I've decided to stay in denial. It isn't just a river in Egypt." Cheyenne waggled her brows.

"That isn't funny enough to distract me, and you know how I like to laugh." Eloise stretched out her bad leg and relaxed against the chair cushions. "You forget I have a romantic disaster in my past, so I know how it can feel when some guy who says he loves you up and ends things."

"Our relationship was convenient for him, that was

all." Cheyenne's face tightened, although she acted light and breezy as if she hadn't been devastated. "I'm over it."

"Wow, your denial is really strong."

"It's made out of titanium. Nothing will crack it."

"Then I guess we'd better change the subject."

"Fabulous idea."

And she knew exactly what the subject would be. The handsome cowboy from the drive-in flashed into her mind. In truth, he hadn't ever really gone away but lurked in the back of her brain like a happy thought. "I ran into your cousin in town today. He has an affinity for ice-cream cones, too."

"Right. Sean. I'm trying to remember the last time you saw him."

"Years and years ago. Probably the summer before we graduated from high school, the last summer I was home." She caught sight of Sierra returning and debated changing the subject. But why? It wasn't as if she were interested in Sean Granger. Besides, she wanted to know more about him. "He's changed. I hardly recognized him."

"He's gotten tall, hasn't he? I think he's taller than Dad."

Sierra set the glasses of icy drinks on the table. "Are you talking about Sean? He's such a nice guy. It's too bad what happened to him."

"Why? What happened?" Inquiring minds wanted to know. She leaned forward, her heart rate tapping inexplicably faster.

"Bad breakup." Sierra added two rolls of cloth napkins to the table. "She shattered his heart, or so I hear. She up and started dating someone else."

Images of the handsome cowboy hopped into Eloise's mind. Of the black Stetson shading his rugged face, the dimples bracketing his grin and the strong dependability the man exuded. "He didn't look too heartbroken to me."

"Are you kidding? It's a Granger family trait not to deal with emotions." Cheyenne took a sip of her iced coffee. "I notice you are doing the same thing, Eloise."

"Me?" She smiled at Sierra as the waitress padded away, knowing she was completely guilty. But did she want to talk about it?

No. Not in this lifetime. The cane leaning against the windowsill was proof. There was no sense crying over what you could not change. "Isn't that like the pot calling the kettle black?"

"Absolutely." Cheyenne smiled and lifted her glass for a toast. "Here's to denial and burying emotions."

"It is the only way to go."

With a laugh, they clinked glasses and the conversation turned to the evening's plans, Eloise's search for horses and Cheyenne's funny tales of her long drive home from vet school.

This was the life. Sean Granger popped the top on the cold can of root beer, waving goodbye to the housekeeper who had left dinner in the oven and the timer set. All he had to do was listen for the ding. Mrs. Gunderson waved back as she hurried around the corner of the house and disappeared, leaving him blissfully alone. Well, almost alone. A clunk on the other side of the screen door reminded him two Grangers still remained in the house. But not for much longer.

He ambled over to the porch swing and settled onto the cushion to watch the sunset. Comfortable. *Thanks for leading me here, Lord. It's just where I want to be in life.* He took a sip of his soda. A cow grazing on the other side of a white fence leaned over the top board and mooed at him. Her bright brown eyes were focused on his soda can.

"Buttercup!" The screen door whispered open and the youngest Granger sister popped out. Addison slung her designer bag over her shoulder. "You can't have fizzy drinks. They give you the burps. Remember?"

The cow's long sorrowful moo may have been a comment that some pleasures were worth a little discomfort.

"Dad should just let that cow live in the house like a dog, she's so spoiled." Addy winked as she waltzed by him. "It's Friday night. You shouldn't be here alone. I can stay with you and keep watch on Sunny. I'm worried about her."

"No way. Don't you change your plans. I can keep an eye on your expecting mare. Besides, I want to spend the evening with my sweetie." He stretched out his legs and crossed them at the ankles.

Buttercup, his sweetie, mooed again as if in total agreement.

"Then enjoy the peace and quiet while you can." Addy's advice was delivered with a grin as she hopped down the steps, strawberry blond hair flying behind her, looking a lot like his baby sister as she hurried enthusiastically down the concrete path. "Don't forget to do your own dishes!"

"I know. My mom trained me right," he called after her as she disappeared around the corner.

"That's debatable." A different voice answered. Cheyenne pushed open the screen door. "I saw the state of your bedroom. Do you know how to pick up anything?"

"Hey, that's my private domain. I know how to do housework, but I'm not so good at doing it without someone telling me to." He may as well be honest. He'd learned that was the best way to go through life, even if he could think of folks who didn't agree—like his former fiancée.

"That's a tad better than my brothers." Cheyenne jingled her truck keys in one hand. "Are you really going to stay here all by your lonesome? It's Friday night."

"I didn't know I'd be here alone, but yeah, I don't mind. I like the peace." It was what he preferred, and he'd had enough drama with Meryl to last him a lifetime. He liked quiet. He liked computers, books and watching time go by.

"It's weird now that Dad's with Cady." Cheyenne hesitated on the steps. "He used to be home every weekend night unless there was something going on at the church. Now, look. I never thought it would happen, but he's dating."

"He sure is. He trailered up his horse and drove off about an hour ago. Said he and Cady were going for a ride. He looked pleased as punch." Sean took another sip of root beer and let the featherlight summery air puff over him.

"What about you?" Cheyenne twisted around to walk backwards. "There's no one you have your eye on?"

"Who? Me?" He stared off into the distance. The cow was going to hurt herself straining over the fence like that. He climbed to his feet, doing his level best not to think of pretty Eloise. "No. I'm done with relationships. They're for the birds."

"I know the feeling." Cheyenne seemed satisfied at last, and he realized she didn't want him to feel alone. That would explain why she was hesitating.

"What are you up to?" He set aside his can.

"I'm having dinner with a friend. Wait, you know her. Eloise, remember? We've been friends forever."

"Blond hair, green eyes, is real quiet?" Surprising how the mention of her could make him smile. "Saw her today at the Steer In."

"Yes. That's Eloise. She's home to stay, just like I am, so we're celebrating with cheeseburgers and chocolate milkshakes. I can bring you an order home."

"No. Mrs. G. left me on casserole duty. She's got the timer set and a salad in the fridge." He ambled down the steps and dug into his jeans pocket. The cow, scenting the molasses treat he found, hopped up and down excitedly. "Eloise is the one who used to skate, right?"

"Ice dancing. She won two world championships." Cheyenne nodded as she hesitated at the corner of the garage.

A long span of mown grass separated them, and he had to speak up to be heard above the mooing cow and the twitter of larks. "What happened? Did she get injured or something? I saw a cane in her car."

"She was in a serious car accident." Cheyenne frowned, sad for her friend. "It's amazing she walks, but she'll never skate professionally again."

Emotion punched him in the gut, reminding him life could be a tough road. He handed over the molasses treat and gave Buttercup a pat as she chewed happily. Sunshine gleamed off the cow's sleek black coat. Her pure white face and white tipped ears made her look as cute as a button. He thought of Eloise and couldn't guess what it would be like to lose a goal like that, although he knew what tragedy felt like. His older brother Tim, an Army Ranger, had been killed in action. The family had gone on but the loss had marked them all.

"Oops! I'm late." Cheyenne darted around the corner and out of sight, her words carrying to him on the breeze. "If you change your mind, you have my cell number. Keep a close eye on Sunny and if you think she's not doing all right, call."

"I know the drill," he told Buttercup as he rubbed her nose.

She gazed up at him with puppy-dog eyes, sank her teeth into his hat and lifted it off his head.

"Funny girl." He rescued it from her and dug another treat out of his pocket. Life was good on the Wyoming range, and he was glad to be a carefree bachelor in command of his life. So what if it got a little lonely? He could handle that. If the thought of Eloise Tipple's lovely face made him reconsider, he had to admit he was lonelier than he'd thought. It wasn't easy being a lone wolf.

"Don't look at me like that," he admonished Buttercup. "I really am a lone wolf."

The cow shook her head as if she didn't believe him for a second.

"Is that you, honey?"

"Yes, Mom." Eloise tapped through the shadowy kitchen and pushed open the back screen. The music of the nearby river serenaded her as she stepped onto the patio.

Helene Tipple looked up from her cross-stitch piece. "Did you have a good time catching up with Cheyenne?"

"I did." She leaned her cane against the patio table and eased into a cushioned seat. Another positive about being back—there was no place like home. Their conversation had covered everything essential while neatly skipping the painful. "Cheye and I are going riding this week. I get to go over to the ranch and see all the new foals."

"That's nice, dear." Mom poked her needle through the embroidery hoop and fussed with the stitch. "I was talking with your grandma today."

"You talk with her every day." Eloise rolled her eyes, already bracing herself. She knew exactly what her mom was going to say because they'd had this conversation many times before. "She told you about my upcoming blind date, didn't she?"

"She is pretty excited about this young man. She wants you to call her. Take a few moments to gather your strength first." Mom's eyes twinkled as if she were enjoying herself.

"Yes, because this is so amusing." Eloise shook her head, laughing, too. "This is my life. My grandmother is finding dates for me."

"And don't you disappoint her." Dad spoke up with a rattle of his magazine page and a grin.

"I wouldn't dream of it." She loved her grandmother with all her heart. No one on earth wanted to disappoint Gran. "Even if she is torturing me."

Her parents chuckled as if she'd made a joke. Sure, her personal life was a laugh a minute. Shaking her head and laughing at herself—what else was a girl to do?—she hoisted up out of the extremely comfortable chair and made her way to the kitchen. As she dialed the phone, her gaze drifted to the large picture window overlooking the patio. Her parents made an iconic picture, sitting side by side beneath the striped table umbrella. Their silence was a contented one, broken by quiet murmurings and gentle smiles, a sign of their long and happy marriage.

Not everyone got the fairy tale. That was simply a plain fact. Eloise leaned against the counter and listened to the phone ring.

"Hello?" Gran warbled cheerfully. "Is that you, Eloise? Your mama promised you would be calling me."

"Yes, it's me, Gran." Theirs was a lifetime love, too. She adored her grandmother. She would do anything for her, which was why she was doomed. "You might as well get to the point."

"I talked with Madge." Gran's excitement vibrated across the line. "This is what I learned about George. He manages an office-supply store over in Sunshine. He's a good Christian boy and he wants to get married."

"Why can't he find someone to marry him who actually knows him?"

"Well, he is terribly short but you don't mind that, do you? A short husband is better than none at all. It's what's inside that counts."

"Yes, it is." Who was she to be arguing with that? She leaned her cane against the cabinet doors and prayed for fortitude.

"I have high hopes for this one. Don't worry, I'm looking out for you, sweetheart."

"I'm looking out for you too, Gran. I'll drop by after work tomorrow." Her grandmother needed a little help around the house these days, and she was happy to do it. That way they could spend quality time together, another very big advantage to being back home again.

After chatting for a few more minutes, she bid Gran goodbye and hung up the phone. The peace of the evening filled the kitchen like the rosy light of the sunset tumbling from the western horizon. The entire landscape glowed as if painted with a luminous pearled paint. Her mind drifted back over her very good day and lingered on the memory of a man with a black Stetson holding a strawberry ice-cream cone in one rugged hand. A very nice image, indeed.

Chapter Three

"Good afternoon. Lark Song Inn." Eloise tucked the receiver between her chin and shoulder. "How may I help you?"

"Yeah, this is Nate Cannon. I need to talk with Eloise."

"Dr. Cannon." The local vet. A kick of anticipation charged through her, so she grabbed a pen off the front desk and poised it over the memo pad. "I'm Eloise. Did you happen to hear about my mission?"

"Cheyenne clued me in. She said you folks are looking to buy horses in need, and I happen to know of a pair."

"Bless you." She'd tried the local agencies and organizations over the last handful of days, but no luck. "Where are they? What are they like?"

"Two geldings, as gentle as could be. Their owner passed away a while back and the folks who inherited the land don't want to keep them. It's hard to sell horses this old, so if your boss is looking to make a difference in an animal's life, she wouldn't regret taking them in."

"They sound perfect." The poor things. She glanced

at her watch. Wendy should be back from her break in a few minutes. "Could I take a look this afternoon?"

"I'll give you the address and phone number. Now, these folks aren't the most agreeable so you might want to bring someone with you who really knows horses. Like Cheyenne. I'd offer, but I've got a show horse with colic to get back to and a busy afternoon after that. You could call my receptionist. She might be able to book you a time."

"Thanks, but I'll call Cheyenne." After getting the necessary information, she buzzed Cady, who was delighted at the prospect of horses for the stables, then dialed her best friend's number.

"Hello?" A familiar baritone rumbled across the line. "Stowaway Ranch."

"Is this Sean?" Why was she smiling? The man simply had that effect on her. She was curious. That was different from interested.

"Eloise. How are you doing?"

"Fine enough." Was it her imagination or did he sound glad to hear from her?

"Are you calling for Cheyenne?"

"Guilty. She promised me use of her horse expertise. Tell me she's there."

"I wish I could but she took off to do some shopping in Sunshine. Should be gone all afternoon. I might not be an expert when it comes to horses, but I'm no slouch either. What kind of help do you need?"

"Uh…" Brilliant answer. Her brain decided to short circuit again. "The vet found some horses."

"Oh, and you need someone to go with you. I can do that."

"Uh…" Was she stuck on that word? What was the matter with her?

"It's a slow afternoon and I like to make myself useful. I can bring a horse trailer."

"I can't say no to that." Especially since she didn't own a vehicle capable of pulling one. But did she really want to spend an afternoon with the most gorgeous man she'd ever met? She was fairly sure judging by the amount of friendliness in his voice that he hadn't noticed her cane yet. She dreaded the moment when he did, but putting horses in the inn's stables was her new assignment. She wanted to do her job well. "Let me give you the address."

"Great. I need something to write with." A drawer banged open before he came back on the line. "Got it."

"You probably know where this is already, but the vet gave me detailed instructions." She gave him the information. "When can you get there?"

"Give me thirty minutes?"

"Thirty minutes it is. Thanks for helping out, Sean."

"Hey, that's what friends are for." He set down the pen and folded the scrap of paper.

"I didn't know we were friends."

"A friend of Cheyenne's is a friend of mine." He ignored Mrs. Gunderson who bustled into sight with a laundry basket balanced on one hip. A lone wolf could have a friend or two and still be a lone wolf, right? "I'm happy to help. I like what Cady's doing. She could be filling her stalls with pampered horses, but she wants to make a difference. I'll see you soon."

"Thanks, Sean." Eloise's gentle alto was about the prettiest sound he'd ever heard. She wasn't fake, like some women he could think of—Meryl came to mind—

but honest and sincere. He liked that. Those were just the right qualities for a friend.

He hung up and caught Mrs. Gunderson's raised eyebrow as she paused midway up the stairs, free hand on the rail. There was no mistaking that motherly look.

"What?" He held up both hands, the innocent man that he was. "I didn't do anything."

"I didn't say a thing." She had raised five sons of her own, so he knew she was wise to the ways of the male mind. "You call me if you aren't coming home for supper."

"Why wouldn't I be home for supper?" He grabbed a chocolate-chip cookie from the jar. "This isn't a date. It's a humanitarian mission. Well, an animal welfare mission."

"You like that girl." Mrs. G. narrowed her gaze at him. "Don't try and fool me."

"I'm not fooling you. I like her. What's not to like? But I don't *like* her." After Meryl, he'd be stupid to. A smart man would be leery after being used like that.

"Sometimes the best things come along when we aren't looking for them." She went on her way, padding up the stairs and out of sight, her words carrying up to him. *"All things are possible to him who believes."*

Boy, did she have the wrong idea. Sean shook his head. Mrs. G. couldn't be more mistaken. When he wiped a crumb off his shirt, he noticed his T-shirt had a hole in it. His jeans sported grass stains and his work boots were dirty.

Maybe he'd better go change. Getting spiffed up had nothing to do with seeing Eloise. It was simply a matter of cleanliness. He took the stairs two at a time, whistling.

* * *

"This must be the place," Eloise said to herself as she glanced at the reflective numbers stuck to the side of a battered black mailbox. Although two numerals were missing, the description matched the vet's directions so she eased her car off the paved county road and onto a driveway that was more dirt and potholes than gravel. She listened to the rush and whap of weeds and grass growing in the center of the lane hitting the underside of her car. Hopefully there wasn't anything big enough to do any damage. She gripped the steering wheel tight and eased up on the gas pedal.

Something dark and large lumbered up behind her, filling the reflective surface of her rearview mirror. She recognized that dark blue pickup. Sean. The sunshine seemed brighter, although that was probably an illusion and had nothing to do with the man's appearance. She eased around a hairpin corner and a dilapidated covering built out of corrugated metal and weathered two-by-fours came into sight. It huddled sadly against a broken-down fence. Barbed wire hung dangerously from listing and rotting posts. Most of the grass had been eaten away from an acre-sized field, where two horses pricked their ears, spotted the truck and came running.

She pulled to a stop in front of a carport that had seen better days. A rusty truck rested in the shade. Overgrown grass danced in the wind as she watched Sean's vehicle pull up beside her. Maybe the last wheeze of the air conditioner was the reason the hair stood up on her arms. She did not want it to be a reaction to the man strolling into sight. She braced herself for the inevitable and reached for her cane.

Sean Granger looked like a western hero in his long-legged worn blue jeans. The white T-shirt he wore emphasized his sun-kissed tan and as he swept off his Stetson, muscles rippled beneath the knit cotton blend. He raked one hand through his brown hair and smiled down at her as he opened her car door. His dreamy blue eyes captured her with a steady stare and then his gaze slid downward as she climbed out from behind the wheel, stood tall and used her cane.

Here was where he dimmed down the smile and his friendliness when he got a good look at her cane. It's what most guys did whether they were interested or not. She braced herself for it as she took one limping step, but it didn't come. Instead Sean closed the door for her, nodding toward the horses. "Did you get a look at them?"

"No, I was too busy trying not to lose my car in one of the potholes," she quipped and was rewarded with a grin as he swept his hat back on.

"They saw the truck and came running. Look at them." His hand settled on the curve of her shoulder, a friendly weight, as he turned her gently toward the fence line. "I wonder if their former owner drove a truck like mine."

"They keep staring at it, almost waiting for someone else who might be in there." She gasped, realizing how they must be feeling. "Dr. Cannon didn't say how long the gentleman who owned them has been gone."

"Three months. Animals don't forget those they love." Sean ambled up to the fence and held out his hands for the horses to scent.

She took the opportunity to put a little physical distance between them. He was more touchy-feely than she was used to or felt comfortable with. "How do you know that?"

"Uncle Frank knew. I told him where I was headed. He knows everyone in these parts." Sean patted one of the horses. The big black gelding lowered his head for a good ear scratch. No one had taken time to comb out the tangles and burrs in his mane, and his hooves needed attention.

"You are a good fellow," Sean mumbled and the horse closed his eyes in trust. There was something deeply calming about the man, Eloise agreed. He made others feel safe.

"Are you the folks the vet called about?" A middle-age man wearing faded overalls and carrying a pipe limped into sight. He didn't seem to be in good health.

"We are." She spun to face him, thinking about the blank check her boss had handed over to her. "I'm Eloise from the Lark Song Inn."

"I'm Harry." He tipped his sagging hat. "Are you still interested now that you've seen them? They ain't much, and I regret to say I'm not up to caring for them."

"I'm sure we can settle on a price." She glanced over her shoulder at the horses, one still accepting strokes from Sean, the other watching the blue pickup sadly. He finally lowered his head, perhaps realizing his beloved former owner would not be emerging from the pickup, and stood still and silent, his dejection as tangible as the wind on her face.

She couldn't bring back to them what was lost, but she could make sure these horses were cherished and pampered. Good things were ahead for them. They just didn't know it yet. She tugged the check out of her purse, wondering how best to proceed.

"Do you trust me?" Sean towered over her, as breath-taking as any hero in a Western legend. "I can negoti-ate for you, if you'd like."

"Yes, thank you." She handed him the check, relieved in more ways than she knew how to say. She had no idea what the horses were worth, and she could see the man had a tough row to hoe. She didn't know what was fair, but she sensed Sean knew how to make it right.

She watched him stride away and offer Harry his hand. They shook, making introductions and small talk about the man who was deceased. A low-throated nicker caught her attention, and she found the friendlier horse watching her with curious eyes.

"Your lives are about to improve." She ran her fin-gertips down the gelding's graying nose. "Just you wait and see."

In the back lot at the inn Sean lowered the ramp with a clatter, surprised as Eloise tapped up the incline with a lead rope in hand. She didn't let her cane slow her down much. A glow of admiration filled him as he followed her up. The horses, not used to the trailer, were in various stages of fear. The black one fidgeted against his gate.

Eloise laid a comforting hand on his flank and spoke calmly and confidently like someone who had been around horses all her life. "It's going to be all right, Licorice."

The gelding blew out a breath, as if he were highly doubtful of that.

"How about you, Hershey?" she asked, unlatch-ing the brown gelding's gate. The bay glanced over his shoulder to study her, his eyes white-rimmed, but he didn't move much as Eloise clipped into his halter and led him out.

Why couldn't he look away? He ought to be paying attention to the horses, but all he saw was the woman. She walked like a ballerina even with an obvious limp. There was strength and a beauty inside her that became clearer every time he looked.

"I know you're worried, Hershey, but trust me when I say you have one of the best stalls in the county waiting for you." Her alto rose and fell like a song over the pad of her cane and the clomp of hooves on the ramp. "Cady went all out when she built this stable. Every stall is huge and it has a view. That's it. Turn for me, big guy. Come this way, that's right."

Kindness made a woman truly beautiful, Sean decided as he laid a hand on the black's neck. The gelding shivered, lunging nervously against the metal barrier.

"It's all right," he crooned, aware of the tension bunching in the horse's muscles. "It has to be hard having no say in this, but you are going to be just fine. No worries, buddy."

He clipped on the lead and backed the horse down the ramp. Every step Licorice took was halting as if he wanted to bolt into the trailer and go home. The unknown can be scary, so Sean used his voice to reassure the horse and led him down the breezeway between large but empty box stalls.

All he had to do was follow Eloise's voice, which felt as natural as breathing. Sunlight found her, burnishing her blond hair and haloing her like a Renaissance painting. Her frilly blouse and slacks weren't typical barn wear, but she didn't look out of place as she secured the gate to the straw-strewn stall. Inside, Hershey gave a snort and paraded around, taking in his view of the grassy paddock and various troughs for water, grain and alfalfa.

"Licorice can have the corner stall." She spotted him coming and opened the gate wide. "Rocco, who's on barn duty, has everything ready for them."

Across the row, a gold-and-white mare raced in from her paddock and clattered to a stop in her stall. Curious to meet her new neighbors, she arched her neck, whinnying in a friendly manner. Her big chocolate eyes shone a welcome.

"This is an exciting day for Misty, since she's been all alone in the stable," Eloise explained as he closed the gate and unhooked the lead.

"It's a pretty good day for me, too," he quipped, not at all sure how to say what he was feeling. "We did good work today."

"Yes, and I am indebted to you, sir." She handed him back the rope she'd used on Hershey. "I couldn't have done this without help."

"You mean without me."

"Well, yes, since you're the one who helped me." She gave her shiny hair a toss behind her shoulder, shaking her head at him as if she didn't know what to make of him. "It was good of you to volunteer. Cheyenne doesn't know what she missed out on. Until next time, that is."

"Hey, I don't mind doing this again." He kept his tone casual and made sure he didn't make eye contact. A lone wolf didn't work at making connections, he kept things light and loose. "I had fun. There's a lot of satisfaction to this. These horses weren't wanted, and now they are. It's a good way to spend an afternoon."

"So, you're really volunteering for next time?"

"Absolutely. Might as well make myself useful. Besides, Cheyenne might be busy and I have lots of spare time."

"Doesn't Frank keep you busy at the ranch?" Her grin hitched up in the corners of her soft mouth.

Cute. He ambled down the aisle at her side. "Sure. I get in a hard day's work. Lately, my personal life has been a bit slow. That's the way I want to keep it."

"Me, too." Was that a hint of sorrow turning her gorgeous eyes a deep, emerald green?

Hard to tell because it was gone as quickly as it came. "That is, if you want me to lend a hand. You know I come with a horse trailer, right?"

"I know." She rolled her eyes at him.

Cuter. "Then you aren't agreeing to this reluctantly?"

"I am." She leaned her head back and gazed up into his eyes full on, a spark of humor lighting her up. "I am very reluctant about you."

"Sure, cuz most folks are." He smiled all the way down to his toes. It was nice being with her. They emerged through the open double doors into the kiss of the late-May sun and heat. Larks warbled, robins swooped by and a sparrow up on the roof chirped at them warningly. Grass whispered in the wind, leaves rustled and he couldn't remember the last time he felt so good.

"My dad didn't want me to grow up to be a cowboy, you know." He knelt to put up the ramp, working quickly, hardly thinking about it. He finished the quick task with a rattle and clang. "Said it was hard work and a hard life. He wanted something more for me."

"Is that why he didn't stay and help Frank with the ranching?"

"Yep, but I guess he didn't have the calling. Ranching is in my blood. That's why I'm here."

"Sometimes you get blessed with the right path to follow in life." The wind tangled her sleek blond locks. Again, that brief flash of sadness disappeared as if it had never been. "It doesn't always last, so you should enjoy it while you can."

"Good advice." He glanced at her cane, wondering if that's what life had taught her. He had some advice for her, too. "Sometimes you feel lost. When you look down, you realize you are already walking the path meant for you."

"You are a glass-is-half-full kind of man, aren't you?" She led the way down a garden walkway.

"Sure. It's a matter of choice. The glass has the same water in it either way." He flashed his dimples at her. "Let me guess. You're the kind who sees the glass as half-empty."

"I'm pleading the fifth." Dimples framed her smile, bright and merry.

The cutest yet. He jammed his hands into his pockets. "Speaking of glasses, I'm thirsty. How about we hunt down something cold to drink? My treat."

"No, that makes it a date." She grimaced in good humor. "Yikes. We probably don't want that. I'll get mine, you get yours."

"Wow, I guess I know where I stand," he quipped, following her down the breezeway.

"I've been on a lot of first dates lately. Did I sound defensive?"

"Only a little." He was glad to be with her. Eloise was fun and interesting. He was looking forward to finding out exactly how much.

Chapter Four

"Thank you, Sierra." Eloise lifted the iced coffee from the silver tray and took a cooling sip. Across from her on one of the inn's comfortable porch swings, Sean did the same.

"That engagement ring looks good on you," he told the waitress.

"Thanks. It's taken some getting used to." Sierra blushed rosily. Happiness radiated from her as she admired the impressive diamond on her left hand. "We have finally agreed on a July wedding."

"This is news." Sean leaned back, stretched his legs out and crossed them at the ankles. He was an interesting man to watch, all long, lean lines, strength and old-West charisma. "Tucker said you wanted to make sure not to interfere with Autumn's wedding next month."

"More like in three weeks. Haven't you noticed the flurry over it? You live in the same house." Sierra shook her head merrily as she padded away, off to wait on the Neilsons who were at the far end of the porch, holding hands and talking intimately.

"A bachelor tries to ignore all conversations, ac-

tivities or magazines with the word 'wedding' in
them," Sean quipped as he sipped at his coffee. "Self-
preservation."

"Typical. I suppose you're the carefree-bachelor type.
Never one to settle down." He was handsome enough
to have his pick of women. "You probably left a dozen
broken hearts behind when you moved here."

"Only one." His grin didn't lessen but the shine
inside him did. His personality dimmed like a cloud
passing before the sun. "And I didn't leave it behind. I
brought it with me. It was mine."

"Yours?" He didn't look like a man with a broken
heart. He certainly didn't act like one, not with his
charm and easy humor. When she looked closer, emotion worked its way into the corner of his eyes, leaving
attractive little crinkles. Perhaps he wasn't as easygoing as she first thought. She gave the swing a little push
with her foot, setting it into motion. "Are you sure you
weren't the one who did the breaking?"

"I was probably responsible for it." His confession
rang low with truth and sincerity. He gave the appearance of a tough, untouchable man but she suspected
his feelings ran deep. His grin was gone along with
his easygoing manner, replaced by a solid realness that
was attractive and manly. He swallowed hard before he
spoke again. "I landed a good job at a software company. I was in management overseeing this great project, but I wasn't happy being trapped indoors all day."

"That can be hard for a country boy." She could
picture it.

"I worked long hours, not that I mind hard work. I
liked being a programmer, but I didn't love it. When
Uncle Frank called on my birthday in February, I ad-

mitted to him that I would rather be in a saddle all day. That he had my ideal life."

"And he offered you a job?"

"He did. Temporary to start. To test the waters, he said, but I think he didn't want to upset my dad too much." He shrugged, glancing over his father's disappointment. He took another pull on the straw, letting the cool settle across his tongue and glide down his throat. It helped wash away the tough feelings he was trying to avoid. "I gave my notice and talked my folks into seeing the positive side of this. I was really psyched. Uncle Frank has a lot of land and livestock. This is a good opportunity for me to do what I love for a living. It was my decision that changed everything."

"What do you mean?"

"A special someone didn't want a blue-collar ranch hand for a husband." He may as well get it off his chest. "Meryl and I were engaged."

"Were?"

"She dumped me."

"Because you followed your dream?"

"That's the long and short of it." The country cliché was easier than admitting the truth. He'd loved Meryl. "I could have stayed, in fact I had the phone in hand to call Uncle Frank and decline his offer when I got the news she was already dating someone else and had been for a while. Hedging her bets, I think."

"I'm sorry. That had to have hurt."

"Yes." He swallowed hard against the pain, which was lessening. Mostly it was the humiliation that troubled him now. "I made a crucial mistake, but I learned a valuable lesson. Never fall in love with someone who doesn't love you the same way in return."

"I learned that hard lesson, too." She bit her bottom lip, the only sign of vulnerability he'd seen her make. With her classic good looks, smarts and kind personality he couldn't imagine she'd been through something similar.

"Who had the bad form not to care about you?" he wanted to know.

"Oh, he cared. Just not enough." Ghosts of pain darkened her green eyes and she shrugged one slender shoulder, as if she were well over it. No big deal.

He wasn't fooled. "Who was he?"

"My ice-dancing partner." She tore her gaze from his and stared out at the horizon, where the jagged peaks of the Tetons seemed to hold up the sky. "Cliché, I know. Gerald and I spent eight to ten hours a day together either on the ice or in the gym every day since I was eighteen. We even took classes together at the nearby university."

"You were truly close to him." He sympathized. He knew what that was like.

"I was." Shaky, she lifted the glass and sipped, still watching the white puffs of clouds in the pristine blue sky and the visual wonder of the Teton Range. Maybe she was trying to keep her emotions distant, too.

"You had been together a long time?" A question more than a statement, but he wanted it to sound casual, as if his pulse hadn't kicked up and he wasn't eager to know why she'd been hurt.

"We were friends for the first three years and then it turned into something more. Something really nice." Maybe she wasn't aware of how her voice softened and her expression grew lighter as if she'd had the rare chance to touch more than one dream. She sat up straighter and set her coffee on the nearby end table. "For a while it was sweet and comfortable and reassuring. He was there whenever I needed him, at least when we were skating partners."

"Sounds as if you two had a good bond." He couldn't say the same. He'd loved Meryl. He hated to admit he might still love her a little bit and against his will. But he'd never had that type of tie with her.

"It was nice." She might think she was hiding her sadness, but she would be wrong. "I guess some things aren't meant to last."

"What happened?"

"Are you telling me you can't guess?" She rubbed at her knee in small circles before turning away from him to fetch her drink. He didn't imagine the hurt in the silence that fell between them.

A car accident, Cheyenne had said. But it was far more serious than that.

"A drunk driver was going the wrong way on the floating bridge when I was coming home after a late night practicing for my church's Christmas pageant. I saw the lights and I tried to avoid him. But I steered toward the right hand shoulder, what little there was of it, and he decided to do the same. I spent the next few months in the hospital and the next year in a rehabilitation center in Los Angeles." She took a sip, letting the pain settle between them. "Gerald couldn't wait, he had to keep training, so he found another skating partner. It turned out my injury and the distance between Seattle and L.A. were problems too big to overcome and our bond faded."

"I'm sorry that happened to you." Sympathy, that was the only reason he reached over to lay his hand on hers. He cared, sure, but he was in control of his emotions. He didn't care for her *too* much. He willed his understanding into his touch. "It wasn't fair."

"Fair? No. God never promised this life would be fair." Her chin went up, not a woman to feel sorry for herself. "But there have been many blessings that have come my way. I survived the accident. I beat the odds to walk again. I'm really very blessed."

"Sure, I see that," he agreed. She was blessed in more ways than he had understood before. She had strength and faith enough not to let the unfairness of her accident and injuries embitter her spirit. It was hard not to like her more, and he twined his fingers through hers, holding on and not wanting to let go. When he gazed into her clear green eyes, a similar tug of emotion wrapped around him. "You've had some tough blows. First the accident, then the breakup."

"Gerald tried. I have to give him credit. In the end he chose someone else." Her fingers tightened on his, holding on to him, too. "Yes, it was his new skating partner."

"Did you feel passed over?" That was certainly how he felt.

"Yes. It was easy for Gerald to move on. Proof his heart wasn't in it as deeply as mine was." She smiled, a mix of poignance and beauty that made her compelling. "Life goes on."

"It does." He was lost in the moment gazing into her, and he couldn't remember the name of any woman previous. The brush of the breeze, the murmur of the other couple on the porch and the faint rasp of the rocking swing silenced. The world narrowed until there was only Eloise and her hand, so much smaller, tucked in his.

Footsteps vaguely drummed closer and a familiar woman's voice pierced into his thoughts, pushing back the boundaries of his world so that Eloise was no longer the center. Cady smiled down at him and she wasn't alone. Two dark-haired girls, one around ten with braided pigtails and the other a little older with a touch of disdain, stood by her.

"Are you boyfriend and girlfriend?" the youngest girl wanted to know.

"No." He abruptly sat up and whipped his hand away from Eloise's. He knew why the kid was asking. It looked as if they were, sitting together with hands linked and sharing secrets. Couples did that sort of thing. He noticed Eloise seemed uncomfortable, too. He caught Cady's curious look and set out to reassure her. "Just talking. That's all. I suppose you heard about the horses?"

"I found Eloise's message on my voice mail when I reached the airport. I had to pick up these two and their father." Cady was honorary family to the girls, and was also their godmother. They all had been close when she'd lived in New York City. Cady gently steered the kids toward the steps. "I can't wait to see our new horses. I didn't think to ask if they were gentle or even trained."

"They appear to be." Eloise grappled for her cane. "Their previous owner took good care of them, rode them regularly and they are steady and gentle. With a little training, they should make good, reliable horses for guests to ride."

"Excellent. What a great job, Eloise." Cady beamed, her happiness evident, before leading the girls away. "Let's go see the horses that were saved because of you, Julianna Elizabeth Stone."

"Do we get to ride them?" the little girl wanted to know as she skipped down the steps, and Cady's answer was lost in a rising gust of warm wind.

"Well, I guess I had better get back to my desk." Eloise checked her watch and grabbed her cane. "I've got just enough of my day left to call the farrier. Tonight I have to get off work on time."

"Why's that?" He climbed to his feet and followed her along the porch.

"I've got a date tonight. A blind date." She let her tone say it all.

"Poor you. Who set you up?"

"My grandma." She liked that Sean opened the door for her and held it. He was a gentleman underneath his cowboy charm. She stepped into the air-conditioning with a sigh. "She is the only person I can't say no to."

"So you are stuck going out on a date when you don't want to date?"

"Exactly." She liked that he understood. Her own mother had little sympathy for the situation with her matchmaking grandma. "But it's only one dinner. I can suffer through anything for an hour or so, at least that's what I tell myself."

"Sure. Who is it with?"

"I don't know him. Some guy who lives in the next town over." She hesitated in the well-appointed lobby, where their paths would part. The front door loomed to the left, the hallway leading to her office to the right. Remembering what Julianna had said made her blush. She wasn't interested in Sean in that way. "The last thing I need is a boyfriend."

"Right, because who wants to be tied down like

that?" He swept off his Stetson and raked a hand through his thick dark hair. "Who needs the heartache?"

"You said it." It was nice that they shared this common ground. Not wanting a repeat of earlier when he'd held her hand too long, she backed away. Maybe a no-physical-contact policy between them would be a good idea. "Thanks again, Sean."

"Any time. I'll see you on the next horse-gathering mission?"

"Absolutely." She spun on her heel so she couldn't be tempted to watch him walk away. So she couldn't be tempted to wonder why any woman would have chosen another man over him. He didn't even seem to notice her disability. He didn't treat her differently because of her limp. He had understood the devastation she'd felt after her accident and her breakup.

He was a nice guy. A really nice guy. That type of man was hard to find, which made her think about her impending date. She gripped her cane tightly and turned her thoughts to the evening ahead. *Please, Lord,* she prayed as she always did before one of Gran's fix-ups. *Let this blind date not be too uncomfortable.*

God hadn't answered that particular prayer yet, but there was always a first. She was determined to hold out hope.

"We have to fend for ourselves tonight." Uncle Frank looked up from his laptop on the kitchen table the moment Sean came through the door. "The girls are in Jackson trying on the dresses for Autumn's wedding and dragged Mrs. G. with them. I told her you and I could throw something on the barbecue or hit the diner. What do you say?"

"The diner." He'd just finished cleaning out three stables and feeding all the horses. That explained where Autumn was, who practically lived in the barns. "Where's Tucker?"

"His fiancée is cooking for him, but he didn't see fit to extend an invitation to us." Frank grinned and pushed away from the table. "Let me grab my hat and my keys. How did the horse rescue turn out?"

"Good. The inn has some gentle animals, and some good horses have a caring home." He turned on his heel and headed right back out the door.

"Then it's good news all around." Frank seemed in an unusually chipper mood but he didn't explain as he hopped down the steps. Buttercup dashed up to the fence and mooed, her bright eyes sparkling. "Hey, girl. I'll come see you later. How's that?"

A discontented moo trailed after them as they headed to the garage.

"Tucker's about ready to take possession of the land he bought." Frank hopped into the driver's seat of his big black pickup.

Sean climbed into the passenger seat and buckled in. He liked his uncle. He couldn't count the number of times Dad had said, "You remind me of my brother." Sean supposed he and Frank were alike in some ways. They both liked the outdoors, loved animals, had ranching in their blood. Sean liked to think he was as even-tempered. "Does that mean the Greens are officially moved off the land he bought?"

"They leave tomorrow for Florida. Retirement. I can't picture that." He started the engine and gunned down the driveway with the speed and skill of someone who had done it thousands of times. Trees whipped by along with rolling green fenced fields full of grazing horses. The view of the Tetons and the Wyoming sky could knock the breath out of you. Frank turned the truck onto the paved county road. "I'm going to wind up like my dad. I'll be here until the end of my days."

"It's not a bad life sentence."

"I reckon not. Say, I hear you're on the rebound," Frank said as if he were discussing the weather and not dropping a bombshell.

"Where did you hear that?" He chuckled. "Who am I rebounding with?"

Then he knew. He remembered Eloise's hand beneath his, the feminine feel of her slender fingers entwined between his. The talk they'd shared on the porch in plain view of anyone walking by. "Cady told you, didn't she?"

"She mentioned seeing you and Eloise together." Frank kept his gaze on the road as if indifferent, but there was no missing his knowing grin.

"We were having a cool drink after fetching the horses. No big deal."

"No big deal. Sure, I get that. Except the two of you were holding hands."

Nothing was private in a small town. Sean chuckled. "Looks are deceiving. Cady saw me comforting a friend, that was all."

"A friend. If that's what you want to call her, fine by me." Uncle Frank's ear-to-ear grin said he knew differently.

He would be wrong. "Eloise has had a tough time. We were talking about it. Friends do that."

"You don't need to convince me."

As if that were even possible. It looked as if his uncle had already made up his mind. Sean shifted on the seat to watch a hawk glide by over the long stretch of field. He and Eloise knew the truth. On the rebound?

He shook his head. It would take a long time before he would be ready to jump in and risk a romantic relationship, rebound or not.

Talk turned to the subjects of the ranch and family until town came into view. The truck rolled to a stop in front of the diner's wide picture windows and a familiar fall of straight golden hair and a cute profile drew his attention. Eloise sat at a booth with a fork poised in midair, listening intently to something her dinner partner said.

Dinner partner. Sean's brain clicked into gear. Her date. She was on a blind date this evening. He frowned at the guy who wore a white dress shirt and dark slacks and had a wholesome, all-American look to him. Sean bristled. He didn't trust that guy. He unlatched his seat belt, opened the door and dropped to the ground. On the other side of the sun-streaked glass, she turned toward the window, toward him, and her gaze arrowed to his.

Surprise flashed in her gentle green eyes before she returned her attention back to her dinner date. In that one moment he felt dismissed, a friend and not more, just as he'd insisted on being.

Chapter Five

He's coming into the diner! That single realization sent nerves zipping through Eloise's stomach as she watched George cut what remained of his chicken-fried steak into tiny pieces. She trained her eyes on her dinner date but her attention slipped toward the opening door even if her gaze didn't. The door swung open and in the background Sean sauntered in. He planted his hands on his hips but he didn't glance her way. His mile-wide shoulders squared as he ambled down the far aisle with his uncle and out of her field of vision.

"…I am up for a promotion right now," George explained as he precisely set his knife on the edge of his plate. With an unsatisfied frown, he moved it slightly until he was pleased with the angle it made on his plate rim. "You could be looking at the next regional manager."

"Wow." What else could she say to that? It was a plus he actually had a job, but he was really hung up on himself. The signs were hard to miss, blaring like a neon banner throughout the meal.

"There would be a lot of travel involved with being

regional manager." He repeated the title, as if simply to hear himself say it. "After that, I could go after the sectional manager position. I have a lot of advancement opportunities, unlike you. That's the problem with thinking small. You have to find a job with room to move."

"Clearly." Yes, that was her problem. She rolled her eyes. She thought too small. Glad she'd met George so she could learn that. She took a bite of grilled chicken and resisted the urge to glance at the clock on the wall behind her. How was it possible that time could move this slowly? Surely the evening was almost over—and the date.

But no, George went right on talking.

"I have a ten-year plan." He precisely speared a perfectly cubed piece of steak with his fork.

"A ten-year plan to be sectional manager?" She tried to listen, she really did, but Sean's magnetism pulled at her attention like he was a black hole sucking up all the gravity in the room. It was his fault, not hers, her gaze slipped just a few inches to the left to bring the farthest booth into her peripheral vision.

Sean. Her hand tingled as she remembered the comfort he'd given her today. She hadn't planned to open up to him or to anyone. She would rather keep the truth behind her breakup with Gerald bottled inside where it was easier to deny. Hearing herself tell part of the story to Sean had helped and she felt better. He'd been easy to talk to.

"No, ten years to realize my plan of being the manager of the entire western half of the country." George chewed exactly twenty-two times before continuing.

"I have a deep understanding of paper products and I want to bring that to the world."

"Good for you." She set down her fork, truly able to say she was no longer hungry. *Lord, please let this date come to an end.*

"Oh, a spill. Here, let me." He scooped up his napkin, reached across the table and dabbed at the base of her water glass. He swiped away the few drops of perspiration that had trickled onto the faded Formica as if it were the Ebola virus needing to be eradicated. He wasn't pleased until he had used a handful of paper napkins from the dispenser to dry off every streak. Once he was satisfied he had decontaminated the site thoroughly, he gave a nod and continued. "I'll be right on schedule if I land the regional position. The key to success is to set short achievable goals that lead you to the end goal."

The waitress must have spotted her distress because she padded over, sneakers squeaking on the tile, and dropped the check on the edge of the table. "Hey, there, Eloise. Do you two need anything else?"

"No, absolutely not," she answered before George could debate the dessert options. It had taken him over twenty minutes to decide on the original meal. The sooner this experience was over, the better. "Thanks, Connie."

She wasn't surprised when George lifted his knife to check his hair in the blade's reflection. He finger-combed a few locks and reached into his pocket.

"You won't mind if we go Dutch, will you?" He tossed her what he probably thought was a charming grin, but it fell far short of the caliber of charm she was used to. He shrugged. "I mean, you understand."

Gladly, she opened her purse and tugged out enough bills to cover her portion and a generous tip. She was just happy the torture was over. "It was interesting meeting you, George."

"So I've been told." He apparently took everything as a compliment. He squinted at the bill, stopped to do the math in his head and reached into his pocket for coins. He left exact change and no tip. He stood and as he watched her do the same, he couldn't quite hide the distaste when his gaze landed on her cane. "Nice meeting you, Eloise."

She clutched her cane's grip, waiting to move until he was safely away from her. From the moment he'd spotted her cane leaning against the window sill, the date had come to a screeching halt. He had only been going through the motions, which she was thankful for because she was definitely not interested in him. But still, it hurt. She wished it didn't, but it did. She was twenty-four years old and she felt passed over and no longer attractive.

Fine, that was vain. The Bible was full of warnings against vanity. But she wanted to feel young and whole and womanly, as she had before the accident, just like any other female her age.

"Whew, dodged a bullet with that one." Connie returned with a pot of coffee in hand. "I saw how pained you looked, so I thought I would give you an out. He looked bored, too."

"Of me, yes, but not when it came to himself," she quipped. Poor George. She hoped he was able to live out his ten-year plan. Everyone deserved a good future. She moved her cane forward and took a step. "Thanks, Connie. I appreciate it more than you know."

"Anytime." Connie went on her way with coffee pot in hand.

"Eloise!" A familiar baritone rang warmly across the diner. Sean studied her over the top of a soda glass. It was hard to say what he might be thinking. His dark blue eyes watched her speculatively as she turned away from the front door and ambled down the aisle. His forehead furrowed. "That date looked painful."

"Yes, thanks for noticing." She stopped at their table, feeling awkward. "Hi, Mr. Granger."

"Hi, Eloise. Haven't seen you around the ranch lately." Frank set his soda glass on the table. "I'm surprised you and Cheyenne aren't out riding. The weather's good for it."

"We have plans later in the week." Another perk about living here again. Horseback rides on lazy summer afternoons had been some of the best parts of her childhood. "I guess that means I'll see you around, Sean."

"I just wanted to make sure you were all right after that experience." He broke off a piece of bread from the basket on the table and swiped butter over it. "It looked as if he wasn't being very nice to you."

"It was a blind date. I wasn't what he was expecting." She shrugged it off. George might not be her idea of a catch, but surely the Lord had made someone just for him. Somewhere there was a woman who cut her steak in precise cubes and chewed exactly twenty-two times and prayed for her soul mate. Eloise liked to think they would find each other. "I can only imagine what my grandmother told his grandmother about me."

"A lot of good things," Sean insisted.

"*Only* the good things," she corrected. "Gran left out everything else, especially the cane."

"Any man who doesn't like your pretty pink cane isn't worthy of you." He spoke up like the friend he had become.

"That's nice. Thanks." Sweetness filled her, which *had* to be gratitude of the highest magnitude and not any other emotion—like interest. "I didn't expect to see you here tonight."

"Wedding stuff. Mrs. G. was whisked away to help view the wedding dress, leaving Uncle Frank and me to fend for ourselves."

"You poor men. Don't either of you know how to cook?"

"Sure, but we didn't want to." He popped a bite of bread into his mouth. His stomach growled, betraying exactly how hungry he was. It would have been expedient to have tossed something on the barbecue. "This way, no dishes. We're smarter than we look."

"So I see." Mirth drew up the corner of her mouth and put little lights into her green irises.

Not that he ought to be noticing. Not that his chest should be tight and achy over seeing her on that date. When the other guy had walked off and left her standing there, relief had hit him in the gut. For a moment he had to wonder if he cared for her more than he wanted to admit, but that couldn't be possible, could it? Ever since his heart was broken, he'd become a lone wolf. A man who needed no one. What he felt for Eloise couldn't be rebound feelings or romantic glimmers or anything like that.

He cleared his throat and washed the bread down

with a few gulps of root beer. "Did you want to sit and keep us company?"

"I'd like to, but I can't. My grandmother is expecting me." As if on cue, an electronic tune chimed deep in her bag. She took a step back. "That would be her. She'll want to know how things went with George."

"Will she set you up on another blind date?"

"Heaven knows she will keep at it." Nothing could hide the love she held for her grandmother, and it was an amazing sight. "Bye!"

"Bye." Sean cleared his throat, doing his best not to watch her walk away. If he had the slightest hook of a grin on his face, his uncle would be sure to notice. More talk of a rebound romance was the last thing he wanted. A man needed his privacy. The door whooshed shut and she was in plain sight through the glass as she ambled to her car.

"Bacon double cheeseburger." The waitress slid the plate on the table in front of him. "And your usual, Frank. I piled on the onion rings. I know how you like them."

"Thank you kindly, Connie." Frank said something else, but the words were lost to Sean as he watched Eloise open her car door.

The wind played with her hair, tossing it across her face. She moved with the grace of a dancer and she shone with the quiet beauty the Bible spoke about. His chest cinched tight, making it hard to breathe. Frank couldn't be right, could he? These feelings he had for her weren't romantic, were they? Was he on the rebound?

No. Sean dismissed the idea and bowed his head as his uncle said the blessing.

* * *

Low rays of sunshine slanted through the orchard of fruit trees and onto the rows of the garden patch. New green sprouts speared through the earth to unfurl their stems and leaves. Eloise, changed out of her work clothes and into something more practical for chores, stabbed her cane into the soft grass as she crossed her grandmother's back lawn.

"There's my sweet pea." Edie Tipple looked up from her weeding. A welcoming smile wreathed her face. "I already got a call from Madge. She said her grandson thought you were real nice."

"He had many good qualities, too." Eloise eased down across from her grandmother. "I'm still not looking to get involved, Gran."

"I mean to change your mind. You never know when the right man will come along." Trouble glinted in her grandmother's green eyes. She tugged at the brim of her hat to keep the sun out of her face. She looked adorable in her pink checkered blouse and pink pants. "I figure on helping you find that right man."

"A woman doesn't need a husband to be happy." As if they hadn't had this conversation before, she plucked at a budding dandelion in the feathery fronds of new carrots, careful not to disturb the growing vegetables. "Look at me. Happy."

"Yes, so I see." Gran didn't sound convinced. "You work all day and spend your evening helping an old lady weed her garden."

"You aren't old to me, Gran, and I like hanging with you, just like I used to when I was little." She plucked a tiny thistle sprout, taking care not to rip the tender roots as she pulled. "Remember when I practically lived here?"

"You, your older sister and I baked every afternoon. Cookies and brownies and pies. Your brothers would eat everything we made." Gran laughed at the good memories they'd shared.

This awesome evening was another great blessing in her life. Time spent with Gran listening to the wind whistle through the grasses and feeling the sunshine on her back made her troubles seem far away. "You don't have to set me up anymore, Gran. I can find my own man when I'm ready."

"I can't seem to help myself." She inched down the row and hunkered over the new section of carrots. Weeds were helpless against her practiced assault. "I can see you didn't fall in love with George. I was hoping he was the one."

"Sadly, no. Not even close." She pulled a buttercup blossom from the feathery greens. The delicate bold yellow petals reminded her of being a little girl running through the fields that would turn yellow with them this time of year. She tucked it behind her ear. "I know that look, Gran. You have someone else in mind."

"I have a backup, it's true. I had you meet the best one first, but this one has prospects, too." Gran glowed with happiness as she worked, considering the possibilities. "His grandmother promises he's a nice boy. He makes up with lots of good traits for what he lacks in other areas."

"Oh, boy." Not again. Eloise laughed. "I don't want to go on another blind date. They're too painful."

"What you need, my girl, is more practice." Gran patted the earth where she'd extracted a particularly

long-rooted dandelion. "It's not fair what happened to
you. The accident. Spending all that time in a wheelchair—"

"I don't like to think about that time and what I lost,"
she interrupted. She could only take so much. The year
she'd spent as a paraplegic had been the most difficult
of her life. "I got through it, but it's over now. I'm looking forward."

"That's wise, dear." Gran swiped her brow and left
a faint trace of dust on her forehead. "It was hard re-
building your life. I watched you do it. You had to leave
so much behind. The skating you loved, the man you
loved, everything."

"I'm all right." She swallowed hard, refusing to
break the cage of denial she'd trapped all her feelings
in. "That's what matters. Please don't set me up on another date."

"Too late. I know what's best for you." Gran, as endearing as could be, reached across the row and patted
Eloise's hand.

All her life she'd looked up to her grandmother, ran
shouting with joy up the front steps to be swept into
Gran's hug. The little girl she'd been still could not say
no. Gran seemed so big to her, more special than anything on earth.

"I hope you have next Wednesday available." Silver
curls fluttered in the wind as she bent over her work.
"If not, clear your calendar so you can meet Craig."

"I'm afraid to ask what he does." Eloise pulled a
handkerchief from her pocket and shook it out.

"He's a technician at one of those oil-changing
places. Now before you think the worst, he's in line
for a promotion."

Memories of George flitted into her mind as she gently brushed away the smudge of dirt on her grandmother's forehead. "Goody."

"That's my girl." Pride lit her up. "You'll find your happiness, I promise you that. You can't give up looking, and you can't give up hope."

"I'm not sure I want my happiness to depend on a man." She thought of Gerald and how he hadn't been as stalwart as she'd believed him to be. She would never forget the phone calls she'd made to him and the last messages she'd left on his voice mail. She'd been lonely for him and needed to hear the sound of his voice after a tough day in physical therapy, and what had he been doing? Taking his new skating partner out to an intimate, romantic dinner. She'd been left waiting while his feelings had turned off for her and on for someone else. Almost a year had passed and it still stung.

"When it's the right man, your happiness is assured." Gran sat back on her heels, growing misty remembering. "When your grandfather was alive, my life was perfect. Love made it that way."

"Gramps was great." She couldn't argue. "I'm not sure they make men like him anymore."

"Sure they do. You just have to find him. Your perfect match. The man God means just for you." Gran returned to her weeding, so sure of her view. "Faith, Eloise. You have to believe."

"Of course." Believe? She wanted to. It was a nice idea, but life wasn't that simple and love was painfully complicated. "How about I take a break from believing and start up again, oh, say in five years?"

Gran laughed. "Don't think you are getting out of this date."

"I wouldn't dream of it." She plucked a dandelion and a long-root system out of the soil. A robin flew overhead and landed on the edge of the grass. The bird's head cocked to one side as she listened, then hopped along in search of her supper.

At least her grandmother hadn't yet heard the news that she'd spent time with Sean Granger. That would come one day, but she decided it wouldn't be today. She let the silence lengthen just like the pleasant evening shadows of approaching twilight.

She separated a fragile patch of carrot tops and hunkered down to do some serious weeding. This was her life and she would be content with it.

Chapter Six

Hard to believe a week had gone by without seeing Eloise. Sean gripped the steering wheel as he slowed for a deer in the fields at the side of the road. He kept an eye on her as he approached, ready to stop if she startled and dashed across the road. This time of year, she would have a fawn or two tucked away somewhere so he wanted to take extra care. But she darted safely into the fields so he kept watch for other animals and gave the truck a little more gas.

A whole week. He hadn't been pining for her or anything as dire as that. He'd simply missed out on seeing her. She and Cheyenne had a riding get-together earlier in the week and he figured he might be able to say hi to her then, since he had the expecting mare to check on in the barn. He had intended to ask about the horses they'd rescued. But no, his cousin Tucker had taken possession of the land he'd purchased across the road and had asked for help walking fence lines and making a few minor repairs in the outbuildings. Couldn't say no to the chance to wield a hammer and restring barbed wire, could he? But he'd wondered about her.

There would be no more wondering. He was about to have the pleasure of her company. He felt as cheerful as the sunlight shining through the windshield. When he hit town, he hung a right and followed the detour on Second Street to avoid the vendors setting up for the town's yearly summer festival. The few miles he had to go seemed like ten. Maybe he was looking forward to seeing Eloise more than he'd thought.

Anticipation buzzed through him as he turned off into the paved lane that rolled through fields, trees and blooming flowers to the Lark Song Inn. When Uncle Frank had called him into the barn with a message to meet Eloise with the horse trailer, he'd had to hide the gladness sweeping through him. He didn't want his uncle to misread things. He didn't bother to hide it now.

Eloise was nice. Who wouldn't enjoy spending time with her? Add to that the fact she was a casualty of romance too, how could he resist wanting to see her? It was a comfort to have a buddy going through the same thing he was. Even a lone wolf needed a buddy.

He parked, grabbed the keys and hopped into the pleasantly warm morning. The parking lot only had a few cars. A middle-aged couple led the way down the porch while a hotel employee carted their luggage after them.

"Good morning." He stepped out of the way to let them down the stairs first. They returned the greeting, quite relaxed and content. That's when he caught sight of Eloise. Wow, she took his breath away. She breezed through the doorway wearing a pink T-shirt, boot-cut jeans and riding boots. She'd obviously changed out of her work clothes for their next horse-hunting adventure.

"Sean. You made record time." She waved the gray

Stetson she carried in her free hand and plopped it on her head as she crossed the porch. "You had to be standing right beside Mr. Granger when I gave him the message."

"No, but he didn't waste time getting a hold of me." He didn't add that his uncle was hoping a romance would develop. Frank was definitely going to be disappointed on that score. Sean waited while she tapped down the steps. "You didn't waste any time finding more horses."

"Actually they found me, or the humane society did. I had spoken to them last week, of course." She joined him on the pathway and they backtracked to the truck. "I—"

"Eloise!" A child's voice rang in the air behind them. Cady's little goddaughter Julianna waved at them, all dressed in purple. "Daddy said I could come, okay?"

She pounded down the stairs in her glittery grape sneakers. Too late to say no to her now. He lifted a brow to Eloise in a silent comment.

"Do you mind?" She bit her bottom lip, maybe worried he might get mad.

"How could I? First I was spending the morning with one pretty gal, now I get to spend it with two." He opened the truck door for her, noticing she smelled faintly like honeysuckle.

"You are a gentleman, Sean Granger."

"I try."

Threads of pure blue sparkles wove through the emerald depths of her irises. He'd never seen a more arresting color. She was wholesome femininity and sunny beauty and he wasn't sure why his chest cinched up so hard he couldn't breathe. Probably any man would have the same reaction to her. It wasn't romantic feelings he felt. Probably gratitude for a friendship that was obviously cementing.

That had to be it. Satisfied with his conclusion, he waited for Julianna to skip across the lot, caught her elbow to help her up into the cab first and turned to Eloise. He knew the touch of her hand and the slender fit of her fingers against his.

Nice. This is friendship, he insisted as his heart skipped a single beat—just one. Nothing to worry about. Once she was helping Julianna with her seat belt, he shut the door and circled the truck to the driver's side.

"Now that I've joined the team," he said as he started the engine. "What are the details? Where do we go?"

"We take a left at the county road and keep on driving for ten miles." Eloise pulled a pink memo out of her jeans pocket. Glossy gold hair curtained her face, leaving only the tip of her nose and the dainty cut of her chin visible. "Angie from the humane society is already on site. She says there are four horses and that's all I know."

"Abused or just unwanted, like the last pair?" He nosed the truck down the lane.

"I don't know." She folded the paper back up into quarters. "They are doing the assessments right now."

"So you don't know if these will have the temperament you're looking for?"

"They are in need. Cady says that's more important."

Julianna nodded. "They need love," she chimed in, as cute as a button.

He remembered when his little sister, Giselle, was that age. Although she was grown up and in college now, she was still as sweet to him. He shared a smile over the top of Julianna's head and the silent connection he felt with Eloise defied words.

Checking for traffic, he saw the road was completely clear and turned left. Fields spread out as far as the eye could see, broken only by trees, a few houses scattered far and wide and the occasional herds of grazing cattle and horses. "How are Hershey and Licorice?"

"Licorice gives kisses," Julianna answered, as serious as a judge. "Hershey likes apples the best."

Not exactly the information he was after and across the cab Eloise's gaze found his again. It was a shared moment where words weren't needed. It was nice to have a real friend, one he was in tune with.

"After they had a good bath and brush down, the farrier came by to tend to their hooves and shoes." She fingered the edge of the paper she held. "They are sweet guys. Licorice seems relieved to have so much attention again. He's already making friends with everyone. Hershey is having a harder time."

"He stares down the aisle all day," Julianna explained. "He's got sad eyes."

"He's grieving. He's especially tenderhearted and he's taken all these changes very hard." She'd spent the bulk of her breaks and lunch hour making friends with him. "We are all trying to comfort him. Everyone already loves both horses."

"I'm sure they aren't being spoiled."

"Not at all." Her day felt brighter. It couldn't be because of Sean, right? She leaned back in the seat and savored the fall of sun on her face and the sense of freedom at being temporarily released from her managerial duties. "I'm certainly not guilty of that, right, Julianna?"

"Right." The girl shook her head emphatically and her twin braids bounced. "Me neither."

Sean chuckled. Eloise felt comfortable in his presence. Not at all like Friday night when it had been a struggle to make conversation with George. "I was going to saddle them up and give them a test ride this afternoon and could use some help. Are you interested?"

"I'm game. Count me in." He squared his impressive shoulders. He had come when she'd asked, and she thought about that, finding one more thing among the many to like about the man.

"Can I come, too?" Julianna steepled her hands as if in prayer. "Please, please, please?"

"After we find out how they handle, then you can see what your dad says." Eloise gave one braid a gentle tug, knowing that would make the girl smile.

"Bummer. I know how to ride, you know. Aunt Cady lets me ride her horse." Sparkles glittered in her eyes full of excitement and childhood wonder. "I love horses, too. I've asked Dad one hundred times and he still says I can't have one. We live in the city."

"Yes, there's no place for a horse in a brownstone." Eloise understood the girl's love of horses. It was a phase she hadn't ever fully outgrown. Her mare, Pixie, lived in her grandmother's field, as she had for the last fourteen years. "I got my horse when I was your age."

"You did? Cool." Julianna sighed. "I know you aren't supposed to pray for yourself. That's not the right way to pray. You are supposed to think of others and pray for them. That's what Dad says. So, do you know what?"

"What?"

"I pray for my horse. She's somewhere and I want her to be happy. Maybe that way she can find me. And if she does, maybe she can be gold with a white mane." Julianna's forehead puckered with concern. "Do you think that's being selfish like my mom?"

On the other side of the truck, Sean caught her eye. He drove with both hands on the wheel and kept most of his attention on the road, but in the brief moment their gazes met an unspoken understanding passed between them. Probably because they were on the same wavelength.

Julianna's mother had left the family for a richer man. She couldn't imagine how much that would hurt a little girl. Eloise cleared the emotion from her throat. Her parents' marriage was rock solid. Her grandparents on both sides had been the same. "No, I don't think it's selfish. You are asking for the horse to be happy first, even if you never get to meet her, right?"

"Right." Julianna sighed. "But I hope I do."

"Me, too." She liked to think there was a very lucky and nice horse out there wanting a little girl to love. She let her eyes drift shut. *Please, Lord, if it's possible, give Julianna her dream.*

"I saw that," Sean said after she'd opened her eyes. "I know what you asked for."

"How?"

"Because I did, too."

It was tough not to like him even more for that. It was a good thing she spotted the road they needed to turn on to so that she didn't need to analyze it. There were horses to rescue. "Take a right there by the pine trees."

"Sure thing."

The truck hit the dirt lane with a bump. They bounced down the wide private road lined by thick trees and she unfolded her memo to make sure she re-

membered the directions correctly. "We're looking for
a mailbox with the last name Noon. It should be on the
left-hand side."

"I see it." He slowed the truck to make the turn. The
driveway was in terrible shape, overgrown as if no vehicle had passed there for some time. Fresh tracks through
grass, weeds and a sprouting blackberry bush testified
it was an actual driveway.

"No worries." Sean gave the wheel a slow spin. "I've
got four-wheel drive."

"Let's hope you don't need it." She couldn't imagine
getting the horses and trailers out if they did. Julianna
seemed to enjoy the jolting and pitching, her eyes shining with the importance of their adventure.

It wasn't long before a clearing gave way to a mass
of parked vehicles and the saddest sight. Eloise gasped
aloud at the four shapes huddled in the shade of a maple
tree in a barren, tumbling-down corral. The shapes were
animals covered with thick layers of dried-on mud and
dirt.

The sharp hint of bones pierced the horses' sides. Her
vision blurred with hot, shocked tears and obscured the
image of the half-starved horses. Sean's truck rolled to
a stop and she wondered if she should make Julianna
stay in the cab or call her father to inform him the situation might be too graphic for her.

But it was too late. Julianna unclicked her belt, rising to her knees on the seat. She gripped the steering
wheel, straining to look. "What happened to them? Why
are they like that?"

"They're starving, sweetie." Sean answered, his baritone layered with sadness. "Someone left them to fend
for themselves."

The place was obviously abandoned. The old farmhouse stood dark and silent with weeds growing on the walkway and obscuring the front steps.

"It's been foreclosed on. When the appraiser came to take a look at the property for the bank, she found this." A woman who must be Angie, the lady from the county shelter, strode over in a simple shirt, jeans and boots. "Nate is taking a look at them right now. They seem glad to see us, poor things."

"It's good to meet you, Angie." Eloise didn't remember tumbling from the truck, only that she was on the ground staring at the horses. She swiped at her eyes. "I'm sorry, I wasn't prepared for this. Julianna?"

"I've got her," Sean answered. The girl's hand was tucked safely in his as they watched Nate work with the animals.

"We're going to help them, right?" Tears rolled down the girl's face.

"That's why we're here." Sean was ten feet tall in her view. Shoulders square, spine straight, unfailingly decent. It was really hard not to look at him and think, "amazing."

"I'm sorry to bring you all the way out here like this." Angie glanced at her cell screen before tucking it into her pocket. "I was just getting ready to call you. It's worse than I thought. I suppose you are rethinking your offer?"

"Not at all." The wind puffed lazily against her as she turned toward the fence. One of the horses lifted her head over the top rail, nostrils scenting the air, chocolate eyes gleaming with the smallest hope. "My boss would not want me to walk away from this."

"Whew. I can't tell you how glad I am to hear that."

Angie tugged at her hat brim. "Our donations are down in this economy, and we are stretched thin as it is. I'm not sure we have the resources for this, even with Nate donating his services. They are good horses, as far as I can tell. Calm. A little skittish, but that's to be expected."

"How long have they been like this?"

"Probably a few months. I talked to a neighbor. No one realized the animals were left behind or they would have done something sooner. The folks who left probably had no money to deal with the animals, but they should have called us. We could have helped. That's why we're here."

A sad situation. Eloise set the tip of her cane on the uneven ground. "At least we can help now. How long before we can trailer them?"

"As soon as Nate is done. I think he intends to follow you back to town. They are going to need some special care."

"We will make sure they get it." Determined, she joined Sean and Julianna at the fence. The horse had poked her head through the wood rungs and buried her rather substantial-size face against Julianna's stomach and chest. The mare leaned into the little girl with obvious need.

"She likes me," Julianna breathed, holding on tightly to the animal so dirty it was hard to make out her original color. "I like her, too."

"So I see. You are friends already." She laid the palm of her hand against the horse's sun-warmed neck, hoping the animal could feel in her touch that everything was going to be all right.

"I'm going to help the vet." Sean reached over to

brush a strand of hair from her eyes. The stroke of his fingertips was brief but tender. Her breath caught, but he didn't seem affected. Calm and collected, he moved away, his gait confident and easy, his movements athletic and sure. He ducked between the rails and paused to reassure the horses before he moved a step closer.

Maybe it was her imagination, but the sunshine seemed to brighten all around him.

"I feel sorry for Julianna's dad." Eloise swung up on her good leg and settled into the saddle. She patted Licorice's neck and tightened the reins to keep him from sidestepping. "The girl refused to leave Dusty's side."

Julianna had named the mare because she was so dusty. The two had bonded and as soon as they'd arrived back at the inn, the horse lumbered down the ramp and ran straight to the child. They were inseparable. Fortunately, the chef had sent a picnic lunch out to the stable for everyone working on the new arrivals, so the girl had gotten lunch.

Eloise reined Licorice around. "I don't know how Adam is going to get Julianna back home to New York."

"I overheard him saying the same thing." Sean eased into his saddle, although Hershey wasn't too sure about a new rider. The big bay gelding danced in place but didn't discourage the seasoned rider who commanded him with a gentle hand and reassured him in low tones. "I think it was love at first sight."

"You are definitely right." She tugged the brim of her hat lower to cut the sun's glare. "That is the most dangerous kind of horse love. I don't recommend it as I'm still in the midst of it."

"Me, too. It's one love that has no end." He felt the

gelding's hesitancy. The animal kept looking around, searching for someone long gone. He laid his hand on the gelding's neck, so the horse could feel the comfort of his touch. "You did nothing wrong, buddy. Are you going to be all right?"

The horse's sigh was answer enough. He plodded along but his feelings didn't seem to be into it. Poor fellow. Larks twittered on branches and jays squawked from the fence line as he guided the horse down the sidewalk, trailing Eloise. She sat straight and tall in her saddle, graceful as always and her long hair trailed in the wind.

"Where should we go?" she asked over her shoulder.

He pressed his heels lightly to bring Hershey alongside the other horse. "Do you know what sounds good after that lunch we had?"

"An ice-cream cone?"

"How did you know?"

"A wild guess."

"Proof great minds think alike." Of all the ways he'd seen Eloise, and he'd liked every one, this had to be his favorite view of her. Astride a horse, she was carefree and relaxed, girl-next-door wholesome and unguarded. On the back of the horse, she seemed less restrained, less careful. Maybe it was because she didn't need her cane to move through the world. She dazzled in a modest, genuine way he could not describe with words but could feel with his soul.

"I'm sorry to tell you this, Sean, but a great mind? You? I don't think so." Humor crinkled attractively in the corners of her eyes.

"Ouch. That's hard on a man's ego."

"I would think your ego would be used to it by now."

Dimples bracketed the demure curve of her mouth. "If it's any consolation, my mind isn't great either. Just so-so."

"I'm mostly so-so," he quipped. "Just ask my brother. He's a decorated Army Ranger and I'm the never-do-well in the family."

"The black sheep?"

"Baaah." So, he liked to make her laugh. Nothing else felt important right now, just that she was happy. The geldings pranced quickly down the lane and onto the shoulder of the county road. No traffic buzzed by, but when a vehicle did it would be a good way to judge how steady the horses were. "How about you? Let me guess, you are the perfect daughter."

"Me? No way. That's my older sister. Gabby is perfect. She was the A student, I was the B student. She has her own design business in Jackson—she was hired to do the inn, that's how I met Cady. I'm the slacker living with my parents."

"You still live at home?"

"Guilty as charged."

"Honestly? I did, too. I came back after college. Now I live with Uncle Frank and my cousins. Although it will be one less cousin in a few weeks. Autumn is moving out after the wedding." He pressed Hershey into a trot. "We have a lot in common, Eloise."

"I know, it's scary." She urged her mount to keep up with him. "Very scary."

"I have a question for you." He nudged Hershey into a smooth canter. Steel shoes rang on the pavement in harmony as they ran along. "You haven't heard from that blind-date guy again, have you?"

"Me? Oh, no. George was never interested in me."

She glanced over her shoulder. "We're in luck. A hay truck is coming up on us."

He hadn't noticed the rumble of the diesel engine closing in. All he could see was Eloise lighting up the world around him. He shook his head, bringing the landscape into focus. The blue sky, green grass fields and the first glimpse of town up ahead seemed distantly dull next to her. The semi's engine whined as it downshifted. "I guess we'll see how the horses take a little distraction."

"My guess is nice and steady. Licorice handles like a dream." Affection and pride for the horse softened her and she'd never looked more awe-inspiring than when she leaned forward to pat the gelding's neck. "Isn't that right, boy?"

The truck rolled by and Sean didn't notice the hit of the back draft or the tiny bits of hay raining down from the load. All he could see was Eloise's tender compassion as she spoke to the horse and her caring spirit as she urged Licorice into a gallop, leaving him and Hershey behind in their dust.

Chapter Seven

"Licorice is really fast." Eloise turned in her saddle. "I wanted to push him and see what he had. Wow."

"Impressive." Sean pulled a winded Hershey into a slow walk. "Like he's part Thoroughbred."

"He's a great horse." She watched the gelding's ears flicker, taking in every word. His neck arched with a touch of pride and his luxurious black mane rippled in the warm breeze. "My guess is he was ridden often. Someone spent a lot of time with him."

"That would explain a lot." He rocked along with the horse's gait. He appeared powerful in the saddle, utterly Western and heroic as if he could right wrongs and fight outlaws into submission.

Eloise shook her head to scatter her thoughts. Highly inappropriate. He was a friend, nothing more. A very handsome friend. Muscles shaped the cut of his T-shirt. He was in incredible shape, but his power was more than physical, it went deeper as if straight to the soul.

"Hershey keeps glancing back like he's expecting someone to materialize and his life can go back to the way it was." Sympathy etched into the hard rugged lines of Sean's face. "He wants to go back in time, and I can't do that for him."

The man was way too gorgeous for his good and for hers. She drew in a deep breath. Time to stop noticing these things. She looked up to realize they were at the drive-in. How did they get there? She had no idea because she'd been watching Sean and not the scenery.

She guided Licorice into the driveway and straight toward the drive-thru lane.

"I can empathize." She drew her horse to a stop in the shade of the building and studied the lighted display. "I remember lying in the hospital staring up at the ceiling tiles and asking God to take me back in time so I could change the events of that evening. I wanted back what I'd lost."

"You knew you couldn't skate again that soon?" Sean sidled up beside her, forehead furrowed with concern, sitting tall and straight. If a girl were to lay her cheek against his wide shoulder, she would feel safe and incredibly protected.

Not that she was that girl. She steeled her spine. "Oh, yes. As soon as they looked at the X-rays, they told me I'd never return to the ice."

Sean opened his mouth to say something, probably to ask the obvious question but thankfully the speaker squawked to life. Licorice stood calmly at the noise. Hershey danced a few nervous steps and then settled.

"Welcome to the Steer In." A cheerful teenage girl's voice popped and cracked over the ancient system. "Is that you, Eloise?"

"Hi, Chloe. How are you doing today?"

"It's a quiet afternoon, so good. What can I get you?"

"A soft chocolate ice-cream cone." She shivered when Sean leaned close.

"A strawberry for me," he rumbled in low, smoky tones.

"Oh, is this like a date?" Chloe blurted over the speaker loud enough to carry to the nearby car parked beneath the awning. Two gray-haired ladies glanced their way, familiar smiles flashing as they turned to watch the proceedings. They were, as luck would have it, friends of Gran's.

It was too much to hope she wouldn't be recognized. Impossible, really, since the women in the car had known her since birth.

"Not a date." She was quick to correct loud enough for her voice to carry. "Don't say things like that, Chloe. You're going to ruin any chance I have of my grandmother abandoning her plans to marry me off."

"Sorry," Chloe laughed.

"You wouldn't happen to know those ladies over there?" Sean leaned in and splayed his palm on the saddle's pommel. "They're waving."

"I know them." All too well. Mrs. Parnell was Gran's oldest friend. Mrs. Plum was Gran's second-oldest friend. They lunched together at least once a week after their church meeting.

No way was she going to keep this private. Her grandmother was sure to find out. As she touched her heels to Licorice's sides and he obligingly stepped forward, she fought off a wave of panic. All Gran had to do was to talk to Frank Granger, and how hard would it be for the two of them to make Sean feel obligated to take her to dinner? Putting him in that uncomfortable position was the last thing she wanted.

"It's my treat." He leaned across her to hand money to Chloe at the window. "Keep the change."

It was too late to protest. Chloe darted away before Eloise could dig out the fold of dollar bills she'd hidden in her jeans pocket.

"The horses are handling all of this just fine, don't you think?" Sean knuckled back his hat, revealing more of his face. His blue eyes resonated the manly kindness she'd come to expect. A girl could lose herself dreaming about him.

But not her. She was thankful for that. She cleared her throat, surprised her voice sounded thin and scratchy when she answered. "Yes, I do. Hershey will be calmer once he gets used to all the changes he's facing."

"He needs time. That's all." Sitting in the saddle, backlit by the brilliant blue sky and the sun-kissed greenery of grass and trees, he was a compelling sight.

Not that she was compelled.

"He might require a bit of work. I'll volunteer to train him, if there's a need."

"Thanks." Her voice sounded squeaky. "I'll keep that in mind."

Chloe popped into view through the take-out window and produced two cones. Eloise handed one over to Sean along with a few paper napkins Chloe also dispensed.

"Have fun!" The teenager called out. Clearly she had high hopes for their "date."

The horses plodded forward lazily. It was a perfect summer afternoon. Not too hot, but hot enough to make the ice cream taste like an icy luxury. Not too windy, just a light puff of air stirring up the scents of earth and grass and horse. The noise from the main street increased as they circled the lot to the exit lane. Colorful booths and awnings stretched as far as the eye could see up the street. A red banner strung from light poles read, "Welcome to Wild Horse, Wyoming's Pioneer Days Festival."

"When do you have to be back to work?" he asked.

"Cady said not to hurry." She leaned back in her saddle, tilting her face toward his. "Are you thinking what I'm thinking?"

"That's an affirmative." He gave his ice-cream cone a taste and let the strawberry sweetness melt on his tongue. "Nothing like hitting the festival on the first day. We'll get the best view of stuff and it's not crowded."

"Yes. Wait until tonight." She gave her cone a twirl, neatly catching all the drips. "I hadn't realized how much I've missed all this. I got caught up chasing after things that didn't last, at least not for me. Now that I'm home, I've forgotten how special this all is."

"Small-town festivals?"

"Yes, and small-town life." She sighed as the horses plodded leisurely down the empty section of the street. "Before I was always so busy and focused. When I was on the ice, I had to shut out everything else. There was only practice."

"And the falls? That ice looks like a hard place to land." He had to quip; it was who he was. It was easier to joke than ask harder questions.

"I don't miss the falls." She had a wonderful laugh, reserved and whimsical. "But I miss the skating. I trained and I trained. It took me an extra two years to squeak in college courses so I could get a degree. Between skating and school, I didn't do a whole lot of living. I put off everything. Fun weekends, vacations, seeing movies and even the idea of marriage and a family."

"Are you second-guessing the choices you made?" He knew how that could be.

"No. I can't imagine following any other dream. It simply hurt when it ended." She looked wistful and not bitter, retrospective and not sad. "If the accident hadn't happened, I would still be skating."

"What was your favorite part?" He took a big bite of ice cream and let it melt in his mouth, watching as she licked a dab of chocolate ice cream off her bottom lip. She was as sweet as could be, trying to eat her cone before it dripped all over her.

His chest warmed with new emotions, which had to be admiration and respect—certainly nothing romantic. He was a lone wolf. Lone wolves didn't do romance.

"The competitions were way too stressful to be my favorite part. The travel was tough because we were focused on our training and our performances." She frowned in concentration and gave her melting cone another lick. "It was the day-to-day skating I loved. Being on the ice when it was just me soaring. I felt like I did when I was little skating on Gran's winter pond. It's all I ever wanted to do."

"You didn't only lose a vocation, but a calling. Something you loved."

"Yes." She turned those incredible, honest eyes at him. "But there are worse things to lose in life. How about you? What have you lost?"

"My older brother a few years back." He bit into the sugary cone, crunching as he gathered the courage to let down his guard. "Tim was an Army Ranger killed in action."

"I'm so sorry."

"Me, too. It was a hard blow for everyone in my family."

"How did you handle it?"

"Mostly, I felt lost. Drifting. As if everything I'd thought about myself and about life changed."

"Trauma will do that to you." Empathy layered her words.

"The earth had been knocked out from beneath me and I no longer wanted the same things I once did." The first vendor's booth was close, so he eased Hershey to a stop. "One loss made everything shift. I couldn't see life the same way. My brother wasn't in it. I knew the phone would never ring with him on the other end of the line. I no longer believed only good things happened."

"Life can change in an instant. I learned that lesson, too." She daintily bit into the rim of her cone. "It makes you appreciate each day more, I think. Here and right now it is such a beautiful afternoon. I want to soak it in, every detail, and remember it always."

"Even me?" He finished off his cone.

"Especially you." She blushed a little, but when he nodded in understanding, she relaxed. They were on the same wavelength, they didn't even need the words. She'd never experienced it with anyone else before. "We can tether the horses here in the shade."

"And bring them some water from the hot-dog vendor." He gestured with a nod at the nearby booth before dismounting in a single powerful movement. His boots hit the ground with a muffled thud.

"Good idea." She managed not to spill her cone as

she swung her leg over and eased to the pavement. "We'll keep an eye on them for a bit. Make sure they don't start worrying about being left again."

"Hershey's already looking nervous. It's okay, boy." He stroked the gelding's nose in slow, gentle glides that made the horse calm.

The moment she let go of the saddle horn she realized her mistake. Too late to get back on the horse without having to explain to Sean. She kept her weight on her good leg and leaned lightly on Licorice for support. For a little while, she'd forgotten about what the doctors had labeled a disability. She had been free from her partial paralysis and the cane she relied on.

"Did you forget something?" Sean ambled closer and tugged her hat brim up a few inches so he could study her face.

"I didn't forget it. I just didn't bring it." Her cane was leaning against the stable wall, right where she'd left it. Self-conscious, she wanted nothing more than to get back on that horse where she didn't have to be less than. On the back of a horse, she could be like any other young woman. That's the way she wanted Sean to see her.

"No problem." He held out his arm. "You can lean on me."

"No, I would be embarrassed." Every step she would take would remind her of how different she was. It would remind her even more strongly of the woman she no longer was.

"What's to be embarrassed about?" He appeared genuinely confused, as if he couldn't begin to see any problems. Proof of the kind of man he was. He caught her arm in his, sun-warmed and substantial. "Don't worry. I won't let you fall."

"I didn't think you would." She took a step with her weak leg, hating the weight she transferred onto Sean's forearm. "I weigh too much."

"You weigh the perfect amount. You don't have to worry, Eloise." He took a step forward to show her he was better than any cane she'd ever used. "I don't notice your limp. When I look, I see you."

"You must need glasses." She had to tease so he couldn't guess what his words meant to her. She would never forget the look on Gerald's face when he saw her sitting in a wheelchair for the first time. It was a blend of horror and pity that was burned on her brain, although he had quickly covered it up well enough. "I could recommend a good eye doctor."

"There's nothing wrong with my vision."

Before she could argue teasingly, the rest of her ice cream was plucked out of her hand. She turned, surprised to see Licorice crunching away on the last of the sugar cone.

Sean burst into laughter. "Next time we'll have to get some for the horses."

"I hope that doesn't give him a stomachache." Good humor chased away her worries. Life was good as she and Sean headed down the street together.

It was easy being with Eloise. Sean tucked his wallet into his back pocket and handed over the twenty. The vendor looked pleased as punch as she accepted it and began to wrap up the sale.

"The wind chimes are lovely, but it's too much." Eloise folded a strand of blond hair behind her ear in a shy gesture that only proved how cute she was.

Cute. He kept using that word for her over and over again. It wasn't the only word. *Awesome* came to mind. So did *endearing. Beautiful* was another that described her in any situation. To think she was self-conscious about her injury. Her limp was invisible, her loveliness outshone it tenfold.

"It will be something to remember today by. Something good, after the rough morning we all had." The neglected horses stayed at the back of his mind. He knew they were at the back of hers, too. The set of halters and leads she'd bought from one of the other vendors was testimony enough they were not far from her mind. At least the animals were more comfortable now. He accepted the bag from the sales lady and added it to the bundle he carried. "Whenever the wind blows, you can think of me."

"Because you're a bunch of hot air?"

"Ha ha." He bit his lip to keep from laughing. Before he could come up with a snazzy comeback, he heard someone say her name.

"Eloise, is that you?" a fragile voice warbled. A delicate elderly lady padded up to lay her hand on Eloise's arm. "Where is your cane, sweet pea? How are you getting around?"

"Gran." Eloise's jaw dropped. As if mortified, she sputtered for a second unable to think of what to say.

Sure, Sean knew how it looked with her hand tucked lightly on his forearm and with him carrying all her purchases. He cleared his throat. "I'm squiring her around this afternoon. Mrs. Tipple, we met a long time ago when I was a teenager."

"I remember. You were trouble, if I recall. Couldn't stop fidgeting during the candlelight service." She smiled, a timeless beauty. "You are one of the Granger boys."

"Guilty. I hope you don't mind I've stolen your granddaughter for the afternoon."

"Not at all." She chirped with happiness. "You aren't married, I take it?"

"No, but I'm not looking to be." He broke the news gently as Eloise gave her grandmother a hug.

"We're just friends, Gran, so don't get any ideas. Promise me?" Unmistakable love made her luminous. "I'm going out to dinner with Craig, but that is the last fix-up. No more."

"Take pity on her, Mrs. Tipple." Sean couldn't resist helping her cause. He liked Eloise. He'd do about anything for her. "I know how she feels. It's humiliating every time a new date doesn't work out."

"Why, I never thought of it that way before." The older lady furrowed her brow, adorably puzzled. "I can't think of why that would be."

"Gran, you found your perfect match on the first try. That's a great gift few of us are blessed with." She probably looked a lot like her grandmother did fifty years ago, Sean decided. She had the same willowy build and oval face and eyes shining like flawless emeralds. There was strength, too, the kind that went all the way to the soul.

"I'd best leave you kids to your fun." A grandmother's love beamed from her as she gave Eloise one final pat. "Don't think you have to hurry over tonight. I've got all the weeding done except for the tomatoes."

"Don't you dare do it without me." Eloise's warning held no bite, only sweetness. "See you later."

Her fingertips settled on his arm as she turned to watch her grandmother join her friends at a nearby booth. He laughed. "I finally have it figured out, chickie."

"What, exactly?" She sparkled as she leaned lightly on his arm.

"You spend a lot of evenings with your grandmother. You live with your parents." He heard his phone ring and pulled it out of his pocket. "I'm starting to see the real you."

"Oh, no. You don't want to be associated with someone so drab. Or would dull be a better word?"

"You? Dull? That's impossible." The experience of holding her on his arm had brought him closer to her than he'd expected, both physically and emotionally. Because she'd left her cane behind he had been near enough to see the twinkle lighting her eyes when she'd spotted the wind chimes for the first time.

Eloise was quietly exhilarating and she was easy to be with. There was no knot of anxiety in his chest. Meryl had always tied him up in knots, leaving him to wonder if he'd done things right or wrong. Being with Eloise was as natural as breathing. He stepped out of the flow of pedestrian traffic. "Is that your phone?"

"Probably. If not, then it's my guilt calling. I'm having too much fun. I should be on my way to work." She tugged out her cell and checked it.

"I heard Cady say not to rush back. No guilt necessary." He liked that about her, though. She was conscientious.

"Cady sent a text. She wants me to stop by the feed store and pick up a few things for the new horses."

"Let me see." He leaned close. His cheek brushed hers as he scanned the list. Her skin felt satin soft and he breathed in another hint of honeysuckle. It was nice. He kept using that word, but it was the truth. Being with her was so enjoyable, he wouldn't want to be anywhere else.

He focused on the list typed across the phone's little screen. "It's all easy stuff to tie on the saddles. It's doable."

"Definitely." She didn't move away.

Neither did he. The breeze danced through her hair, sending a stray wisp against his jaw. "The feed store is across the street from the horses. It couldn't be an easier errand."

"True."

Time stood still. The noise and heat and scents from the nearby hot-dog vendor became background to the slow, drum-like thud of his heart. He leaned in, so close their noses almost bumped. Her soft mouth opened slightly, betraying her surprise. The same surprise tapped like mad through his veins, but he couldn't seem to jerk away and put proper space between them. All he could see was her. Her big soulful eyes, her incredibly beautiful face, her lips. She was sugar-cookie sweet. He wanted to kiss her tenderly to match the tender adoration filling him.

Adoration? He furrowed his brow. That wasn't what he wanted to feel. What he wanted was to be unattached, a male wolf prowling the wilderness on his own answering to no one. So why was he inching closer?

Don't do it, he told himself. Kissing her wouldn't be right. It wouldn't be fair.

It was all he wanted.

Chapter Eight

"No." Her slim hand shot out and splayed across his sternum. "Sean, what are you doing?"

He swallowed. Good question. He was obviously being stupid.

Except it didn't feel stupid. It felt right to care for her. He shrugged. "I'm a man. Do we ever really know what we're doing?"

The quip worked. The tension taut in her shoulders relaxed a smidgeon. The stress tightening her jaw eased. Confusion continued to cloud her eyes as she stood like an island in the moving stream of the crowd, and he had to make that right. He hated to think he'd hurt her or caused her turmoil of any kind.

"Proof there really is something wrong with men." Her puzzlement turned to a chuckle.

"True. We're deeply flawed. Forgive me."

"I'll think about it." She tilted her head to one side, considering him. She held out one hand, since she couldn't take a decent step without him. "I think you have had too much fun, mister."

"Guilty. I have a weakness for street fairs. I lose all

common sense." His arm linked with hers, offering her his strength and his friendship as if the moment had never happened. "Let's stop and get water for the horses before we hit the feed store."

"It's a plan." She pasted on what she hoped was a smile, one that wasn't too bright and yet neatly hid the knot of confusion and disappointment tangled inside her.

They said nothing more, just little necessary things, as Sean ordered two big cups of water and they took them back to Licorice and Hershey. He tried to hide it, but she noticed the tension bunched along his square-cut jaw and the crinkles etched into the corners of his eyes. The friendship between them was strained. The easy camaraderie vanished. Sean had crossed a line she hadn't been comfortable with and she didn't know how to repair it.

He probably hadn't been thinking, just like he'd said. Maybe he was lonely, too. Maybe for a moment he'd felt less so and that's why he'd moved in to kiss her. She was convenient, she acknowledged silently as she held the cup for Licorice. Sean couldn't possibly have actually meant that kiss.

Sadness eked into her, and she gripped the side of the hitching post to balance her weight. Why did that make her so sad? As the horse lipped and slurped, she watched Sean out of the corner of her eye. He stood stoic in front of Hershey, holding the cup of water at an angle.

"If you want to hand me your phone, I'll run across the street and pick up the stuff." His words were nearly monotonous with strain as he held out his hand, wide palm up. Apology shadowed his gaze and she looked away.

She fished her phone from her pocket and handed it

over. But as he strode away without a word, dependable shoulders straight, gait athletic, an impressive man of good character, she felt her heart tug.

If only her gaze didn't follow him across the street. When he strode through the door and out of her sight, it was as if the sun dimmed.

Don't start feeling for him, she warned. No matter what she could not start to wonder what would have happened if they had kissed. She would be foolish to start wanting what she could not have.

Dumb. That's how he felt, like the biggest doofus in the county. Sean dismounted swiftly as soon as they reached the shadow of the inn's stables to fetch Eloise's cane. It was right where she'd left it, propped against the wall in the breezeway outside Licorice's stall. He seized the handle and hurried back just as she was dismounting.

"Thanks." She broke the silence, which had haunted them on the ride back.

He didn't know what to say after nearly kissing her. He couldn't bring up the subject again because it would only make those unhappy lines etch into her face. He didn't want that. Mom always said, "Less said, soonest mended," so he decided to go with the age-old adage, but he remained troubled. He'd hurt their friendship over an almost-kiss she hadn't wanted.

He had.

Clearly his feelings were bigger than he wanted to admit, even to himself. It was a lonely place to be. Disappointment crept around him like talons, digging deep. He prayed it didn't show as he took Licorice by the bit.

"I'll walk them in to Rocco. He's the one in charge of the horses?"

"Yes. I'll come with you. I want to see how the new additions are doing." She kept her gaze on the uneven gravel path ahead of her, as if that required her concentration.

He wasn't fooled. She did very well with her impaired walk. She didn't need to put so much concentration into it. She wanted to, and he didn't blame her.

He'd acted on feelings, not on thought. Maybe Uncle Frank was right. Maybe he was rebounding and he didn't even mean to be. Rebounding was not his style. He had decided to be a loner. He wanted no connections to any woman. That was the best way to heal from a broken relationship instead of jumping feetfirst into a new one.

Something tugged on his shirtsleeve. Sad-eyed Hershey lifted his horsy eyebrows in a show of sympathy.

"You're a good guy, Hersh." He patted the horse's nose.

The gelding nickered low in his throat, as if in perfect agreement.

"Eloise!" A child's voice echoed in the rafters above, accompanied by the patter of running feet. Julianna charged around the corner like a cute, purple butterfly. "You gotta come see! I have Dusty's stall real nice for her. And she just got a bath, and guess what?"

"My, you have been busy while I've been gone." She brightened at the girl's approach.

He winced. Eloise had said "I" instead of "we."

"Rocco and Dr. Nate gave her a bath and she's a palomino! She's gold with a white mane, just like I wanted." Julianna's hand crept into Eloise's and clung tight. "Do you think she's the horse I prayed for? I love her so much."

"So I see." She gazed down at the child with gentleness.

What he saw on her face blew him away. He leaned against Licorice for support. She would make such a good mom. He had never had a thought like that about a woman. Not even Meryl, whom he'd planned to marry. It was strange how he would see Eloise as a mother, kind and patient and always smiling. He gulped, afraid to guess where this line of thought might take him.

"Sean? Are you all right, boy?" Uncle Frank strolled into sight, dapper in a new T-shirt and jeans as if he were ready for a date with Cady. "You're lookin' a mite pale."

"I'm fine. It's nothing." He glanced around, surprised they weren't alone. Aside from Julianna and Frank, there were a handful of other people in the aisle tending to the stabled horses. He spotted a couple of wall rings and drew a rein through one of them. "What's going on here?"

"It's Friday evening. I came by to pick up Cady for dinner and look at what I found." Frank was sharp-eyed. He didn't miss much. Along with the knowing grin was a look of understanding. "I thought I could lend a hand."

"Yeah. Me, too." Lending a hand, that sounded like as good a reason as any to be here. As long as he didn't have to admit to the truth. Eloise caught his attention as she followed Julianna through an open stall gate and closed it behind her. The palomino nickered gently and lowered her nose for the girl to pat. The mare closed her eyes, looking mighty glad to have attention.

Sean swallowed hard. Maybe his feelings had been

stirred up by coming across this kind of neglect; they had overwhelmed him. Perhaps that's all his new, tender feelings were toward Eloise. That meant their near-kiss was nothing more serious and neither was his glimpse of Eloise as a future mom. Wouldn't that be a relief?

"How did the horses ride?" A woman's voice drew him out of his thoughts.

The horses? He shook his head, realizing Cady was asking about the trip to and from town. He looped another rein through a ring and loosely tied it. "Good. I think Licorice is going to do just fine for you. Hershey might have a hard time adjusting to different riders. Maybe at first, maybe not. I can work with him if you'd like."

"Yes. Absolutely." Cady had a serene gentleness about her that made her likeable and a good match for Uncle Frank. "I would pay you."

"Not necessary." As if he would accept her money. If she could take in animals in need without complaint of the vet bills it might cost her, he could offer his time to help.

"Then perhaps you would accept goodies from the kitchen now and then." She strolled up in her designer boots to offer Hershey a hunk of carrot. "After all, you have to keep your strength up."

"I wouldn't argue that." Especially since everything that came out of the restaurant's kitchen was fantastic. He untied the sack of molasses treats from the back of the saddle and caught sight of Eloise in the stall with Julianna.

The rush of tenderness he'd felt at the street fair when he'd been a fraction away from capturing her lips with his hit him full force. He felt as if caramel were melting in the middle of his chest. It was friendship, that was all. It couldn't possibly be anything more. From here on out, he wouldn't let it be.

He hefted the feed bag on one shoulder and grabbed the pack of supplies in his free hand. Every step he took past Eloise, he wanted to look at her. He wanted to grin at her over the top of the stall gate and know what she was thinking by the set of her expressive eyes. He wished he could see the uptilt of her mouth without remembering what it had been like to almost kiss her.

He let the bag slide down to the floor in the feed room. Tucked out of sight from the breezeway, he didn't need to look up to know who was coming down the aisle in his direction. He recognized Eloise's gait and the faint tap of her cane on the concrete. He straightened up, and the melted caramel feeling in his chest increased as she approached.

"Oh, hi." She appeared startled to see him. "I'm leaving for the day."

"I guess it's quitting time already." He stood as still as stone. Not a muscle quivered. "Are you going back to the festival?"

"Not tonight." She took a step, hating that the palm of her hand had gone damp against her cane.

"Meeting someone?" He stepped into the aisle to call after her.

"You could say that." She didn't turn around. If she did, she would have to face him. "I'm having dinner again."

"Not another blind date?"

"Yes." She feared he saw her the way she saw herself—as someone with her best years behind her. Sean clearly was carried away when he'd tried to kiss her, but that didn't change the situation. Blushing, she took another step, painfully aware of the drag of her leg. Her limp would always be a part of her. She could not wish it away.

"Have a good evening, Sean," she called over her shoulder and kept going.

"I never thought that boy would leave," Frank quipped as he poured sparkling water into two crystal glasses.

"I think he's sweet on Eloise." Cady leaned forward on the blanket set in the soft green grasses in the shade of the stable to take one of the glasses.

"And then some." Frank grinned. He was sweet on Cady.

She was elegance in motion. Every little movement she made was graceful as if timed to music as she lifted the glass to her lips and sipped. The wind blew her soft brown hair against the side of her face and she brushed it away with her free hand before he could put down the bottle and do it for her.

"That's why I suggested they ride the horses to town to test them out." Cady traded her glass for her fork and daintily pierced a bow-tie pasta with the tines. "I thought the time together would do them good."

"Agreed. I think they need a push." He set down the bottle, making sure it didn't tip over in the uneven grass. He'd also liked Cady's suggestion they stay close to the horses instead of heading into town so the employee in charge of the barn could take a dinner break. He liked everything about her, especially her sensitivity to others. "Sean's been hurt, so he's holding back."

"Eloise, too."

"I know how that is." He took hold of his fork and loaded up. The meaty tomato sauce on the pasta was tasty and he ate so he didn't have to elaborate.

"Everyone knows what that's like." Cady's fork hovered in midair. "How long do you think it will be before he asks her out?"

"Probably not as long as it took me to ask you," he joked. He was always lighthearted with his Cady. He thought of her as his these days, not that he'd told her so yet. They had been having dinner and going riding for the past three months and each outing had gone well. Every time he was with her, he cared about her more. After being a widower for seventeen years, it was comforting to have someone to spend time with. Reassuring to know someone cared for him in return.

"You did take a long time." She laughed, nibbling on the pasta. She may have been a respected personal-injury attorney when she'd lived in New York, but he knew the reason she had been so successful was the quiet strength and steady kindness that shone from within her. It was easy to spot on an evening like this with the birds chirping and butterflies dancing from wildflower to wildflower. Her guards were down. Small-town life agreed with her.

"I didn't think you liked me at first," she confessed.

"Sure I did. What's not to like? I was fairly sure a gorgeous woman like you wouldn't look twice at an old rancher like me."

"Old?" That amused her. "Watch it, mister. If you are old at fifty-three, then I am old at fifty-one. I would rather not think of myself as old."

"I don't see you that way. True beauty is ageless and you are truly beautiful." He meant the words, but he also liked the way their impact moved across her face. Her honest eyes brightened and the radiance of her spirit somehow made her heart-shaped face more comely.

"You know how to charm a lady, Frank Granger." She rose onto her knees with poise and brushed her lips against his clean-shaven cheek.

"That's not the kind of kiss I was hoping for."

"It's not?"

"Maybe I should show you what I had in mind."

"Maybe." His kiss was perfection sugarcoated with reverence. The brush of his lips to hers made her feel cherished. His hand cupped her jaw, cradling her as the sweet kiss lengthened. Her heart skipped three beats from the sheer exquisiteness of his gentlemanly kiss.

No man ever had made her feel cherished the way Frank did. Romantic love had eluded her all her adult life, but no longer. It had found her in this little Wyoming town. Moving here to follow her dream of owning a country inn had been the best decision of her life.

"Aunt Cady! Aunt Cady!" Julianna's voice echoed through the stable's wide breezeway and across the meadow full of wildflowers. The little girl burst into sight, as dear as could be, skipping ahead of her sister and father, Adam.

Love filled her as it always did for her goddaughters. "Julianna. Why are you so excited?"

"Cuz Daddy said we can stay for another whole week." She bounced to a stop at the edge of the blanket and dropped to her knees. "Both Jenny and me. We can stay if you say yes. Please, please, please?"

As if she had what it took to say no to those big Bambi eyes and little girl fingers steepled as if in prayer. She melted like an ice cube in Tucson.

"It's just us." Jenny, a serious twelve-year-old, tucked a lock of dark hair behind her ear. "Daddy has to go back to work."

"It's all he does," Julianna added sincerely as she plopped down on the blanket and sidled close. "He's a workacolic."

"A workaholic," Jenny corrected coolly. "When we're home, he never spends time with us anyway, so we may as well stay here with you."

Cady recognized the hope buried in Jenny's aloofness, and it was just as strong as Julianna's glittery excitement. She wrapped her arms around the littlest girl, who was within reach, holding her close. These girls and their father were family.

Adam planted his hands on his hips and raised one eyebrow, and she recognized his grave look. She had seen it many times before. He had a hard time juggling single fatherhood, his demanding job as a cardiologist and the emotional aftermath of his divorce. He hadn't always been terribly somber. She gave Julianna another quick snuggle. "I would love to have you girls stay with me."

"Yay!" Julianna bounced happily. "I get to stay with Dusty. She needs me."

"I get riding lessons," Jenny announced primly, clearly trying hard to contain all her secret happiness.

"I'm getting the short end of the stick." Adam winked as he strode closer, no longer quite as somber. "Girls, let's leave Frank and Cady to their dinner. Sorry, we didn't mean to interrupt."

"No problem," Frank spoke up, easygoing as always. That was one thing she adored about him. He was a powerful and rugged man, and strong of character, too.

Not much rattled him. He always went with the flow of things with good humor and steady confidence. "You're welcome to stay."

"Okay." Julianna bounced onto her knees to inspect the food and helped herself to one of the colorfully decorated cookies the inn's chef had packed in the picnic basket.

"I want one." Jenny dropped down to choose a cookie for herself.

"The more the merrier," Frank said, his deep baritone rumbling like a song. He winked, clearly not minding the intrusion. It was easy to see the father he'd been when his children were small, and the combination of might and gentleness made him more of a man in her eyes.

"This isn't the date you were hoping for." She lowered her voice, speaking over Julianna as the girl plunked down into Cady's lap. Adam came to peer into the basket too, interested in a selection of sliced fruit. She lightly wrapped her arms around the girl, holding her close. "First the horses and now this."

"Don't you worry about that. Any time I'm with you is a gift." So sincere. The power of his spirit made her world stop turning. He held out one big hand in silent invitation. "I'm glad to be here with you."

She laid her much smaller hand in his. Perfection. Their fingers linked, her soul stilled and she felt with her heart what he was too bashful to say with words.

Chapter Nine

Eloise. Against his will she dominated his thoughts on the drive home. As Sean cleaned and unhitched the horse trailer, images of the day with her overwhelmed him. Memories of her racing away from him on Licorice's back, the ring of her unguarded laughter, her look of shock when he'd tried to kiss her. He cringed and gave the garden hose a tug. He could still feel the imprint of her hand on his chest, blocking him from moving in to cover her lips with his.

He'd messed things up royally. He gave the nozzle a final blast, chasing the last of the soap bubbles from the tire rims. The trailer was clean inside and out and his work was done, but he didn't want to head down to the house. He knew it would probably be empty. He hadn't stopped by to see for sure on his way up the hill, but over breakfast this morning he'd overheard his cousins making plans to hit the street fair. Mrs. G. would have gone home. He didn't want to be alone battling thoughts of Eloise.

He coiled up the hose, working fast, trying to forget their awkward conversation in the inn's stable. When she'd walked away from him, it had felt final. He sighed, frustrated with himself. He hadn't even seen that attempted kiss coming.

A plaintive moo caught his attention. He glanced up. A white-faced Hereford leaned over the fence begging for attention. A half dozen other cows ambled over too, probably hoping for treats. He dug some out of the bag in the back of his truck and crossed the lane to greet them.

"Howdy, Buttercup." He rubbed her poll. She lowered her head to go after the treats. Being with animals made everything better. He chuckled as he held the goodies out of her reach. "You only get one, cutie. You have to share."

Buttercup's friends mooed in agreement and pushed against the fence too, eager for pats and treats of their own. Jasmine's long pink tongue stretched out. Lily, not to be outdone, caught hold of his T-shirt with her teeth and tugged.

"Girls, girls." He began handing out the treats since he was outnumbered. "There's enough to go around."

"You're popular with the ladies." Addy tromped into sight in the field, flanked by yearling cows who danced and hopped and skipped around her. "I can't believe you're not in town. Scotty can keep an eye on our expectant mare tonight so you don't have to stay. You should be having fun."

"I've already had all the fun I can handle." He held out the last of the treats to the cows, who devoured them cheerfully. He rubbed Buttercup's nose and Jasmine's poll. "Besides, the company is better here. Isn't that right, ladies?"

Buttercup mooed at him, as if in perfect agreement.

Addison laughed at the yearlings tumbling and playing around her and swiped a lock of straight strawberry-blond hair out of her blue eyes. "I've done nothing but work all day. Not that I mind but I'm dying to shop. I've got money to burn, or I will once I get a hold of Dad."

Addison reminded him again of his younger sister and he fought off a pang of homesickness. He missed his family. He was close to them. Maybe it was time for a call home. He put that on his mental to-do list. "The yearlings look good. They've been keeping you busy."

"Always. I've got the babies in the barn fed, so I'm heading down to the house." She patted a few eager heads. "Daisy, you be good while I'm gone. You too, Violet. Rose, don't even think about trying to get out of this fence. Are you sure you don't want to come?"

"I'll think about it." The evening was perfect, but the thought of spending it in an empty, echoing house made his stomach tighten. If he wanted to be a lone wolf, he would have to get used to it.

"C'mon. You really need to come." Addy climbed through the fence and bobbed to a stop beside him. "It won't be just us girls. We're all meeting up in front of the cotton-candy booth. Justin, Tucker and Ford will be there. You can hang with the guys."

"Good, because I don't think I could take hanging out with the likes of you." He gave her ponytail end a tug, just like he did when they were kids and was rewarded with her big, infectious grin.

"Fab! I'd better hurry. I promised I wouldn't be late." She took off at a dash down the lane. "Give me ten minutes, and I'll meet you at the truck."

"It'll be fifteen," he joked, as the cattle called out, saying goodbye in their cow-like way. His cell rang and drew their attention. Bovine ears pricked and eyes brightened in excitement as he fished it out of his pocket. Tongues reached, trying to grab the contraption from him and he chuckled. Cows were great.

He rubbed Lily's nose, stepped just out of reach of Buttercup's tongue. He expected to see his mom's number, but when he squinted at the display he couldn't believe his eyes. Meryl's name stared up at him. It was really her. She was calling. His palms went damp.

Three months ago, he used to pray for this. When his phone rang, it had been her name he had most wanted to see. Times had changed and he couldn't move his thumb to hit the button to answer the phone.

Something tugged at his hat brim. Teeth clamped on the neckline of his shirt. Yearling noses poked between the rails to sink their teeth into the legs of his jeans and tugged. The cows and their bright eyes were as affectionate as could be and a great comfort as he stared at the screen.

How could Meryl call after the way she'd left things? And why? It was like a sudden icy downpour had pummeled from the sky, drowning out the warmth and sunlight. He shivered in the eighty-degree temperature.

He hit Ignore and jammed the phone into his pocket safely out of sight but not out of mind.

"How did you like Craig?" Gran stepped onto the shaded old-fashioned porch with two glasses of icy lemonade in hand. The wooden screen door slapped shut behind her as she set the glasses on a pretty cloth-covered table. "Was he the one?"

"He was the last one." Eloise gave her car door a shove and trudged up the walk. Her weak leg seemed to drag more as she climbed the steps, but maybe it was her spirit that was lagging. She'd endured an hour and a half of Craig's flat monotone, his endless fascination with some video game he couldn't stop talking about and the fact that he looked just past her right shoulder whenever he spoke to her. Predictably he'd been quietly distasteful when he'd spotted her limp. Getting through that dinner had not been easy.

"No more, Gran. Take pity on me." She collapsed onto the closest cushion and leaned her cane against the side of the wicker chair. "Promise me you won't put me through another minute of this."

"I don't make promises I can't keep." Gran eased onto the neighboring chair. "Why is this so hard for you, sweet pea?"

"I would rather not talk about it. I'm here to weed." She had stopped quickly at home to change into an old T-shirt and shorts. She sipped the ice-cold lemonade and let the tangy sweetness sluice over her tongue. "I'm going to take this with me, though. Delicious."

"Don't you go anywhere, young lady. I already did the weeding." Gran's chin lifted with a touch of defiance. "I'm not too old yet to weed my tomatoes. Now, answer my question."

"I'd rather go back and have dinner all over again with Craig."

"Was it really that bad?"

"Gran, you are torturing me. The CIA could use this as a method for extracting information. It was agonizing." She may as well tell the truth. "Please stop fixing me up."

"What's so bad about meeting a nice young man?" Gran's face scrunched up, bewildered. "I know Craig had nice manners. I asked his grandmother to make sure."

"Yes, but you could have asked if he had a personality."

"Oh, my." Gran put her hand to her mouth and chuckled. "I had no idea he was lacking. I'll do better next time."

"Next time I'm going to bring you with me so you can see what I'm up against. There are no good men left." That was her argument and she was sticking to it.

"He is out there, mark my words." Her grandmother appeared certain, unfailing in her belief. "I've been praying."

"Fine, but can we change the subject?"

"The right man will love you the way you are, for all that you are." Gran took a dainty sip of lemonade.

I don't notice your limp. When I look, I see you. Sean's words rolled into her mind and so did the memory of the kiss they'd almost shared. She swallowed hard and set down her glass before she spilled it. She'd been terrified of his rejection. That was the reason she'd stopped him before his lips claimed hers.

What would his kiss have been like? She blocked her mind from envisioning that little scenario. Imagining the tender brush of his lips to hers would only make it harder to forget. She wanted to slap her forehead because she'd visualized exactly what she'd been trying to avoid—Sean's kiss.

"How did your date go with that nice Granger boy?" Gran asked as casually as if she'd asked about nothing more personal than the weather.

Eloise inhaled, sucking lemonade into the wrong pipe. She coughed and sputtered, gasping for air. Her face turned red. Her eyes watered. She could see the tip of her nose shining like a beet.

"It was not a date," she wheezed. A few chugs of lemonade got everything going the right way, but it didn't begin to soothe the turmoil roiling up within her. "Sean and I were taking two of the inn's new horses for a ride."

"I didn't see any horses."

"Trust me, it was work-related, not personal." Although it might have been. She gulped another swallow of lemonade, hoping Gran hadn't happened to witness their almost-kiss.

Maybe she had. Nothing went unnoticed in a small town. Gran looked merry over the rim of her glass. "You're a heartbreaker, Eloise. Just like me in my day. Oh, I had them lining up for me, too."

"I'm not sure I should be hearing this." She blushed harder.

"Your grandfather wasn't just the best of the bunch, he was simply the best. I knew it the moment I saw him. He was new to town, the owner of this ranch right here. I remember it as if it were yesterday. He moseyed into the diner and my heart stopped beating. Time stood still and I felt wonderful down to the soul. As if I had taken my first breath and my life was about to start anew."

"I know the story, Gran." Everyone in the family had heard it a hundred times, but it was sweet enough to savor again. "He looked at you, lifted his hat and told you he'd just met the lady he was going to marry."

"He did and I was charmed." Gran looked happy and sad in the same moment. Although Gramps was gone, her love for him had not dimmed. "I caught that Granger boy looking at you and I saw the same look in his eyes."

"Wishful thinking." Her heart felt ready to crack

apart, which made no sense at all. Sean was *not* falling for her.

She grabbed her cane, gathering her dignity. Sean had admitted he hadn't even meant to kiss her, and that was no surprise. She was painfully aware of the tap of her cane and her limping gait as she rose to fetch the pitcher from the kitchen. The breeze from the open windows scented the room with the fragrance of blooming flowers and warm summer air and made her rebellious mind boomerang right back to Sean, wondering what he was doing.

She hated to admit it, but she wasn't as unaffected by him as she wanted to be.

The muted light of evening hazed the town with a Norman Rockwell glow. Sean jumped into the back of the truck, since they'd picked up Cheyenne and Autumn in town. The last thing he wanted to do was to be stuck in the cab with three women bent on talking weddings. Not that he objected to matrimony, but a bachelor was required to avoid the topic. It was the manly thing to do.

"Are you sure you're okay back there?" Cheyenne peeked out the back window.

"I'm used to being hauled around like a bale of hay," he assured her. "It's how my family always treats me."

"Sure they do." Cheyenne laughed at him, shook her head as if to say there was no understanding the male species and told Addy to hit the gas.

The truck rolled forward away from the curb leaving the hubbub of the street fair behind. Some vendors had closed up for the day, others were doing a stellar business. In a few minutes' time, they hit the outskirts and the vehicle gained speed on the country road.

Since he had a moment to himself, he yanked his phone from his pocket. With the breeze whipping his face and hair, he studied the screen. One voice mail, it said. If he pushed the button, then he would hear her voice. He still smarted somewhat fiercely at the thought.

He drummed his thumb on his knee, debating. What did she want? If he deleted it without listening, he would never know. She might have apologized. Maybe listening to something like that would give him closure. Or, he thought with a leap of his pulse, she might want to get back together.

What do I do, Lord? He had moved on without Meryl and he was finally happy. Why mess that up?

Eloise. She was the one he wanted to talk with about this. She would understand. Was it wrong to want to see her? He frowned, belting out a frustrated sigh, angry with himself. After that debacle with the failed kiss, he didn't think he had the right to count on her friendship. He moved his thumb to the number pad of his phone, wishing he could call her.

He couldn't.

The truck swept around a long, lazy country corner heading directly into the sun. The shade from the cab fell over him, and his screen glowed brightly like a sign. He would face his problems on his own. He hit the voice-mail call button and waited, palms damp and respiration sketchy. Meryl's ingenuous alto lilted from the speaker.

"Sean. I know it's been a while and you probably don't want to talk to me. That's fine, I understand. I really do." Her voice hitched, as if she were in pain. "Please call me anyway. I need you to know how I feel. I made a mistake. A big mistake. Have you ever made one that you feel so bad about you are afraid nothing you can do will ever make it right? Well, that would be me. I'm praying there's a way to make things right, Sean. God is guiding me back to you."

A big mistake? He hit Delete. That tore him up. Things hadn't worked out with the dentist, huh? He was sorry for that, but he felt stirred up. The old wound became fresh.

This was why love was a bad idea. It should be avoided at all costs.

The back window slid open and Autumn smiled out at him. She shone with deep, contented happiness, the kind that polished her from the inside out. True love had done that. He was glad it had worked out for her. Concern creased her brow as she studied him. "Hey, are you all right?"

"I'm okay." He shrugged, hoping to dislodge the pain. It didn't work, but he wasn't ready to talk about it.

"I just heard the scoop about you and Eloise." She brushed her auburn curls behind her ear as the wind caught them. "I think it's great, by the way. We've all known Eloise forever."

"That's the way things go in a small town. People leap to the wrong conclusions awful fast." He loved this way of life, but he could use a little more privacy, at least where his heart was concerned. He'd taken two blows all in one day, first Eloise's rejection and now Meryl's apology, and it was about all he could take. "I'm just helping her with the inn's horses."

"It's so sad about those poor things." Autumn grew serious. "Is there something I can do?"

"You'll have to ask Cady. They're in relatively good

condition, considering. No major illnesses, no injuries, and they are being well cared for now."

"Still, I feel like I should do something. Maybe I'll swing by the inn and see them."

"Sure." Inspiration hit. Maybe he should ask her to take over his offer to help Eloise instead. If Autumn stepped in, he could retreat into the background and keep his distance. It would be safer to bow out. It was a good idea, except for the matter of the quickly approaching wedding. As busy as Autumn was, he figured she would shuffle around her responsibilities.

He couldn't ask her. He couldn't say the words.

Chapter Ten

$\sim$

The Pioneer Days rodeo was in full swing. Eloise eased onto the hard bleacher seat, tucked her cane against her knee and resisted the urge to scan the rest of the arena for a certain somebody. Sean Granger was not on her mind—at least that was her goal.

"Oh, good, we haven't missed the barrel racing." Mom twisted open the small thermos she'd brought in a big wicker basket. "Do you want some, sweetie?"

"No thanks." While she listened to her mom pour a cup of iced tea to share with Dad, she did her best to watch the last of the event on the grounds below. Two riders on horseback swung lassoes after a wily black calf who was good at evading them.

"Oh, ho!" The announcer, Tim Wisener Junior, called out. "Looks like the Walters brothers have to try again." The speakers blared and echoed as the mid-afternoon heat blazed like an oven.

Just like old times. She found herself smiling. She'd forgotten all the many things she'd missed over the years about small-town life. A hometown rodeo was one of them. Half the county crowded onto the bleachers or milled around on the adjacent street. The wind brought the scents of dust, hay and popcorn from a nearby vendor's kiosk.

Everywhere she looked, she saw someone she recognized and exchanged smiles. Sierra Baker sat beside her fiancé, Tucker Granger, with her young son, Owen, tucked between them, pointing excitedly to the goings-on below. Sierra's parents sat on the bench above. The group made a pretty picture of a family gathered for a fun day together and they weren't alone. Nearby Frank Granger sat next to Cady, surrounded by his family. Oops—she averted her gaze. Best not to look at that section of the bleachers where Sean was sure to be.

Down the row, she spotted the Parnell girls, all four of them blonde and as golden as could be, and her grandmother's friend, Mrs. Plum, sitting hand-in-hand with her husband of over fifty years. She noticed Jeremy Miller and his kids. The Bakers, Chip and Betty, looked happy and content surrounded by their immediate family. Their daughter, Terri Baker-Gold, sat with her husband radiating happiness, her hand resting lightly on the small bowl of her abdomen. Word had it their first baby was due in November.

So many happy families. Eloise blew out a breath but it didn't ease the painful tension bunched up in her chest. Since she knew who and what was responsible for it, she tried to ignore it. Not exactly easy, since every time she took a breath the tension refused to budge.

"Helene." A friendly woman's voice spoke from the row behind them. The scent of chocolate-chip cookies filled the air. Eloise glanced over her shoulder to see Martha Wisener holding an open plastic container full of treats. "Would you all care for some? I went on a baking binge this morning and made way too much."

"They look delicious," Eloise heard her mom say. "I'm going to get that recipe out of you one of these days."

"You and everyone else." Martha laughed. She tipped the container closer. "Eloise, you must have one. I've heard all about your quest."

"My quest? Do you mean finding the horses?" She thanked Martha and took a cookie. They looked buttery and chocolaty. How could anyone resist? She took a nibble and the soft chewy center and melty chips were bliss.

"Everyone's talking about it." Martha, who was also the mayor's wife and the town realtor, was up on all the latest news. She missed nothing. "I hunted down Cady a little bit ago to hear all about it. Abandoned horses. Such a terrible thing. I hear you were the one to find them."

"Actually, it was the humane society. They called me."

"Sad. I'm thankful they were found. Can you imagine? You just know God intervened at exactly the right moment. Any longer and who knows what would have happened to the poor things?" Martha tipped the cookie box in the other direction, offering it to Gran. "You have to be proud of your granddaughter, Edie."

"She's a keeper." Gran beamed sweetly. "How many horses are you going to find for Cady, dear?"

"I don't know. I'll stop when she tells me to or when the stable is full." The announcer hollered over the speaker, excited by a time earned by the next team-roping pair to finish—the Granger girls. Eloise turned back to her grandmother. "Knowing Cady, she will simply build another stable and fill that one also."

Down below, Addy lifted both fists in victory, while Cheyenne coiled up her lasso and rode her horse toward the gate. Apparently the team had won. Eloise cupped her hands to her mouth. "Yay, Cheyenne! Yay, Addy!"

Her call was lost in the crowd, but she was happy for her friends and in that unguarded moment she forgot to keep her gaze averted from the section of bleachers directly ahead of her.

Sean. Her focus zoomed straight to him. He sat one row behind his uncle, his hat shading his rugged face. He was magnificent in a navy T-shirt shaping his impressive physique and jeans. So handsome, he made the knot in her chest multiply and she gasped for air. Time reeled backward and she remembered the moment on the street when he'd leaned in and she'd panicked.

What if she hadn't stopped him? The thought made her pulse bump to a stop. What if she had let him kiss her? Would he have pushed her away when he came to his senses? When the kiss was done and he stepped away, would he have regretted his impulsive act?

Probably. The sunlight glinted off her cane, propped against the bench beside her. What other outcome could there be?

His head shot up as if he'd sensed her interest and across the arena their gazes fused. The sounds and sights of the stadium faded until there was nothing but the intensity of his bold blue eyes rooting her into place. She could not move or blink, not even breathe. Could she rip her gaze away from his?

No. She felt an incredibly powerful pull on her heart, which felt like regret. She missed him. She remembered his stalwart kindness as he'd tended the starving horses and assisted the vet with competence and compassion.

She recalled the strength in his arm when she'd needed to lean on him at the street fair when she'd forgotten her cane. Would his kiss have been gentle?

"Eloise?" Her gran's voice came as if from a far distance. "Is that Sean Granger? You should go say hi to the boy."

"N-no." The word stuck in her throat and sounded unnaturally loud and defensive. Oops, she hadn't meant to sound that way. She cleared her throat and tried again. "I mean, yes, it's him, but no, I don't need to say hi."

"Sure you do," Gran insisted. "After all the time you two have been spending together. You don't want to let a man like that get away."

"Get away?" She highly doubted she had a chance of ever holding Sean Granger. "He's just a friend."

"Famous last words," Martha interjected. "Although in this case, it might be wise. I hear he's nursing a broken heart."

"Eloise, you've been spending a lot of time with one of the Granger boys?" Mom sounded bewildered. "Why didn't I know that?"

"Because it's nothing." She wished she could focus on anything else but her gaze remained glued to his. Sean and his riveting blue stare, the strong lines of his face, the cut of his high cheekbones and the unyielding angle of his jaw—she couldn't see anything else.

They'd had fun together. She wished it could be more. But she had learned a painful yet important lesson from Gerald. Her disability was a liability to men. Hadn't all her blind-date fiascoes proven it? No, she'd been right to stop Sean before he'd kissed her. They had to stay friends.

Tossing him an uncertain smile, she ripped her gaze

from his. She felt winded from the superhuman effort that took, and her vision couldn't seem to focus on anything else. The blur of a horse and rider in the ring below would not become clear.

The barrel racing events had obviously started, but she hadn't heard Tim Wisener Junior announce it nor could she hear his comments as a horse spun around a barrel and knocked it over. Why couldn't she concentrate?

Because her attention was still on Sean. She could see him in the corner of her vision. He leaned forward, planted his elbows on his knees and rested his chin on his fists. He looked frustrated. He looked to be thinking. Was he regretting that she'd pushed him away? Or was he glad he hadn't kissed her?

You're not whole, Eloise. Gerald's words rolled up from her memory. *Nothing is ever going to change that. I can't keep pretending it doesn't matter. I've tried, I really have.*

She bowed her head, remembering how painful the lesson was. Her pink cane glinted in the sun, a reminder that her condition was never going to improve.

"Next up, we have Cheyenne Granger." Tim Junior's friendly tenor blasted across the open-air arena. "She's riding Dreamer, and she is our returning champion. Eight times she's won this event. Will she do it again? Here she comes, so let's find out."

Eloise swallowed and ate the remaining bite of the cookie before cupping her hands to cheer for her friend. When she was a girl, she used to race barrels and not well, so she knew it was harder than it looked. Cheyenne and her horse worked like a flawless team in a mad dash toward each barrel, each turn neat and tight before the all-out sprint for home.

"A new rodeo record!" Tim Junior proclaimed as the speaker crackled. "With a whole list of competitors to go, this is gonna get real interesting. Up next is Addison Granger. Let's see if she can steal the title from her big sister."

"Eloise?" A familiar baritone rumbled next to her ear. A familiar riding boot stepped into view.

Since her palms went damp and the knot sitting against her rib cage tightened, she didn't need to look to know who settled on the bleacher beside her.

"Are you enjoying the rodeo?" he asked in a low voice, perhaps aware of her family and Martha on the row behind them leaning just a bit to try to listen in.

"S-sure." The word caught in her throat. "Are you?"

"I always like a good rodeo. Look at Addy go." He nodded toward the ring where Addy's dappled gray American Quarter Horse executed a neat, hairpin turn around the second barrel. The crowd went wild as the mare dug in, stretched in an all-out sprint and pivoted around the final barrel. "She just might do it this year."

Sean's presence rattled her and she couldn't concentrate as Addy rode to the finish. Bless him for coming over and making the first move.

"I can't believe it!" Tim Junior's excitement echoed across the arena. "A tenth of a second short. Cheyenne holds on to first place, but barely. That was a great run, Addy! Next up we have Ashleigh Parnell—"

"I never apologized to you for the other day." Sean knuckled back his Stetson. "I should have and I didn't. I'm sorry."

"Don't worry about it. It's already forgotten."

"It is? Whew."

"Sure." She wanted those words to be true. She showed how aloof and cool she could be, casual and unaffected. "It was no big deal."

"I think it was." He straightened his shoulders as if with an iron resolve. "It upset you and changed things between us."

"Everything is fine, Sean." She could practically see Martha Wisener ready to tumble off the edge of the bench straining to hear more. Gran wasn't even trying to mask the fact that she was eavesdropping.

Great. The last thing she wanted was for everyone to know what had happened. That Sean Granger *hadn't* kissed her. In the ring below, Ashleigh Parnell raced to the finish and Tim Junior belted out her time, the third best, a hair below Addison's. Eloise glanced down at her cane and wished with all her heart that she could be whole, the way she was before the accident. "Believe me, Sean, I understand completely."

"That's a relief. It won't happen again. One thing about me, I can be taught. I never make the same mistake twice."

"Then I guess we're still friends."

"Sure, you can't afford to stay mad at me."

"I wasn't mad at you."

"I have a horse trailer, remember? You need me."

"Cheyenne has a horse trailer, too. I could replace you."

"Don't do it. I'm a horse lover from way back. After finding those starved horses, I'm more committed than ever. This cause is too important to me." Even a lone wolf needed something to believe in and a purpose to his life. Even he needed a friend. As a small smile hooked the corners of her rosebud mouth and she returned her attention to the ring, he felt better. Happier. Her Stetson shaded her lovely, wholesome face, and looking at her gave him a sweetly warm feeling.

He didn't want anything serious, so he figured it was wise not to analyze his feelings any further. This was friendship. That was his story and he was going to stick with it. Eloise clearly didn't feel anything else for him.

Good thing, he thought ignoring a sting of disappointment, the lone wolf he was determined to be.

Tim Junior belted out the name of the next contestant and the noise and commotion of the spectators reminded him they were far from alone. An electronic jingle interrupted whatever it was Sean had been about to say. He tugged his cell from his jeans pocket and answered the call. It was from the ranch. "Scotty?"

"Sunny's finally decided to have her foal. Of course it's when everyone but me is away."

"That's the way it always works." A foaling mare he could handle. "Did you call Nate?"

"Yep, got him in the stands a few minutes ago."

Sure enough, a Stetson-wearing man was making his way through the grounds. Nate, off to the Granger ranch. Sean set his shoulders. The timing was bad, but duty called.

"How are the girls doing at their events?" The longtime ranch hand was practically a member of the family.

"So far, Cheye and Addy have come in first in their team events, first and second in their individual ones." He tried to focus on what he was saying, but Eloise stayed on the forefront of his thoughts. Her brow furrowed, a question pinched the corners of her eyes, and she leaned toward him with concern. He tried to focus. "Does Uncle Frank know?"

"You were the one on call, so I dialed you first," Scotty explained.

"Good, let him enjoy his date with Cady. I'll be right there." He pocketed his phone, hating to have to leave Eloise. He wanted to fix what was wrong between them.

"You have to go?" she asked.

"Sunny has decided to have her foal." Bad timing, he thought, tugging out his keys. But then again, God's timing was always perfect and that gave him an idea. "Want to come?"

"With you?" Surprise twinkled like pretty spring-green specks in her eyes.

"Why not? Don't you want to see a little foal born? I'll let you pet the baby."

"I'm not tempted." Her resistance was melting. He could see it as she tugged her bottom lip between her teeth, debating.

He didn't want to leave without her.

"C'mon, Eloise." He held out his hand, palm up. "Cute little foal. How can you resist? Maybe we should take a poll."

"A poll?" Amusement stretched her soft mouth into a dazzling smile.

He glanced around for support. He didn't have to look far. Martha was balancing precariously on the bench one row up. Eloise's mom had a pleasant smile of surprise. Mrs. Tipple seemed about ready to burst with excitement. Looked like he had all the backing he needed. "What do you all think? Should Eloise come along with me or keep hanging out with you?"

An easy question, since he already knew the outcome. Eloise knew it too, judging by the way she shook her head at him, scattering the ends of her gleaming gold hair.

"Don't you bring my family into this," she warned, but it was too late.

"I'll choose for you," Mrs. Tipple called out. "Eloise, looks like you've got a live one."

"I'm not fishing, Gran." Eloise bit her bottom lip, as if holding back a laugh. Merriment made her brilliant and made his heart notice. "And if I was, then I would throw him back. You do that with the ones too scrawny to keep."

He liked that everyone laughed. He laughed, too. He knew good and well he wasn't scrawny.

"You've hooked a good one." Martha leaned in. "Eloise, you don't let him get away."

"I haven't hooked him." She grabbed her cane and pushed off the bench. "If I wanted to hook some man, I could do better."

"You definitely could," he agreed and held out his hand to help her down the crowded aisle. Funny how calm he felt the moment his fingers twined between hers, like everything was going to be all right.

"You two have fun," her grandmother called and gave two thumbs-up. "I think it's a date, Helene. It looks like one to me."

"I hope you didn't hear that." The breeze scattered Eloise's gossamer wisps of gold curls that had tumbled down from her pony tail. "You know about my grandmother's plan to marry me off, right?"

"How could I forget? She's responsible for your last two dates." He led the way down the row, excusing them as he went. A lot of inquisitive gazes took note as they made it down the steps. "I saw her two thumbs-up. I rate better than I thought."

"Don't take it personally. Remember George? She gave him two thumbs-up, too."

He chuckled, protecting her from the tussle of the stragglers heading into the grandstand. It was a perfect afternoon without a cloud in the sky. He felt as bright as the sun and with Eloise beside him, his world seemed promising. As much as he wanted to deny it, his feelings were changing against his will.

Chapter Eleven

What she liked most about Sean could be best seen in the little things he did, Eloise decided as she clutched the top rung of the gate in the Grangers' main horse barn. She couldn't tear herself away from the sight of him kneeling inside the birthing stall with the vet, the mare straining in the throes of her contractions. This was a deeper side of Sean than she'd seen before, mighty and yet calm, sure of himself in a humble but amazing way.

"You're doing good, Sunny." Sean stroked the horse's neck like the accomplished horseman he was, his tone soothing and musical. "What a good girl you are."

She'd seen foalings before but each one was special. She loved watching Sean be part of it. She was fascinated by the unfaltering comfort he gave the mare. His capable manner gave the horse confidence.

"I've got two hooves," Nate announced in a steady, assured voice. He gently uncurled a leg and held the two tiny hooves in his palms.

"You're doing great, Sunny," Sean encouraged. "Your baby is almost here."

Good decision to come along, she thought. She wouldn't trade this for anything.

The man belonged in this environment, with the sun slanting over him and the soft straw beneath his boots. She remembered the way he'd helped her into the truck back in town, his care as he found the seat belt for her and closed her door. He lived with confidence and thoughtfulness. Everything he did, he did well, big tasks or small ones, important or insignificant. His good heart shone through.

Very, very hard not to admire that.

"Is she here?" A little girl's voice echoed down the breezeway, followed by an older sister's scolding *Shhh!*

"Hush, Julianna. You are supposed to be quiet or you'll scare Sunny." Footsteps tapped closer. "She's having a baby, you know."

"I know, Jenny. Frank said I get to name her."

"He said *we* get to name her."

Both of the Stone girls tromped into sight with identical dark brown hair and beautiful button faces. Julianna's pigtails bounced with her gait, while Jenny's dark locks were sleek and freshly tended to. She slipped her comb into her pocket. "Hi, Eloise," they said in unison.

"Come see." She inched aside to make room for the girls. With one final thrash, a tiny brown bundle tumbled into the straw at Nate's knees.

"Wow." Julianna curled her fingers around the gate rung. "Look at the baby."

"It's so cute." Jenny stared, unblinking.

The baby studied them all with a startled look. Fuzzy ears stood straight up as the newborn took in its new surroundings. Inside the stall the mother rested, catching her breath.

"We've got a little filly," Sean announced as he gave the mare one last neck pat and strolled up to the gate. "Do you girls have a name picked out?"

"Tomasina," Julianna announced.

"Angelina," Jenny argued.

"I guess you two have some negotiating to do." He climbed between the rungs, broad-backed and with every muscle rippling. At his six-foot-plus height, he towered over her, a giant of a man in her estimation.

Such a good man.

"Are you glad you stayed?" he asked, smiling because he already knew the answer. Somehow, he knew. Although several feet separated them, the distance shrunk.

"Very." Danger, her instincts shouted at her, but did she listen?

No. It was impossible to see anything else but Sean.

"What's going on here?" a man's baritone boomed cheerfully. Frank Granger, hand in hand with Cady, ambled into sight.

"We've got ourselves a new filly," Sean answered, staying close, his hand gently closing around the curve of her shoulder to keep her from sidling away.

Panic popped like little bubbles in her midsection. At least, she thought it was panic. Maybe it was better not to analyze her feelings too much.

"So I see." Frank Granger with Cady at his side stopped to peer in over the bars. "Good job, Sunny girl. That's a fine baby you've got."

The mare lifted her head, her dark eyes finding Frank. She nickered low in her throat in answer and rolled off her side onto her folded legs.

"The baby is so pretty," Julianna chimed in. "Can we pet her?"

"Not yet, Julianna," Jenny answered.

"Maybe in a bit," Frank said.

Eloise tried to focus on the animals inside the stall, but the pressure of Sean's hand on her shoulder riveted her attention to him. She could hear the faint regular rhythm of his breathing. She couldn't help noticing the dark blue specks in his irises and the five-o'clock shadow beginning to darken his iron jaw.

"Look! She's getting up!" Julianna clung to the gate, fascinated as the mare climbed to her feet and gave the top of her baby's head a lick.

The filly blinked, still busy taking in her new surroundings. Nothing could be more adorable than her perfect dishpan face, long lashes and big chocolate fudge eyes. Her mane was short and coarse, sticking up like broom bristles. A white star crested her forehead.

"I've never seen anything so precious," Cady cooed.

"We get a lot of that around here. Every single foal is precious." Frank looked content with the life he had built here, but it was a different kind of contentment that lit him up when he looked at Cady.

True love. It was easy to see, and no one deserved it more.

"Oh, we missed it!" Addy interrupted, tromping in, followed by her sisters.

"Only by a few minutes." Sean didn't remove his hand and he didn't step away, but held her in place—not that she was complaining—as Cheyenne and Autumn ambled into sight, trailed by the rest of the Granger family. Justin appeared, walking hand in hand with his wife,

Rori. Tucker came last with six-year-old Owen riding on his shoulders and Sierra by his side.

"Good job, Sunny." Autumn ducked between the rails. The mare nickered in greeting and proudly licked her filly's face as if to show off the baby. "She's a beauty, just like you."

"Aren't you glad you came?" Sean whispered so only she could hear.

"Maybe," she hedged but inside she thought, *definitely.* Tingles skidded down her spine, which probably came from standing so still for so long. That combined with the excitement of the newly born foal, well, that was probably the explanation. Those tingles had nothing to do with Sean.

"I get to do this for a living." He looked pretty happy with that.

"You are blessed. Not everyone can say the same." A wisp of sleek gold slipped from beneath her hat to fall in her eyes. He brushed it away, letting his fingertips linger on the silken skin of her forehead.

Another little tingle, but surely it could not be from the sweetness of his touch.

"I consider myself a pretty fortunate man," he went on. "As long as Uncle Frank decides to keep me on. This is a temporary position."

"Yes, we all know." Frank chuckled easily and winked. "Temporarily is about all I can put up with you, boy."

"So everyone tells me." He shook his head, his dimples dazzling.

Those handsome dimples would make any female in the state of Wyoming notice, so it wasn't anything to worry about. No reason to read anything into her reaction. That was probably the hazard of having a drop-dead gorgeous guy for a friend.

"Why do you think I'm here? My parents wanted to get me out of the house." That made everyone chuckle in agreement, although beneath the banter there was a loving acceptance of Sean that was hard to miss.

"Answer a question that is puzzling me," Cheyenne asked, turning to her. Friends that they were, it was easy to recognize the sparkle of amusement in Cheyenne's blue eyes. "Why are you putting up with our cousin? Surely there is some better guy to hang out with."

"You know it." Eloise felt more lighthearted than she had in years as the wind gusted down the breezeway and the filly splayed out her thin, impossibly long legs. "I keep him around mostly because of his horse trailer."

"That explains it." Frank Granger roared. "We have all been wondering what a fine gal like you is doing with the likes of that boy."

"I'm the disappointment of the family," Sean explained with a shoulder shrug, as if it didn't trouble him one bit. "It's always a topic at all the family get-togethers."

"Better you than me," Addy quipped, hanging off the rail beside the little girls.

"I have a horse trailer," Cheyenne chimed in. "Now you don't have to hang with Sean."

"True, but I come with mine lickety-split whenever she calls." Sean winked. "I'm no dummy."

Everyone's laughter rang merrily in the barn, and he didn't mind that they were all laughing with him. He caught the look in his uncle's gaze, the one that said, "Told you so."

Uncle Frank was wrong. Everyone was. Even if his

feelings were starting to change, it didn't matter. He had supreme self-control. He was in charge of his feelings. No problem.

"Eloise, why don't you stay for supper?" Uncle Frank asked in that sly, knowing tone. "We've got plenty, and you haven't lived until you've tasted Mrs. G.'s potato salad."

"I don't see how I can say no to that," she said. "Only someone particularly daft turns down the chance for some really great potato salad."

"My sentiments, exactly," Sean added, fighting a brightness taking root in his heart he did not wish to claim.

At least the tingles in her spine had stopped and Eloise took comfort in that. She swiped the dishcloth across the kitchen table, brushing up crumbs from a tasty and fun supper. That was the Granger way, she'd learned long ago. Good food, better conversation and the family's lively interaction had been more entertaining than the rodeo. Even cleanup was fun.

"Mrs. G. works too hard," Cheyenne said from the sink where she was dealing with the hand washables. "We should do something for her."

"Dad pays her. A lot," Addy spoke up, standing next to her sister and drying dishes. "I caught a glimpse of the check he writes her every week. Wow."

"She earns it." Rori set the last of the leftovers into the refrigerator with orderly care. "Don't think it's easy taking care of all of you. I've done it, so I'm speaking from experience."

"We *are* a tough bunch." Autumn sidled up to Rori at the refrigerator and snagged a bag of carrots from the produce drawer. "I think we should do something for Mrs. G., too. Maybe a day at Cady's spa."

"Ooh, that's a great idea." Addy gleamed with enthusiasm. "We should all go."

"You just want to be pampered," Cheyenne argued with a laugh. "We're talking about Mrs. G. here, not you."

"I know, but I was just saying." Addy grinned sweetly and popped a plastic colander, newly dried, onto the counter. Sierra swept it up and put it away.

"I agree with you," Sierra put in her two cents' worth. "I could use a little pampering, too. Why limit it to Mrs. G.?"

Amused, Eloise scoured away gravy drippings and cherry pie filling that had landed on the vinyl cloth during the meal. The TV in the next room blasted a Mariners game, the noise only to be outdone by the outcry of the men seated around the room, bummed at an umpire's call.

No one else in the kitchen reacted to whatever was going on in the living room, but if she leaned slightly to her right she could see a sliver into the living room where Sean sat, leaning forward on the sectional, elbows on his knees, groaning along with his cousins and uncle. His dark hair stood on end, tousled as if he'd run his fingers through it in frustration.

"Yes. Doesn't Mrs. G. live all alone?" Cady said as she swiped a cloth over the countertops. "She might like a girls' day out instead of going to the spa all by herself. It's always fun hanging out with you Granger girls."

"We are keepers," Addy piped up cheerfully.

"*We* are, but not you, little sister," Cheyenne teased.

"Hey! You splashed me."

"Then you owe me a splash."

"Don't think I won't forget," Addy warned, glittering with humor. "Sometime in the near future when you least expect it. Splash!"

"Ooh, I'm scared." Cheyenne rolled her eyes and drained the sink. "Eloise, are you okay?"

Vaguely she heard her name as if from a great distance but she was too busy watching Sean rock back against the cushions looking unhappy. His team must not be doing well. He was terribly handsome, even when bummed. The strong blade of his nose and the chiseled cut of his jaw could have been carved out of marble. No man had ever captivated her the way he did."Eloise?"

A touch brushed against her shoulder and she startled, gazing up into Cheyenne's concerned blue eyes. How long had she been staring at Sean? Heat crept across her face. "Sorry. I guess I was staring off into space."

And at a really amazing guy, but she kept that part to herself.

"I do that all the time," Addy commented across the kitchen as she hung up the dish towel on the oven handle.

"Sure, you do." Cheyenne's gentle teasing held a note of caring. "But Eloise has more common sense than you."

"Hey!" Addy countered good-naturedly.

"Is your injury bothering you?" Cheyenne asked with a good friend's concern and a doctor's skilled eye. "You have been on your leg all day."

"I'm fine." Her weak leg was a little prickly from so much activity but that wasn't out of the ordinary. Her neurologist had said she would always face limitations, and she was deeply grateful to God that those limitations weren't what they once were. At least for now. "I'm just overwhelmed by you all. It's been a while since I've hung out with the Grangers."

"We are a rowdy bunch," Cheyenne agreed. "Not me, but others are."

"I am, definitely," Autumn chimed in with a bag of carrots in hand. "Anyone want to come with me to the barns?"

"Me!" Addy called out. "I want to see how the new baby is doing."

"Me, too," Cady said above the sudden jingle of a cell phone in the adjacent mudroom. "Oh, I think that's mine."

"Look at Dad," Cheyenne whispered as Cady slipped from the room. "He doesn't want us to know, but he's keeping an eye on Cady. He's always aware of her."

"They seem really serious." Eloise managed to find the words, but she couldn't take her attention away from Sean. Distantly, she realized the dishcloth was missing from her hand.

"Dad is completely head over heels when it comes to Cady." Cheyenne balled up the cloth and tossed it. It sailed across the island to land in the sink.

"Two points." Addy headed to the living room, gripped the sides of the archway and leaned in, pitching her voice to be heard above the roar of the game. "I know it's exciting in here and everything, but we're heading out. Anyone want to come?"

"It's batter up," one of the brothers said.

"Yeah, bases loaded." Little Owen's sweet voice made everyone smile. "Tucker and me gotta see what's gonna happen next. Then can we go to the barn?"

"Then we can go, buddy." The love for his soon-to-be stepson was impossible to miss.

More conversations rose up, but Eloise heard nothing other than silence as Sean rose from his seat. The distance between them zoomed like a camera in a movie, focusing in until there was no one in the house, no one in the room but him and his slow, incredible smile. Dimples framed the corners of his mouth like a dream, stealing her breath. She leaned on her cane, a little dizzy, a little overwhelmed. Her pulse tripped over itself as she grabbed the edge of the table for balance. Strange how he affected her equilibrium, and it worsened as he paced closer. His bright blue gaze latched onto hers with uncomfortable intensity.

Why was the tingling back? Shivers snapped like bubbles in her spinal column. She gulped, realizing she was alone to face Sean's approach. Cheyenne had moved away and headed toward the back door with her sisters.

"You look like you're having a good time." He ambled up. "Although it can be overwhelming. This branch of the Granger family is just plain crazy."

"In the best possible way." She didn't remember deciding to join him. She fell in stride beside him. The sunshine slanting through the wide picture windows brightened inexplicably. "This reminds me of all the times I stayed over with Cheyenne for supper and sleepovers when we were kids."

"Good times?"

"The best. I come from a big family too, so I'm used to all the action."

"Life would be dull without it. That's the problem with being a lone wolf." He held the screen door for her.

"*You* are a lone wolf?"

"Don't act so surprised. I thought my solitary wolf thing showed."

"Not even close."

"Really? I was sure I radiated aloofness." Those dimples ought to be illegal in every corner of Wyoming. "I'll have to try harder."

"Much harder." Her cane tapped on the porch boards.

At the rail, Cady smiled as they passed, phone to her ear.

"Yes, Adam. The girls are doing fine. No, Jenny was a gem today. As happy as could be. You're still coming to pick the girls up on Friday?"

"Daddy! Daddy!" Julianna dashed up the steps with a clatter, hand held out for the phone. Jenny jogged behind her at a slower pace, but judging by her look she was eager to talk to her father, too.

Such nice little girls. Eloise couldn't help feeling a little wishful. She'd always planned on having kids one day, always wanted to be a mom. She leaned on her pink walking stick on the way down the steps. No man was going to marry her now, so motherhood wasn't going to happen. It was another loss she had to learn to live with.

"I don't know how anyone is going to tear Julianna away from the horse she rescued." Sean matched his pace to hers as they crossed the lawn. "The Stone family should just move out here."

"I agree. She and Dusty are bonded. It's been adorable to see how they need each other." She glanced over her shoulder to watch the girls trade the phone back and forth, the din of their merry chatter as sweet as lark song on the breeze.

"Their father might not be as interested in moving here."

"Why not? He's a surgeon. We could use one of those in these parts. There are a few specialists over in Sunshine, but mostly we have to go to Jackson, Boise or Salt Lake City. When Owen had his heart surgery, Sierra took him to Denver."

"I remember. I had just landed the job with the inn at the time." She wondered how difficult it had to be for Adam Stone to be separated from his children. His daughters clearly loved him, chattering merrily away, eager for the chance to tell their dad everything they had been up to.

A cow's moo cut through her thoughts.

"We're coming, Buttercup. No one has forgotten you." Sean chuckled. "Buttercup is my sweetie. Isn't that right, girl?"

The cow lowed, pleased with her status as Sean's beloved. She wore a necklace of buttercups. A single daisy was stuck jauntily on the fluffy tuft of hair between her ears. Clearly Julianna and Jenny had been spending time with her before their father's call. Buttercup's big puppy-dog eyes beamed as she placed her nose in Sean's outstretched hands and sighed with emotion at seeing him again.

"You have a way with the ladies," Eloise quipped. "Too bad it's only with the bovine variety."

"It's my lot in life." He winked, unaware of the image he made with the sun's low rays painting him in a golden glow. "That's why I'm a lone wolf. It didn't always used to be by choice."

Buttercup batted her long curly eyelashes at him and

lipped at the collar of his T-shirt. She drew the fabric into her mouth, holding on tight to him, adoringly.

Yeah, Eloise thought, she knew just how Buttercup felt.

Chapter Twelve

The sound of voices filled the breezeway as Sean knelt to check Wildflower's cinch. The mare watched him curiously, her ears twitching as she listened to the rise and fall of familiar voices a few feet away. He resisted the urge to pick out one soft alto among all the others just like he was doing his level best not to let his gaze drift over the horse's gold rump to where the women congregated in front of Sunny's stall, cooing over the newborn foal.

Lone wolves did not moon after pretty gals. They stayed remote, defenses up, in control of their common sense.

Satisfied the cinch was tight enough, he patted the mare's neck.

"Looks like we're ready to go," he told the mare. "You don't mind taking Eloise home, do you?"

Wildflower, the good girl that she was, whickered low in her throat, an affable agreement. He walked behind her, placing a hand on her flank and did the same to his gelding, Bandit, who arched his neck and stomped his foot, eager to go. He'd spent the day in his corral, and he was a horse that liked to stay busy and on the move. Sean knew just how he felt.

"Don't worry, we'll head out in a minute, buddy, I—" He looked up, spotted Eloise, and forgot whatever else he'd been meaning to say.

She blew him away. Slim and willowy, she leaned against the gate, transfixed by the foal, wonder on her face. She was golden goodness as she glided her fingertips across Star's forehead—Julianna and Jenny had agreed on the name for the new filly.

"Hi, little one." It was her musical words that stopped him in his tracks, her delight that stole the air from his lungs. Happy, she glowed as bright as the sun's rays slanting through the open door, a rare and arresting beauty. The newborn foal's eyes drifted shut at her tender touch.

"She likes you, Eloise," Cheyenne said, and Addy chimed in something too but he didn't register what.

It was nearly impossible to hear a thing over the rush of his pulse thudding in his ears like a death knell.

"I don't know how you Grangers get any work done." Eloise stopped stroking and the foal's eyes opened.

"It's tough," Cheyenne agreed. "There's nothing but foals in the fields with their dams and calves in the pastures with their mamas. Most days all you want to do is play with the little ones."

"She is amazing, wobbling on those long, awkward legs. Adorable."

"I don't know how many foals have been born on his ranch, and I am in awe every time," Cheyenne agreed. "They are so innocent and sweet and knock-kneed. Just too cute."

Cute, sure. He was in awe, totally. But it wasn't the

foal that captivated him. Not even close. Eloise's gentle laughter radiated joy as the filly clamped onto the hem of her pink T-shirt with her velvety muzzle. With care, Eloise gently freed her shirt from the little darling's clutches.

Something nudged his hand, dragging him out of his reverie. It was Sunny, who gave him a look that plainly said she was waiting.

"Sorry, girl." He tugged a chunk of carrot out of his pocket. She grasped it with her big horsy teeth and her whiskers tickled his palm. As she crunched contentedly, his attention drifted back to Eloise. "Are you ready to head home?"

"I'm not sure I can tear myself away." Elation rolled through her words.

"I can't compete. I'm definitely second fiddle to a filly like Star." He approached the throng of women, knowing full well what his cousins thought about his friendship with Eloise, but he didn't let other people's suspicions bother him. "We can stay here as long as you want, but I've got the horses saddled and ready."

"I don't want to make them stand too long. It's a beautiful evening." Eloise swept a lock of silken hair behind her ear and pushed away from the bars. "I wouldn't want to be tied up in the stable, not on an evening like this. Goodbye, little baby."

The foal's ears swiveled, taking in the sounds. Her chocolate fudge eyes were wide and curious as she watched the human walk away from her. Her mother, at her side, gave a low whicker of reassurance. His cousins called out their goodbyes and Eloise returned them. Could he listen? No, not with Eloise at his side.

"I saddled Cheyenne's saddle horse, Wildflower, for you." He slowed his gait to match her uneven one.

"Hey, girl." She held out her free hand for the mare to scent. "We know each other from way back, don't we?"

In answer, Wildflower lowered her head for a scratch, which Eloise obliged. His spirit brightened simply from watching her.

"I thought that might be the case." He knelt and laced his fingers together. "Need a boost?"

"No, but since you are already down there…" Trouble twinkled along with dark green flecks in her irises as she turned her attention to him. "You may as well make yourself useful."

"Useful." The full focus of her gaze walloped him, leaving him breathless. It was all he could do to stay steady as she planted her foot in the palms of his hands. "Glad to know I'm good for something around here."

"Oh, I'm sure you must have some value in addition to being useful."

"If I do, that's news to me." He lifted effortlessly, boosting her into the saddle. "If I have so much value, you might have to hang out with me more often."

"I'm not sure I would go that far." Leather creaked as she settled into place, towering like a princess on a throne.

"It seems to me if I have such merit you wouldn't hesitate." He snatched the cane she'd left behind and tucked it behind the saddle, then tightened the ties until it was secure.

"Oh, there's the male ego. I knew it was there. Every man has it."

"Please, don't go confusing me with other guys. I'm

not that bad, am I?" He untied Wildflower's right rein from the wall hook and drew it up for Eloise to take.

"I said you had some merits. That doesn't erase your many, many flaws." Dimples hooked the edges of her pretty mouth.

No one could make him laugh the way Eloise could. He untied Bandit and swung into the saddle. "Fine, I have a few flaws. More than a few flaws. See, I'm better than other men since I can admit it."

"Yes, clearly superior."

His big black gelding tossed his head, ready to roll. Sean pressed his heels and the horse responded, eager to get out in the summer evening.

Birds chirped and flitted from fence post to tree. Horses grazed. In the fields far up the hillside cattle lounged, looking like a mass of black dots against the stunning grassland. The clomp of hooves as he and Eloise rode together down the hill was about the most companionable thing he'd ever known.

Now this is friendship, he thought, watching the gentle breeze flutter through the ends of Eloise's hair. He and she were two like souls out for a ride, enjoying the summer evening. He wasn't noticing in the slightest that she was the most beautiful woman in the world. He'd hardly even glanced at her soft rosebud mouth upturned in a smile. As for his crazy attempt to kiss her?

Forgotten. Wiped from his memory permanently.

"Let's cut through the fields," he suggested. It was shorter than following the roads to her house and more scenic.

"Just what I was thinking." She tugged the brim of her Stetson lower against the sun. "It's a perfect evening for riding."

"That it is." Perfect. That was the exact word he'd been searching for. Nothing could be finer than being on the back of his horse with her riding at his side. He breathed in the fragrance of the windswept meadows and felt her shadow fall across him as he sidled Bandit up to the gate to unlatch it.

"I was just wondering why Buttercup wasn't dashing up to us." Eloise rode past him into the field, stirring his heart like ripples in a pond.

Remember, you don't feel a thing, he told himself and followed Eloise into the pasture. Feelings were what got a man into big trouble. Heartbreak trouble. He swung the gate closed behind him. The horse waited with a swish of his tail while Sean secured the latch and double-checked it.

"No wonder," Eloise said as if from a thousand miles away. It was hard to hear anything over the crazy drumming in his ears. She sat straight in her saddle, gently gorgeous and quietly dazzling. "The girls are busy adoring Buttercup appropriately."

"That cow is the most spoiled bovine in the state. Maybe in the entire country."

"Perhaps the whole continent?"

It took all his effort to focus on the gathering at the far end of the field, since his eyesight seemed fixated on Eloise against his will. He tried to focus on the two little girls flanking tall, slender Cady, but everything was blurry. The trio were petting Buttercup and adding a crown of daisies to the top of her head. "There ought to be a law."

"Yes, animal pampering ought to be regulated," she quipped, although a layer of seriousness remained beneath.

He knew what she was thinking. He winced because he didn't think he could ever get the sight of those half-starved horses out of his head. That had been an emotional day. Proof that emotions were best avoided, since they had led to his disastrous attempt to kiss her. From here on out, no emotions allowed. "Here's my law. All animals should be pampered."

"I would vote for it. That's always been my rule." She patted Wildflower's neck and the mare nickered as if she were in total agreement, too.

"That's why I love working with Uncle Frank." He steeled his chest so no emotions could sneak in and cause all sorts of trouble. "I love ranching, I love working outdoors, I love cows. I could have hired on at a lot of other big operations in the state. There are always openings."

"But you wanted to work with your uncle."

"Yes. Not just because he's my dad's brother, but because of what he stands for." He liked that Eloise understood that and understood him. He relaxed a little, rocking in the saddle slightly in time with Bandit's gait. "He's a top-notch rancher and he treats his animals right."

"You want to learn from him."

"I want to be like him." He kept his attention on the ground ahead where a worn trail wove its way through the tall grass and nodding wildflowers. Amazing that Eloise could instantly see what his parents had not been able to get. "He has a gift with animals, and he's good to them. He respects them. There's never a harsh word used, never a whip, never an electric cattle prod. Every steer, cow and calf has a name and they aren't solely a means to making a profit, but they are the point of the ranch. There is a reward in ranching the right way that no amount of money made can begin to compete with."

"Sounds noble to me."

"Glad you think so." Her opinion mattered to him. He let silence settle between them, broken only by the occasional creak of a saddle and the rhythmic plod of horse hooves. Bandit's mane rippled when he lifted his head to scent the wind. Wildflower danced closer to avoid a sudden flurry of a killdeer bursting out of the grasses and crying out, feigning an injured wing to lead them away from her nest.

"I think that's the secret to a happy life." She didn't rein Wildflower away but let the mare walk alongside Bandit, so close Sean could reach out and catch her hand with his.

Not that he wanted to hold her hand. But he could.

"What's the secret?" he asked.

"That happiness can't be found necessarily in the big successes of life or the material benefits, but in the things that can't be measured. In knowing you are doing things the right way. Living your life with honor. Living with your heart." She caught her hat with one hand as she tipped her head back, breathing in the scent of the winds and letting the gold-layered sun rays paint her with sepia tones. "It's also pretty nice riding horses on an amazing summer evening like this."

"It is pretty amazing. The evening, I mean. The horse ride." And her. She was awesome and so full of life that her emotions tugged him along with her, forcing him to feel. Not the easy things like the warmth of the sun on his face, but the hope that could be found when he peeled back the scars on his heart and looked beneath the surface.

"It's what I've been struggling with," she confessed. "I've had so many losses since the accident, not just having to give up skating."

"It sounds to me like you had to give up everything."

"Not everything, but it felt that way. One day my life was going great. The next what I'd worked for so hard for years was gone. My career, my life in Seattle, my relationship with Gerald." Along with the chance to be married, to be a mom and raise kids of her own, but she couldn't admit that aloud. Not to Sean. Not to anyone.

The pink glint of sunshine hitting her stowed cane was the reminder of why. Seated in a saddle, her disability didn't show, but it would always be with her and always a part of her. She set her chin, determined to stay positive. "Somehow I have to live with those losses and not let them diminish my life. Whew, that's a really heavy subject. I say we change topics."

"If you want." His expression had turned thoughtful. Nothing could be dreamier than his blue eyes. He could see right through her barriers to places she liked to keep hidden, which was the last thing she wanted.

Yes, a change of topic was definitely a good idea. An electronic chime chose that moment to fill the air, emanating from Sean's back pocket. Wildflower pricked her ears, listening to the tune, and Eloise patted the mare's neck in reassurance. She wasn't noticing how attractive Sean was as he tugged his cell from his back pocket. A shock of dark hair tumbled into his eyes as he studied the screen. Her fingers itched to brush it back into place.

"A rancher's work is never done," she commented. "Is it your uncle? If you have to head back, I can find home on my own."

"No, that's not it." He hit a button, silencing the

phone, and jammed it into his pocket. He didn't sound as breezy as he probably meant to. "Personal."

"Personal? Oh, you so aren't getting away with that." She squinted against the sun as the trail wound due west where light glinted off the wide snake of the river. "Tell me."

"It's nothing." A muscle jumped along his strong jaw line. He shrugged one wide, capable shoulder. "No big deal."

"I know a big deal when I see one." He wasn't fooling her. She'd caught the flash of pain in his soulful blue eyes. The tension ratcheting through him was plain to see. She leaned toward him in the saddle, wanting to reach out and afraid to do so. "Avoiding someone?"

"My ex." He concentrated overly hard on guiding Bandit through the grass.

That was it. No explanation. No elaboration. He turned to marbled stone before her eyes, shutting down, closing up. He was hurting.

Caring poured into her heart, caring she had no right to feel. She brushed a strand of windblown hair out of her eyes, debating what to do. Did she give him his privacy? Or did she express her concern the way any friend would?

"Can I ask why she is calling you?" She tilted toward him, amazed by the display of emotion warring beneath the surface of his set face. He wanted to appear unaffected but that was far from the truth. She read the wince of pain and the shadow of regret. "Didn't she break up with you?"

"This is the second time she's called." Tendons corded in his neck, as if he were holding back pain.

He must have loved her very much. Of course he

had, since he'd proposed to the woman. He wasn't like Gerald, who had been able to move on so easily. Sean felt deeply and truly.

How could any woman not have wanted him? Meryl didn't know how blessed she was to have had Sean's love and devotion. Anger speared through her, and she had to look away, take a few deep breaths and focus on the serenity of the daisies dancing in the wild grasses. How could anyone have treated him that way?

"Seems things didn't work out with the dentist, so she's decided to apologize to me." He tried to sound aloof.

He almost pulled it off. She would have believed him if she didn't know him so well. She tried to sound aloof too, as if she wasn't hurting and upset on his behalf. "Apologize? Or do you mean she wants you back?"

As he casually shrugged one brawny shoulder again, an attempt at being aloof, muscles rippled beneath his T-shirt and corded in his neck. Her pulse tripped over itself in the silence. Was he going to forgive the woman? Would he go back to her?

That thought doesn't hurt at all, she told herself, ignoring the arrow of pain burrowing into her. She adjusted the reins and concentrated on getting the sun-warmed leather straps just right between her fingers.

"I don't want her back." Sean broke the silence, resolute. "I don't want to be second-string. Not when it comes to being loved."

Whew, that was a relief. Tension rolled out of her and she almost slumped in the saddle. "I've been there, done that, bought the T-shirt."

"I have that shirt, too. I was a fool letting her dupe me like that. I didn't even realize she was seeing someone else." He tugged his Stetson a notch lower to shade his eyes against the sun, but it also hid the emotions he had to be fighting. "My mom and stepdad have one of the best marriages I've seen. I never really thought about it. All those years growing up and watching them, I just thought that was how relationships went. You got along, you were happy and you put the other person first."

"That was my experience, too." It felt as if they were in sync as they rode the gently sloping hillside together. Copses of cottonwood and groves of pine cast shade here and there and hid them from the houses popping up at the edge of town. "I just assumed any relationship I had would be the same as my parents'."

"That's what I did. I was probably naive, but I couldn't see the little things that were wrong. When I did, I argued them away." He guided his big black horse off the trail, turning onto the residential road. His long, wide shadow fell across her. He cleared his throat, but his emotions lingered in the deep notes of his baritone. "If I'd paid attention, maybe I could have ended things earlier and saved myself a lot of agony. I tried too hard to make it work."

"Me, too." It was really hard to think straight with Sean at her side. She had to resist the pull of his attractiveness. She had to hold down wishes that could not be brought into the light. "There were little things that were off, things I told myself not to be so picky about. Gerald always wanted things his way, he forgot the courteous little touches, he always picked the movie we watched. Now and then I worried I was an afterthought to him."

"You told yourself he was busy or had a lot on his

mind or that no one is perfect and that you weren't being accepting enough?"

"Exactly." That was it. "Gerald was good to me, not great, but good. I could explain everything away because of the stress of our constant training and competing. We were world champions. Maintaining our title was hard work and pressure. The excuses I made for him came very easily and I didn't even realize it."

"I understand. Once my eyes were opened, I felt stupid because I settled for so little. I couldn't see her behavior for what it was. She didn't want me to see it, but she was biding her time with me." His voice steeled, rising powerfully above the knell of the horse hooves on the paved street. "When she thought she could do better, she did."

"She could not do better, Sean. Not by a long shot." For all his manly strength, he was as vulnerable at heart as she was. He had been devastated as thoroughly. Heartbreak played no favorites but hurt equally. "You loved her truly."

"I thought so, but now I'm not so sure. If it were true love, then my feelings toward her would never fade. They did." He shrugged, sitting taller in his saddle, his chest up, his shoulders straight, his dignity showing.

She admired him so, so much. She feared she liked him even more.

The leisurely dance of a country sunset was deepening with its last chorus. The underbellies of fluffy, marshmallow clouds blazed with bold purples, pinks and reds. Sunset cast jeweled tones into the light that enveloped them like a sign from above. Tall trees cast long shadows over the land and over the occasional house lining the road. Her driveway came into sight and she sighed with sadness. Their ride was at an end.

She hated drawing Wildflower to a stop. For a while, for the length of the ride, she had been able to forget about the cane tucked into the saddle straps. She dismounted, struggling to keep the smile on her face and to hold on to their moment of closeness. She gripped her cane tightly and handed over the reins to Sean. "Thanks for riding with me home."

"I could have taken you in the truck." He tied a loose knot in the end of the reins and looped them over his saddle horn. "But I thought this would be nicer."

"It was." Nice. That was one word for it. Illuminating was another. She tried with all her strength to keep from feeling a single thing as Sean tipped his hat to her.

"Good night, Eloise. I'll see you." He wheeled the horses around to retrace his trail home, sitting so strong and tall in the saddle he took her breath away. "My horse trailer is ready to roll any time you need it."

"I'm still keeping Cheyenne as an option."

"Funny." He held up one hand, riding away into the shadows and the dying rays of light.

Do not fall, she warned herself. Do not even start to fall for the man. He was certain heartbreak waiting to happen.

Chapter Thirteen

In the heat of the mid-afternoon sun, Frank Granger strolled into the main horse barn, whistling. His sons were busy walking the north herd's fence line checking wire. Autumn and Addy were working horses in the arena; he could hear the faint ring of his daughters' laughter as he ambled down the breezeway. The stalls were empty this time of day, smelling of fresh straw and hay, the horses out grazing in the shade of the cottonwoods. It felt good knowing everything was going fine, his kids had the place running like a top and for the first time in years he had leisure time. May as well make good use of it.

"Got Rogue saddled and ready," Scotty called out, giving the gelding a pat. The ranch hand had been working for the Granger family for too many decades to count. "You've been taking off a lot lately."

"That I have." Rogue gave a deep-throated nicker, one of welcome and friendship. He and Rogue had been together a long time, too. He loved his horse because Rogue didn't toss him the knowing grins everyone else in this town did. Rogue held his tongue and didn't ask questions about a certain lady Frank was seeing. Rogue understood a man liked to keep some things private.

"Going to see Cady again?" Scotty stood there grinning, silvered hair slicked back. He crossed his arms over his barrel chest, expecting a confession that wasn't going to come.

"Thought I'd take Rogue out on the river trail." He untied the rein from the wall ring and stroked Rogue's nose. The gelding leaned in, a whicker rumbling deep in his throat.

"The river trail. That goes all the way to the other side of town." Scotty didn't give up. His grin broadened. "Cady's inn is on the other side of town right along that trail."

"What's your point, Scotty?" He swung into the saddle. With a touch of the reins, Rogue backed and moved into the aisle.

"You're spending a lot of time with that fine lady." Humor twinkled in dark eyes. "When are you gonna get up the gumption and propose to her?"

"Just you mind your own business." Frank laughed, shaking his head. Wasn't that everyone's question these days? "I've been a bachelor a long time. I might just be stringing her along, unable to commit."

"I say it's soon." Scotty, more friend than employee, belted out a laugh. "You've been bitten hard. You're in love with her."

"The better question everyone should be asking is how she feels about me." That concerned him. Heat stained his face as Rogue trotted into the sunny yard. His romance with Cady Winslow was as sweet as could be, but it was hard to know if the hopes taking root in his heart matched hers. He nosed Rogue out of the barn and down the hill.

"Dad, are you going to see Cady?" Addy's singsong alto lilted across the fields where horses grazed. She sat on the back of her dappled mare, ponytail askew and grinning wide. Looked like she'd been racing barrels.

"Where else would he be going?" Autumn sidled the mare she was working on up to the end of the arena, opened up to let in the fresh air and sun. She beamed happiness as she waved. It was good to see his girls on top of the world, Autumn about to be married, Addy home graduated from college. "Have fun! Give Cady a hug from me."

"And from me, too!" Addy chimed in.

"Will do." He held up a hand and kept riding, glad for the expansive distance of the fields because they made a long conversation impossible. Horses looked up from their grazing and whinnied, others bounded across the grass toward him. On his other side the yearling calves bawled and leaned against the wooden fence. Buttercup and her troop joined in.

"No time to chat, ladies," he called out to all the creatures on both sides of the fence. "I'll make it up to you later, promise."

Buttercup mooed as if her heart would break. Jasmine and Daisy joined in, their lows rising above the horses' disapproving neighs. Cheyenne would spoil them appropriately in his stead after her long day at the vet clinic was done. He swelled with pride at his daughter, who was doing so well. Mrs. Gunderson climbed the porch steps with a basket on her hip, done with her work in the garden.

"Looks like it's just you and me for a bit, Rogue."

The gelding answered with an agreeable nicker. Larks sang, robins hopped along searching for an early supper and on the far rise of the hill he caught sight of the faint figures of his sons bent to their work stringing wire. He swelled a little more with pride in his boys, working the land. Justin happily married, Tucker about to become a husband. Life was good.

The Lord had blessed him richly in all his children, no doubt about that.

His phone rang, proof his day was never done. He hoped it wasn't a problem that would pull him back to the ranch. He dug his phone from his pocket and checked the screen. It wasn't work, which puzzled him. "Sandi Walters, what can I do for you?"

"You have the nicest housekeeper, Frank. I just talked with her up at the main house. I invited her to our Bible study at the church on Thursday." Sandi Walters worked at the diner and had always been as friendly as could be to his kids. Hard not to appreciate that, even if she'd always been a tad too friendly to him ever since her divorce.

"It's awful kind of you." He leaned back in his saddle guiding Rogue onto the stretch of the county road. The empty ribbon of blacktop was framed by overgrown grass nodding in the wind. "I'm sure Mrs. G. was glad for the offer."

"She was. Say, the reason I'm calling is about the rumor I've been hearing."

"Which one would that be?"

"That your nephew and the youngest Tipple girl are taking in unwanted horses?"

"For once, a rumor in this town is true." Frank chuckled, relieved he didn't have to try to dodge any rumors about his personal life. "You wouldn't happen to know of a needy horse?"

"I do. Would the kids be interested?"

"I'm sure they would. I'll let Sean know."

"Wonderful. It was good talking with you, Frank. I suppose everything is going well with your family?"

"Just fine. Hope everything is well with yours." Rogue turned down Tucker's dirt access road, already knowing where they were headed. Not much got past that horse. The gelding lifted his head, scenting the air, and swiveled his ears. Sean must be nearby. Rogue was an eavesdropper from way back.

Frank said goodbye, pocketed his phone and patted Rogue's neck. "As you heard, we are on a detour. Sean must be around here somewhere."

The spread Tucker had bought shone like an emerald in the sunshine, green fields, growing crops, reaching trees. A small herd of sheep dotted the hillside like dollops of white fluff. Lambs played tag, running and frolicking under the watchful eyes of their mothers. A figure rose out of the herd and lifted a hand.

Sean. The boy had a way with all creatures, cattle, horses, even sheep. He scribbled on a notebook. Must be updating records now that the lambs were tagged and their inoculations were due. Frank urged Rogue up to the fence line. While Sean hiked across the field, Frank texted him Sandi's number. "Found another horse for Cady's stable," he called out.

"Great." Sean might think he was fooling everyone, but the only one he was fooling was himself. The young man's eyes didn't light up because of a horse. No, a certain young lady had something to do with that. Sean hauled out his phone and glanced at the screen, acting casual, as if the gal was no big deal. "I'll give Eloise a call. She'll be pleased."

"Sure, and it's fortunate you have a horse trailer to help out." He held back any teasing remarks because he knew what it was like to be a man deeply in love. "Looks like Cady is going to have a full barn if this keeps up."

"This economy has been tough on horses, too." Sean moseyed up to the fence, shoulders wide, unaware of the sheep, Cotton Ball, trailing him. "Do you think Tucker will mind if I take off?"

"No, I'll give him a call for you. You just go with Eloise and rescue that horse. That's important." Frank tipped his hat in farewell and reined Rogue away from the fence. Cotton Ball gave a protesting baaah.

"Then I'd better get my trailer hitched up." Sean probably figured he'd kept the anticipation out of his voice and the twinkle from his eyes, but he would be wrong.

The boy was head over heels. It took someone in the same spot to recognize it. *Lord, please watch over my nephew. He might need a little bit of help.*

Frank shook his head, chuckling to himself as he and Rogue headed in the direction of Cady's inn.

See how he didn't feel a single thing when Eloise breezed into sight? Sean grinned to himself, pleased his strategy was working. He opened the truck door for her as she padded down the inn's front steps, leaning on her cane. He hardly noticed the dip of her gait, for her beauty outshone everything. Her hair was down, unbounded, falling across her slender shoulders like liquid gold. She'd pulled on blue jeans, although she wore a ruffled blouse, which obviously had been meant to go with a classy blazer and a skirt.

"Word is spreading around about your rescue mission." He gripped the door handle tightly as she approached. "Now folks are starting to call us."

"It's Cady and Julianna's rescue mission," she corrected sweetly, bounding past him, and leaving a scent of honeysuckle in the air and a tug on his ironclad heart. "But it is an awesome thing. Cady has a lot of empty stalls to fill."

"How are the horses we've already rescued?" He watched her avoid his attempt to help her as she hopped onto the seat.

"Settling in, improving, eating." When she smiled, she could make him forget every one of his troubles. "They have names. Since Julianna named her favorite one Dusty, Cady is calling the others, Rocky, Clay and Pebbles."

"Funny. Cady has a sense of humor. I'm sure the horses are lapping up all kinds of attention."

"More than they know what to do with. Our employees head to the stable on their breaks, Cook saves carrots and apples to bring out to them and as for Jenny and Julianna, they are majorly attached. They hardly leave the stable. Their father arrived yesterday to take them back home. Apparently he didn't want the girls flying by themselves. They leave tomorrow."

"How is he going to pry the girls away from the horses?"

"I don't know. I wouldn't have the heart."

Speaking of hearts, his was still successfully barricaded. He closed her door and circled around the front of the truck, pleased because he hadn't noticed how lovely she was today, more lovely every time he saw her. He'd hardly glanced at her mouth that looked sugar-cookie sweet. Pleased with himself, he yanked open his door and hopped onto the seat. Not a single feeling crept in, other than the cheerful joy lighting up inside him. Joy from taking an afternoon off work, that was the only reason.

"Adam and the girls aren't going to stay for Autumn's wedding?" He put the truck in gear and hit the gas.

"I don't know. We'll see how persuasive Cady and the girls turn out to be." She shrank the passenger compartment, making it seem much smaller than it had been before. Unaware of what she'd done, she clicked her seat belt. "I do know that Cady saddled up Misty not long ago and left to meet with your uncle."

"Frank was mighty chipper earlier. He's awful serious about your boss."

"What was that? I saw that scowl."

"I was just thinking that he'd been single for so long. I don't know how he can give up his lone-wolf status after all this time."

"Maybe he turned in his membership card?"

"Funny. Or maybe he forgot to pay his annual dues and he got tossed out. He used to be my role model, but now? Not so much." He shook his head, feigning disappointment. The gentle notes of Eloise's laughter didn't touch him. Nothing could. His emotions were stone, his will unbreakable, and if he faltered just a little, he knew he would be in big, big trouble.

"Look, there they are."

Her voice changed, holding a hint of a wish, a touch of a dream and his impenetrable defenses wobbled a tiny bit before he could get them under control. Oblivious, she pointed in the direction of lush green fields and leafy cottonwoods to where the river glinted and two horses stood side by side, their riders holding hands. The tilt of Frank's Stetson, the upturn of Cady's face and the gild of the sun radiated an immeasurable tenderness.

The barriers Sean had up slid right down. Fortunately he could concentrate on his driving and pretend it hadn't happened.

"It's nice to see Cady so happy." Eloise turned her attention forward, since the speeding truck had left the couple behind. "I think she's been alone for a long time."

"Just like Frank," he said, although that wasn't new information. He couldn't seem to think straight. What he needed was a safe topic of conversation, one that had nothing to do with love or romance or happy couples. "Did you get any information about this horse we're going to see?"

"All I know is that they have a stray horse they don't know what to do with." She settled back against the seat. "Troy sounded busy when I called. You know what ranch work is like."

"I do. It's always something, which is what I like about it." He hit the signal and turned onto the county highway heading north. Town was a distant blur of color as they sailed by. "I'm a temporary hire at the Granger ranch, but I'm hoping I will be so invaluable after Autumn comes back from her honeymoon Uncle Frank will keep me on. It helps that Tucker has moved into his place across the road. There's more acreage and more livestock to tend. Everyone is spread thin."

"Will they be combining the ranches?"

"Looks like it. It will make both spreads easier to run." He eased off the gas and pulled off the highway. "That's a lot of acreage, so I'm hoping it means long-term job security for me. Plus, Autumn might not want to work so many long hours when she's married."

"All excellent news for you. So this means you have a fair chance of sticking around?"

"Just try and get rid of me."

"Good." The effect of the man's dimples could make any girl forget to breathe. It didn't mean a thing that she couldn't draw in air. Any female would naturally feel a little dazzled by his smile.

The wide gravel lane spooled between rows of fence posts and verdant pastures. Cattle lifted their heads from grazing to watch their approach. Calves ran alongside the fence line, kicking up their heels and chasing the truck. Up ahead, a brick ranch house rose into sight. A row of barns and outbuildings marched along the base of the low hill. Sean navigated toward the buildings, bumping along the private drive, hands on the wheel, shoulders wide, simply his ordinary self but he made her rib cage tighten with wishes she could not acknowledge.

"Sean. Eloise!" A man in his thirties looked up from working a horseshoe, released the animal's hoof and stood. "You didn't waste any time gettin' here."

"Cady wanted me to follow up on this right away." She rolled down the window, squinting against the sun. "She's on a mission to save as many horses as she can, for little Julianna's sake."

"So I hear. I applaud it, too." Troy left the horse cross-tied and ambled over to the truck. "Sean, long time no see. It's good of you to lend a trailer to Cady's cause, although I'm bettin' your uncle has something to do with it, huh?"

"Maybe, but that's all I know. I don't have any scoop about his intentions." Sean hopped from the truck.

"Hey, I was only speculating!" Troy chuckled as he opened Eloise's door with a slight squeak, the sound startling her. It took effort to force her gaze away from Sean, tall and muscular, bounding around the front of the truck. Warm air breezed over her and she grabbed her cane.

"Everyone in this town is speculating." Sean still smiled, nothing about him had changed except for a harsh twist in his words. "Since there's no movie theater in these parts, folks have to have something to watch."

"You know it," Troy agreed good-naturedly and held out his callused hand, offering to help her down. His dark gaze lingered on her cane and pity wreathed his features.

Pride kept her from taking his hand. Any moment Sean would march into range and see the expression on Troy's face. Aware of the weakness in her left leg, she eased off the seat and landed on her good leg, dug the tip of her cane into the powder-soft dust coating the driveway and tried to stand straight and strong as if she were fine, just fine.

"I'll get the door," Sean said tersely, which was strange because he was an easygoing guy, but he was definitely ruffled about something. "Where's the horse, Troy?"

"This way." Unconcerned, the cowboy knuckled back his hat and headed in the direction of the nearest gate. A cloud of dust rose with each step. "The poor thing showed up about a few days ago."

It was hard to guess what Sean was thinking. His dimples had faded into a stern frown as he shut the door. He kept at her side, his impressive shadow tumbling over her as they walked together toward the rails. She gripped her cane tight until her knuckles went white, sorely aware that every other step she took was imperfect. What if Sean looked at her the way Troy had? What would it do to her heart if he ever did?

"Come on, girl." Troy chirruped, gesturing toward a sad-eyed mare who hung back from the rails. "She showed up just hanging around the fields looking in at all the horses safe in the pasture."

"Poor girl." The mare was thin, not emaciated, but lost looking as if she had known too much disappointment in her life. There was no hope in her gaze, no spirit in her stance as she lifted her head to scent them. Wariness haunted her.

"Pretty girl." Sean leaned against the fence, his tenseness faded. "Is she lost?"

"That's what I thought at first," Troy explained. "I brought her in but she doesn't have a microchip or a brand. There's no way to identify her."

"She's a sweet thing." Sean held out his hand, palm up.

"Do you think she was abandoned?" Eloise watched the mare stretch out her neck and creep toward Sean's hand one hesitant step at a time.

"That's my guess," Troy answered. "Folks are pretty vigilant here. A missing animal wouldn't go missing for long so it stands to reason she was probably let go. I think she's put a lot of miles on her hooves. She's walked so far on bad shoes, she could have gone lame."

Another needy creature found just in time. *Thank*

You, Lord. Eloise was truly grateful as the cautious mare tentatively brushed her nose against the tip of Sean's fingers and jumped back, as if waiting to see what would happen next.

"Don't worry, sweetheart," he murmured, kindness and warmth layered in his voice, and the mare responded to it. She shook her mane, nickered nervously and reached out again.

"That's a good girl." When he spoke, it was as gently as a man's voice could be. He brushed his fingertips over the velvet curve of the mare's nose with infinite caring. No man could be more gentle. "That's right, I'm not gonna hurt you, beautiful."

Worry slid from big brown eyes as the mare inched closer and offered more of her head. As handsome as Sean was, nothing could be more attractive than his compassion as he befriended the horse.

"You are wanted now," Eloise told the mare quietly and earned a nod of understanding from Sean. Her entire heart seemed to be falling and she could not let it. Somehow she had to find a way to stop it. She could not afford to adore this strong man with a depth of caring and kindness.

I wish, she thought wistfully. I so, so wish. It was too bad some things were never meant to be.

Chapter Fourteen

"My boss put an ad in a few local papers." Troy backed away from the trailer, the mare successfully loaded. "If we get a call about the mare, who should I contact, you or Eloise?"

"Eloise." Sean gritted his teeth. Me, he'd wanted to say, but that made no sense. He couldn't explain why he didn't want Troy to talk to Eloise. The thought made his jaw clench so hard his teeth hurt.

"Yes, or Cady." Eloise folded a windblown lock of hair behind her ear, beautiful as always, possibly more beautiful than the last time he'd looked at her about three seconds ago. "You have my cell number. The inn's number is in the phone book."

"Easy enough." Troy knuckled back his hat and apparently figured he had the right to open the truck door for her since he paraded beside her in that direction.

Wrong. Sean yanked open the door, fighting a wave of red hot, boiling jealousy that flashed into existence with a force that rivaled spontaneous combustion. Jealousy wasn't like him, but he couldn't deny the fact that his entire field of vision flashed crimson as Troy made small talk with Eloise.

"Cady and the girls are going to love the mare." She planted her cane in the dust beside the truck, unaware that she was the reason he couldn't breathe. Troy probably felt the same way and that made the shade of crimson darken.

I'm in big trouble, he thought and stepped around the door to block any attempt by Troy to help her into the cab.

"Then I can stop worrying about that lost little horse," the cowboy drawled. "She's in good hands now. The Lord provides."

I'm not a jealous man, Lord. Prayer seemed the only way to deal with the scalding rise of emotion that rocked through him like a lightning bolt. *Please help.*

No answer came on the gust of warm wind or in the call of larks singing from their perch on the fence rails. He took a shaky breath and the rushing in his ears dulled enough so that he could make out the sound of human conversation. He caught Eloise's elbow and helped her up, although she didn't seem to need it.

He was in a fix. He couldn't breathe, he could barely hear or see. It wasn't as if he was looking for a relationship. He wasn't about to turn in his lone-wolf club card.

"Thanks for coming by, Sean." Troy turned to him, affable as always. "You saved me a trip trailering the mare to the inn."

"It was no problem at all. Thanks for the call." It was a total surprise he sounded normal. As he circled the truck red faded from his vision and the rushing in his ears calmed. He felt completely normal as he dropped behind the wheel.

"Another deserving horse to cherish," Eloise said in her soft, musical alto that made him want to listen forever. "Cady and the girls are going to absolutely adore her. She's just the kind of horse Julianna wanted to save."

"She's a gem," Sean agreed, fairly sure he didn't mean the horse. He could not take his gaze off Eloise as he turned the key and the engine roared to life. Where were his ironclad defenses, the barriers he'd put up, the resolve he'd made not to feel one single thing for the woman?

Gone. They were all gone, as if blown to dust. He didn't know why. He gripped the steering wheel tight and steered the truck back down the driveway, the tires kicking up a thick plume of dust. None of his current feelings were intentional. After his last bout with romance, he wasn't eager to dive back into a relationship. So, what was wrong with him?

"You have saved the day again." Eloise tossed that perfectly sweet smile at him, the one he couldn't resist. The one that played havoc with his heart.

"Hey, all I'm doing is driving."

"Cady and I can count on you, and that means a lot. I wasn't even tempted to call Cheyenne."

"Funny. Frank was quick to let me off work." He couldn't take too much credit. Sure, he wanted to help out as much as the next guy and he cared about animals. He appreciated what Cady was trying to do, but that wasn't the biggest reason he was in this truck with Eloise. Did he want her to know that?

Not a chance.

"I'm going to make a few calls to make sure no one

is looking for the mare." She looked relaxed with him, so beautiful he kept forgetting to watch the road.

"Good." The word stuck in his throat—the only word his brain would produce. His gray matter decided to freeze and he couldn't think of a single thing to say.

Eloise didn't seem to notice. She smiled over at him as the air conditioner carried a hint of her honeysuckle fragrance. Being with her, letting silence fill him, made his soul stir. Emotions threatened to carry him away, but he held fast. He didn't let his heart give a single bump, beat or tumble. He might not be in control of much, but at least he was in command of his feelings and he would stay that way.

"Are you going to the wedding on Saturday?" The words popped out of their own account, as if his brain had decided to ignore his resolve.

"Of course. Do you know anyone who isn't? It's the talk of the town. No one thought Ford Sherman would last as sheriff. No one has stuck around for very long, but he's putting down roots." She adjusted the air-conditioning vent so it blew on her face. "It will be nice to see Autumn happily married. She's waited a long time for true love to find her."

"True." He couldn't deny that. He also couldn't deny the basic truth that love tended to find a person. You could go looking for it, but that didn't mean you could locate it. And if you did, it might not be a love that would be as true or as durable as the one looking to find you.

Maybe that had been his problem with Meryl. He'd wanted to find love. He'd wanted the blessing of it in his life. What he felt for Eloise was different. It was spontaneous and quiet and illuminating, and he couldn't allow himself to acknowledge it, couldn't tumble one tiny bit.

"Things must be getting pretty crazy in your house with all the wedding preparations." She glanced across the fields as he navigated the county road that would bring the inn into sight at any moment. "I imagine there's so many last-minute things that crop up."

"I wouldn't know about that, as I duck my head and try not to listen whenever something comes up." He winked, keeping it light and friendly. "Autumn handles everything well and planning her wedding is no exception. She also has Mrs. G., who is phenomenal. Nothing gets past her."

"Doris is also the best wedding planner in town."

"She's the only wedding planner in town."

"True, but she's also very good." Eloise shrugged, determined not to give in to the wish gathering like a lump behind her ribs. "Autumn deserves a trouble-free day. A perfect day."

"That's what all the fuss has been for," he agreed, keeping his eyes on the road.

"This is making you uncomfortable, isn't it? The confirmed bachelor talking about marriage."

"I'm tough enough to handle it. I think," he added as a quip, using his dimples to his advantage.

If only she were immune. She sighed, unable to stop herself and the wish that could not be buried. Some day, Sean was going to fall head over heels for a woman. He was going to propose to her, marry her, be a fantastic husband to her and raise a family with her. Some woman was going to be greatly blessed to know his kindness, his tenderness, his gentle kiss.

I wish it could be me, she thought. I wish I could be

the one he will love. Not possible, she knew, as the truck turned into the inn's driveway and the white building with a wide front porch, picture windows and roof gables came into sight between the rustling cottonwoods. Windshields glinted in the sunshine from the guests' cars parked in the lot. Sean kept right, following the trail of blacktop around the gardens to the shining new stable in back.

"Eloise! Eloise!" Julianna came running all in bright pink, from her hair ribbons to her sandals. "Did you bring her? Oh, you did! I can see her through the window."

"We've got her stall all ready." Jenny came at a less enthusiastic jog, but her dark eyes glittered with anticipation. "Aunt Cady put a call in to the vet, and Nate says he is on his way."

"Excellent." It was a relief to hop out of the truck and escape Sean. As much as she cared, it was starting to hurt to be near to him. She welcomed the kiss of the hot sun and the puff of a lazy breeze against her skin. "She is a dear. I think you are both going to love her."

"I love all the horses," Jenny admitted, following her little sister around to the back where the clunk and clatter of the metal ramp going down told her Sean was there. If she listened she could just make out the low murmur of his baritone reassuring the mare.

"Guess what?" Jenny lingered, hands clasped, dark eyes unguarded. "Dad said we could spend the summer here. The whole summer. He's gonna get a house and stay here with us and everything."

"That's great. You seem happy about that."

"I am. I like it here. Julianna does, too. Besides, the horses need us."

"Yes, they do. Very much." There was no doubt the horses had flourished with two little girls to love them. Love makes everything better. Wasn't that one of life's secrets?

Julianna's voice rang like musical chimes, muffled by the trailer. Hooves clomped on the ramp and the little girl raced into sight. "Jenny! Come see her. She's so pretty!"

"Ooh, she's like red velvet."

"She's called a sorrel." Sean strode into sight, leading the horse by a halter and lead rope. The mare stared at Jenny. Sean held the mare capably, crooning to her in reassuring tones and with his easy confidence.

Somehow she had to resist the incredibly powerful pull of gravity on her heart.

I will not fall, she vowed. I won't do it.

"Look, she's taken a liking to you, Jenny." Sean gave the mare her lead and she walked straight to the older girl. Big brown horse eyes gleamed hopefully.

"She's so nice," Jenny breathed, holding out her hands as the mare placed her face in them. "She really does like me."

"Maybe she used to have a girl about your age," Sean suggested as the mare nickered low in her throat, a contented, welcoming sound. Julianna held out her hand to stroke the horse also.

Over the arch of the mare's neck, Sean's gaze found hers. It was more than horses they were rescuing, and she knew by the poignant set of his gaze that he knew it, too. They were repairing wounded hearts and broken promises and giving animals the chance for happiness to find them again.

I cannot fall for him, she told herself, holding on tight

with all the strength and willpower she had. She was not in love with Sean. Teetering on the edge, maybe, but she had not made that long, perilous tumble.

Yet.

"Eloise, you brought us another keeper." Cady breezed into sight, the tall solemn figure of the girls' father trailing behind her. "Come, let's show her to her new stall."

Sean handed over the lead to Jenny and stepped away, saying nothing as he backtracked around the truck. It was easy to say goodbye if she didn't look at him. She gripped her cane and headed to the barn, not daring to turn around and wave as he drove away.

Thoughts of Eloise trailed him all the way to the ranch. Images of her burnished by the sun, tenderly petting the new mare, just being Eloise with the air conditioner blowing her hair. He banished them but those images kept coming, impossible to stop. By the time he'd unhitched and hosed out the trailer, he'd lost the battle.

Footsteps knelled behind him when he was winding up the hose.

"Heard Dad took you off sheep duty." Tucker ambled over, dusty from a hard day's work repairing the fence. "Were you able to get the mare?"

"That's an affirmative. She's being properly spoiled in Cady's stables as we speak." He attempted to keep the vision of Eloise from popping into his mind, but it was a half-hearted attempt. He had to accept he had no power when it came to her. Maybe he never truly had. He could see her with the Stone girls, luminous and hopeful as the mare basked in the children's attention.

"Nate's coming over first thing in the morning." Tucker strolled on by with a chuckle. "Earth to Sean. Do you read me?"

"Sorry, guess I'm a little spacey." He shook his head, the understatement of the year.

"Yeah, I remember feeling that way. Still am ever since Sierra and I set a wedding date." There was no disguising the understanding grin one man gave another when he'd been lassoed in by marriage. "There's no way to avoid it now."

"You're doomed, buddy," Sean jested, as it was the lone-wolf way.

Stop thinking of Eloise, he told himself in the silence left behind as Tucker strolled out of sight. Work was done for the day, and he needed to do something to keep his mind from boomeranging back to her.

He hopped in his truck and his phone rang. He whipped it out of his pocket so fast, he didn't even glance at the screen. His palms went damp, his pulse galloped as he imagined Eloise on the other end. "Hello?"

"Sean." A woman's overly bright voice burst across the line.

"Meryl." Shock left him so stunned, he nearly steered right into the fence. His mind spun, too shocked to engage. Utterly blank, he listened to her chatter on.

"I'm so thankful you took my call. Finally. That must mean you listened to my messages. I know you're upset with me, but you took my call." She emphasized the words as if he'd saved the world from a killer asteroid and lived to tell the tale.

His guts clenched. His throat ached. The memory of her betrayal lingered, souring his mouth. "I wouldn't have answered if I had known it was you." He said the truth as gently as he could. "I don't want a second chance with you, Meryl. The first time around was more than enough for me."

"But I made a mistake. You can forgive me, I know you can."

He pulled into his slot in the garage and cut the engine. Yes, he was capable of forgiveness. "I can't forget and I'm not going to. This really is over."

"I was hoping we could meet. I could drive up your way."

"No. Sorry." He opened the door and let the sweet grass-fed breezes tumble over him, breathed in the fresh air and wide open spaces. The bitterness vanished. He was over her, he realized, thinking over his afternoon with Eloise.

He was losing the battle to deny his feelings. He didn't know how much longer he could hold out.

"You have a nice life, Meryl." He meant it as he hung up, feeling chipper. The tension bunched up behind his rib cage melted away as both boots hit the ground. He jammed his phone into his back pocket, whistling as he crossed the yard and pounded up the porch steps. Buttercup called out, batting her long lashes at him.

"I won't be long, sweetie," he called over his shoulder as he swung open the door. "I'll bring you a treat. How's that, darlin?"

The cow lit up like a puppy at her favorite word, "treat," and did the bovine equivalent of a happy dance.

Female voices rang like music as he kicked off his boots in the mud room. He balked at the circle of women at the kitchen table, most likely busy doing something for tomorrow's wedding. Maybe he could sneak on by before any of them noticed, but Mrs. G. was a sharp tack. She didn't miss much as he padded stealthily into the room.

"There you are." The housekeeper looked up from her place at the table. "Guess you'll be here for supper after all. Frank said not to count on it."

"Uncle Frank doesn't know everything." He tossed her a big grin because he saw her starting to get up. Probably to fetch him something cold to drink from the fridge. Before he could stop her, one of his cousins did.

"I don't know. Dad is usually right." Cheyenne hopped up instead and circled around the island. "Isn't Eloise with you?"

He saw how deftly she was trying to get information out of him. He wasn't about to be fooled, so he changed the subject. "Shouldn't you be at the vet clinic doctoring animals?"

"Yes, but since my sister is getting married I scheduled the afternoon off." Cheyenne grabbed a trio of pop cans from the fridge. "Don't ignore my question."

"Yeah, we know you're sweet on Eloise." Autumn made a neat little bow out of thin ribbon wrapped like a noose around a bunch of lavender netting. Wedding favors, apparently.

"Ooh, romance." Rori smiled as she leaned back in her chair. "Tell us more."

"I'm down on love, but that doesn't mean I don't want to hear all about it," Addy added.

"Mostly because you're nosey," Cheyenne teased as she distributed the cans.

"Sure. Inquiring minds want to know."

Mrs. G. took a can from Cheyenne, plopped it onto

the table and patted an empty chair. "Sean, sit. Make yourself useful. Answer the girls' question."

"You're a romantic, aren't you, Mrs. G.?" He didn't miss trouble gleaming in her eyes. "You were a heartbreaker in your day."

"I still am." She laughed and the kitchen rang with laughter as everyone joined in.

"Maybe we should be talking about your love life, Mrs. G." He plopped into the chair, not complaining as Addy on his left pushed a mound of ribbons his way and Mrs. G. set her pile of the lavender mesh stuff between them.

"Is it my imagination, or is the boy trying too hard to change the subject?" Mrs. G. asked.

"He's definitely trying to dodge the question," Cheyenne agreed as she wrapped two cookies with care. "That speaks for itself."

"Sure I'm sweet on Eloise. Who wouldn't be? I'm also sweet on all of you and Buttercup." He popped the top on his can and took a gulp of root beer. Good stuff. "Guess what I saw today? Frank and Cady out on a ride together."

"Yeah, we know all about it. If Dad isn't here, where else would he be?" Addy asked with a dimpled grin.

"I'm surprised Cady isn't here helping out." He spread out a piece of the mesh stuff and grabbed two cookies from the bowl. "Isn't this her kind of thing?"

"We wanted to have her here," Autumn explained. "I was going to invite her but then Dad took off to go riding and I thought that was more important."

"Cady's awesome." Addy fussed until she got the bow just right. "I love her. Anyone who makes Dad whistle is primo in my book."

"I can't ever remember him being so happy," Cheyenne agreed as she snapped open her strawberry soda.

"He seems really serious about Cady," Rori said.

"I think he's going to propose." Addy opened her soda. "Can you imagine? After all these years, we'll have a stepmom."

"She will be a great one," Autumn predicted.

"She sent me care packages when I was at school." Cheyenne got busy wrapping up more cookies. "Really nice ones."

"Ooh, me, too." Addy agreed as she lifted her pop can.

"And she emailed me all kinds of encouraging quotes when I was putting in long hours on my rotations."

"I got quotes and nice chatty emails."

"Friendly," Cheyenne agreed. "She didn't have to do that. She was busy getting her inn off the ground, but she took the time to really care."

"That's it. She's genuine. I'm glad Dad has someone like that to care about him." Addy took a sip of her soda. "Ooh, this is fizzy. Cheyenne, did you shake my can?"

"No, but it was tempting."

Laughter filled the kitchen again, the conversation steered well away from Eloise, but that didn't stop him from thinking of her. Knowing she would be at the wedding made him peaceful, as if a great calm were settling inside him. He couldn't wait to see her.

Chapter Fifteen

Maybe she wouldn't run into Sean. Maybe she could safely avoid him. Those thoughts were what got Eloise up the church steps when she wanted to go back to the car. Yesterday's outing with him remained at the forefront of her mind. The million little reasons she cared for him tormented her as she stepped through the doorway and into the sanctuary. Everyone had showed up for Autumn's wedding. The aisles were packed, the pews stirred with folks settling in, visiting, calling out howdy to friends and neighbors.

No sign of Sean anywhere. Major relief. Maybe she could scoot into an aisle and become part of the crowd and when he arrived he would never spot her. Avoiding him was the only plan she could think of to keep her heart safe from the torment troubling her. If she didn't see him, then she didn't have to fight for control of her heart.

"Excuse me, dear." Doris, the minister's wife, bustled by glancing at her watch. She'd been organizing the town's weddings for the last thirty years. She disappeared down the aisle and into a throng of more guests crowding through the doorway.

Eloise gripped her cane and took one step. She didn't get any further before the air changed. She knew he was close even before her gaze found him striding down the lane looking like a Western movie hero come to life in a dark jacket and trousers. All that was missing was his Stetson.

"Eloise." The way his voice warmed around her name made little bubbles pop in her midsection. "I was hoping I might find you here."

Joy inexplicably burst inside her. She tried to stop it, but she couldn't. Her emotions tumbled in a freefall because of the man who strode toward her with his long-legged, confident gait. The afternoon brightened. She became fully alive as if for the first time at his slow, dazzling smile. It was as if she took her first breath.

"I think everyone on this half of the county is here." She feared he could hear the strain in her words. Tension coiled through her, making her feel awkward and anxious.

"The church is packed," he agreed amicably, at ease. "Let's go find a place to sit while we still can. Come sit with me."

Say no, she told herself. Make an excuse. Find Gran. Escape him while you still have your heart. But when he held out one hand in silent invitation, she was helpless to say no. Her hand automatically met his and the drone of conversations faded. At the twine of his fingers through hers, her spirit quieted. Peace permeated her, soul-deep.

Don't start wishing, she thought. Not one wish.

"The house was crazy this morning." Amusement

vibrated in the low notes as he shortened his stride to match hers. "There were women, lace, dresses and flowers everywhere before I left. It's too much for a bachelor. I barely survived it."

"You do look worse for the wear," she quipped.

"Thanks. You look amazing."

"Now you are fibbing. You better be careful as you're in a church. Lightning could strike."

"Well, it wouldn't hit me." He'd never seen anything more stunning than Eloise in her summery pink dress. The swingy hem swirled with each step, and her golden hair tumbled in soft bounces to frame her incredible face. She'd blushed at his compliment and the light pink stealing across her nose and cheeks only made her more amazing. He had no clue how she managed to get any more beautiful.

Time to accept he couldn't win the battle. His heart was full of feelings he could not stop.

"What's the latest word on the little mare we rescued?" he asked.

"She settled in just fine. Jenny named her Princess. I think those two are going to be close." She glanced toward the middle of the church. Midway down a row Mrs. Tipple gave him a two thumbs-up.

Poor Mrs. Tipple had way too high an opinion of him. She was the most hopeful one of all. "I'm guessing Nate turned up to give her a good exam?"

"He did. She needed some care, but she will be fine. She needs to be reshod, so the farrier is dropping by on Monday."

"Excellent. While I hope there isn't another horse in need anywhere, if there is we can ride to the rescue. It's been rewarding. I'm glad we're doing this together."

"Me, too." She did her best not to let her adoration show. Tiny wishes kept threatening to rise to the surface that he would look at her and think, wow, and that his feelings were changing, too.

Of course they weren't, but her stubborn hope would not die. No matter how much she knew it had to.

"I need to sit with my family." The words rushed out, more strained than she'd intended. She wanted to come across as unaffected. She wanted to seem like a cool, casual and independent woman who didn't need a man's affections. He would never know how much she wanted him, how he was the man of her dreams.

"Sean, the ceremony is about to start." A man in his sixties moseyed down the aisle, Stetson in hand. "Howdy, Eloise."

"Hi, Scotty. You clean up nice." She'd known the Grangers' ranch hand since she was a small child, although it was rare to see him out of a T-shirt and jeans. "Don't let me keep you. I'm going to sit with Gran."

"Sure." Surprise flashed across Sean's handsome face but it fled quickly. "I'll see you after."

"Sounds great." That came across as breezy and easygoing, didn't it? Pleased with herself, she headed down the row, refusing to give in to the need to glance over her shoulder. She knew better than to fall in love again.

"Hold still, Dad." Cheyenne leaned in to fuss with his tie.

Frank Granger scowled. He wasn't fond of monkey suits, as he called the black tux, but it was his oldest daughter's wedding. He could survive the insult to his rancher's dignity for a few hours.

The room in the church's basement reverberated with excitement. He gazed around, proud of what he saw. His beautiful daughters were dressed up and as grown-up as could be. Maybe it was wishful thinking, but his daughter-in-law, Rori, appeared a bit peaked as she fussed with Addy's hair do. Maybe it was from the excitement, but he suspected it was more than that.

Autumn shone like the happy bride she was, wearing one of her mother's diamond necklaces and decked out in a white lace and pearl dress with some designer label that had taken a chunk out of his savings account—not that he minded. All he'd ever wanted in life was for his children to be happy.

"Doris gave me the two-minute warning." Cady bustled into the room, tall and slender and as pretty as a magazine picture. She was elegance in an understated, dark emerald-green dress to match her eyes and tapped crisply on her coordinating heels. Her soft bouncy locks were tamed into a fancy do that only enhanced the beauty of her oval face. "Are you ready, Autumn?"

"Ready? I was about four minutes ago. Now I'm mostly really nervous. Look, I'm shaking." She held out one hand, which wobbled somewhat terribly.

"Remember how nervous I was when I married your brother?" Rori took Autumn's hand in her own and they leaned together, talking away.

"Ooh, I'm not happy with this," Cheyenne muttered and went to loosen his tie. "Dad, you're not holding still."

"This is good enough. I'm an old man. There's only so much improvement anyone can make with me." He gently tweaked her nose, as he'd used to do when she was small. He could still see her freckles and pigtails, trailing after him when he doctored an animal.

"You aren't so old," Cheyenne quipped gently as she picked a tiny dab of lint off his collar. "Addy! Dad's ready for his picture."

"Ooh, goody!" His littlest bounced up in a swirl of silk, prancing across the room with a contraption in hand. "Dad, you look fab. Gather up, everyone. Group picture!"

It was too late to duck out the door. Cheyenne had a hold on him. That girl wasn't just good at barrel racing and doctoring animals. She was sharp-eyed and she had a strong grip. But he wasn't born yesterday; he knew how to handle a pack of women.

"Addy, give me that camera. I get to do the honors. You all cozy up together so I can get a picture of my girls." He flashed a grin at them because he knew how tough it was for his daughters to say no to his dimples. "C'mon, make your dad happy."

He watched with love in his eyes and a catch in his throat as Rori and Autumn joined Cheyenne and Addy. With the bride in the center and her bridesmaids surrounding her, he positioned his camera. Although his attention was on his girls, he was aware of the other woman in the room, hanging back and quietly watching. Cady had an effect on him, one he couldn't deny. "Alright, big smiles. Say cream cheese."

"Cream cheese," they chorused as he clicked. "Cady! Come join us."

"Oh, no, I couldn't." She was blushing. He forgot anyone else was in the room as she leaned one shoulder against the wall. "I try to avoid cameras at all costs. I take terrible pictures."

"No one here believes that." Autumn floated around him to take Cady by the hand. "I'm the bride. It's my day. You have to indulge me."

"I can't say no to you, sweetie." Cady patted Autumn's cheek. It was a gentle gesture, one of caring that a mother might give a daughter.

His throat tightened up. He knew Autumn and Cady had gotten close over the last year. His daughters pulled Cady into their circle, fussed with her and showed in little ways of tone and gesture that they cared for her. Truly cared. It meant so much to him his vision went a little fuzzy as he snapped the picture. He took a second one just in case. He wanted to make sure to capture this moment in time.

"Calling all bridesmaids!" Doris charged in like a general preparing for a siege. "It's time to go! Follow me. Frank, are you all right? You look a bit overwhelmed."

"I'm the father of the bride. It's my prerogative." He held out Addy's camera, hoping no one noticed he'd managed to avoid getting into the picture.

"Frank." Cady's caring alto and her gentle touch drew his attention. She took the camera before Addy could reclaim it. "Let me take a picture of you and your daughters."

He could read the unspoken understanding in her eyes. She knew what his kids meant to him. He didn't have to say a thing nor did she, but with the comfort of her touch a current zinged between them—a bond of connection and emotion that defied words.

"I've got the music cued, Frank Granger." Doris, whom he'd known since grade school, gave him a scolding look that didn't stymie him any. One flash of his dimples had her reconsidering. "All right, but make it quick, Cady. Autumn, are you ready, honey?"

"Now I am." Her arm hooked into his. Frank gazed down at his little girl and he knew he had to give her away. Not that she was going far. The construction on her house was finished, and it was less than a quarter of a mile from his driveway to hers, proof life was changing. He thanked God for it, but it hurt to know this fork in the road would take her a little away from him.

Cady clicked the shutter, Addy confiscated the camera and Doris steered the bridesmaids out of the room, straightening bows and handing out bouquets as they went.

"This is it, Dad." Autumn's arm tightened in his. "I'm steady now. Whew, glad those nerves are gone."

"Perfectly natural. Same thing happened to me when I married your mom." It was bittersweet to remember that day when his hopes had been sky-high. The road had been tough. In the end Lainie hadn't been a good fit with ranching life, but many of his other hopes had come true. Five perfect children, grown up to be five good people. And as he sensed Cady step from the room to give him and Autumn privacy, he was thankful for a new dream that had come to him in the middle of his life. "Good things are on the way for you and Ford, Autumn. Don't forget. Always be loving and enjoy the journey."

"Thanks, Dad." She went up on tiptoe to kiss his cheek, his sweet little girl.

God was good, he thought as he led her from the room. Never had there been a man more blessed than he.

Eloise stood in the church hall listening to the string quartet. The lilting notes rose over the dozens upon dozens of conversations. So far, she'd succeeded in her latest mission of avoiding Sean at any cost.

"Dad has a hidden ballroom dancing talent. Who knew?" Cheyenne sashayed up in her bridesmaid's dress and doled out the three cups of lime punch she carried. "Look at him go."

"I would give him a perfect ten," Addy declared as she took a sip. She studied her father over the rim of the cup. Frank Granger with Cady in his arms sailed modestly around the dance floor as if all he could see was Cady, as if she were the only person in the entire world.

If only, Eloise wished. She could not hold it back. If only Sean would look at her like that.

"They make a handsome couple." She managed to clear the wistfulness from her voice and took a sip of punch. It rolled over her tongue, sweetly tart. Cady deserved a fine man like Frank Granger. "I'm happy for them."

"We are, too," Addy answered for her sister.

Happy couples were everywhere. Eloise spotted her parents toward the back, waltzing rustily. Silver-haired Hal and Velma Plum waltzed as if they were fifty years younger. The bride and groom gazed into each other's eyes, cocooned in their happiness and love for one another.

"I have to say Autumn and Ford make a beautiful couple," Eloise heard Martha Wisener comment in the crowd behind her. "The town finally found a sheriff who will stay."

"About time, too," Sandi Walters added. "He might be a city boy, but he fits in around here like a stitch in a seam."

"That he does," Arlene Miller concurred.

"Aren't you glad this is not going to happen to us any time soon?" Cheyenne asked with a grin.

"Or ever," Addy concurred. "All that lace and ruffles and being tied down. No thank you."

"Who needs it?" Eloise found herself saying to cover up the sadness of the truth. Romance was not going to find her again. Gerald's words remained like a thorn in her soul she could not pluck out. *No man is going to want that kind of burden. I've tried as hard as I can, and I can't do it. I don't want to marry you now. You're not what you used to be.*

"I am thankful Autumn found a great guy. Those don't come around every day." Cheyenne ran a fingertip along the etched pattern of her glass cup. "They might be much rarer than first thought."

"I'll agree with that." In the crowd, Eloise spotted a familiar shock of dark hair. Wide shoulders. Six-foot-plus height. A dimpled smile and a rugged, handsome face.

Sean. Her pulse screeched to a dead halt. Every neuron she possessed went into a ceasefire. She could only stare, captivated against her will as he moseyed up to Tucker and Owen. Ever since Tucker had proposed to Sierra, her little boy had been glued to his future father's side. It was nice to see the happy child holding on tight and trustingly to the man he clearly adored. Sean lit up as he talked with the little guy. He knelt so he was eye-to-eye with the child, his masculine strength and kindness the most attractive thing she'd ever seen. She caught the word "horse," and "Bandit," so she didn't have to wonder about the topic of conversation.

He would make a good dad. That realization sailed right past her defenses, another wish she could not give voice to. Good men might be rare but they were out there. Sean was the best of the best. She tamped down the dream before it took form. Whatever God had in store for Sean's future, one thing was for certain. She could not be a part of it. She breathed slowly, carefully past the knot of pain behind her ribs and took another sip of punch.

"I never thought the day would come," Martha spoke up again. "Frank has chosen a bride."

"Oh, they aren't engaged so soon, are they?" Sandi Walters commented. "I'm never going to get over the fact that he didn't choose me."

"Me, either. My heart is forever broken," Arlene Miller agreed. It was no secret to anyone the two middle-aged women had been holding out hopes for Frank's interest over the years, but it had never happened. "I keep praying and praying for a handsome widower to move to town. But so far, God hasn't seen fit to answer that prayer."

"It sounds like a good one to me. I wonder what the holdup is?" Sandi quipped.

"Ooh, look who's coming this way." Addy leaned close. "He doesn't seem to be looking at either one of us, Cheyenne."

"No, I think you're right. He seems awful focused on someone else. I wonder why?"

"Ooh, romance." Addy grinned. "I'm all for it, as long as that dreaded disease doesn't come my way."

Eloise swallowed, unable to speak. The sisters' conversation faded, drowned out by the mad drumming of her pulse pounding in her ears. Her neurons began to fire again, but the rest of the world was fuzzy. Only

Sean was clear as he shouldered his way closer. Be still my heart, she pleaded.

It was already too late.

"Looks like I've found the prettiest girls in the room." His easygoing charm was turned up to full wattage.

"What did I just say about great guys being hard to find?" Cheyenne teased.

"I can't win with you two." He grinned, unthwarted. "Eloise. I was hoping you wanted to grab some fresh air with me. I've had about all the wedding festivities that a lone wolf like me can stand."

"A lone wolf?" Addy laughed at that. "Try again, Sean. Eloise, we'll see you later."

"I don't even get to say no?" she protested as Cheyenne plucked the nearly empty punch cup out of her hand and Addy spun away on her heels.

"I'm not sure they agree with the whole lone-wolf thing." He shook his head and nodded toward the open doors nearby, where green leaves rustled and a patch of blue sky beckoned.

"You can try to be something you're not, but it doesn't always work out." Her tone remained light. Golden hair tumbled forward like a curtain, shielding her.

"You're right." He agreed, shoving his hands in his pockets, determined to stay casual. "I'm not a loner type. I would like to be, but I may have to admit defeat."

"You can only be yourself." She led the way into the bright fall of sunlight searing the steps. He'd never recalled a time when the green had been greener. The deep verdant color hurt his eyes. The sky burned a bright robin's-egg blue, so stunning the only thing rivaling it was Eloise in her light pink dress, the hem swinging knee length, making her look like a little piece of cotton candy. Nothing on this earth could be sweeter.

He may as well face it. He'd failed because of her. He hadn't been able to wall off his heart or keep himself from tumbling head over heels.

"You are right." He let humor sound in his words but he kept back other emotions. Ones that he might not be ready for, but they came anyway as purely and truly as a Sunday morning hymn. The musical sweetness enveloped him, leaving him forever changed. Tenderness rolled through in persistent and powerful waves, drawing him inexorably closer to a truth he had to confront. "It's time to face the truth."

"What truth?" She curled a strand of hair behind her ear, deliberately avoiding his gaze.

"There's something I've been fighting. I've tried to forget it, ignore it, deny it and it hasn't worked." He drew her to a stop with a hand on her arm.

"What do you mean?" Nerves quaked through her and a spike of fear she couldn't explain stabbed at her chest.

"I know you have said you aren't ready for this, but I want to talk with you." His amazing blue eyes darkened, so deep they revealed his heart. "We have been spending a lot of time together lately."

"We have. It's been nice." What she saw in him made her palms go damp. The nerves quaking through her turned into tremors.

"Nice?" He shook his head. "No, it's been more than that. Being with you has changed me."

"For the better, I hope. Isn't that a sign of a good friendship?" Keep it breezy, she told herself. He didn't ever need to know how much the word "friendship" hurt. He didn't need to know how much she wanted the affection she saw in his heart.

"Friendship, sure." He nodded, no longer easygoing as everything about him became serious. "It's turned into something more. My feelings for you have deepened. I'm hoping yours have, too."

How was she going to stay in denial now? Air hitched in her throat as he leaned closer. The nerves tremoring through her became a full-fledged earthquake as his gaze focused on her mouth. No, she thought, don't give in. Hold on to the denial.

"We agreed on friendship, Sean." She gasped for breath, taking a rapid step back. "That's all it can ever be."

"It's true. I've been fighting it for so long. I've come up with all kinds of excuses but none of it is the truth. It's time to be honest, Eloise, both of us. I can't help how I feel."

"Sean, I am definitely not ready. I'm not going to be. Ever." How could he do this? His feelings may have changed, but they couldn't last. She gripped her cane tighter, feeling wrenched apart. In front of her was everything she wanted and everything that she couldn't have.

"I don't want to look back in life and wonder, what if?" He brushed the pad of his thumb against her silken cheek. "I don't want to stay silent and think about what my life would have been like if only I'd had the courage to speak my heart."

"Sean, this has to stop." Pain laced her plea. "Please."

Didn't she see? From the moment he'd spotted her at the drive-in with his ice-cream cone, he'd been caught like a fish on a hook doing everything possible to try to get away. But watching Autumn pledge her love to Ford made him realize how deeply he felt about Eloise. To have and to hold, in sickness and in health, through good times and bad. That was how he loved Eloise. With all he had, with everything he was, and he could not get the images of the future he wanted out of his mind, images that came from his soul.

"Don't push me away, not again. Not this time. Please." He brushed at the fine, flyaway strands of hair stirred across her face by the wind. "Let me show you how I feel."

"Sean, I—"

"Just close your eyes." Tenderness rose within him like a summer's dawn, gentle and cozy and certain. There would be no going back and he didn't want to. As he cupped her face with his hands, devotion shimmered within him like the rarest of gems, perfect and flawless and valuable beyond all measure.

The images began to unfurl. He saw sunny summer days and cheerful banter over the supper table with Eloise. He saw weekend horse rides, ice-cream cones at the drive-in, a ring on her finger and a baby cuddled in the crook of her arm. He envisioned everything when he gazed upon her. His hopes, his happiness, his dreams. This was what he wanted her to feel in his kiss as he slanted his lips over hers and opened his heart.

Chapter Sixteen

Panic rattled through Eloise's system, but she hadn't believed it was real until his mouth captured hers. Time stood still, their surroundings vanished and there was only the tender, reverent brush of his lips to hers. Her pulse halted, her soul stilled and she prayed the moment would never end.

It was perfection. Never had there been such a kiss. Fairy tales ended with kisses like this. All the wishes she had fought against rose as if they had sprouted wings. Affection welled up through her, affection she'd tried to banish, but hadn't been strong enough to. Love ebbed into her and she reached out to lay both hands against his chest.

For one breathless moment, she had the dream. A fairy-tale ending could be hers. It was just a breath away. Then the metallic clink of a cane striking the concrete shattered the moment and reality rushed in. The dream vanished. She opened her eyes, back to herself, and broke the kiss. Sean's poignant gaze searched hers.

For one blissful minute she'd forgotten who she was. The cane lying at her feet reminded her.

It would always remind her. The joy ebbed away.
The hopes uplifting her now gently lowered her back
to the ground. The happy-ending wishes evaporated
like mist in a wind, leaving her with a reality that she
could not dream away.

"That was some kiss." He cradled her face in his
hands with infinite tenderness. She wanted his tenderness more than anything. Sincere affection transformed
him. He seemed taller, a bigger man in her view. The
corners of his mouth hooked into a quiet grin. "I say
we do that again."

"You, sir, have an inflated opinion on your kissing
ability." She had to let go of the moment. She had to
step away from the closeness and she had to end things,
but the very essence of her being wanted to hold on, to
keep dreaming, to never let him go. "It was a perfectly
adequate kiss."

"Adequate?" Humor danced in his tender blue eyes.
Affection warmed the low notes of his voice. "That kiss
was a good deal more than adequate. I'm a great kisser."

"I'm not exactly sure where you got that idea." She
smiled, fighting to keep things light but the grief inside her began to grow. She could not stop it. It wrapped
around her in icy swirls.

"I'm apparently misinformed. That means only one
thing." Unaware, Sean gazed at her with honest love,
tall and stalwart and everything, just everything. She
wanted his love so much, but her injury was a burden.
He leaned in, his fingers featherlight against her chin.
"Practice makes perfect. I'm going to need a volunteer
to practice on. Interested in the job?"

"That sounds like cruel and unusual punishment to
me." Just a little longer, she hoped. Maybe she could

hold on to the gift of being close to him, laughing with him, just a little longer. She drew in a shaky breath, straightened her shoulders and grabbed hold so very hard to the moment. "You might have to find someone else."

"Sadly, there have been no other takers. I can't think why." Gentle amusement stretched his kissable mouth, softening the lean lines of his face. A face she could gaze on forever and never get her fill. A face she would never forget through the years. He leaned in closer still. "Are you ready for kiss number two?"

Yes, her heart answered. No, her common sense insisted. No. Misery pulled her down and she felt smaller, shorter, diminished. Unable to hold on, the dream slipped through her fingers. This perfect moment shattered and time rolled forward again. She could not deny the past or wish foolishly for the future that the accident had taken from her. Gerald's words rolled into her mind, no matter how hard she tried to stop them. *No one wants a burden for a wife. No man can take that long-term liability. It's too much sadness.*

She steeled her spine and took a step back. She had to do the right thing. She had to be realistic.

"No more kisses, Sean." She hated the shock that swept across him. He stared at her for a moment, blinking, as if not sure he had heard her correctly. His brows arched in confusion. Crinkles dug into the corners of his eyes in bewilderment.

"I hadn't thought. You're right." He glanced slowly from side to side. A soccer ball rolled with two grade school kids in pursuit. "This is a public place."

"A really public place," she agreed.

"What we feel for one another is private. Just between you and me." The tenderness within him deepened with a strength he'd never known before. It bound him to her with a steadfast connection that would never break. "Why don't we take off? Autumn is happily married, they are about to leave for the airport at any minute. No one will miss us if we don't stay for the send off."

"I can't go with you, Sean." Her words were heavy with sadness. "That kiss was wonderful, but it never should have happened."

"Shouldn't have happened? I don't understand." He couldn't wrap his mind around it. Maybe because he didn't want to. The depth of devotion he felt for her was greater than anything he'd known before. How could something this powerful be one-sided? Didn't she feel the same way, swept up by feelings too amazing to deny?

"I shouldn't have let you kiss me," she confessed. "I should have stopped you."

"Just like last time?"

"Yes." She sounded as though she were strangling, as if she were breaking apart from the inside out, just like he was. "This is all my fault. I shouldn't have let it happen."

"What do you mean? You kissed me back. I felt it. I know this is right." He raked a hand through his windblown hair, frustrated. "I am in love with you, Eloise. More than I ever thought possible."

"Maybe you just think so." Didn't he know how his words were tearing her apart? With as much dignity as she could summon, she knelt to retrieve her cane. "You called off a wedding. Seeing Autumn get married today affected you."

"Sure it did. I was happy for her." He straightened his spine, drawing himself up taller than ever. "The past is over. I've dealt with it. You are the one who affects me. Just you, Eloise."

She barricaded her heart so those marvelous words would not penetrate. He really meant it. He loved her. She took a step back, holding her cane so tight because her knees went shaky. His love was the one thing she wanted above all else and the one thing she couldn't have. Agony sliced through her like a sharpened blade. Her dear, sweet Sean. He'd done what she hadn't thought was possible. A man had fallen for her, cane and all.

But it couldn't last. She knew better than to believe.

"This is the part where you say, 'I love you too, Sean.'" He swallowed hard, tension bunching along his jawline. He towered over her, magnificent and vulnerable. He was all she could ever want, her most cherished of dreams, a prayer she dared not ask for.

"I can't." Tears pricked behind her eyes. She would give anything to simply savor this precious moment, forget the past and lay her cheek against the unyielding plane of his chest. To know what it would be like to be enfolded in his strong arms and to feel the beauty of his love.

But she had been down this road before. She didn't want to hurt him, but she had to be honest. He deserved no less.

"Sure you can," he persisted, fighting pain that crept across his face and cut grooves around his failing smile. "You might add how you didn't expect to feel this way for me, too. It's overwhelmed you but it's everything you want."

"I wish." She wanted that more than her very breath.

The words stuck on her tongue, the ones that would drive them apart forever.

"Then we don't have a problem." His smile won out, driving away his hurt. Nothing was more dear to her than a loving smile on his face, than the amazing truth of his devotion twinkling like a promise in his eyes. "Now, about that kiss."

"There can't be another." How could she end this, if there was? No, she had to hold on to her resolve. She gripped her cane tightly, drawing herself up as straight as she could.

Lord help me, please. Help me to do this the right way. She swallowed hard. Hurting Sean was the one thing she'd never meant to do. The notes of the string quartet wafted on the wind, the faint drone and laughter from the church hall, the merry sounds of a wedding party all reminded her of what she could never have.

"Sure we can kiss again. It's entirely possible." He winced, as if he were in pain, but he was stubborn. He didn't want to let go either. "You just lean in, close your eyes and we kiss. It's that simple."

She wanted to fight for him. If she did as he asked, if she accepted his kiss and grabbed the wonderful lifeline of the love he offered her, then what would happen? What would their future be?

She knew the outcome. She'd already lived it. She knew how hard he would try to love her over time, as her disability became a bigger and bigger issue between them. How could she hold a man like him? He was outdoorsy, he was always on the move, he lived a physically active lifestyle. His precious love for her would fade and so would the amazing love in his eyes when he looked at her.

How could she survive that? Imagining it crushed her as if an essential part of her was dying. Ending this now was the only choice for either of them. If she rejected him now, one day he would have the happy future he deserved with someone whole, with someone who would never let him down.

"I don't want another kiss." The words felt torn from her, leaving her raw and bleeding. She could not endure the flash of agony darkening his gaze. "Trust me, you feel this way now but over time that will change."

"Impossible. My love for you will never fade, never alter, never diminish." So sincere. He braced his feet, mighty shoulders squared, looking like a Western hero to whom legends could never do justice. He was bigger than life and genuine to the core, everything she'd ever wanted, every dream she'd ever had.

Everything she had to walk away from.

"You say that now. You have the best intentions. But this is for the best." She leaned on her cane and backed down the sidewalk. "From now on, I'm going to have Cheyenne help me with any horses that need rescuing."

"Don't do this, Eloise." He clenched his jaw until it hurt, until tendons stood out on his neck. "At least give us a chance."

"I can't." Tears swam in her eyes but didn't fall. The silent plea pinched her lovely face. Silently, she begged him to understand. She wanted him to let her go.

"Goodbye." She choked on the word. Misery wreathed her features as she spun around, tapping down the sidewalk away from him with great determination. As if she could not get away from him fast enough.

Crushing pain left him in tatters.

"At least tell me why." His call echoed down the

sidewalk and she stiffened. Her shoulders straightened. She stopped, clutching her cane. The wind swirled the hem of her skirt around her slim knees and ruffled the straight fall of her glossy blond hair. Alone, a solitary figure on the empty sidewalk, she broke his heart. The pain he felt was nothing compared to hers.

"Why do you think this can't last?" He jogged to catch up with her. She could end this, push him away, never want to see him again, and all the resulting pain would be nothing compared to the torture of knowing she was hurting.

"You know why." She kept walking, the tap of her cane counterpoint to the strike of her low heels on the concrete.

"I'm a man. I don't know anything." Humor had always worked with her in the past. "You have to clue me in."

"Look at me." She tapped faster, chin up, jaw set, so tense she looked fragile, as if she were holding herself so tight because she was ready to crack apart. She might think she was hiding her despair, but not from him. Never from him.

Tenderness deepened, becoming impossibly profound. In all the world, nothing could matter more to him than her. "I'm looking. I see a beautiful woman who has made me fall in love with her."

"I made you?" She stopped, faced him, her eyes dark with sorrow. "I did no such thing."

"Yes, you are completely to blame." He brushed windswept bangs from her eyes, moving in close because he could not stay away. "You captivated me right from the moment I saw you at the drive-in. Then you roped me into helping you with the horses, and I was a goner. The least you can do is tell me why I'm not good enough for you."

"Not good enough?" Her face twisted. Concern for him layered her voice. "You are entirely too good. Don't you see? The problem is me."

"How could you be a problem, darlin'?" He'd never seen anyone look so defeated, as if the sun would never shine again. His soul buckled and he fell harder, loving her more. Maybe he'd been so busy trying to be a lone wolf protecting himself he hadn't realized that she had been doing the same. "Maybe now is a good time to let me know. So I can understand why you have shattered my heart."

"Oh, Sean, you already know the answer." Tears pooled in her eyes, but they didn't fall. Tears for him, he realized. "It's because of this."

She tapped her cane.

"I told you, I don't see that. Eloise, I only see you."

"Yes, but you said that as a friend." A friend was different from a boyfriend. She'd learned this the hard way.

"I mean it always." Stalwart, that was Sean.

He didn't know the truth about her injury. What if she leaned on him, opened her heart without reservation and gave him all the trust and devotion she possessed? All she could see were her fears that Gerald had been right. No man was going to love her enough to stay. She squeezed out the images of Sean growing tired of the challenges, of Sean leaving her for someone else, of Sean breaking her heart.

Too late for that. She was already shattered. She had to tell him the whole story.

"I remember the exact moment when Gerald fell out of love with me." She hated the tremulous sound in her voice and the catch in her throat that she could not swallow or clear away. "It was when he came to visit me at the hospital as he'd been doing faithfully, but it was the first time he'd seen me using a wheelchair."

"You were in a—?" He didn't finish. He looked startled.

She nodded. Here was where Sean would see her differently. She straightened her spine, steeling herself for it. It had to be done. He deserved to know why. He would want to end this.

"For how long?" he asked.

"Six months. They were the hardest of my life." She could not bear to watch the caring slide from his gaze, so she stared at the sidewalk ahead. She caught a glimpse of the main street and the Steer In, where the lot was empty. The bright sun tumbled over her with summer's heat and light, but she felt locked in the shadows of the past. "Don't get me wrong. I was deeply thankful to have survived the car accident. When I was trapped in the driver's seat, terrified and unable to move, I thought I might die there. I thought it was the end."

"I'm sorry you had to go through that." Sympathy layered his words. He didn't sound distant, as if he was emotionally withdrawing yet, but it would come. She had to prepare for it.

"So I tried to be positive when they told me my spinal cord injury was complete and permanent and I would never walk again. I fought hard, and I walked again." She pushed away the crushing grief that had consumed her at the time and that was consuming her now.

"But you were in a wheelchair for a while," he empathized.

"Yes." The lazy summer breeze rustled through the leaves of the trees marching alongside the curb, and the world so bright and colorful and summery made her want to believe that a man's love might be strong enough to accept all her imperfections.

Except she knew better.

"There's no guarantee the paralysis won't be harder to compensate for as I get older." She squared her shoulders, ready for the rejection she knew was coming. She'd known it from the moment she'd met Sean and been attracted to him. She had plenty of experience with this moment, thanks to her grandmother's fix-ups. "Over time, it is likely I may be a paraplegic again."

"I see."

No man, not even Sean, could love her now.

She did her best not to let it show as she took a wobbly step forward. Her knees were far from steady. Any moment he would turn away. Since it was Sean, he would be kind, gallant, gentlemanly, but he would not look at her with love in his eyes. Never again.

"This was the biggest reason behind your breakup with Gerald?" He dug his fists into his pockets. "He bailed on you when you were injured?"

"He was a nice guy. He wanted to do the right thing. He wanted to behave the right way. He tried to be there for me, but it was hard. When I was in the hospital, the prognosis was so grim. When I was in a wheelchair, there were a lot of adjustments to get used to. There were logistical challenges like sidewalks and finding the wheelchair-accessible ramps instead of stairs, which is harder than you think. So much had changed between us, I had lost so much. The sadness was simply overwhelming." She bowed her head, her hair cascading forward to hide her face. Now he knew the truth. He was free to go. He would be polite, he would be sympathetic, but he would leave.

"You said there were other things wrong with the relationship." He watched her carefully. His gaze had darkened, his forehead furrowed with thought.

"Yes. Our relationship wasn't as solid as it should have been, but nothing could have withstood the strain. Sometimes love isn't enough."

"Sometimes." He had to agree with that. But at least now he knew what had wounded Eloise so badly she had lost her faith in the fairy tale. He had, too, until she saved his heart. "You would be worth all of that and more. My love for you is strong enough."

"What did you say?" She gazed up at him, disbelieving.

"I love you now, I'll love you then, I'll love you forever. No matter what." He towered over her, more breathtaking than any hero could possibly be. "Nothing is ever going to change that."

No, it couldn't be true. She felt wrenched into pieces, wanting to believe. He was being chivalrous. Optimistic. He was such a good man, he was saying what he wanted to be true instead of what actually was.

"Love is kind." As if he sensed her reluctance, he bridged the distance between them and cradled her chin in his hands. *"Love bears all things, believes all things, hopes all things, endures all things. Love never fails."*

"First Corinthians." How could she not recognize those words? They stirred her soul and lifted her hopes, but how could she believe? She had been through sadness and loss and had worked hard to rebuild her life realistically, so she could never be hurt like that again. How could she be sure?

The truth was in Sean's eyes. He gazed at her with endless, abiding love, more powerful than it had been before he'd known about her prognosis. He knew the whole truth and he loved her more.

Joy rolled through her like a prayer answered and she leaned into his touch, savoring the warmth of his fingertips against her face, the bliss of this moment, knowing she was truly loved.

"Now that I've bared my soul, that only leaves one question." Vulnerability flashed across his rugged features. "How do you feel about me?"

She laid her hand on his chest, remembering how gentle he'd been with the mare. How good he was to all God's creatures. He would never hurt anyone intentionally. He was one man who would always cherish her.

I love him, she finally admitted. I truly love him.

When his hand cupped her chin, she went up on tiptoe. His lips brushed hers with a beauty that brought tears to her eyes. She hated for it to end. Sean must have felt the same way because his hand lingered against her jaw and his gaze locked with hers. It was like being soul-to-soul.

"I love you with the kind of love that never fails." Love sailed through her so forcefully, it nearly lifted her from the ground. Bliss drove out all doubt as she wrapped her arms around Sean, her Sean. Being enfolded against him was the sweetest blessing, the only one she could ever want. Dreams she thought long lost burned as bright as the sun. There was so much good ahead in store for her life she could not hold the images back—glimpses of Sean proposing on bended knee, a wedding in the town church, a little home made happy with their lasting love. So very much good ahead, she held him more tightly, determined never to let go.

"There is one more thing we have to talk about." Sean stepped back just enough to meet her gaze. "I would like to discuss the possibility of more kisses."

"I would be in favor of it."

"Good, then we are in perfect agreement." He claimed her lips in a kiss that dimmed the sun with its beauty and captured her soul with its sweetness.

Romance had found her, after all.

Epilogue

"Do you know what your problem is, Eloise?"

"I didn't know I had a problem, Gran." Eloise adjusted her cell phone against her ear as she reined Pixie off the country road and onto Main. Town was busy for a hot June Saturday afternoon. A couple of vehicles were parked in front of the diner, she recognized a Granger pickup, and a truck or two at the feed store. Yep, there was nothing like small-town living. Enjoying the peace, she lifted her face and let the temperate winds puff her bangs off her forehead. "My life is nothing but blue skies. Not a cloud in sight."

"You spend way too much time helping in my garden instead of with that young man of yours. Next time you come over to weed, you bring along young Mr. Granger."

"I might consider it."

"I'll make him some of my homemade lemonade. I'm pleased you found Mr. Right, but I'm bummed I didn't find him for you."

"Yes, sadly my blind-date fix-ups have come to an end. Forever." Hallelujah. That wasn't the greatest thing about being with Sean, but it was a definite perk. She'd found the best man, the very best. "Now that my blind-date days are over, whatever will you do to amuse yourself?"

"You need to ask? I've already got your wedding figured out. The minute he pops the question, you let me know. I've got a notebook started and the church hall booked."

Help me, Lord. She sent the prayer heavenward. Was her grandmother ever going to stop meddling? Not that she minded, but it was the principle.

"I just want you to be happy, sweet pea."

"I want that for you, too." She so loved her grandmother. Pixie lifted her head, neighing in welcome at the sight of the black gelding standing in the drive-in lot where a car should be parked. Bandit lifted his nose in an answering welcome, and a cowboy moseyed into sight.

Handsome.

"Gran? I've got to go."

"All right, dear. I'll see you this evening. Don't forget to bring that boyfriend of yours."

"I'm making no promises." She didn't remember disconnecting the call or stuffing the cell into her pocket. The man beside his horse with a Stetson shading the splendor of his face commanded every shred of her attention.

"Hey there, pretty lady." He tipped his hat, his deep baritone layered with warmth and humor. "How would you like to join me for an ice-cream cone?"

"I could be tempted." The strong, lean lines of his cheekbones, his sparkling blue eyes and his chiseled jaw held her captive. Wow. "What is a handsome man like you doing here all alone?"

"Trying to pick up a gorgeous chick." Humor flashed in his bright blue gaze. "Interested?"

"Very." She slipped off the saddle and into his waiting arms, such strong arms. There was no place on earth she would rather be than enfolded against his chest, so near to him their souls felt as one.

His chin rested on the top of her head as she snuggled closer and cozy feelings left her smiling into his sun-warmed T-shirt. He smelled like summer and hay and leather. She never wanted to let go. If she could stay just like this cuddled in Sean's strength, she would ask for nothing more.

"Guess what I did today?" His lips brushed her hair.

"Did you end up going to the sale with your uncle?"

"Sure did. I tagged along at the auction over in Sunshine. The ranch did real well selling off some of the cattle." He paused, remembering. He was a permanent employee now and the excitement of the bidding, all the cows to check out and spending time with his uncle and cousins had been fun. But it wasn't the highlight of his day. "Frank came on an errand with me to offer his opinion."

"An errand? You didn't say anything about that before."

She leaned back in his arms, so lovely she knocked the air from his lungs, so beautiful his spirit ached with adoration. Spending time with her and opening his heart to her had been the greatest reward of his life. He was no lone wolf, never had been. He could admit it. He was a pack man, a family man, and he was proud of it. He thanked God daily for the blessing of Eloise in his life.

"It was a top-secret mission." In the bold summer sunshine he saw another piece of his future. A little toddler clinging to her knee and a new baby in her arms. Birthdays, holidays, anniversaries spent with her, years rolling by, each one better than the last. A sense of rightness filled him up until his vision blurred and all he could see was her, Eloise, the reason for his life.

"Ooh, sounds mysterious. Top secret." She dazzled, from the inside out. "Don't tell me you made a stop at your favorite pizza place and didn't bring home any leftovers for me?"

"No pizza, no leftovers. It wasn't that kind of mission." Behind him he heard Bandit snort his opinion, as if he disapproved of the place and time, but Sean could not wait. Love overwhelmed him and his decision was made. Pixie nodded at him, as if she were saying to go for it. So, he did.

He tugged the ring out of his pocket. The gold band gleamed warmly in the light. The square-cut diamond framed by emeralds winked like a promise made to be kept. His entire spirit stilled with the importance of the moment.

"I was going to do this tonight at sunset in a field of wildflowers," he confessed. "I hope you don't mind we are in a parking lot, but where I am standing is where I first was bedazzled by you."

"That's an engagement ring." She stared wide-eyed, surprise on her dear face. "That was your secret errand?"

"Yes. The diamond is forever, the emeralds are because they match your eyes, which are now my favorite color. You are my favorite gal." He took in a shaky breath. Worry crinkled his forehead. Love warmed his voice, so much love. "Do you know what I see when I look at you? A porch."

"A porch?" Fine, not what she was expecting but the adoration on his face made her pulse skip three beats. Anticipation left her breathless. "Why a porch?"

"Because on that porch I see a gray-haired couple sitting side by side on a porch swing, holding hands."

"Are they watching the evening unfold?"

"Yes. They do that every warm summer evening, just as they've done every year of their married life. They are happy together." He towered over her, stalwart and incredible and true. "You can tell how much the man adores his wife every time he looks at her."

"That couple is us?" she asked, her eyes growing watery.

"Yes." His eyes deepened with emotion as he cradled her hand in his. Such a gentle touch. "That is what I see when I look at you. I want to marry you. I want to raise a family with you. I want us to be that silver-haired couple happy with a life well spent adoring one another through thick and thin. With every day that passes, I promise to cherish you more. Please marry me, Eloise. I love you so much."

"Not more than I love you." How could she say no to that? It was every dream she'd lost, everything she'd ever wanted with the one man she treasured above all. The sun chose that moment to brighten, as if heaven were trying to spotlight the moment. She realized this is where God had been leading her all along, that He had given her more than the accident had taken away.

"Y-yes." Happiness made the word stutter like a sob in her throat. Tears filled her eyes, and she blinked hard. Joy was too small of a word to describe her feelings. "I want to marry you more than anything and spend all my days loving you. It's a fairy-tale ending."

"This isn't an ending. It's a beginning."

"The best beginning."

He slid the ring on her hand and his gaze locked with hers. She felt the impact all the way to her soul. She twined her hand with his, overwhelmed with emotion. Their hearts, now in synchrony, beat as one and always would. Their bond was unbreakable and everlasting.

"Hey, Eloise! Hey, Sean." Chloe clumped up on her skates, carrying two ice-cream cones. "I was right! You guys *were* dating. Now you're engaged. I *so* called it. Hey, a guy was just in for lunch. He's from the next town over and he asked me if the inn was still taking in horses. Are you?"

"Absolutely."

"I have an address. I'll get it." Chloe thumped off, her skates clumping on the blacktop.

Eloise saw the spark of happiness in Sean's eyes as the sunlight caught the diamond on her left hand. Life was good, so very good. "Can you believe it? More horses to rescue."

"Looks like our mission continues, gorgeous." He knelt to boost her into the saddle. "Let's go."

* * * * *

Dear Reader,

Welcome back to Wild Horse, Wyoming. I hope you have been enjoying the Granger Family Ranch stories as much as I have loved writing them. This time cousin Sean has hired on at the ranch to help out. He is recovering from a broken engagement and has decided that no woman is ever going to threaten his lone-wolf status again. Until he meets Eloise, who is in need of a horse trailer, and he can't say no to helping her. While the two of them rescue homeless horses, what are the chances that God will rescue their hearts, too?

In these pages, I hope you have fun visiting returning characters, both human and animal, and lose yourself in a small-town rural way of life. Once again I have tucked favorite things from my childhood into this story—leisurely horse rides, pet cows and chocolate ice-cream cones—and I hope you are reminded of some of the golden memories from your childhood. Thank you for journeying to Wild Horse, Wyoming, with me.

As always, wishing you love and peace,

Jillian Hart

Questions for Discussion

1. What are your first impressions of Eloise? How would you describe her? What do you think she is looking for? What does she fear most when Sean spots her cane?

2. What are your first impressions of Sean? Are you surprised at his reaction to Eloise's disability? What does this tell you about his character? How do you know he's a good man?

3. What do you think of Eloise's grandmother? What role does she play in the story? What advice does she give Eloise? Have you ever had a family member like Gran?

4. What do you think of Sean's intention to be a lone wolf? What function does this serve for him? How does he use the excuse to keep his heart safe?

5. How did Eloise's accident affect her? How have all the losses that followed affected her?

6. Family, friends and the town speculate about Eloise and Sean's relationship. What part do they play in the budding romance? How does this affect Eloise? Sean?

7. Why does Eloise reject Sean's kiss? How does this affect her? Affect Sean?

8. What are Sean's strengths as a character? What are his weaknesses? What do you come to admire about him?

9. What values do you think are important in this book?

10. Little Julianna Stone wants every homeless animal to be saved and to find a home. What Biblical basis is there for her wish? What impact does Julianna's hope have on the story? On Eloise and Sean's romance? What impact does one little girl make?

11. What do you think are the central themes in this book? How do they develop? What meanings do you find in them?

12. In the beginning of the story, Eloise wrestles with the losses resulting from her car accident. What does she learn by the end of the story? How has God given her more than the accident took away?

13. How does God guide both Eloise and Sean? How is this evident? How does God gently and quietly lead them to true love?

14. What role do the animals play in the story? Have you ever helped an animal in need?

15. There are many different kinds of love in this book. What are they? What does Eloise learn about true love?

RODEO SWEETHEART

Betsy St. Amant

To Cindy—for your strength and your fight.
We love you. Never give up!

Acknowledgments

As always, I couldn't have done this novel alone,
especially with the timing I found myself in.
I'd like to thank Lori and Georgiana, for your quick
crits, your friendship and your prayers. Also my mom,
for giving me that one day of baby-free writing a week
that really does make a difference. Thanks to my
amazing editor, Emily, for your fresh insight, and to
my sweet agent, Tamela, for backing me 100 percent.

Fear not, for I am with you; be not dismayed,
for I am your God. I will strengthen you,
yes, I will help you, I will uphold you
with my righteous right hand.
—*Isaiah* 41:10

Chapter One

If wishes were horses, the Jenson family breeding farm would be full of stud mares and furry new foals—not teeming with greenhorn tourists in stiff new jeans and shiny cowboy boots.

Samantha Jenson loosened the lead rope in her hand, allowing Diego another couple inches of leverage. The hot Texas sun glinted off the gelding's chestnut hindquarters, and she swiped at the sweat on her forehead with her free hand. It looked as if this weekend would be another scorcher.

She clucked to the gelding as she studied his limber gait. "Just another lap or two." Diego's ankle injury was slowly healing. A few more days of exercise in the training pen and he'd be ready to hit the trail—though probably just to be manhandled by another wannabe cowboy.

Sam's lips pressed into a hard line and she drew in the rope, slowing Diego's willing pace to a walk. "Good boy." It wasn't the gelding's fault he'd fallen a few weeks ago. Thanks to a careless rider who'd ignored the rules of the trail, Diego had been pushed too hard over uneven ground and tripped in a hole. It was by the grace of God he had only sprained his ankle, rather than broken it. Of course, the tourist hadn't even been bruised—didn't seem very fair.

Sam pulled the rope in closer until Diego's gait slowed to a stop. That probably wasn't the most Christian attitude to have, but it was hard to feel differently in the circumstances. At least God was looking out for her and her mother with the little things if not for the bigger things Sam would prefer. Avoiding a vet bill was nice, but it wasn't going to help bring back her father's dream.

Sam met the horse in the middle of the paddock and patted his sweaty muzzle, drawing a deep breath to combat her stress. No, nothing other than a big wad of cash would bring back the Jensons' successful breeding farm. She and her mother had turned the farm into a dude ranch to earn income, but to Sam, the problems that came with it weren't any better than avoiding the debt collectors. Sure, the new dude ranch business paid the mortgage and had kept the farm from going completely under last winter—and Sam would grudgingly admit running a dude ranch was better than being homeless—but Angie Jenson wasn't the one dealing firsthand with all the tourists. That job fell to Sam, as did filling all the proverbial holes that tourists left in their unruly wake—like horses with sprained ankles.

Sam gathered the lead rope around her wrist and trudged toward the barn, Diego ambling behind. To her left, green hills stretched in gentle waves, trimmed by rows of wooden fences. The staff's guesthouses to her right had been converted into cabins for the vacationers, tucked in neat rows like houses on a Monopoly board. One didn't have to look close to notice the chipped trim, peeling shutters and threadbare welcome mats. Angie was counting on her customers being so mesmerized with the horses that they wouldn't care about the less than pristine living quarters. Talk about pipe dreams. Her mom had suggested selling the ranch several months back, but after seeing Sam's reaction, she hadn't brought it up again. How could they sell? It was all they had left of Sam's dad.

Things sure had changed. Once upon a time, when Wade Jenson was still alive, one would be hard-pressed to find a single repair waiting on the farm. The grounds stayed kept, the paint stayed fresh and the ranch resembled exactly what it was—a respectable, sought-after breeding farm that had been in the Jenson family for three generations.

In a paddock nearby, Piper whinnied hello at Sam and Diego—or maybe it was a cry for help. Sam tipped her cowboy hat at the paint horse as she passed. "I'm working on it, Piper. I'll get things back to normal for us one day." She fought the words *I promise* that hovered on her tongue, afraid to speak them lest she end up like her father—a liar. Promises from Wade Jenson hadn't stopped the bull's thrashing hooves or the heart monitor from beeping a final, high-pitched tone, and they wouldn't make Sam's dreams come true, either.

She dodged a young boy kicking a soccer ball across the yard and narrowed her eyes at the kid's father, who stood nearby talking to Sam's mother. The man was so enamored by Angie he apparently didn't notice the glittering diamond ring still on her finger—or his son wreaking havoc. The ball slipped under the last rung of the wooden fence containing Piper and several mares, and Sam made a dive before the boy could do the same.

At least the ball hadn't gone into the adjacent paddock, where several stallions left over from the breeding-farm business grazed. Gelding and mares were much more docile in comparison.

"Whoa there, partner. What's your name?" Sam caught the kid's belt loops just in time.

"Davy." He struggled against her grip.

Sam couldn't help but smile at the freckle-faced kid. A toy water gun stuck in the waistband of his jeans and dirt smeared across his sunburned forehead. How many times as a child had she probably looked the same, playing in the yard between chores? Her anger cooled like a hot branding iron dunked in water and she ruffled the boy's already mussed hair. "You can't go in the paddock with the horses, Davy. They might step on you."

Davy crossed his arms and glared a challenge at her. "My ball went in and they're not stepping on it."

Sam's grin faded at the sarcastic logic. "Park it. I'll get it for you." She shot him a warning look before she easily scaled the fence and jogged toward the black-and-white ball. She rolled it to him and hopped back over into the yard. Davy scooped up the ball and took off without even a thank you.

Sam's annoyance doubled as she led Diego into the cool shadows of the barn, the familiar scent of hay and leather doing little to ease her aggravation. She secured the gelding and forked over a fresh bale of hay, then yanked a halter from its peg and headed for Wildfire's stall. If this was still an operating breeding ranch, there wouldn't be little terrors running around scaring the horses while their dads flirted with her mother. Sam's father died only two years ago, and this was the way they honored his memory? By catering to city greenhorns and risking the welfare of their livestock? Tears pricked her eyelids, and Sam roughly brushed away the moisture. *Cowgirls don't cry,* her dad always said. *They get back on the horse and keep riding.*

But Sam's dad never told her what to do when he wasn't there to give her a leg up.

A horn honked from the parking lot near the barn, and Wildfire startled, kicking the stall door with his foreleg. "Easy, boy." Sam soothed him with a gentle touch on his muzzle before peering through the barn window.

An expensive luxury sedan was parked near the first guest cabin, its shiny rims catching the July sun and nearly blinding Sam with the glare. The windows were tinted so she couldn't see inside, but it had to be the Ames family. They were scheduled to arrive within the hour, and Angie had already cautioned Sam on being extra attentive to the wealthy guests. Apparently this family owned a multimillion-dollar corporation of some kind in New York. How they ended up in the nowhere little town of Appleback, Texas, remained a mystery to Sam. But VIPs were VIPs.

"They're staying three solid weeks, and if they tip like they should," Angie had said earlier that morning, "we'll be able to make all of our bills and have money left over for the first time in ages." Her eyes had shone with such excitement at the prospect Sam almost didn't notice the heavy bags underneath them or the frown lines marring the skin by Angie's lips. But Sam had noticed, and it was the only thing that kept her from protesting. That, and the prospect of having to waitress again to make the house payments. Those exhausting months last year were definitely not ones she wanted to relive.

The doors of the car opened and a well-dressed couple in their early fifties exited the vehicle. The lady smoothed the front of her white pantsuit as she cast a gaze over the horses in the pasture. The car's trunk popped open, and the man emerging from the driver's seat shaded his eyes with one hand as he looked around—probably searching for a valet or bellhop.

Great. One more chore for Sam to pull off—like acting as full-time stable hand, groom and trail guide wasn't enough to keep her busy. She considered hiding in the hayloft like she did that time she was ten and failed her math test. But avoiding reality didn't work—she should know. She'd been trying that for two years now.

"Guess it's now or never." Sam slipped the halter back on its peg, and Wildfire snorted his disappointment. "I'll be back for you in a minute." She looked out the window again to see if the couple had managed to grab their own luggage, just in time to see a silver convertible squeal to a stop beside the sedan. A dust cloud formed around the tires, causing the woman to take several steps backward and cough.

The driver's side door of the sports car opened and a guy in his mid-twenties slid out. He surveyed the ranch over lowered sunglasses, his expression shadowed.

Wildfire ducked his head and blew through his nose, pawing at the stall floor. Sam rubbed the white splash of hair on the gelding's forehead, a frown pulling her brows together. "I know exactly how you feel."

Ethan Ames never thought he'd see the day where his mother teetered in high heels on dirt-packed ground—

on purpose. Then again, he never thought he'd see the day he joined his family on a rural working vacation, either. He shouldn't have taken that back-roads exit off the interstate. Nothing was stopping him from speeding farther west and finding some real fun in Vegas—nothing more than his mother's disappointment, anyway. Or his father's incessant phone calls and threats. On second thought, Vegas wouldn't be much fun without an expense account—and his father knew how to hit Ethan where it hurt.

One would definitely have to pay Ethan a bundle to get him to admit that deep down, he was a little curious about this country life thing, after all. He shut the door to the convertible and pulled his duffel bag from the backseat. At least the rental company had given him something decent to drive this time.

"You really shouldn't speed like that, Ethan." Vickie Ames touched her hair, as if the motion could protect it from the country air.

The passenger door slammed, saving Ethan from answering. His cousin Daniel slid over the hood and landed beside Vickie. He looped an arm around her shoulders. "Don't worry, Aunt Vickie. Ethan never passed ninety-five miles an hour." He winked and slung one booted foot over the other.

Ethan rolled his eyes. Leave it to Daniel to blend in with new surroundings like a chameleon. He'd picked up those stupid cowboy boots before they'd even left New York and propped them up on the dashboard for the entire drive from the airport. Ethan didn't think real cowboys would splurge on designer tooled leather like that for a three-week vacation. And what was with that *Dukes of Hazzard* move he just pulled on the car hood? Ethan snorted.

His father, Jeffrey, cleared his throat. "If you two would quit clowning around and find the valet, we could get settled a lot sooner."

Ethan shouldered his duffel. "I don't think this place has staff like that."

"The boys will get the bags." Vickie shot Ethan a pointed glance that clearly said to get busy.

Jeffrey looked around, the permanent frown between his bushy brows tightening even further. "This place is more run-down than I thought. We should get it for a song." His lips stretched into a line. "It better be worth this charade."

"It will be." Vickie gestured around them, her red manicured nails startling against her white suit. She looked as out of place as a bull in Saks Fifth Avenue, just smaller and better dressed. "You know we just need to find a reason to get the owner to sell to us for cheap— before she gets wind of the highway relocation. You said yourself this would be the perfect place for a mall after they move the interstate. So quit complaining—a dump is exactly what we're looking for."

Ethan shook his head. Only his mother could get away with telling Jeffrey what to do. If he or his cousin had tried that, well, it wouldn't have been pretty.

Jeffrey's face purpled. "I still don't see why we all had to come down here to the middle of nowhere and cut a work week short. We could have just sent the boys to make the offer—"

"It's about appearances," Vickie hissed under her breath. "You know the owner is hesitant to sell in the first place. She doesn't even want her daughter to know why we're here. She wants to feel like the person who buys it will take good care of it. You think she'd be more willing to warm up and accept an offer from two businessmen in suits, or to a vacationing family of four? She'll never believe that we want to keep the place as a ranch if we make an offer from New York."

Jeffrey's lips disappeared beneath his mustache. He looked as if he wanted to argue, but wasn't sure what to say.

"Uncle Jeffrey, we'll handle the bags. No problem." Daniel grabbed the largest of the suitcases from the trunk and hefted it to the ground. "Where to?"

Ethan took a second bag, trying not to snicker at Daniel's obvious attempt at kissing up to his father.

"I think check-in is inside there." Vickie pointed to a two-story farmhouse with a wraparound porch. Paint peeled near the faded trim and the stairs leading to the front door looked saggy, as if they'd held up one person too many over the years. "They'll have our cabin numbers. I requested the two biggest ones they had."

Ethan's mouth twitched as he studied the crumpling architecture of the house. "After you, Daniel." He wasn't about to stand on that top porch step with a suitcase. He was likely to go straight through to the grass.

"I'll check us in." Vickie brushed them aside. "You boys get the rest of our luggage." She lightly scaled the steps and disappeared inside the run-down building, an unspoken warning floating in her perfumed wake. *Don't upset your father.*

Ethan grabbed another bag and passed the next to Daniel. Jeffrey stood by with his hands in his pockets, letting others do the work. The familiar claws of resentment dug once again into Ethan's back, and he set his father's suitcase in the dirt a little harder than necessary.

"Watch it, boy." Jeffrey didn't even bother with a glance in Ethan's direction, just kept staring out across the fields spotted with wildflowers. "There are break-ables in there."

Ethan bit the retort on his lips and set his father's suitcase upright. Three weeks of this? He must be crazy. No, his mother must be crazy to insist they come. She'd played it up as a huge business opportunity, a real work-ing vacation—heavy on the vacation. But so far, the Jenson ranch was nothing to get excited about. Who cared if the family had been here for three generations? That didn't make the property a steal—it'd just make it even more expensive to buy because of the owner's hesitation to sell, especially if she heard of Jeffrey's plan to develop a mall on site. Families didn't like get-ting rid of memories.

Normal families didn't, anyway. The only thing sen-timental to Jeffrey Ames was his collection of gold money clips. Maybe Ethan and Daniel should go ahead and hightail it to Vegas after all.

Ethan turned his back to his father and shot a grin toward his cousin, the same easy, cover-up smile he'd spent years perfecting. Jeffrey would never know how badly he got to Ethan, and neither would anyone else if he could help it. Ethan had buried so many emotions over the years, what was a few more? He lowered his voice. "I don't know about you, man, but I could go for a little fun instead of playing this charade. You want to get out of here?"

Daniel sat on the top of his suitcase and rocked back, balancing on his heels. A gleam sparked his eyes. "You know I'm up for anything. Just say the word. Where do you want to go?"

Ethan started to answer, and then stopped as a woman about his age stepped out of the shadows of the giant red barn and headed in their direction. Underneath a tan cowboy hat, her light brown hair was streaked with natural blond highlights, not the fake stuff his mother used every six weeks. Her slim jeans were peppered with dirt and her boots clomped across the dirt-packed earth as she strode confidently in their direction.

A slow grin spread across Ethan's lips. "Who said anything about leaving?"

Chapter Two

"Welcome to Jenson Farms." Sam greeted the guests with a smile, trying not to cringe at the amount of luggage surrounding the three men. Wasn't the family only here for a few weeks? "I'll be happy to show you to your suites."

The older man sized her up with a quick nod. "Jeffrey Ames."

Sam shook his offered hand. "I'm sorry for the delay in coming out. I had business to tend to in the barn." She started to add they were shorthanded, but thought better of it. Her mother had warned her not to say anything that would make these guests think the Jenson ranch was less than top-notch—although it wouldn't take more than a cursory glance to determine that particular truth.

"Not a problem." He gestured for Sam to lead the way. She hefted a bag on her shoulder and turned toward the two adjoining VIP suites. They were really nothing more than two small wooden cabins joined with a narrow porch, but these particular cabins had full kitchens, unlike the partials in the other guesthouses. Good thing her mother had added those big garden tubs in the bathrooms last summer, or the Ameses might make a dash for civilization. Why was such a wealthy family on vacation in the nowhere town of Appleback, anyway? If Sam had money, she'd vacation in Europe. Or some deserted island in the middle of the ocean where she could ride bareback in the sand and sip fruity drinks with umbrellas.

"Dad!" The sharp voice sounded seconds before the duffel bag was tugged from Sam's grasp. She turned to find the young sports car driver holding the luggage and scowling at Mr. Ames. "She doesn't need to carry our luggage."

"We can get it." The passenger from the convertible winked at Sam and she quickly looked away from the leer in his eyes.

"Nonsense. It's her job." Mr. Ames turned back to Sam. "I'll make sure you're compensated for it." He motioned her along with a wave of his hand.

Sam's stomach clenched at the flippant dismissal. She'd never been talked to like the hired help before, although with the Jensons' new business venture into the tourist world, that's exactly what she was. Her father's image flashed in her mind, and Sam forced tidbits of pride down her throat. Without money, she'd never get the ranch back the way it was, and the Ames had it to spare. Time to work. She picked up another suitcase, this one heavier than the first.

"Here, let me." The son's warm voice and sudden nearness filled Sam's senses. "I'm Ethan Ames. And this is my cousin, Daniel."

"Sam Jenson." She set the bag down and shook Ethan's hand, noting its smoothness. The men in Appleback all had work-worn hands, calloused from hard work. This guy must not be used to handling anything other than a leather steering wheel or computer keyboard.

"You don't look like a Sam to me." Ethan's dark hair, short and spiky, heightened the deep brown of his eyes. If it wasn't for the fact that he was a dreaded tourist, she might actually find him attractive. He was taller than Daniel, and didn't seem to have an agenda in his eyes like Daniel did, either. More maturity lurked in Ethan's gaze, along with a heaviness that suggested secrets. Maybe there was something substantial to this greenhorn after all.

"It's really Samantha." She allowed Ethan to take the suitcase handle from her. "But I go by Sam." No one but her father had called her Samantha, and if she had her way, no one ever would again. Some rights were reserved for the dead.

"Samantha." Ethan's smile turned slightly flirty, heightening Sam's first impression when he'd arrived in his convertible. "I think I'll call you that instead. You don't mind, right?"

The respect he'd earned by helping her with the bags faded into oblivion, and Sam flashed her own smile as she hoisted another duffel bag in her arms. "Only if you like boot prints on your back."

Sam strode past the men toward the cabins, ignoring Daniel's burst of laughter. She kept her head high and refused to give them the dignity of a backward glance.

"You really said that?" Sam's best friend Kate Stephens laughed, leaning forward to momentarily rest her head on the top rail of the fence. Her curly red hair gleamed in the setting July sun. "Only you, Sam."

"He had it coming." Sam stuck a strand of hay in her mouth and chewed as she looked out over the pasture, unable to hide her smile. "I wish I could have seen his face."

"Priceless, I'm sure." Kate cupped her hands and motioned as if reading a headline. "Preppy City Boy Told Off by Overworked Cowgirl."

Sam shoved Kate's arm down. "It wasn't that big of a deal." Though Ethan had yet to emerge from his cabin, and the incident happened hours ago.

"I better get back home. It's feeding time." Kate dug her booted foot off the lowest rung of the fence and stretched. "For me *and* the horses."

"I hear that." Sam tossed the piece of hay on the ground. "I'm glad Mom finally found another cook for the guests. Mom can make breakfast food all right, but dinner is another story." Sam and her father used to joke about corn bread that could be used as horseshoes and chili that would keep a body in the restroom for a month of Sundays. She squinted against the memories, determined not to cry. Not again, not today. She swallowed.

"Oh, I almost forgot!" Kate clapped her hand on the fence. "I came over here to tell you something important, and you distracted me with your story of charming guest hospitality." Her green eyes sparkled with amusement. "Guess which horse my father is selling now?"

"Viper?" The mustang gelding was the oldest horse still living at the Stephenses' busy racing stables down the road from the Jensons'. Kate's father, Andrew Stephens, was known for his champion racehorses in southern Texas. Last year, Kate had bought a few acres and a small farmhouse not too far from her family and Sam's, where she ran a successful boarding and grooming service for animals. Despite her own proverbial plate staying so full, she still occasionally helped out with the inner workings of her family's business.

Kate shook her head at Sam's guess. "Think black stallion."

Sam's breath caught in her throat. "No way. Noble Star?"

Kate's red curls bounced as she nodded. "He called me this morning to tell me he's decided to retire him. Dad said he'd rather sell Noble and obtain the cash upfront then try to breed for money later. He and Mom don't have the time for new ventures right now." Kate grinned. "I know you've been waiting for something like this."

More like praying for it every night. If Sam could buy the sought-after ex-racehorse, he would be just the ticket to bring back the Jenson breeding farm. Mares for miles around would be brought in to get a shot at those champion bloodlines. Their business would soar and things could finally go back to the way they used to be—as normal as they could be without Wade Jenson, anyway.

Sam's mind raced in a blur of tallying numbers, and the end result brought a sharp jolt of reality. Her shoulders tensed. She could empty her meager savings and still not have enough to buy the blanket off Noble Star's back.

Kate pulled her keys from her jeans pocket. "I just wanted you to know before Dad started advertising. He's going to spread the word this week."

"Price?" Sam closed her eyes for the verbal assault.

The number Kate named was pretty reasonable, considering Noble Star's champion bloodlines and success on the track—but still many thousands more than Sam could dream of obtaining in years, much less the next few weeks. She let out her breath in a slow sigh. "Thanks for the info."

"No problem." Kate sent Sam a sympathetic smile. "I could talk to my dad for you. Maybe he could shave a bit off the price for you and your mom."

"Unless he shaved off half, it wouldn't really matter." Sam forced a laugh. "But thanks for the thought."

"Call me tomorrow." Kate started walking backward to the parking lot. "And watch out for greenhorns!" She grinned before slipping inside the cab of her pickup.

Sam waved, then grimaced as the door to Suite A opened and Ethan stepped onto the porch. She probably should apologize to him. Her mouth was always getting her in trouble, and her mom had a point—the Ames family had the potential to be big tippers. The last thing the farm needed was their sudden departure—especially over something Sam said.

She sighed and trudged toward the cabin. Time to cowboy up.

Ethan let the cabin door slam behind him as he stepped outside onto the porch. The term *suite* had to be a joke—or else the Jensons had never been in a real city before. A suite meant space. Not semi-new bathtubs and adjoining porches. He'd also have to share the bathroom with Daniel. At least he was far enough away from the adjoining cabin not to hear his parents fight. Unless they were making money, they were fighting—and with Jeffrey remaining unconvinced this venture would turn a profit, the arguments were already starting. They had to secure this property as quickly and as cheaply as they could in order to ensure a profit large enough to make it worthwhile in Jeffrey's eyes. But his mother would win. She always did.

Ethan gripped the wooden railing, staring out across the green meadow. Horses grazed, their tails swishing at flies, while a fiery July sun set behind the farthest hill. The longer Ethan watched, the looser his grip became, until finally his shoulders relaxed and he breathed deeply. Maybe there was something to this country air thing after all. Ethan would never admit it in front of Daniel—or his parents—but sometimes, he wished for something other than the late nights in his office, pushing paperwork to further pad his father's bank account. There had to be more to life than money. The church he'd once attended as a child with his grandmother confirmed that suspicion, but once Ethan hit the work world after graduating, time for God seemed to be crowded out as deadlines and marketing the business took first priority.

A paint horse whinnied from the pen, and Ethan studied the brown-and-white animal through narrowed eyes. If Ethan stretched low, really low to the depths of all his childhood memories, he'd admit to having cowboy dreams once upon a time. What little boy didn't? He used to squirrel away books on horses, Jessie James and the Old West, tucking them inside textbook covers so his father would think he was reading "productively." When Ethan reached high school, girls and cars became top priority until his gun-slingin', lassoing, bareback riding dreams were all but forgotten.

Until he pulled up on the ranch and breathed the air

laden with horse sweat, leather and dust. Now those dreams were slowly resurrecting, a fact that would have Daniel doubled over with laughter and his dad smirking beneath that thick mustache. What would it be like to have the freedom to chase his dreams, rather than follow his father's plans? Ethan didn't want to take over Ames Real Estate and Development.

He didn't know yet that he wanted to ride a horse for a living, either, but surely there was something in between.

Footsteps thudded on the porch stairs and Ethan turned with a start. Samantha—no, Sam—joined him on the porch, her hands shoved in the back pockets of her jeans.

"Back for more insults?" Ethan shifted to face her, resting his weight against the railing and crossing his arms over his chest. His heart thudded louder than her boots on the wood floor—real working boots, not the useless designer ones Daniel brought.

Ethan fought to keep his expression neutral, his mind reliving Sam's snappy comment from earlier in the day. No woman had ever spoken to him with such an attitude before, and to be honest, he was impressed. Sam was different from other women he knew—that was certain—and it had nothing to do with her cowboy hat or plaid Western button-down.

Sam's chin lifted a fraction as she stopped a few feet away. "I came to apologize. You're our guest, and I was rude." Her lips twitched. "I just really don't like being called Samantha."

"I gathered that." Ethan tapped his chin, pretending to be in deep thought. "Why not a compromise— Sammy?"

Sam rolled her eyes. "Just stick with Sam and we won't have any problems, okay?"

"Deal." Ethan studied her guarded pose, then held out his hand, for some reason anxious to make her smile. "Don't real cowboys shake on truces?"

Her brows rose. "I don't see a real cowboy here."

Ethan's hand fell to his side and Sam's eyes widened to giant blue orbs. "I'm so sorry, there I go again." She slapped her hand over her mouth and groaned. "I don't mean to—I just—"

"Have a lot of pent-up frustration?"

Her arm lowered. "You have no idea."

"Don't worry about it." Ethan shoved aside the bruised portion of his pride and shot Sam a sideways glance. "Samantha."

Her eyes, greenish now that anger sparked inside, narrowed. "You're impossible." She clomped back down the porch steps and Ethan watched her leave, an unexplainable joy rising in his chest at having gotten to her once again.

"See you on the trail, partner." Ethan grinned as he braced his arms on the porch railing and watched her stalk to the main house. He had a feeling this working vacation was just getting started in more ways than one.

Chapter Three

Sam was up at dawn the next morning, partially because of her growling stomach and the full schedule for the day and partially because Ethan's face had teased her dreams all night. There was nothing worse than tossing and turning in the midst of a dream you didn't want to have—make that a nightmare. Who did Ethan Ames think he was, riding into her life as if he belonged there? So what if he was handsome? There wasn't enough room in all of Texas for the size of his ego. Teasing her about her name, as if he should automatically be granted special privileges, was the last straw in Sam's hay bale of tolerance. If money meant instant ego, Sam was glad she hovered on the poor side of the spectrum.

But poor wasn't going to bring back her father's legacy.

Sam dressed quickly in jeans and a button-down, then grabbed her cowboy hat off her dresser. Her eye caught the photo of her dad, taken nearly twenty years ago at the height of his rodeo fame, and she gently touched the worn wooden frame. She often wondered what their lives would be like if her father hadn't quit the circuit when she turned seven. Would she and her mom still be following him around in that beat-up RV, touring city after city, winning prize after prize? Maybe if her dad hadn't quit and taken over his grandfather's breeding farm to provide a safe life for his family, he'd still be alive.

The irony was what ate at Sam for years, and still occasionally nibbled on her thoughts. Wade Jenson gave up his dreams and his talent to avoid danger and be there for his family—yet the tragic accident happened during his first tribute appearance years after quitting. Angie had told him not to ride, that he hadn't in too long and it'd be dangerous. But Wade Jenson was never one to displease a begging crowd of fans, so he took on the infamous bull Black Thunder. It was the last time he ever rode anything. The injuries from being trampled lingered, and Sam and Angie spent the next several weeks at the hospital until Wade's body gave out—along with their family savings.

What if Wade had recovered, and the breeding farm could have continued as planned? What if Sam didn't have to help her mother carry the burden of providing for their livelihood, and could have moved out? Gone to college? Felt free to date and marry?

She turned away from the picture before the familiar sting of tears could burn her eyes, and shoved her cowboy hat on her head. She was through with the what-ifs. All that mattered were the what-nows. And right now, she had a trail ride to lead, an annoying man to ignore and a farm to save.

Sam pressed her knee into Piper's side, waiting for him to exhale before tightening the girth of the saddle.

The paint gelding was known for holding his breath during the tacking process, leaving a loose, comfortable girth and a rider hanging on for dear life. "I know your game, boy. Give it up."

Piper exhaled in defeat and Sam quickly cinched the girth strap. She rubbed briskly under Piper's mane, her fingers immediately coated with sweat and little white and brown hairs. "Just a short trip, boy. I know it's hot out here." Even though it was only nine-thirty on a Friday morning, the summer sun inched along its path in the sky, blazing the ranch with heat. Only a handful of tourists had shown up for the ride—unfortunately, Vickie and Ethan Ames included.

Sam gathered the reins and clicked her tongue at Piper. He followed her to the edge of the paddock, where she looped the reins around the hitching post. After last night's drama with Ethan on the porch and her round of bad dreams, she'd hoped he'd sleep in and mercifully spare her his presence at the morning ride. He'd skipped breakfast, so Sam figured there was a good chance. But no, there he stood beside Vickie, dressed in designer jeans and a short-sleeved polo shirt that revealed the tanned lines of muscle in his arms.

Sam adjusted the blanket under Piper's saddle with a sharp tug. Where did a city boy like Ethan get a tan? Must be all that driving with the convertible top down. She would imagine he hadn't earned it with sweat and honest work.

Same with the muscles.

"Is that my horse for today?" Vickie Ames gestured to Piper.

Sam nodded and introduced the painted gelding to Vickie. "He's a sweetie, sort of like a big puppy. Just don't spook him with any sudden noises." All the working ranch horses were docile and well-trained, but they still had spunk. Piper hated loud noises, a fact he reminded them of every time it thundered. Sam had fixed more than her share of stall doors and fences after one of Piper's episodes.

"Of course I won't." Vickie patted Piper's nose, then winced at her hair-covered hand. "I forgot my handkerchief."

"Use your jeans, Mom." Ethan sidled up to the paddock fence beside Sam. He winked. "Good morning, Sam."

Sam gritted her teeth, remembering how her mother had specifically asked her to be nice. Her mother was right across the corral, so Sam better fake it for a while. She drew a deep breath. "Mornin'."

"Where's my horse?"

Sam pointed to a chestnut mare that Cole Jackson, one of the longtime stable hands, was saddling a few feet away. "You'll be riding Miss Priss."

"Miss Priss?" Ethan smiled. "You did that on purpose, didn't you?"

Sam shrugged, not wanting to admit he was right. The mare's name was girlie, but the older horse was stubborn. Sam had a feeling if anyone could put Ethan in his place, it would be Miss Priss.

"Well, I'm sure me and the little lady will get along great." Ethan brushed his hands on his jeans with a pointed look at his mom, who was still picking horse hair off her palm.

"Mrs. Ames, would you like help mounting?" Sam turned her back to Ethan.

Vickie looked up with a relieved smile. "That would

be great. I don't know if you can tell, but I'm not used to being around horses much."

No kidding. Sam worked to keep her smile natural as she boosted the woman into the saddle, glad Vickie was at least wearing jeans and riding boots, even if they did look so new she'd surely have a blister by the end of the ride. Angie made a point of stating on the ranch's website to bring comfortable, worn-in clothing for riding, but ninety percent of their guests ignored the suggestion and were usually miserable by the end of the week. Sam had never understood the fashion-over-function mindset.

Beside her, Cole shook back his dark hair in frustration as if he'd noticed the same thing. "Greenhorns," he mumbled as he handed the reins to another tourist.

"Can I get a leg up, too?"

Sam ignored Ethan's taunting call from two horses away, focusing on adjusting the stirrup length for Vickie instead. He was apparently determined to get to her again today, and Sam was just as determined not to let him.

"You know, since I'm not a *real* cowboy." His teasing continued.

Sam moved to work on the second stirrup, keeping her eyes averted from Ethan's position beside Miss Priss. *Ignore him, ignore him.* Cole could help him mount. Not that Ethan actually needed help mounting, he just wanted to rub in Sam's face her verbal mistake from last night.

"Please, *Samantha?*"

Sam dropped the stirrup abruptly, jostling Vickie's leg, and glared across the fence at Ethan. "You know, I thought they said mules were stubborn. Not—"

Angie bumped into Sam as she appeared next to her, effectively cutting off Sam's sentence. "Lovely day, isn't it, Mrs. Ames? Hot, but beautiful. That's Texas for you." Angie finished adjusting the stirrup and shot Sam a warning look. "Go help him," she whispered. She smiled back up at Mrs. Ames. "I love that blouse."

Sam rubbed her face with both hands before slowly walking to Ethan's side, leaving her mother and Vickie chatting about clothing labels in her wake. She hated that her mother had arrived to hear her comment. *God, I'm losing it. Please cool my temper. I don't know why this guy gets to me so badly.* Sam sucked in a fresh breath of air and forced a smile at Ethan. "Need a leg up, you said?"

"Nah, I got it now." He swung into the saddle and reached down to adjust his heel in the stirrup.

Sam fought to keep the shock off her face and nodded stiffly. "Fine." She *knew* he'd been faking asking for assistance. Sam felt Ethan's eyes on her back as she quickly moved to finish saddling Diego, and stifled a groan. This was going to be the world's longest trail ride.

Would this trail ride never end? Ethan shifted in the saddle and his thigh muscles screamed in discomfort. How did Sam do it? She rode like she'd been born in a saddle, leading their small group through the shaded woods, pausing occasionally to gesture to a particular grouping of trees or a historical marker. Her back stayed straight, her hips relaxed, moving like she and that red horse were one being.

He and Miss Priss, however, were getting along more like a bull and a rodeo clown. He nudged her forward, she stopped. He pulled on the reins, she picked up her pace. He said "whoa," she tossed her head and insisted on moving forward.

Apparently real horses were nothing like that carousel his mother made him ride as a boy in Central Park—a fact Vickie must be realizing herself right about now. Ethan twisted around to catch a glimpse of his mom aboard Piper, one hand clutching the reins, the other in a white-knuckled grip on the saddle horn as the paint horse ambled along. At least Jeffrey had stayed at the cabin, determining that "appearances" could only be taken so far. No telling what Daniel had found to occupy his time. For all Ethan knew, the two could be plotting together a new scheme for making money. Jeffrey had always preferred Daniel's input on such concepts to Ethan's.

"We'll stop at the clearing ahead for a snack and to stretch our legs." Sam's voice rang from the front of the line, and Ethan could barely contain his relief.

As soon as the horses came to a stop in a flowered field, he slipped from the saddle, hoping Sam didn't notice the way his knees almost buckled when his shoes hit the grass. After the way he'd teased her earlier, he more than deserved any return insults.

There was also something intriguing about the fact that she hadn't shown any interest in Daniel. Usually women sensed him and his cousin's money a mile away. A cash radar, Daniel joked. He never seemed to mind, but Ethan wanted more. Was it possible he'd finally found someone oblivious to their financial charms?

Ethan pressed his hands into his lower back and stretched as the other riders were doing, then bent down and tried to touch his toes. Pain shot through his hamstrings, and he quickly straightened.

"Having trouble?" Sam appeared beside him, cheeks flushed with the summer heat, a water bottle dripping with condensation in one hand. She offered it to him.

He took the water with a tight smile and twisted off the cap. "Not at all." His right thigh suddenly cramped as if insisting otherwise. But he couldn't let Sam see his weakness, not after all the grief he'd given her. Apparently running on the treadmill required different muscles than horseback riding. He shifted uncomfortably.

"Good for you. So you'll have no trouble making it back? A lot of first time riders get pretty sore their first day on the trail." She took off her cowboy hat and shook her hair off her forehead. The feminine motion almost made Ethan forget her question.

He downed a quick sip of water to clear his head. "It'll be a piece of cake." More like a piece of prickly cactus.

Sam opened her mouth, probably to question his statement, but was interrupted by Vickie's yelp. Ethan turned to see his mother hanging half off Piper's saddle, one foot stretched toward the ground, the other stuck in the stirrup. Her dangling leg was at least a foot from the ground. "Help! He won't let me off!"

Her panicked cry flattened Piper's ears and the horse snorted in distress. Sam rushed to Vickie's side seconds ahead of Ethan, and grabbed Piper's reins. "Easy, boy." Her low tone perked Piper's ears, and he stopped the anxious shuffling of his legs.

Ethan helped support his mom's weight while Sam worked Vickie's boot free of the stirrup. Once her feet were on solid ground, she released a relieved sigh. "He started moving while I was getting down. I tried to get back on, but couldn't get enough momentum. He's so big!"

Sam's mouth twitched. Even Ethan could see Piper was several inches shorter than most of the other horses in the group. He patted his mother's arm. "You're safe now, don't worry."

"Do you want me to call the ranch to have someone pick you up?" Sam held Piper's reins, and the horse blew on her shoulder. She didn't even flinch as his flabby lips worked against her hair. How did she know those giant horse teeth wouldn't sink into her neck?

Vickie brushed the front of her stiff jeans. "I'll be fine. Walking around a little will help."

"It's good to keep moving," Sam agreed. "There are water bottles and packages of crackers in my saddle bag. Please help yourself."

Vickie thanked her and headed in that direction, while Sam briefly closed her eyes and exhaled.

Ethan quirked an eyebrow. "Something wrong?"

"I warned her not to make any sudden or loud noises." Sam patted Piper's hairy cheek. "He's skittish about that. She really could have gotten hurt."

Ethan remembered all the times growing up where his mother's voice had startled him, as well, and he reached out to rub Piper's ear. "Hey, I can relate." He smiled at Sam.

The edges of her mouth started to curl in response, but just as suddenly, she gathered Piper's reins. "Let's get you grazing with the other horses." She clucked twice to the paint before leading him away—without a second glance at Ethan.

* * *

Sam's heart raced, and it wasn't from the near incident with Mrs. Ames and Piper. No, it had everything to do with that brown-eyed stranger and his deadly smile. She pressed a hand against her stomach and drew a tight breath. So what if Ethan was handsome? She'd been around attractive men before, and most of them turned out to be completely full of themselves. If she had time for romance—which she didn't—she needed a man who spent more time outdoors than looking in a mirror. Attractive or not, Ethan Ames was still a rich guy bent on teasing her. He might have had a humane moment there, relating to Piper, but she couldn't forget the incessant teasing he'd doled out to her earlier that morning while saddling up.

Sam tugged on Piper's reins, urging the paint to follow. There was the point, however, that Ethan could have gotten angry with Sam for venting about his mother, and didn't. That showed something decent lurked in the heart underneath that polo shirt of his. Regardless, she'd have to watch her mouth around the tourists from now on. Her unedited remarks could easily come back to bite her—and the ranch's business.

Piper snorted as Sam released him next to the other horses in the field. His black patches gleamed in the noon sun, reminding Sam of Noble Star's midnight-blue coat. She'd better quit wasting time thinking about Ethan and focus on finding a way to earn money to purchase the stallion. She needed a plan, and fast—before someone else realized the stallion's worth and beat Sam to it. He could very well be the ticket for getting them out of their financial crisis.

The wind lifted Sam's hair and cooled her neck. She

soaked in the breeze, tilting her face to the sun, and then turned back to the group of riders just in time to see Ethan look quickly away from her.

Sam started back toward the tourists, purposefully heading away from Ethan. If she wasn't careful, *he* could very well be the ticket for messing up her plans—and her heart.

Chapter Four

The alarm clock on the nightstand glowed three o'clock in bright green digital numbers. Sam sat up in bed, wide-awake. She should have been out the moment her weary shoulders hit the mattress, but her mind kept racing with the events of the day. The trail ride. Ethan. Mrs. Ames scaring the horses. Chores, both inside the house and out. Ethan. Answering the tourists' endless questions about ranch life. Helping Cole finish mucking out stalls. Ethan.

His creeping into her thoughts was even more annoying than the fact that she couldn't sleep.

Sam clicked on the lamp, and then slowly slid to the floor. Sitting cross-legged, she reached under the bed. The navy dust ruffle was, ironically, covered in dust, and she sneezed. Who had time to vacuum under the beds when there was so much else to do? Wishing for a housekeeper was ridiculous when they were having trouble even paying their mortgage, but Sam couldn't help but wish anyway. Her searching fingers found the edge of the cardboard box and she tugged it free.

Shiny gold medals stared back at her as she peered

over the rim. This was foolish, going through her father's box of rodeo awards in the middle of the night. She hadn't pulled the box out in months, not since Angie finally took them down from their display in the den. Her mother had put the box in the storage shed, but Sam had snuck back outside and grabbed it hours later. She could understand her mother needing to pack it away, needing closure, but the contents of the box represented her dad. Painful as it was to sift through the mementos, Sam at least wanted the option of doing so.

She ran her fingers over an engraved belt buckle. BULL RIDING CHAMPION, 1990. Another medal. SECOND PLACE TEAM ROPING, 1985. Several ribbons nestled inside the box, along with her dad's bull-riding gloves and his favorite black cowboy hat. A local newspaper article about his tragic death lay on the very bottom, and Sam quickly covered it up with the hat. It was too late at night for that level of emotion.

She picked up the flyer advertising the annual Appleback Rodeo, dated over two years ago, and smiled. Bittersweet memories. Every year, the town of Appleback hosted a two-week series of events, starting with the Appleback Street fair, ending with the infamous rodeo, and offering a string of cooking and eating contests, concerts and everything else one could imagine in between.

Sam absently traced the lariat border design on the flyer. Once upon a time, she had dreamed dreams similar to her father's. As a child she loved riding, roping and all things adventurous. One of her favorite childhood pictures was her and her dad on horseback, Sam wearing nothing but a diaper and a big baby grin. Wade Jenson taught Sam to ride not many years later, and she barrel raced in local junior rodeos until she turned sixteen. Even after her dad quit the rodeo circuit, his tips and tricks still seemed to subconsciously leak out of his sentences. *Heels down, Sam. Don't look at your rope, look at your target. You'll never earn the title of Rodeo Sweetheart with that form. Let go of that saddle horn, girl, what are you afraid of?* Sam eventually felt more comfortable around horses than people—a fact she proved by skipping her prom to tend to a new baby foal, and standing up more than one date in favor of helping her dad trailer horses to a new client.

When Wade passed away, the thrill seeker in Sam died along with him. She watched herself—and her life—slow down until it nearly stopped. Afternoons galloping bareback across meadows were suddenly spent soaping up saddles and hosing down horses. The chores had to get done, but she could have snuck away for some fun once in a while. Could have—but didn't. Fun meant danger, and that first year after Wade's death, Sam couldn't even mount a horse without thinking of her dad. It seemed wrong to be the same person she always was when he wasn't there to see it, wasn't there to offer his advice and big congratulatory hugs.

Sudden tears stung her eyes and Sam's grip tightened on the advertisement in her hands. The annual rodeo was coming up in August—only a few weeks away. A couple of years ago, she would have entered the barrel racing or roping competition as usual, and would have already been practicing for months.

The writing on the flyer blurred before her eyes, and Sam blinked rapidly to clear the moisture clouding her vision. Her life wasn't about the rodeo anymore, couldn't ever be again. Even if she wanted to compete,

Angie would never allow it. At twenty-four, Sam was obviously long past grounded as a means of discipline, but putting disappointment or fear in her mother's eyes was far worse than any childhood punishment. Things changed, and Sam had to change right along with them.

She started to put the flyer back in the box, but the bold numbers on the bottom stopped her hand midreach and Sam's eyes widened. Things changed, all right. The grand prize a few years ago for the bull-riding competition was the exact amount she needed to buy Noble Star. Add two years' increase, and it was more than enough to get the breeding farm in the black.

The paper rustled as she stuffed the flyer in the box and shoved the entire thing under the bed. Maybe obtaining Noble Star wouldn't be a matter of luck after all, but rather, divine providence. Surely it wasn't coincidence about the money being the amount she needed. Was God finally going to offer assistance to get the Jenson family out of their financial crisis?

It'd be about time He stepped in.

Sam slipped beneath the cotton sheets and lay staring at the ceiling, arms crossed behind her pillow. Her heart hammered, and this time it wasn't from bad dreams, a busy day or thoughts of Ethan.

She had a plan.

The sun streamed through the miniblinds, scrawling patterns of light across the worn bedspread. Ethan grunted into his pillow but made no motion to move. He couldn't if he tried. He needed an ice pack. Or maybe a hot compress. Anything to ease the soreness that glazed his muscles with a constant, annoying ache.

He closed his eyes, then blinked them open at a

snicker. Daniel sat on his bed a few feet away, pulling on his ridiculous boots and grinning. "You should have played darts at the lodge by the main house with me yesterday instead of going on that ride, man. I warned you."

Ethan pushed himself into a sitting position, wincing against the pain. He refused to look like a sissy in front of his cousin—but the grimace probably gave him away. "Yeah, right. You said be careful, riding a horse would make me sore. You didn't say riding a horse would make me feel like I'd been trampled by one."

Daniel shrugged as he stood. "I'm heading to the main house for breakfast. You coming, or do you prefer to limp around here instead?" His boots clomped on the wooden floor.

"I'll be there. Go ahead without me." Ethan slowly eased off the bed. "It'll take me a minute."

"Might be lunchtime before you make it."

"Very funny." Ethan winced. No wonder all the cowboys in those books he'd read as a child walked with such a wide stance. It was the only way to compensate. He swaggered toward the dresser and winced as he pulled out a pair of jeans.

Daniel tugged a cowboy hat down on his head and swiped his room key off the nightstand. "I'll save you some bacon."

"Why are you wearing all that stuff anyway?" Ethan gestured toward Daniel's Western gear, and his biceps quivered. Probably from that death grip he had on the saddle horn yesterday, despite making fun of his mom for doing the same. If Vickie felt even half as sore as he did, she'd probably already changed her mind about "appearances." He hated to agree with his dad on, well, anything—but this time, Jeffrey had a point about not all of them having to keep up the charade at every moment. Ethan would be more likely to see his dad hanging out the moonroof of a limo than he would ever see him aboard a horse.

Daniel tapped the brim of his hat. "Hey, I think I look good. Or at least, the girls I met at the lodge last night thought so." He winked.

"So that's why you stayed out so late." Mystery solved. Ethan shook his head and pulled on a green polo.

"Nothing wrong with mixing a little business with pleasure." Daniel paused at the front door. "Aren't you doing the same? I know you took that trail ride to check out the owner's daughter—Sarah, or whatever her name is."

Ethan worked to keep his expression neutral. "It's Sam—and hardly. I went riding so my mom wouldn't be alone."

Daniel's eyebrow twitched. "Right."

"Believe what you want. I have no interest in Sam." Her full name hovered on Ethan's lips and he couldn't but smile at her ire if he were to say it. Somehow, he suspected she could sense it even from across the ranch.

"Of course not. You always grin real goofy when you're not attracted to someone." Daniel rolled his eyes.

"Whatever." Ethan grabbed a pair of socks. It wasn't true—was it? Sure, Sam was pretty, and there was something different about her, something that went beyond the Western attire and massive chip on her shoulder. But Sam wasn't his type. So what if he'd wanted to tease her a little on the ride? There were worse motivations to have—and his had nothing to do with attraction. He was an Ames. An Ames wouldn't date a cowgirl.

Apparently, they just bought out their land.

Ethan brushed aside the sudden burst of conscience. It wasn't his plan, it was his dad's—not like Ethan had much of a choice. He never had, and at this rate, never would.

Daniel shook his head. "Send me a postcard from your vacation in denial, dude. I'm going to breakfast."

The front door had just shut behind him when a knock sounded. Ethan finished buckling his belt and opened the door. Jeffrey Ames waited with a frown on the other side. "Morning." Ethan fought back a sigh and moved aside for his father to enter.

Jeffrey strode inside the cabin with his usual air of dignified expectation. "What's wrong with you, boy?"

Ethan shut the door. "What do you mean?"

"You're moving like a robot."

"Sore muscles from the ride yesterday." Ethan eased onto the bed and reached for his loafers under the nightstand.

Jeffrey's frown deepened. "Your mother is fine."

"Mom does Pilates and yoga three times a week." Ethan slipped his feet inside the leather shoes, hoping his lowered head hid the shock he felt claiming his expression. His mom had always been a fitness guru, but he'd figured she'd be at least a little sore like he was. Was he that much of a Wild West sissy? He quickly stood, hoping to put an end to the conversation. "I was just heading to the main house to eat."

"I'll join you. But first, we need to talk." Jeffrey shoved his hands in his pockets of his slacks and jingled the loose change. The corners of his lips tightened beneath his mustache—the closest Ethan had ever seen his dad come to a real smile. "There's been a new development."

Ethan bit back a groan at the overused pun. "What's that?" Better not to encourage him with a forced laugh. Humor and Jeffrey Ames went together about as well as fast cars and speed limits.

Jeffrey's eyebrows furrowed. "I had a brief conversation with Angie Jenson yesterday. It seems like we're going to need more ammunition than we thought in order to convince that Jenson woman it's in her best interest to sell." His lips quirked. "To us."

"I don't get it. Why are you smiling? How is that good news?" Other than the fact they could possibly give up now and go back to New York. But for some reason, the thought of leaving so soon seemed more disappointing than alluring. Ethan frowned. Must be that country air getting to him. He needed Starbucks, a massage and a good couple miles on his treadmill. That'd get him back to thinking more like a businessman and less like John Wayne.

"It's good news because her daughter is the reason she's hesitating, and I now know who is going to help fix that." The twinkle was back in Jeffrey's eyes, and worry churned in Ethan's stomach.

"Who?" He didn't want to ask, but he and his father had played the cat-and-canary game for so long now, Ethan just automatically fluffed his feathers.

Jeffrey clamped his large hand on Ethan's shoulder, his diamond-and-gold ring digging into his collarbone. "You are."

Chapter Five

Sam still hadn't gotten used to eating her breakfast at a table full of strangers, but it beat sitting alone in her room. She scooped a spoonful of eggs on her plate and tried to ignore Daniel, who sat to her left, Ethan, who sat to her right, and Jeffrey, who chugged coffee directly across from her. Talk about a bad way to start her Sunday—sandwiched between two preppy, clueless tourists. Daniel had been trying to get her attention ever since he sat down, and Sam could have sworn she even saw him flexing beneath that striped Western shirt. Strangely enough, Ethan hadn't spoken a single word to her yet—just kept darting glances at his dad across the table. Jeffrey in turn would cough and send pointed glares right back.

Men could be so weird.

Sam peppered her eggs and focused her attention on the other end of the large table. Her mom nibbled delicately at a piece of bacon while the same flirtatious man from yesterday—Mike—chatted her up. His troublemaking, ball-kicking son, Davy, sat ignored to his left, building a waffle sculpture on a plate covered in syrup. The sculpture wobbled on its liquid foundation, and if Sam's predictions were accurate, it would go sloshing into Mike's lap any minute now. It would serve him right.

She blew out her breath in an impatient huff. At least the group of vacationing, giggly college-aged girls were absent from breakfast this morning—the ones she'd seen Daniel eye more than once. It also appeared that their resident honeymoon couple was sleeping in. Sam really missed the mornings when Sunday breakfast consisted of just her and her parents—not a host of strangers and hired help. Sure, the food was better now than the cold cereal or lumpy oatmeal they used to have before rushing off to church, but it had been family. Familiar. It had been home.

A concept that apparently died along with her dad.

Sam gave a tired smile to Clara, the newly hired cook, who hovered over Sam's shoulder with a fresh pot of coffee.

"Refill?"

"Yes, thanks." Sam inched her cup closer. She needed the caffeine after last night's 3:00 a.m. stroll down memory lane. If her family went to church anymore, she'd probably have yawned through the entire service. But the work—and the animals—couldn't wait, and with the addition of a busy new dude ranch came the loss of a church home for Sam, at least until they could afford to hire more help. But despite the fact she couldn't quit yawning, the emotional journey last night had been worth it. She knew how to get the money to buy Noble Star. She just needed a fresh supply of courage—and someone to help her.

Clara stretched over with the coffeepot. "Not a problem, Ms. Sam." The hot liquid bubbled into the mug.

"You can just call me Sam." She lowered her head and breathed in the hearty aroma of the brew. One sip of that strong concoction and she'd wake up for sure.

"Okay." Clara moved to refill Daniel's cup. Her tight black curls and ebony skin heightened her youthful appearance, but Sam knew Clara had to be closer to a grandma's age herself. She nodded at Daniel. "Coffee?"

Daniel shook his head, his mouth full of toast. "I've reached my limit." Crumbs sprayed on his nearly empty plate and Sam winced. And he wondered why his charms weren't working on her.

"I'll take a refill." Ethan twisted in his seat to offer his mug. His eyes caught Sam's and he smiled.

Sam decided to blame the accompanying jitters in her stomach on the greasy bacon, and forced a tight-lipped smile in return before focusing once again on her food. The eggs were suddenly tasteless in her mouth despite the salt and pepper she'd heaped on them. She was probably too nervous too eat. She really needed to talk to Cole about her plan before the day got fully started. If he refused to help her, she'd be right back to square one.

The fact that Ethan's presence radiated on Sam's right side like a portable heater had nothing to do with her lack of appetite. Nothing at all.

"Samantha?" Ethan's quiet voice sounded in her ear.

She dropped her fork with a clatter. "It's Sam. Why is that so hard for you? I don't call you Evan, or Eric. My name is Sam. You want me to start calling you Elvira?"

Ethan held up both hands in defense, eyes wide. "I'm sorry. It was an accident."

"I bet." Sam tossed her napkin on her plate. She needed to find Cole, now—before she lost her opportunity to talk to him alone and before she completely snapped and threw a piece of bacon in Ethan's face. Never in her life had anyone so adamantly insisted on calling her Samantha. That was her father's right, and no loafer-wearin' city boy was going to take that away.

"It really was a slipup. Look, I was going to ask if you wanted to take a walk. Show me around the ranch or whatever."

Sam studied Ethan. His cheeks pinked the longer she stared, and the expression in his eyes didn't quite match his tone. He looked guarded—almost annoyed. She glanced across the table at Jeffrey, who beamed and nodded at his son.

Something was up. Sam shoved her chair away from the table. "Sorry, I've got things to do."

"Sam!" Angie looked up from the other end of the table in surprise. "Don't be rude." Mike smirked and Sam wished she could shove her mother's glittering diamond ring in his face.

"Duty calls, Mom." Sam gulped a mouthful of coffee, then wished she'd let it cool just a moment longer. Refusing to water down her dramatic exit with a wince, she stoned her features, bumped her chair under the table with a scrape and stalked toward the back door.

The satisfying slosh of waffles and syrup, followed by Mike's squeal, sounded just before the door slammed shut behind her.

Rejected. Ethan excused himself from the breakfast table and hustled—well, limped was probably more accurate—outside before his dad could finish his breakfast and come after him. Ethan refused to stick around for a lecture on failure from his father. Before breakfast, his dad had directed Ethan to strike up a friendship with Sam in order to make Sam's mom see her having a good time. One of the reasons Angie was considering selling the ranch over Sam's objections was because she wanted her daughter to have a chance to live her life and not be burdened by a failing business. It was also his chance to get inside information about the ranch. Any pitfalls, any problems, any information that could be useful for their securing a low offer on the property was now Ethan's job to report.

Ahead of him, Sam blazed a trail to the barn as if her boots were on fire. It was surprising the grass at her feet didn't puff up in smoke as she passed. Ethan hesitated. He'd never been the type to pursue a woman scorned—Shakespeare definitely had that one right— and that's exactly what he'd done to Sam with his incessant teasing.

But Shakespeare hadn't met Jeffrey Ames, and any minute now, his father would be about five steps behind Ethan, demanding to know why he wasn't trying harder to weasel into a friendship with Sam.

Ethan kicked at a rock in the dirt with his loafer. Take a walk? Pretty lame. Not really surprising Sam turned him down after that ridiculous attempt. He really hadn't meant to say her full name, it just slipped out while he was mentally rehearsing his next line.

A rehearsal that led to a less than successful opening curtain. Why was she so picky about her name, anyway? Samantha was a beautiful name. He understood she was a tomboy, a cowgirl, but that shouldn't be enough to make her hate her full name. It didn't make sense.

Sort of like how what happened at breakfast wouldn't make sense to his dad. Ethan could just hear his response now. *Daniel wouldn't have that kind of problem with a woman. Daniel could get any girl he wanted. You should learn from your cousin.* Yeah, right. One day Daniel and Jeffrey both would wake up and realize there were more important things in the world than money and manipulative games. One day they'd come to the same conclusion Ethan eventually had come to—that they wanted something more from life than just a trust fund, a successful if borderline shady business and empty relationships.

If you could even call them relationships. Ethan lifted his face to the morning sun and let the warm summer breeze dry the sweat on his forehead. He wasn't foolish enough to believe his parents lived in marital bliss. He purposefully tuned out the details he didn't want to know.

His parents were glued together only by money, and if that ever changed, they'd probably head to divorce court faster than a Ferrari off the line. Ethan wanted something more solid than that, something to really stand on. No wonder he'd never felt a true connection before with the girls in his past—as much as he loved his mother, they all seemed like carbon copies of her. Materialistic, superficial.

Every girl but Sam, that is.

He shoved his hands in his pockets and continued his slow trek to the barn. He could move out and avoid the drama, but his parents' house was big enough for him to be out of the way, and it was rent-free. If he hoped to break away from the family business one day, he'd more than likely be cut off financially and would need a decent amount of cash saved—in a place his father couldn't access. All the more reason to save money now.

A horse whinnied from the other side of a nearby fence, and Ethan squared his shoulders in determination. His plan A in reaching Sam might have been a bust, but that didn't mean plan B couldn't succeed. If he needed to amp up the flirty image, so be it. Ethan hated the pretense—it reeked of Daniel—but if it would get his father off his back, then it'd be worth it. Plus he'd like to see her smile more. No twenty-four-year-old should have to work so hard just to stay afloat.

He just needed to remember not to use her full name.

Ethan turned up the collar on his polo, cracked his neck and strode inside the barn with a slightly crooked smile.

"Crazy city slickers." Sam ran the grooming brush over Wildfire's back in short, firm strokes. Loose hair flurried in her face like miniature red snowflakes, but she didn't care. Who did Ethan think he was, asking her to go for a walk while his father grinned from the sidelines? The invitation was probably a joke, some "let's tease the cowgirl and make her think I'm interested" ploy so he and his dad could laugh behind her back later. Like she'd ever be interested in some New Yorker who didn't know which end of the horse went first.

Sam brushed faster. The only bright spot on this cloudy morning was that Cole had agreed to help her out. The loyal stable hand had assured her he'd have a steer in the north paddock by eleven o'clock that night for her to practice riding, and that her secret was safe with him. Apparently Cole hated dealing with the downfalls of the new dude ranch business as much as Sam and was game for her plan—absurd as it must have sounded.

She looked up as a dark figure, silhouetted by the sun, strolled inside the barn. The cocky gait seemed familiar, and within moments Ethan's features became distinguishable. *Great.* He was back for round two. She kept brushing and refused to acknowledge his presence.

Ethan stopped in front of Wildfire's stall and hooked his arms over the closed gate. "Mornin', again." He smiled and Sam couldn't help her eyes darting to meet his. She quickly ducked under Wildfire's neck to groom his other side. It put her closer to Ethan but at least her back was to him.

"You missed one of the guests swimming in waffles." Ethan's voice sounded smooth and rich over Sam's shoulder, much like the syrup that must be clinging to Mike's pants right about now. Too bad those waffles couldn't have fallen in Ethan's lap, too.

She dropped the grooming brush in the bucket in the corner behind her. "Sounds like fun." She bent and snatched a comb from the same tub, and began picking through Wildfire's tangled mane. "Is that all you came to tell me?" She felt more than saw Ethan's startled response, and couldn't but grin.

"No, I, just—well…" Ethan's voice trailed off and he coughed. "I thought maybe I could help out, if you were too busy to take a walk."

Sam turned to face him, the blue comb dangling from her fingers. Even Wildfire snorted, as if shocked. "You want to do chores?"

"Sure." Ethan straightened his slumped position on the gate and smiled. "Why not?"

"Why not?" Sam laughed as she turned back to Wildfire's mane. "Because you have no clue what you're doing. Because you could get hurt. Because this is your vacation and you shouldn't be working. Because—"

"Okay, I get it." Ethan held up both hands. "But I don't mind. I can learn."

"Thanks, but no thanks." Sam tossed the comb in the bucket and clipped the lead rope that she'd draped over the stall door to Wildfire's halter. "Excuse me."

Ethan backed away from the gate as Sam and Wildfire walked through, giving Wildfire's back legs a wide berth. "Then what about a walk later tonight? After dinner?" His tone held a hopeful edge.

Sam clucked to Wildfire and led him down the barn aisle. His shoed hooves clacked on the hard floor. "Again, thanks—but no thanks." Sam refused to feel even slightly sympathetic or look back at Ethan standing alone in the barn aisle. She had zero interest in being a pawn for some rich boy's family to manipulate with their weird games. She had chores to do, a ranch to save and a bull to ride.

Starting with a steer tonight at eleven o'clock.

Chapter Six

The moon hung low in the velvet night sky, a shiny silver orb against a sea of black. Sam trudged through the shadows toward the north paddock, her boots silent on the dewy grass. Despite the late hour, adrenaline pulsed in her veins and her hands shook. She shoved them into the back pockets of her jeans as she walked.

Maybe she was crazy. Riding a steer was nothing like riding a bull, as steers were significantly smaller, but it was all she had access to for practice. She'd sat on a bull once before on a dare—for about two seconds at a friend's ranch as a young teenager. Of course, that was before her friend's father ran outside, yelling at them for taking the risk and looking much scarier than the bull. After watching the competition at the local rodeo each year, Sam figured her brief stint couldn't even come close to being the same.

She rounded the corner of the barn, and the outline of the steer's narrow horns inside the paddock siphoned into view. Cole, dressed in dark denim from head to foot, waited by the fence, one boot hung lazily on the bottom rail. A long rope was coiled over his shoulder. He straightened as she approached. "You ready for this, kid?"

Sam nodded. Only Cole could get away with such a nickname. He'd started work at the Jenson farm right after he graduated high school, when Sam was a child, and stayed on full-time these past twenty years. Now he was more like a big brother than a hired hand. "Of course I'm ready. Bring it."

The tremor in Sam's voice almost canceled out the confident words, but to her relief, Cole didn't seem to notice. "That's what I like to hear." He opened the paddock gate and motioned for Sam to go through first.

She strode into the pen, keeping a wary eye on the steer. The miniature beast looked up from inside the makeshift chute Cole had concocted, and blinked lazily, grass dangling from its flabby lips. At this rate, riding would be a breeze—downright boring, even. But once Cole tied that rope around the steer's hindquarters… Sam swallowed. "Where'd you get him?"

"A friend with a cattle ranch a few miles west owed me a favor. He said we can borrow Lucy here for as long as we'd like."

"Lucy?"

"Short for Lucifer." Cole winked.

Sam's stomach flipped.

"I know he looks calm now, but this here is a flank strap." Cole gestured with the fleece-lined leather rope he uncoiled off his shoulder. "Don't worry. It'll get him bucking good."

That was the problem. Sam forced a smile, hoping the evening shadows hid her apprehension. She couldn't back down now, not after Cole had gone to all that effort to bring the beast. Besides, kids rode steers in rodeos all the time—it was considered a junior event. If some 4-H preteen could do it, Sam could, too.

She just wouldn't think about her father's last bull ride in the process.

"What do we do first?" Sam crossed her arms, hoping to keep her pounding heart from bursting through her long-sleeved T-shirt. Too bad Cole couldn't have found a steer with shorter horns.

Cole started toward the animal, which backed up a step. "I'll tie the flank strap and bull rope on him, and you hop on."

"And then what?"

"Hang tight." Cole grinned, his teeth a white splash against dark stubble.

Easy for him to say. He wasn't about to mount a giant cow with horns. Sam took a deep breath as Cole straddled the fencing between the rail and the makeshift pen and went to work securing the flank strap. Cowboy up, as her father always said. She could do it—for him, for the farm. Winning the rodeo competition was her only immediate chance at earning enough money to buy Noble Star from Kate's dad. Without the stallion, the farm would continue having to front as a tourist trap. Going from trail rider to bull rider would be hard enough with months of training—and Sam only had a few weeks. There was no time to waste.

"All set." Cole gave a final tug on the rope and sat back on the fence. The steer snorted his disapproval. "Need a leg up?"

She ran her hands down the front of her jeans. *Get on the steer, Sam.* She took a steadying breath, trying to envision the finish line—Jenson Farms, back the way it used to be. "Sure." She climbed the fence before she could change her mind, and hooked one leg over the top rail. Holding on to Cole's arm for balance, she brought in her outside leg and eased onto the steer's leathery back. Heavy muscles twitched under her weight.

Sam gripped the bull rope around the steer's neck and held tight, just as Cole advised. "Any last words of wisdom?" Her voice shook again and this time she didn't care.

Cole shrugged. "Don't fall off?"

"Thanks." Her nervous laugh punctured the weighty silence resting on her shoulders and she rotated her neck. She could do this. It was a new adventure, one she probably would have pursued long before now if things had turned out differently for her family. No reason to be scared—as long as those horns stayed up there with the steer's head where they belonged.

"Ready?" Cole hopped from the fence to the dirt, patchy with mud from a recent rain, and reached over to unlatch the chute's gate.

Yes. No. Never. She squeezed her eyes shut and nodded.

Her world exploded.

Hooves thundered. Dirt pelted her face. Sam's arm wrenched against the bull rope, yet her fingers refused to let go. She clung tighter with her legs and forced her eyes open. Sky, earth. Sky, earth. It was like riding a hairy, out-of-control rocking chair. How could her dad have ever done this for fun?

The steer snorted, his horns twisting to the left and then to the right. Sam bounced hard against his thick neck. From her peripheral vision, she glimpsed Cole clapping his hands. "You're doing great!"

She was? Maybe she could do this after all. Her biceps screamed in protest and Sam winced as mud slung in her face. She instinctively twisted away from the dirty onslaught just as Lucy turned—in the opposite direction.

Sam hit the ground hard, mud oozing into her ears and down the neck of her shirt. She raised her hands to protect her face, but Lucy, free of her burden, had harmlessly trotted back toward the chute.

Sam lowered her hands, aware of a fiery ache in her quivering right arm and thighs, aware of Cole yelling for her not to get up yet, aware that had she been thrown just a few feet farther to the left, she would have landed on the paddock rails.

But mostly, she was aware of Ethan Ames standing on the other side of the fence, his face a mixture of shock and amusement.

Ethan wasn't sure if he should offer his hand, laugh or run away. He was tempted to do all three. But the stable hand he recognized from the trail ride yesterday beat him to his first instinct, and pulled Sam out of the dirt.

"What are you doing here?" Her wary eyes met Ethan's as she slapped at the mud clinging to her jeans.

Ethan braced both arms against the top rail dividing them. "The better question is why are you riding a bull?" Dirt speckled Sam's honey-colored hair, but he wasn't about to point that out.

"That ain't a bull, greenhorn." The stable hand spit in the paddock dirt. "That's a steer." He held Sam out in front of him by her shoulders. "Are you okay, kid? That was some fall."

"I'm fine, Cole." Sam wrestled out of his concerned grip, a dark red flush working up her neck. She met

Ethan at the fence and glared. "Why are you up this late?"

Ethan checked the Rolex on his wrist, visible by the light of the moon. "Late? It's not even midnight."

Sam's eyes snapped. "Guests aren't supposed to be roaming the property all night long. This isn't a country club. People could get hurt."

"Hurt like when they fall off a bull?"

"It's a steer," Cole reminded.

"Bull, steer, cow, whatever." Ethan shrugged. "Why were you riding it?"

Sam hesitated.

"Trying to ride it, I guess I should say." If she wouldn't be honest, he couldn't help teasing her a little.

Sam's head jerked. "You want to give it a shot, if it's so easy?"

Ethan laughed. "No, thanks. I value my life."

"I do, too." Sam's voice quieted and she turned to stare toward the main house. "That's why I'm doing it."

Cole broke the ensuing silence. "Hey, kid, I'm gonna go put this steer up for the night."

"Wait, what if my mom—?" Sam's voice broke off and her eyes widened, flickering from Ethan, to the animal, to Cole.

Ethan frowned at the exchange. What was Sam worried about? More importantly, what was she so concerned about him knowing?

Cole strode toward the steer, which was now attempting to pull grass through the bottom rail of the paddock. His long horns knocked against the post and Ethan shuddered. What on earth could have possessed Sam to mount such an animal—practically in the middle of the night? There were obviously secrets here—

maybe ones his father would be interested in. The faster this sale went through the faster he could break out on his own and leave Ames Real Estate and development in his dust.

"I'll handle it. Don't worry." Cole tipped his hat at Sam before reaching the animal. His low voice murmured softly through the night air, and the steer remained calm long enough for Cole to tug a rope around his neck and untie the one around his hind legs.

Something was definitely not right with this picture, and it had nothing to do with a steer-whispering stable hand. Ethan turned back to Sam. "Seriously, what's going on?"

"It's none of your business." She grabbed the fence and began climbing over. Ethan sidestepped to avoid getting hit in the face with her swinging boot when she reached the top.

"Fine. I'll just go back to my cabin." Ethan walked backward two steps.

"Thank you." Sam landed on the ground and rubbed her right shoulder, which was more than likely bruised from her fall. She'd taken quite a hit. "See you tomorrow, I guess."

"No problem." Ethan turned, walking faster. He decided to take one last stab in the dark—literally. "I'm sure I can find out from Mrs. Jenson in the morning what all this was about."

Sam's hand snagged the back of his shirt and tugged, pulling Ethan to an abrupt halt. *Bingo.* He controlled his smile before turning around to meet her anxious expression.

"You can't ask her."

"Then tell me."

"I can't." Exasperation laced Sam's tone but Ethan stood his ground. If Sam confided in him, he'd be one step closer to friendship. One step closer to getting the information his dad needed before Jeffrey sent for backup—namely, Daniel.

The thought of Daniel weaseling his way into Sam's life sounded so much worse than Ethan doing the same. At least Ethan had no intentions of manipulating Sam's emotions. He just wanted to be friends, get the info his dad needed, and get back home to start his new life. Daniel, however, would prey on her emotions, attempt to mix business with pleasure and get something for himself from the deal. Ethan had to find out what Sam was up to first. His cousin had already taken enough from him, including Jeffrey's respect.

He didn't want Daniel anywhere near Sam.

He cleared his throat. "Why don't you want your mother to know?"

"I just don't. Are you going to tell her?"

"Maybe not, if you'll do something for me."

Sam crossed her arms. "What do you want out of this?"

What *did* he want? A gentle breeze caressed Ethan's neck and he shivered. He wanted to leave the real estate business, wanted to get as far away from his father as he could. He wanted to find what he was really good at and make an honest living, rather than be a pawn in his father's devious plans. He wanted independence, respect—and, watching the wind tease tendrils of hair around her dirt-streaked cheeks, what he really wanted was to kiss Sam.

He'd settle for two out of three. "I want to learn about ranching."

She snorted. "You can't be serious."

"I'm completely serious." Ethan straightened his shoulders, trying to imitate the way he'd seen Cole standing earlier—straight back, cocked hip, loose leg. Seeing the ranch from an insider's perspective would provide Ethan ample opportunity to discover any issues about the property his dad hoped to find. He'd do his job, make his father happy and get out of Dodge—or, rather Appleback—of his own will, and not because he was being replaced by Daniel. And maybe he could even show Sam how to enjoy life a bit and put a smile on her face. Everyone won.

Until your father buys Sam's beloved ranch.

Ethan quickly squelched the thought and held out his hand. "You teach me about horses and running a farm, and I'll keep your secret."

Sam shook on their deal. "You're rotten, you know that?"

Yes, Ethan did. Some days, he knew it all too well. That's why he needed to be free of his father's influence. He tightened his grip when Sam tried to pull her hand away. "One last condition."

Sam raised her eyebrows. Good thing looks couldn't actually kill. "What else could you possibly want?"

"I want you to tell me why you were riding that bull."

"Fine." She sighed.

"Promise?" He shook her hand again so she couldn't back out of the new condition. Weren't handshakes as good as a signed contract back in the Wild West days? He shook it harder.

"Promise." She wrestled her hand free and rubbed it.

"So why were you?" Ethan tilted his head, eager to hear what could possibly make a woman desperate enough to hop on a wild animal in the middle of the night with only the moon for a seatbelt.

"Why was I what?" Sam smirked and Ethan's smile slid off his face. "I promised to tell you why I was riding a bull. I never promised to tell you why I was riding a *steer*." She abruptly strode toward the barn.

Ethan ran his hands down the length of his face, once again not sure whether to laugh, go after her—or run far, far away.

Chapter Seven

A sudden pounding on the cabin door shook Ethan from a sound sleep. He groggily sat up in bed and moved to look out the front window. The sun was barely up—so why was he? The knocking continued.

"Coming!" He wiped at his bleary eyes. Daniel stirred under the covers from his bed across the room but didn't wake. Ethan threw on a pair of jeans and a T-shirt and yanked the door open with a scowl.

Sam stood on the front porch, hands tucked in the back pockets of her jeans, wearing a blue-and-white flowered button-down shirt that brought out her eyes. "Morning, sunshine."

Her smile, pretty as it might be, was much too bright this early on a Monday. "What do you want?"

"That's no way to greet your boss."

"Boss?" Ethan hit his ear with the palm of his hand, certain he'd heard wrong. His boss was his father, and Jeffrey Ames was thankfully nowhere in sight. What was Sam talking about?

"Well, maybe not boss, technically, because you're not getting paid." Sam smirked. "But you are here to learn, so you're sort of like my apprentice—which means I'm in charge. Which means you need to get ready. We're behind schedule."

"Impossible. The sun just came up." Birds chirped from a nearby tree, and Ethan felt like throwing his pillow at them. He never fully woke up until consuming a massive amount of coffee—preferably Guatemalan dark roast, but he'd made do yesterday at the main house with the generic brand. Looked like he'd have to do it again.

Talk about living off the land.

"Ranchers get up before the sun, partner. Welcome to farm work." Sam quirked an eyebrow. "Of course, if you'd rather back out of our agreement..."

Agreements. Steers. Secrets. The previous night rushed at Ethan like a sports car on the autobahn and he groaned. No wonder he felt so exhausted. He'd gone back to bed after his midnight bargain with Sam, but had lain awake for at least another hour reliving his sudden rash of good luck. It was the perfect setup for getting his father off his back and putting his plan for future freedom into action. "You're not getting out of it. I'll be ready in two minutes." He closed the cabin door, leaving Sam to sulk on the porch. He refused to let her out of their deal—not when there was so much to lose.

Daniel sat up as Ethan flicked on the lamp and pulled a pair of socks from his dresser drawer. "What's going on, man? Breakfast isn't for another hour or more."

Ethan hesitated, hopping on one leg as he tugged his sock over his foot. He hated to tell Daniel the details of his arrangement, but Jeffrey would tell him eventually anyway. Besides, Daniel didn't have to know Ethan's true motivation for getting close to Sam—just the same reason that Jeffrey would hear. "I have a meeting with

Sam." Hopefully that sounded vague enough to hide his growing feelings for her.

"Meeting, or date?" Daniel grinned, and then squinted outside. "Is the sun even up?"

"Meeting. Definitely just a meeting." Ethan slid into his loafers, thought better of it and grabbed his running shoes instead, the ones he'd ridden in two days ago. He hadn't packed cowboy boots—at the time, he hadn't imagined ever using them. Looked like he'd have to find a pair if he was going to be doing ranch work. At least these tennis shoes could get dirty with little consequence. He wrestled them on without untying the laces.

"What kind of meeting is worth a dawn appointment?" Daniel yawned and flopped back against his pillow. "You've got it bad, dude."

"You're dreaming—literally. Go back to sleep." Ethan automatically grabbed his watch, then realized there was no point in wearing it, not to do stable work. What exactly had he gotten himself into? This idea seemed much smarter in the middle of the night, staring at Sam's desperate blue eyes.

Sam didn't even bother to hide her smile as she watched Ethan grapple with the pitchfork inside Piper's stall. "You have to scoop it, Ethan. Not stab it." Across the pen, Piper flicked his tail as if agreeing.

"This is disgusting." Ethan swiped his hair off his forehead with one shirtsleeve. Sweat glistened on his hairline.

Sam couldn't help the bubble of satisfaction fizzing in her stomach. She leaned back against the stall wall and let it hold her weight. Served Ethan right. If ranching was so easy, every city slicker would hustle down from the North and give it a whirl. Ethan deserved a good dose of reality. And if that came by pitchfork and manure, then all the better.

"You do this for every stall in the barn?" Ethan dropped a load from his pitchfork into the wheelbarrow and wrinkled his nose.

"Every single day. Cole helps, usually. But this morning I told him we'd handle it." Sam grinned.

"We?" Ethan stopped shoveling and stared, resting one arm atop the long wooden handle of the fork. "You've done nothing but point."

"Hey, you're the one who wanted to learn about ranching." Sam adjusted the rim of her cowboy hat in an exaggerated air of indifference. "I'm just trying to help."

"Quit the sarcasm. It's too early in the morning." He went back to scooping, watching Piper as warily as Piper watched him. "Couldn't you have taken her out of the stall for this?"

"Him. And there's no reason to. He only uses this one corner."

"Who teaches them that?"

"It's a natural instinct that most animals have." Sam watched Ethan work a moment longer, than sighed. "All right, fine. I'll shovel the next one." She didn't feel guilty, exactly—just wasn't used to standing around without purpose. She reached for the pitchfork.

"No way. I asked for this, remember?" Ethan refused to relinquish the handle.

She tugged back on it. "I can manage—apparently better than you can."

"What's that supposed to mean?" He pulled harder.

"It means I'm used to hard work."

"And I'm not?" Ethan's expression tightened.

Sam gripped the handle with both hands. "I didn't say that."

"But you thought it." Ethan let go and Sam stumbled backward several steps. "You sure do lose your balance a lot."

She quickly regained her stance and pointed the pitchfork at him. "At least I'm not afraid to try."

"Look, I know what you're thinking." Ethan waved both hands in the air. "The rich city boy never had to do anything but learn how to feed himself with a silver spoon. Right?"

Sam opened her mouth, then snapped it shut. He was dead-on—and why should she think differently? He flaunted his self-importance. Kate had warned her the Ameses' first day at the ranch to watch out for tourists. She'd been joking, of course, but Sam would be better off taking the remark seriously. Ethan was the exact image of the stereotypical, heartless guy, searching for a new hobby that he would inevitably tire of. But what if he tired of it before his vacation ended and broke his end of their deal? Angie would be devastated, Sam would have to quit the competition, and there went any chance of buying Noble Star or bringing back the breeding business. Sam's home would forever be a tourist trap.

No, as much as she wanted to throw the pitchfork at Ethan and walk away, she had to keep him happy. There was too much at stake. She gritted her teeth. "Why don't we start over?"

"With the stall?" Ethan's eyes widened in alarm.

"No, not with mucking out the stable. With us. With this." She gestured between them.

"What's the catch?" Ethan's chocolate-brown gaze turned cautious.

Sam rested the pitchfork against the gate. "No catch. I just think if we're going to be around each other, the least we can do is be civil about it."

"Civil, as in, no more sarcasm?"

"I make no promises." The corners of Sam's mouth twitched into a grin.

Ethan's eyes shimmered in amusement as he held out his hand. "Fair enough. Truce?"

"Truce." Sam slipped her palm against his and a spark ignited at contact. She quickly pulled it back, wondering if he felt it, too. From the way Ethan wrung his hand once before reaching to pick up the wheelbarrow, she could only assume he had.

"Which way?" He gripped the handles and maneuvered the full barrow toward the door.

Sam opened the gate and pointed toward the far end of the barn. "Outside and to the right is a compost pile. You can't miss it."

Ethan squeezed past Sam through the opening. The lingering look he shot over his shoulder before he headed down the barn aisle made her breath hitch.

Sam secured the gate and paused a moment to give Ethan a much-needed head start.

Couldn't miss it, indeed.

Never in his life had Ethan imagined he'd be dumping horse manure into a compost pile. Even more than that, he had never imagined he'd be doing it with a ridiculous smile on his face that wouldn't quit. Good thing Sam stayed in the barn or else she'd think he was nuts.

Ethan turned the empty wheelbarrow away from the

compost pile and back toward the stable. That electric spark he felt when Sam shook his hand wasn't imaginary—it was real. Which meant he was either losing his mind—or falling for the enemy. His dad would panic for sure if he knew Ethan had felt something, really felt something, at that contact.

Truce. He snorted. Making that kind of agreement with Sam was more dangerous than continuing the sarcastic battle of wills they'd had before. He'd much rather shoot barbs than sparks.

Ethan straightened his shoulders as he pushed the wheelbarrow down the stable aisle. It didn't matter whether Sam's touch made his entire arm feel as if he'd been struck by lightning. It didn't matter if she was intriguing, sweet and spicy all at the same time. It didn't matter, because she was an obstacle, the barrier to navigate on the way to his dreams. If he'd learned anything worthwhile from Jeffrey Ames, it was that goals on the road of life were never reached by stopping to pick wildflowers along the way.

Ethan cracked his neck in one quick motion and schooled his features as he handed over the wheelbarrow handles to Sam. Her eyes, wide and luminous beneath the brim of her hat, made his stomach flip—eyes the exact color of the periwinkle wildflowers in the meadow behind the barn. He drew a steadying breath. This was ridiculous. He was Ethan Ames. No way would he be bested by some tomboy in boots.

Even if she had him thinking about wildflowers.

Chapter Eight

Sam shut the dishwasher with a clank and turned it on. She straightened, pressing her hands into the small of her back. Nothing worse than completing a day of outside chores just to come in and work equally hard in the kitchen. But she'd taken one look at Clara buried under a mountain of dishes, and couldn't let the older woman handle it by herself. Besides, Angie was paying bills in the computer nook off the den, and the kitchen was the farthest room away from the bitter mutterings and frustrated pen clicks.

Clara tossed a sponge in the sink and untied her apron from around her ample waist. "I think that does it. Thank you for helping me with the dishes."

"No problem. After that meal, how could I let you do them alone?" Sam patted her stomach with a smile. "Good thing I work so hard, huh? I think I had three helpings of mashed potatoes."

Clara tsked as she hung her apron on a peg by the industrial-sized refrigerator. "You could stand a few more pounds, if you asked me. I've never seen such skinny women like you and your mother."

"We burn a lot of calories."

"Ain't right for a woman to be skin and bones." Clara winked as she shouldered her purse and draped her navy sweater over one arm. "I'll fatten you both up yet."

"I have no problem letting you try." Sam patted Clara on the arm as she walked with her to the door. "Thanks again for the pot roast."

"Just doing my job. You all have a good night." Clara shut the door behind her and once again, the Jenson household was silent.

Sam turned off the kitchen light and released a heavy sigh. She needed a hot bath—would maybe even throw some bubbles, a book and a soda into the mix. Working so hard every day did have at least one silver lining—Sam had basically become immune to caffeine. She could drink coffee in bed if she wanted and still sleep soundly.

She wiped her tired eyes with the back of her hand. On second thought, maybe she'd skip the bath and the drink and head straight to her room. She could use a solid eight hours of sleep—too bad she'd only get three at best before having to sneak out for her midnight ride with Cole and Lucy. Maybe this time Ethan wouldn't crash the practice session. Even with Ethan shadowing her around the stable all day, Sam had still successfully avoided telling him why she was determined to ride the steer in the first place. That was one more complication she just didn't need.

Sam tiptoed past the computer nook. Hopefully her mom wouldn't hear her on that squeaky bottom step—

"Sam? Is that you?" Angie's voice sounded more exhausted than Sam felt.

Sam hesitated on the staircase. Then guilt took precedence over exhaustion and she shuffled into the den. "How's it going?"

"Same as always." Angie pushed her short, sandy-colored hair back from her face. The light from the desk lamp shone on her tanned skin and she rested her elbows on the tabletop.

Sam swallowed the pride lingering in her throat and forced the words she'd hoped to never utter from her mouth. "Do you need me to get a second job again?" She held her breath.

Angie sighed. "That's thoughtful, but we'd be worse off losing the work you do around here."

Relief crowded Sam's already full stomach. She couldn't handle an outside job, not among her other daily chores on the ranch and her new hours of training for the upcoming competition.

Sam studied her mother's scribbled notes in the margins of the ledger book. If only she could tell her mom her plan to save the ranch she would, but the timing was more than a little off. As soon as Angie heard the words *bull* and *rodeo,* she'd go berserk—even under the best of circumstances. Bill paying was probably the worst timing of all. Until Sam was positive her mom would understand that the end result was well worth the risk, she'd have to stick to her original plan of keeping the secret. Sam peered over her mom's shoulder to better read the bottom line. "Are we going to be okay?"

"We'll make it." Angie shoved up the sleeves of her shirt and bent over the pile of envelopes and the ledger book, shielding it from Sam's view. "We always do, somehow. But if we considered selling..."

"Things will get better soon." The promise rolled off Sam's tongue before she could stop it, desperate to ease the stress lines tainting Angie's once-young face. Sam hoped she'd be able to make the assurance true and keep the farm where it belonged—with the Jensons.

"I know. God always provides, doesn't He? Your optimism is contagious." Angie's smile appeared slightly more sincere this time and she squeezed Sam's hand. "Go to bed. You've done enough for tonight."

Sam squeezed back before turning and heading silently up the stairs to her room. She hadn't done anything yet, not anything that mattered, at least—but she was about to, starting with round two on Lucy.

Would it be enough?

Ethan's muscles ached, his head throbbed, and his eyes felt sticky from lack of sleep—yet he'd never felt so good in his life. Who knew hard manual labor carried even more endorphins than his logged treadmill miles?

He glanced at the digital alarm clock on the nightstand. Only fifteen minutes until Sam would be at the north paddock with Cole and that crazy bull—no, steer. The scariest part of the whole experience was that he hadn't minded the chores nearly as much as he'd expected. Mucking out the stables wasn't exactly fun—especially after the sparks with Sam when they touched hands—but grooming the horses, learning how to saddle them for trail rides, and helping distribute fresh hay to all the stalls hadn't been bad. Pleasant, even, once he and Sam kept to their no-more-arguing truce.

Now if only his emotions could stick to the pact he made with himself.

Ethan tapped his watch with his finger. Ten minutes until practice time. He hadn't told Sam he was coming, but it should be assumed. They were in it together. He just still didn't know what this "it" was. Sam had yet to tell him why she was on that steer last night—a fact Ethan planned to remedy in a few short minutes.

He eased out of bed and slipped into his running shoes, careful not to disturb Daniel. His cousin had returned to the cabin earlier in the evening, griping about how the girls he'd been flirting with earlier in the week had already gone back home, their vacation over. Daniel had crashed in his bed and immediately started snoring.

Ethan shook his head at Daniel's sleeping form and crept out the front door, wincing at the loud click. He waited, but Daniel didn't make a sound from inside. With a relieved sigh, he turned—and bumped straight into Jeffrey's broad chest.

"Dad!" Ethan gulped, hoping his surprise didn't show on his face. To Jeffrey Ames, being unprepared was an indicator of weakness. No matter that his dad was skulking around the cabin porch in the dark—it'd still be Ethan's fault for being startled. He straightened his shoulders and lowered his voice. "What are you doing?"

"Coming to wake you up to talk." Jeffrey gripped Ethan's elbow and led him down the stairs and around the corner of the cabin. The grass squished under their shoes. "What progress have you made with the Jenson girl?"

"Sam?" Ethan's heart raced and again, he hoped his dad wouldn't notice. He'd definitely have to work on his poker face when it came to Sam—at least until logic overtook his emotions.

"Sam, Pam, whatever. I haven't seen you all day. What do you know? What have you been doing?" Jeffrey crossed his arms.

Ethan recognized the pose—the businesslike, get-it-done posture that Jeffrey took on regardless of the cost. His dad wanted answers, and he wanted them now. "I've been with Sam all day. Like you wanted me to be."

"Has she mentioned anything that could be useful for our cause?"

Ethan winced, remembering the ignited handshake in the barn, Sam's melodic laugh and the way his eyes stayed drawn to her all day as if they'd been taken over by a magnetic force. "Not yet."

"Well, you need to step it up. We're running out of time."

"Already? We've only been here three days."

Jeffrey shook his head impatiently. "Business waits for no man, you know that. Your mother is afraid Ms. Jenson will hear about that highway relocation before we can make our offer. If she does, she's more likely to discover our intentions of building the strip mall—and then she'd never sell to us. We're having enough trouble convincing her to sell under the pretense of keeping the property exactly as it is. We have to move fast—before Sam realizes why we're here, and before Ms. Jenson decides not to take an offer. She's wavering because of her daughter." Jeffrey scoffed. "Something about so many memories here."

"What do you want me to do? I can't make up reasons to offer less money." Ethan quickly replayed the events of the past two days for his father, omitting the details of Sam's secret riding plans. No use in sharing private, personal matters with Jeffrey. The man didn't have a personal bone in his body. "Maybe we should just offer them a fair price. We'd still make money off the deal when the highway comes."

"Are you crazy? After spending time on this ramshackle place, the last thing I'm going to do is offer more money." Jeffrey brushed at his forehead and the moonlight caught in the reflective face of his watch. "We're going to have to go a step further."

"What now? You want me to date Sam instead of just trying to be her friend?" Some tiny, twisted part of Ethan's psyche hoped his father would say yes. Not that Sam would ever agree. She probably only fell for real cowboys—men who smelled like sweat and earth instead of expensive cologne. Ethan brushed away the pinch of rejection at the idea. This was business. He didn't need romance.

Especially with a woman with eyes like periwinkle wildflowers.

"Don't be ridiculous." Jeffrey's harsh laugh jerked Ethan back to the conversation. "If I wanted someone to romance the girl, I'd ask Daniel." He scoffed and Ethan tried to ignore the way the barb pierced the same, worn dent in his emotional armor. "Maybe you can find proof that the ranch is failing, specific proof. If she has to sell, she won't worry as much about her daughter's feelings."

"What if there isn't any?" Ethan adjusted his stance to mirror his dad's.

"Then make some."

Ethan flinched.

"Keep on befriending the girl. She needs to trust you." Jeffrey looked over his shoulder and lowered his gruff voice to a near whisper. "But in the meantime, look for ways to sabotage the property. Cut fences. Destroy feed. Poison it, for all I care. We need Angie to accept our offer, and we need her to do it now."

Ethan's stomach twisted. He could never purposefully hurt any of the horses, or Sam. Besides, Ethan *wanted* to be near her—and not just because he was ordered to for his job. He opened his mouth to object.

Jeffrey caught Ethan's shoulder in one large hand and bent down to his level. "Do it, or I'll get your cousin to handle things for you." He straightened, lowering his hand to his side, but the weight of it continued to rest on Ethan's shoulders. "It's your choice."

Jeffrey turned and strode back to his cabin, his back ramrod straight in the lengthening shadows. Ethan trudged in the opposite direction toward the north paddock, the excitement of seeing Sam suddenly ruined. He spun his father's words over and over in his mind, the meaning striking with new clarity at each rotation. *It's your choice.*

None of this was Ethan's choice. That was the whole problem in the first place. Ethan didn't get to choose his career. He didn't get to choose how he did his job, or which bank to use or even which college to attend. He had no choices at all. But there was no way he'd allow his father or Daniel to sabotage Sam's ranch.

Ethan's eyes narrowed at Jeffrey's retreating form, growing smaller the more distance he put between them. He'd show his father about choices, all right.

Starting with Sam.

Chapter Nine

The next morning, Sam jerked the cinch strap and adjusted the saddle pad on Diego's back. Then she looped the reins over the fence post, grabbed Piper's blanket from the top paddock rail and moved toward the gelding waiting on the other side of Diego. At least the chestnut's ankle had finally completely healed.

She blew an annoying strand of hair out of her eyes as she slid the checkered blanket over Piper's sweaty back. It seemed like every guest on the ranch had showed up for the Tuesday morning ride and was waiting impatiently for a horse—even the honeymoon couple. She and Cole had their hands full trying to get the animals ready, and the sun already shone hot on Sam's head. A fly buzzed by Piper's mane and she swatted it. Thankfully, the wind was blowing, a welcome respite from the July heat.

"Miss Priss is ready." Cole patted the mare's cheek as he ducked under her neck. "I'll start helping the riders mount."

"Thanks, Cole." Sam yawned and noted the matching fatigue shadowing Cole's face. She pushed aside a wave of guilt. She might owe Cole for helping her practice in the middle of the night, but the end result would benefit the generous stable hand, too. They'd both be free from the guests, the endless questions, and the commercialization of the only home they'd known—although at this point, they were also both in danger of falling asleep in the saddle.

"Mornin', partner." Ethan's exaggerated cowboy drawl sounded over Sam's shoulder and she couldn't help but smile. Ethan had watched her practice session last night on the steer, and she didn't know what was more amusing—her own efforts to stay on Lucy's back or the look on Ethan's face every time Sam fell off. If panic had a tangible form, Ethan would have been wearing it.

Sam handed Piper's reins to Cole so he could lead the gelding to a guest. She turned to Ethan, the wind whipping her hair in front of her eyes. "Is the rest of your family joining you for the ride?"

"My mom probably will, as long as she's nowhere near Piper again." Ethan laughed. "Do you have a deaf horse?"

"Very funny." Sam glanced over her shoulder as Vickie Ames strode into the mounting area in a stark white button-down and jeans. That shirt probably wouldn't stay pristine for long, but if the Ames family were as wealthy as Sam's mother kept hinting, Vickie could easily get another ensemble. She could probably fully outfit every rider on the ranch for their entire vacation and never even notice the expense. What did the Ames family do that they were so successful with? She should ask Ethan about his career. Not that it really mattered—the knowledge wouldn't change the dwindling dollars in the Jensons' checking account.

Sam's mood darkened as she took Miss Priss's reins and strode toward the start of the trail where the others waited. What would it be like to have that kind of money? Ethan and his family had never wanted for a thing, while Sam and her mother struggled just to pay the electric bill and the gas bill in the same month.

"Are you okay?" Ethan caught up to Sam and touched her shoulder. "You walked off pretty fast."

She eased away from the innocent contact, too upset to care how the touch held just as much spark as it had yesterday in the barn. Fireworks were dangerous, and so was Ethan Ames. She forced a smile. "Fine. Just busy."

"Can I help? Partner?" Ethan smiled.

Sam winced at the teamwork reference. She should have never made a bargain with Ethan, though she supposed it was better than the alternative of him blabbing her secret to her mom. It wasn't his fault that he had money and a successful family business. There was no reason to take her anger out on him.

She blew out her breath and fought for control of her exhausted emotions. "I think Cole and I have it under control. Looks like you're riding Miss Priss again." She handed Ethan the reins, careful to avoid brushing his fingers in the process, and strode toward Diego. Ethan's gaze burned into her back the entire way.

Sam and Ethan might be forced together for the time being, but she didn't have to like it—didn't have to like him. He was on vacation, and while it was nice having the extra help for the chores yesterday, Ethan was bound to get bored soon. And once he did, the workload would fall once again on Sam's weary shoulders, along with everything else that had taken permanent residence there.

She gripped the saddle horn in one hand and easily swung onto Diego's back, automatically dropping her heels and squeezing with her lower legs to urge him toward the rest of the group.

It was a wonder the poor gelding didn't collapse from the weight of all the problems Sam bore.

Ethan couldn't stop staring at the back of Sam's head. At least this time on the trail, he felt somewhat more comfortable in the saddle, and could afford the time spent thinking now that he wasn't worrying about falling off. His upper body swayed in rhythm to Miss Priss's smooth steps as the sun warmed the tops of his shoulders. What was Sam's problem? She'd smiled like she was happy to see him, then turned distant so fast he'd almost gotten whiplash.

He adjusted his hands on the reins, ducking along with the rest of the string of riders as they cleared a low-hanging branch. *Women.* Changing their moods more often than Daniel changed his socks. But Sam didn't seem the type to play the same mind games that the women he was accustomed to often did. Something specific must have happened to douse her spirits during those few minutes in the paddock.

Only one way to find out what. Ethan clucked to his horse as he'd seen Sam do and sidled the mare up to the front of the line, next to Sam. Her eyes widened beneath her cowboy hat and she slowed Diego's pace to match Miss Priss's. "Is something wrong? Is it your mom?"

"No, she's fine. I just wanted to talk." Ethan glanced at the trail ahead of them. Plenty of room for two horses to walk side by side, so she'd have no reason to avoid talking to him. "Are you feeling all right?"

"I'm fine." Sam faced forward again, her expression stony.

"Are you mad that I wasn't at the stable this morning? I meant to be, but I forgot to set the alarm after the late night."

"It's okay. You're on vacation. You shouldn't be working in the first place." Sam's shoulders tensed and Diego tossed his head, pulling against the reins.

"We have a deal, remember? I don't mind working. I asked to." His father's manipulative plan pressed on Ethan's conscience, and he shifted in the saddle. He should tell Sam the truth about why his family was there. But then she'd never talk to him again. Plus, if he backed out of his father's schemes now, he'd be outside the loop and would have no idea what his family was plotting against Sam and her mom. How could he protect her if he was cut off from the information?

Ethan cleared his throat. "Really, I don't mind the chores. I like learning about the ranch."

"Why?" Sam turned toward him so fast Ethan wondered how she didn't fall off Diego's back. "Why do you care so much?"

Ethan's mouth opened, then closed. "I guess if you get to keep your secret about why you're riding a steer, then I get to keep mine." He smiled, and Sam's lips turned up at the corners before she schooled her features back into stone.

"Fine. Be stubborn." She nudged Diego with her knees and pulled ahead.

Ethan tapped Miss Priss's sides with his heels and caught up. "About your riding that steer—" His voice broke off as Sam edged ahead once again. He pressed forward. "Listen, I'm serious. You don't have to tell me why if you don't want to, but whatever the reason, isn't there a better way? It seems dangerous. You fell a lot, and those horns—"

Diego stopped suddenly and Sam's eyes flashed with fire. Ethan reeled backward at the burn. "Don't you dare pretend to understand me." An almost tangible tension filtered through her tight-lipped words.

"I don't." Ethan shook his head to clear the shock residue. Of all the women in the entire world, Sam was probably the least predictable and easy to understand— and he'd been to a lot of places.

"There isn't another way. Trust me." Sam urged Diego into a walk. "You wouldn't get it."

Ethan followed. "You're trusting me with your secret in general—so why not the details of it?"

Sam's jaw clenched and she looked away.

Ethan waited, but didn't push. He was already threatening their delicate truce, but Sam didn't realize Ethan was doing her a favor by not following his dad's orders to sabotage the ranch. She had no idea what was at stake, and the more Ethan knew, the better he could protect Sam from his father's manipulation—and try to reach his own goals without picking wildflowers along the way.

Sam avoided his eyes. "It's not a matter of trust, Ethan. You forced this deal."

Guilt pricked Ethan's heart like a tailor's pin. "For good reason."

"A reason you're going to share?" The silence between them pulsed heavy with expectation.

"I just wanted to spend time with yo—just wanted

to learn about working a ranch, and I knew you'd never agree without some kind of extra motivation." Ethan shook his head at the near slip. He *had* wanted to spend time with Sam, and not just because his dad insisted— but because Ethan wanted to be around her, wanted to soak in her presence like a much needed rain shower.

"I find it hard to believe you're actually interested in cleaning stalls and grooming horses." Sam's eyebrows rose and her face shadowed under the brim of her hat.

"But I am." Again, it was the truth. There was something rewarding about rising early and working with his hands, not just pushing papers around on a mahogany desk while staring at the view from his twentieth-floor, high-rise condo. "Sam, please. Just tell me what's going on."

She tossed her hair, the sun highlighting the honey strands brushing across her back, and inhaled deeply. "I need money, and there's a bull-riding rodeo competition in a little over a week."

"Why do you need money?" What could be so important that she'd risk her life? Was the ranch struggling that badly? At that point, Ethan and his family had less "work" to do than they'd thought, but right now he only cared about finding a way to make Sam smile again.

Sam looked over her shoulder, and Ethan's head automatically swiveled with hers. The rest of the riders in their group were several paces back, talking and gesturing at the meadow view to their left. Sam turned back to Ethan, apparently satisfied no one was listening. "My best friend's father is selling a stallion. Noble Star could help my family resurrect our old breeding business."

Ethan's lips pressed together. Sam was entering the rodeo to win a horse. How could one stallion make or break an entire business? He still didn't get why Sam felt compelled to ride a steer—a bull—when there were more conventional options of obtaining money. "What about a loan?"

"Not possible."

The firm set of Sam's jaw convinced Ethan not to force that route. Sam was a smart woman—if there was a way to get money from a bank, she'd have done it by now. There were probably credit issues involved, and logically so considering the state of the ranch and his own family's presence. "Why not sell the stallions in that fence by the guest cabins? They're not being used anymore, are they?"

"Not for guests. Cole and I still work them regularly to keep them exercised. But if we sold them and were able to start the breeding farm again, then we'd have nothing to start with. They could still earn us some money, but it'd be too time-consuming to get off the ground without a head start like Noble Star." Sam shrugged. "Not to mention we have zero free time right now running the dude ranch business."

"Is the dude ranch not bringing in enough income?"

"It pays the bills. Barely." Sam shifted her weight in the saddle, the brushed leather creaking beneath her. "But this isn't what it should be. This isn't home anymore." Sam leaned forward to pat Diego's neck, but not before Ethan saw a single tear track her cheek.

He let the silence protect her misery, and waited until she wiped her face and cleared her throat. Then he smiled. "I'm sure if anyone can meet their goals, Sam, it's you."

He'd always been a sucker for wildflowers.

Chapter Ten

Sprawled on packed dirt, staring up at the stars dotting the inky black sky, Sam wondered if this whole brilliant plan of hers was worth it. Divine providence, or just a really stupid mistake? She pushed herself into a sitting position and brushed at her dusty sleeves, ignoring Cole's amused grin, Ethan's furrowed brow and the throbbing of her right shoulder. At least Kate's expression was one of sympathy and respect.

"Need a hand?" Cole called from the chute. He grabbed the rope around Lucy's girth and began freeing the steer.

"No." Sam stood on her own, despite the soreness. What she really needed was a stun gun, one to point first at Lucy, and then at Ethan. If he didn't knock off that parental worry he wore on his face like a permanent mask, she'd clobber him. It was bad enough having Cole treat her like she was made of china, another for Ethan to watch and cringe as if she would break. Why did he care so much? Ethan barely knew her, and yet his tenderness earlier in the day on the trail ride tugged at Sam's heart. It'd been a vulnerable moment on her part, moments that grew rarer and rarer the busier Sam stayed, and she could have kicked herself for crying in front of Ethan. The stress of the past few weeks—make that years—had gotten to her. It figured her weakness would bloom in front of a guest—one with chocolate-brown eyes and a smile that beckoned, despite the warnings screaming in Sam's mind.

Avoiding Ethan's gaze, Sam turned to Cole. "How long that time?"

Cole checked the stopwatch he held between calloused fingers. "Four seconds. And that's giving you a tenth."

Kate clapped her hands. "Not bad!"

"More like awful." Sam groaned. "This isn't working. Lucy isn't even a real bull, and I can't manage."

Cole pocketed the watch. "You can't expect to be a pro after a few days of practice, kid."

Kate shook her red curls back from her face. "Yeah, Sam. It takes time. But you've made amazing progress."

"I don't *have* time." Sam pressed her fingers against her forehead. No time, no money, no patience. Nothing but a big balloon of stress pressing against her temples. "I might as well be a rodeo clown. I'm a joke."

Ethan straightened from his slumped position against the fence beside Kate. "No, you're not. That's ridiculous."

She briefly squeezed her eyes shut. "What's ridiculous is me riding Lucy." Sam had gotten in over her head—and now was sinking faster than a baby calf in quicksand. Good intentions didn't hold nearly as much merit when she was on the ground staring up at the horned beast. At least her father wasn't here to see her failure. Tears burned the back of Sam's throat.

"Nothing is ridiculous. You just expect too much of yourself." Cole tossed the rope over the fence and slapped Lucy's rump. The steer ambled out of the chute and began nibbling at the grass growing through the rail.

They really should hedge around the posts, the weeds were practically inside the paddock. Though if the grass kept growing inside the fence, it'd just be extra padding to land on when flying off Lucy. Sam swallowed back a rush of overwhelming emotion. Would the to-do list around the ranch ever be caught up? Not without money. Not without Noble Star. She groaned. If only Kate's father could lower the price of the stallion. But even if he would, could she accept charity like that? She and her mom had made it on their own this long, even if they were a little worse for the wear because of it. She couldn't let someone else pave the way now, even if that meant she had to take the bull by the horns—literally.

Ethan climbed on the top of the fence and hesitated, as if he wasn't sure he wanted to jump to the ground on the other side or not. "Look, I'm sure there's a better way for you to get money than this whole bull-riding thing." He wobbled, and grabbed the rail with both hands.

"And I'm sure in *your* world, there's plenty of ways." Sam glared. "But welcome to reality."

Cole cocked his head to one side and crossed his arms. "Why is this guy still here, anyway? You want me to get rid of him?" He directed the question to Sam but stared at Ethan. Ethan shifted again on the fence and nearly toppled off. Kate shot out her arm to steady him and grinned at Ethan's responding scowl.

"It's a long story." *Too long.* Sam tucked her hair behind both ears and sighed.

Cole shook his head as he began coiling the rope. "Seems to me your list of debtors is getting longer every day, kid."

"Sam, seriously, you can find other ways to earn money." Ethan landed awkwardly on his feet inside the pen. "This is crazy. Let me help you."

"This is not crazy. My dad did it." A rapidly fraying thread inside Sam snapped and fresh tears added to the pressure pounding in her head. She jerked away from Ethan's outstretched hand. "And I don't take charity."

"I'm not talking about charity." Ethan looked at Cole, as if for help.

The cowboy's features tightened, and Sam welcomed the rush of warmth that Cole's protection offered. At least someone was looking out for her. Her surrogate big brother believed in Sam's riding ability, so who cared if a near-stranger did not? The flippant thought tugged at Sam's stomach. She did care what Ethan thought, more than she had the strength to acknowledge.

Kate quickly climbed the fence—much smoother than Ethan had—and looped her arm around Sam's shoulders. "Maybe Ethan has a point. We should try to come up with another plan. I don't want you to get hurt."

Flashbacks of hooves, horns and hospital beds filled Sam's mind and she blinked against the torrent. She didn't want to get hurt, either. But if a simple bake sale or car wash could solve the farm's problems, Sam would have been whipping up cupcakes and lathering trucks long ago. It wasn't as if she had a long list of options. She sank against the fence. "It's not that easy."

"It can be if you get creative." Ethan stepped beside her.

A frown crinkled Kate's eyebrows. "Sam, do you really want to do this? Is it that important to you? If it is, we'll support you. Or at least I will." She shot a wary look at Ethan.

Ethan's eyes narrowed. "It's not a matter of being supportive. I just don't want Sam to end up under some bull's hooves."

The audible blow landed like a sledgehammer to Sam's heart. She gasped in pain and Cole's face darkened. "Drop it, Ames. You don't know what you're talking about." Without waiting for a reply, Cole grabbed Lucy's rope and led her toward the barn, his boots clomping loudly on the packed dirt. The shadows swallowed them whole as they disappeared inside the stable.

"Was it something I said?" Ethan winced.

Kate's eyes bugged. "You mean, you don't know?"

Sam quickly interrupted. "Kate, it's okay." Ethan didn't know the details of her father's death, or else he'd probably have used better terms. But she wasn't ready to tell him—not now, maybe not ever. Sam drew a shuddery breath. If that look on Cole's face had been any indication, he'd felt the sting of Ethan's unintentional barb, too. Sometimes Sam forgot she wasn't the only one hurt when Wade Jenson died. He'd been like an uncle to Cole.

Kate's lips pressed together and she nodded in understanding. "I'm gonna take off, then. I'll call you tomorrow." She glanced at Ethan, shook her head and made her way silently toward her pickup parked across the field.

"So is Cole just your spokesman?" Ethan leaned his

elbow against the rail beside Sam. A strand of dark hair, long ago having lost its gel, sagged against his forehead. "Or something more?"

Sam turned to face the same direction, lodging one booted foot against the bottom rail. "He's more like a big brother than anything else. He watched me grow up."

"Stable hand by day, protector by night."

"Something like that." Sam tossed back her hair. "But I speak for myself." She always had, after her father died. If she didn't, no one would.

The breeze stirred Ethan's hair and puffed the sleeves of his polo shirt. At least he hadn't resorted to wearing those designer shirts with the pearl buttons that Daniel wore. He must have thirty of those things and changed them twice a day. Sam wasn't sure what was more annoying—that Daniel was trying too hard to fit into the ranch world, making a mockery of it in the process—or that Ethan fit in without seemingly trying at all. He simply did the work like any other stable hand, minus the traditional attire. Hard as she tried, Sam couldn't picture Ethan in anything other than his signature jeans, khakis or polo.

Although a black felt cowboy hat would really bring out his mysterious dark eyes.

Sam jerked, stung by the errant thought, and slid away from the fence. "I've got to go. It's late."

"If I said something to hurt you, I'm sorry." Ethan's quiet voice broke the silence of the night.

"It's not your fault." In a way she wished it was. Then she could channel the anger and frustration toward someone, toward something tangible. But she had no one to blame for her and her mother's current situation.

It wasn't her father's fault, and Sam knew better than to blame God—completely, anyway. His grace had been the only thing to get them through the blindingly dark days after Wade's death. Maybe riding that bull would be the therapy she needed. Not only would it accomplish her goal for the farm, but it could release the years of buried tension. Is that why her dad rode all those years?

Too much to think about on sore muscles and no sleep.

"I'll see you tomorrow." She lifted her hand in a wave to Ethan and quickly slipped away toward the main house, toward the solace of her bedroom, toward precious sleep that could numb the emotion for another night.

Toward the pillow she'd already sobbed into enough for one lifetime.

Ethan watched Sam walk away from him, and not for the first time. He thought he'd found the perfect opportunity to talk Sam out of this crazy bull-riding idea and into something tamer. But she seemed determined to do this, and for reasons he hadn't yet grasped. How many more secrets were hovering over the Jenson ranch?

Ethan gripped the paddock fence with both hands and winced at a splinter that worked its way under his skin. Sort of like a certain cowgirl. He'd known Sam for, what, a week or less? And he was already overly concerned about her well-being—his heart pounding every time the steer bucked, his stomach tightening every time Sam fell. This was foolish. It was a crush, at best. Sam was different from the women he was used to dating, so she seemed appealing. That was all, right?

Opposites might attract, but they rarely meshed. It'd be stupid of him to think otherwise.

He shoved away from the fence and headed toward his cabin, the lie stinging worse than the splinter in his palm. He didn't need this. He was here to make a sale, gain financial independence and hit the road. Figuratively and literally. Sam was a distraction—a beautiful one, but still a distraction. He had to find a way to get this whole business scheme of his father's over with before he did something stupid.

Like fall in love.

There was a note scribbled on Ethan's nightstand informing him that Daniel couldn't sleep and had gone to play pool in the lodge. He wanted Ethan to come meet him when he got back from his date. Ethan's lip curled as he tossed the letter in the trash. Watching Sam get trounced by a beast wasn't a date, and definitely not with that Cole guy watching his every move.

Ethan stood in the middle of the room, halfway between his bed and the door. He could go put up with Daniel and his competitive streak, or he could go to bed.

And dream about Sam all night.

With a scowl, Ethan yanked the door open and shouldered through the cool night air toward the lodge. At least he could be certain Sam went to her home to sleep and not to the big game room off the main house.

Daniel waved from the back corner of the room and tossed him a stick. "Glad you made it. Now I can beat someone instead of playing by myself." He broke and the balls scattered across the green felt. "Stripes." He missed the next one.

"Nice try. You're going down." Ethan leaned over the table and lined up his shot, eager to vent his frustration. The cue ball ricocheted off a solid orange and slid easily into a corner pocket.

Daniel grunted his approval. "So where were you tonight? And don't give me that meeting junk again."

"It was a meeting."

"Right. And I'm Annie Oakley."

Ethan aimed for the solid green and overshot. "Your turn."

"You didn't answer me." Daniel sunk a striped ball in the left corner. "You were with Sam."

"It was work-related."

"I'd like to work with her." Daniel winked as he studied the table for an opening.

Ethan gripped the cue stick with both hands. He knew Daniel would try to weasel into his relationship with Sam, had seen it coming a mile away. Ethan blinked. Wait a minute. What relationship? He shook his head. This entire process was getting too confusing. One thing he knew for sure, he didn't want his womanizing cousin anywhere near Sam.

Daniel powered another ball into the hole. "Is she seeing anyone?"

"I don't think so." He'd never asked, but there was no way Sam had time for dating. It was obvious her focus remained solidly on the ranch and her goals. Ethan cleared his throat. "But she's not your type."

"I like all types."

"Just leave her alone." Ethan's voice rose and he quickly bit his lip. But it was too late. The truth glimmered in Daniel's eyes and he grinned.

"No problem, man. You can have her. I won't give you any competition, even if your dad did ask me to."

Disbelief clouded Ethan's vision. His father had just

said the other night that he didn't want Ethan getting close to Sam romantically. In fact, Jeffrey's exact words were *Don't be ridiculous, if I wanted someone to date Sam, I'd ask Daniel.*

Reality struck hard and Ethan's heart stammered. His dad was manipulating them all. It was so obvious now. If Jeffrey could ask Ethan to lie, then he wouldn't have any problem lying in return—even to his family.

Daniel leaned over, aimed and sunk the eight ball into the corner. "That's the game."

Ethan swallowed the mixture of anger, embarrassment and denial rising in his throat as he returned the cue stick to its stand by the wall.

It was a game, all right.

Chapter Eleven

"You didn't have to come." Sam shot a sidelong glance at Ethan, who ambled along beside her on Miss Priss. A breeze chilled the morning heat on Sam's back. Even Diego's withers felt warm under her fingers. Just another typical July day in Appleback, Texas. She pushed at the cowboy hat on her head, knowing her hair must be a sweaty mess underneath. "You could have gone with Cole and the others on the regular ride."

"Checking fences is part of ranch life, isn't it?" Ethan grinned and the sun highlighted his brown hair. "I want to learn it all."

"It might get boring."

"I doubt that." Ethan's eyes held a deeper meaning and Sam quickly looked away, her heart stuttering.

Beneath her, Diego stirred and Sam tried to calm the rush of emotion her mount noticed. "Better you than Ethan," she mumbled to the horse.

Ethan leaned over in the saddle. "What's that?"

"Nothing." Sam smiled, hoping it covered the confusion she knew lingered in her eyes. She squeezed Diego's side to urge him into a trot. "Let's go. At this rate, we'll never finish checking the borders."

They rode toward the east perimeter, the weeds and overgrown grass parting around the horses' legs. Ethan didn't bounce nearly as hard in the saddle as he did on their first trail ride, and Sam shoved back the smidgen of pride for her part in the improvement. She might be a good teacher but Ethan, as much as she hated to admit it, had natural ability on a horse. He just needed the time and confidence—which he was obviously gaining as he no longer clung to the saddle horn—to develop it.

"What happens if we find a break in the fence?" Ethan's eager expression seemed as if he hoped they would.

"We note it and send Cole back later to fix it."

"You can't fix it yourself?" Ethan's cocked eyebrow held a challenge, and Sam bristled.

"Of course I *could*. But it's barbed wire and Cole's stronger. He can pull it three times as fast as me." Not to mention she hated messing with those sharp barbs. Besides, it wasn't like she didn't already have enough on her cracked, overflowing plate. "Time is money on a farm."

Ethan's mouth twitched.

"What? You think *you* could do it?" Sam pulled Diego to a halt.

Ethan stopped Miss Priss and urged the mare in a circle to face Sam. She tried not to be impressed at the easy movements he used, as if he'd been doing it for years instead of days. Ethan shrugged. "It can't be that hard."

"In that case, why don't you come out with Cole later and let him show you the ropes?" Sam snorted.

Less than a week on a horse and Ethan thought he was a real working cowboy? Typical. "You'll think twice."

"Oh, yeah?" Ethan shifted in the saddle. "I think I could pick it up after one try."

"One section of fence, and you're an expert? I'd let Cole be the judge of that."

"Then let him." Ethan grinned. "What do you say?"

Sam tilted her head. "All right. Kate and I were planning on going to the Appleback street fair tomorrow night. I say if you don't—under Cole's supervision—fix any broken fence within two hours' time, then you have to sign up for the dunking booth."

"And if I make the deadline?"

Sam pursed her lips. "You won't."

"But if I do…" Ethan's eyes glimmered in challenge. "You have to enter."

Sam sidled Diego up close to Miss Priss and offered her hand to Ethan. "Deal."

They shook, and Sam smirked. She couldn't wait to see Ethan and his trademark polo floating in a pool of water.

Ethan winced as another barb bit into his glove. Cole, several feet down by the post, shot him a knowing look and Ethan tugged harder at the fencing despite his screaming biceps. He couldn't let Cole know he was struggling, or the cowboy wouldn't tell Sam that Ethan did the job correctly. The only thing worse than splashing into a small town's annual dunking booth would be the gloating look on Sam's face if he lost.

He pulled again. No matter who won, at least Ethan had a date to the fair. Sam never would have considered inviting him to come with her and Kate otherwise.

Ethan wrinkled his brow. Invited, challenged—same difference, right? Regardless, Ethan now had tangible proof to show his father he was spending time with Sam doing fun things. Bottom line—if he was with her, Daniel wouldn't have a chance to move in. Never had appearances become so important.

And never had a work project become this complicated.

He shuddered at the thought of his father finding out Ethan's real plans to leave the company. He pushed aside the thought and concentrated on the physical ache in his muscles. He'd never worked so hard, but the thought of getting to spend tomorrow with Sam in a non-chore atmosphere made sweating over a prickly pile of fencing almost worth it.

Although, on second thought, it would be awfully hard to explain to his dad why he was out in a pasture in the middle of the afternoon, helping to repair a fence instead of working to destroy it as Jeffrey requested. The complications kept piling up. It'd be pretty simple to sabotage the fence, even under Cole's scrutiny. But Ethan refused to participate in his father's devious plans. He'd rather make excuses to his dad than hurt Sam any more than he was already going to have to.

"How does this work, exactly?" Ethan strained harder and his gloves slipped. The fencing snapped free and fell to the ground in a messy tangle of wire. He sucked in his breath. Now he'd done it. Once Sam heard about this, he'd lose for sure. He turned his gaze to Cole, who snickered.

"Guess this might be a good time to introduce you to a little thing I like to call a fence stretcher." Cole held up a long yellow tool and grinned.

Ethan's mouth opened. "You've got to be kidding me. How long were you going to let me pretend that I was being productive?"

"I reckon 'bout 'til you gave up."

"Great." Ethan ran his gloved hand over his face and groaned.

Cole began stringing the wire through the machine. "Don't worry, I won't tell Sam. I know about your little challenge."

Ethan's eyes narrowed. "Why would you help me?"

"Sam needs a dose of her own medicine now and then." Cole pushed his cowboy hat back with one hand. "Besides, it'd be pretty funny to see her in that dunking booth. She takes herself too seriously."

"So you're going to tell her I fixed the fence?" Ethan couldn't believe what he was hearing.

"Reckon there's no reason not to—because that's exactly what you're going to do." Cole's face drifted back into his usual scowl. "Now get over here, you're not getting out of this without some work."

Ethan scrambled to follow the cowboy's orders, his heart light for the first time in days. He couldn't wait to see the look on Sam's face when Cole gave her the progress report, or hear the inevitable scream when Sam realized what she'd agreed to. He checked his watch and winced. They'd be cutting it close.

He took the tool from Cole and got to work.

Sam almost swallowed her gum as she glimpsed Ethan and Cole riding toward the barn on Miss Priss and Salsa—laughing. She'd figured Cole would have torn Ethan to shreds after hours of fence repair—both physically and emotionally. But the smile Ethan wore as the twosome dismounted by the stable was brighter than the stars beginning to poke through the navy sky.

She hesitantly made her way toward them, automatically reaching out to take Miss Priss's reins from Ethan.

"I've got her." Ethan's hair, mussed, sweaty and without an ounce of leftover gel, flopped on his forehead and he shook it back with a grin. "A man's got to finish what he starts, right?" He nodded once at Cole before leading Miss Priss into the barn.

Sam turned toward Cole and fisted her hands on her hips. "Okay, what happened out there? You two left as Felix and Oscar from *The Odd Couple,* and came back all buddy-buddy."

Cole unbuckled the girth and tugged the saddle from his mount's back. "Ethan did it." He hefted the saddle onto the fence rail.

"Did what?" Sam reached out to balance the saddle while Cole removed the blanket from the horse.

"Repaired the fence."

Sam shook her head. "Impossible."

"He did the work. Why would I lie?" Cole draped the blanket over one arm and held out both hands for the saddle.

Sam dropped the leather seat over Cole's arm a little harder than necessary and he staggered backward under the sudden weight. "He knows nothing about fences. Or riding. Or horses." Her blood pulsed fiery hot in her veins. No way did Ethan stroll out to the pasture and easily repair a barbed-wire fence, even with Cole's help. Who did he think he was, The Lone Ranger?

"He's a fast learner." Cole turned toward the barn with a little shrug. "What can I say?"

Sam's eyes narrowed as Cole disappeared into the

shadows of the stable. Beside her, Salsa nickered and Sam rubbed his hairy cheek. "Those two are up to something." Salsa tossed his neck as if in agreement.

Reality sounded like a clanging dinner bell and Sam sucked in her breath. If she kept to her word, she was now officially an entrant in the Appleback fair dunking booth. Her stomach flipped at the thought of that cold, dirty water. Cole must have somehow heard about the challenge and lied about Ethan's progress as a joke. That would explain Ethan's sudden aptitude for fence work.

Ethan strode back outside to the paddock and looped his arms over the top rail. "Did you hear the good news?" He grinned.

She tugged at Salsa's reins to lead the horse forward, but Ethan followed close beside her. "So? Did Cole tell you?"

Sam turned to go around him, but it was like backing a trailer into a narrow driveway—hard. She stopped walking. "He lied to me about your work, if that's what you mean."

Ethan's expression tightened. "Do you really think I'm that incompetent?"

"Maybe not at accounting or consulting or whatever it is you do for your millions." Sam sidestepped him again, and Salsa's hoof narrowly missed Sam's boot. "But at ranch life, yes."

"So all this work I've been doing the past several days—none of it matters to you?" Ethan's features hardened to stone.

Sam's mouth opened and closed. It did matter—that was the problem. Ethan was picking up the rhythm of the farm faster than Sam could have ever expected, and for some reason, it bothered her more than she wanted to admit. "Whatever." She started once again for the barn. No time to think about such things, not with Salsa needing to be untacked and Sam's midnight practice ride on Lucy to think about. There were bigger issues at stake, bigger than a street fair and bigger than Ethan's wounded feelings.

Bigger than her heart demanding an evaluation.

Ethan caught her arm. "Listen, Cole knew about our deal. He said he'd cover for me, because he wanted to play a joke on you. But I really did the work on the fence after he showed me how the fence stretcher operated. He isn't lying."

Salsa snorted over Sam's shoulder and she leaned against the horse's neck, enjoying the warmth against the cool evening air and the comfort of the familiar touch against her back. If people could be even half as understanding and sympathetic as horses, the world would be a better place.

"Do you believe me?" Ethan inched closer, his breath teasing her hair.

She didn't want to say yes. It'd be much easier to believe Ethan was just a rich New Yorker who couldn't put his boots on the right feet; much easier to believe the guys just wanted to pull a prank on her over the dunking booth. But the look in Ethan's gaze proved it was more than that. And if she looked closer—*way* more.

Sam abruptly straightened. "I believe you." She had to tell the truth. But she didn't have to tell how her stomach did a boot-scootin' line dance at Ethan's close proximity.

"Good." Ethan eased slightly away, not breaking eye contact. "So, tomorrow night? You, me and the fair?"

"And Kate," Sam reminded. Her heart stammered

and she blamed it on too much caffeine. Definitely not because of those heartfelt brown orbs trying to burrow into her defenses.

"Right. Well, you better bring your pitchin' arm."

Sam paused. "Me? What do you mean?"

"You never let me finish. I did the work—but it took longer than two hours." His lips twisted to the side in mock disgust. "Two hours and twenty minutes. I'm pretty sure Cole won't ever let me forget that."

Sam's eyes widened. "So you're going to sit in the tank?" Him. Not her. She let out a slow breath of relief. Talk about a close one.

"That was the deal, wasn't it? And here you thought I wasn't honest." Ethan shoved away from the fence with a smile.

As hard as Sam tried to pull up her previous frustration, all she could do was smile back.

Chapter Twelve

"Step right up, folks. That's right, step right up here and I'll show you a cowboy in a box." The man in a large hat and striped pants on stilts, who Sam knew was really Bobby Gillum from the Grill My Grits Diner on Main Street, teetered near the tank where Ethan perched on a wooden collapsible seat wearing an oversize rubber cowboy hat. "That's right, a cowboy destined to get soaked."

Sam laughed at Bobby's circus-announcer impersonation—he really should have practiced his bit a little more—and waved at Ethan, who adjusted his position on the wobbling board. She couldn't help but grin. He waved back, his expression dubious as he glanced down at the water lapping at his dangling feet.

Kate and Daniel—he just *had* to tag along uninvited when he'd heard of their plans—had left a few minutes ago to snag some cotton candy for the three of them. Sam was waiting until they got back to take her turn. So far, Ethan had been fortunate. There'd been nothing but a crowd of overeager Little Leaguers with bad aim and a few gnarled old-timers who'd attempted to soak him. He remained dry—for now.

Kate appeared at Sam's side, cotton candy in hand. "What'd I miss?"

"Nothing yet." Sam turned to Bobby. "I'll take a shot." The gathering afternoon crowd parted and murmured their approval as she made her way to the front. She handed Bobby three red tickets and plucked a softball from the bucket.

"Give the lady some room, folks," Bobby boomed, stumbling toward the crowd and waving his hands to clear the area. "This one looks like a winner!"

Ethan crossed his arms over his chest and waited, his dimples making a defiant appearance on his tanned cheeks. He shook his head. "She needs all the room she can get—and a little luck!"

"Sounds like fighting words," Bobby teased. "Come on, Miss. Let's see what you got."

Sam wound her arm a few times to loosen the muscles and drove the ball toward the target. It bounced harmlessly off the plastic net. The crowd booed.

"Wow, look at those muscles." A college-aged girl standing near Sam nudged her friend in the side, her eyes riveted on Ethan.

A prick of jealousy snagged Sam's stomach. She shouldn't care what a bouncy little blonde teen thought of him. But Ethan didn't even seem to notice the girls, as he kept his eyes trained on Sam—and winked.

Her heart stuttered, and she quickly prepared her next shot. *Focus, focus.*

Bam. The ball slammed against the target and Ethan splashed into the murky water. Sam gasped and then threw her arms in the air in victory. "Yes!"

He resurfaced with a gasp for air and sloshed his hair back from his eyes. The crowd roared with laughter and Sam offered a sheepish shrug. Kate grinned around her cone of cotton candy and Daniel shook his head with a smile, as if he knew Sam was going to hear about it from Ethan later and he couldn't wait to watch.

With all the dignity Ethan could muster—which wasn't much, as most of it still floated with the dirty water in the tank—he struggled back onto the seat and waved good-naturedly to the taunting crowd.

Then his eyes met Sam's and she felt as if she was the one drowning.

Ethan changed clothes inside the public fairground restrooms and joined Kate, Daniel and Sam back outside. He shook his head at Daniel's offer of cotton candy.

"Good thing you don't have my red hair and matching temper." Kate grinned, bits of pink sugar stuck to her cheeks. "Or Sam would be in trouble right now."

Ethan shoved his hands in his jeans pockets, and offered Sam an easy smile. "Hey, I agreed to the dare, fair and square. I had to pay my dues—even if she was the only one to soak me during my entire shift." He nudged her with his elbow.

"What can I say? I have good aim." Sam nudged back, her light brown hair pulled up in a high ponytail. Already loose tendrils escaped around her face. She looked prettier than any city girl he'd ever seen in New York—and with apparently little effort. Ethan's breath hitched and he tried to cover the hiccup sound with a cough.

"What, no fight? That's no fun." Daniel tossed his

cone into a nearby trash can. "I was all fired up for a blow-out between you two." He laughed.

"You want fun? Let's hit the Gravy Train. It's the fastest roller coaster this side of the Mississippi." Kate threw away her nearly empty cone of sugar and wiped her hands on her jeans. Pink tufts stuck to the back pockets but she didn't seem to care as Daniel offered her his arm.

"M'lady." He winked over his shoulder at Ethan as they led the way toward the rides.

Ethan fell into step beside Sam. "Looks like those two are hitting it off."

Sam's eyes narrowed as she studied the couple in front of them. Daniel ducked his head low and Kate laughed at his murmured comment. "Seems that way."

"Do I detect a bit of regret in those words?"

"I don't know about regret, but I don't see anything positive forming out of a friendship with those two."

"Why not?" Ethan slowed his pace to match Sam's, ambling beside her as the sun set behind the Ferris wheel in the near distance, scattering bits of pink and purple and orange across the sky. *He* knew why Daniel shouldn't get close to Kate, or any other self-respecting woman, but Sam couldn't know that about him this soon.

"They're too different." Sam gestured toward the couple now several steps ahead. "City boy, country girl. What does Daniel know about horses and ranch life? And what does Kate know about designer labels or foreign cities? They have nothing in common."

"Sort of like us." The blow of Sam's words hit a soft spot in Ethan's heart that had long been forming. He'd hoped it would have calloused by now, but no such luck.

The words pricked sharper than Cupid's bow but without the mushy, pain-relieving side effects. He averted his gaze so Sam wouldn't see the disappointment he knew welled in his eyes.

Sam stopped. "I didn't mean it like—I just..." She blew out her breath and shoved her hands in her pockets. "Forget I said anything." She began walking again, faster than before.

"It's true, though, isn't it?" Not wanting to continue the conversation but somehow unable to stop himself, Ethan hurried after her. "Just say it."

"Say what, Ethan?" Sam wheeled in front of him, and he nearly ran into her. "Say that we're from two different worlds and have nothing in common, either? Why does it matter?" Her gaze searched his, undefined emotion deepening the blue to cobalt.

Ethan looked over her shoulder at the Ferris wheel on the horizon. A dozen thoughts vied for release in his mouth, but he swallowed them as a new idea struck. "Take a ride with me."

"What?" Sam's eyebrows shot up with surprise.

"Take a ride with me." He grabbed her hand, pulled her toward the ticket booth and handed the cashier a ten dollar bill. "Come on." He pocketed the string of red squares and plowed through the throng of people.

"Where are we going?" Sam tugged at his grip, but Ethan held her hand tighter as he maneuvered a path through the thickening evening crowd. He couldn't let go now, or the crowd would swallow her whole.

"Here." Breathless, Ethan drew Sam to a stop at the line for the Ferris wheel. She tilted her head back, peering up at the brightly lit cars making their way around the giant circle.

"The Ferris wheel?" Her brow furrowed with doubt.

"It's a classic."

"What about the Gravy Train?"

"I get enough of the fast life in New York." He paused until Sam's gaze locked with his. "I'm ready to slow things down."

Their car stopped two from the top of the wheel, and Sam didn't know if it was the height or Ethan's nearness that put her nerves on red alert. What had he meant by saying he wanted to slow things down? Was he talking about life in general, or about her? She drew a deep breath, her mind racing almost as fast as the Gravy Train she could see across the park, a whirl of lights and music as the cars raced around a shiny red track. Apparently Kate and Daniel hadn't missed them after Ethan's mad dash to the ticket booth, as Sam's cell phone hadn't vibrated once in her pocket.

"It's nice up here, isn't it?" The wind brushed strands of dark hair out of Ethan's eyes. He must have skipped the gel after the dunk tank, and Sam was surprised at his hair's length. It seemed longer than a typical cut for a business professional, and she couldn't imagine Ethan doing anything outside the book. But maybe there was more depth to him than she'd originally thought.

The idea struck Sam with a shameful dose of clarity. Hadn't Ethan already proven that enough times with his hard work around the ranch? No wonder he'd been so offended when she questioned his capability on repairing fences. An apology rose in her throat and stuck on her lips. "Ethan, I—"

He turned to her, their faces only inches apart. Her

stomach tingled and Sam froze. Ethan's hand found hers and he ran his fingers lightly over her knuckles. "Yes?"

She tried to breathe, but couldn't remember her name, much less what she'd been about to say. "I—" She swallowed. His gaze bore into hers, drawing her in as he leaned closer. Sam followed the magnetic pull, the lights of the Ferris wheel a romantic glow in her peripheral vision. "I—" Her hands shook, and she clenched her free one in her lap. Desperate to speak but scared of the words that might roll off her tongue.

Ethan's cell rang, jangling Sam out of her thoughts and jarring her back to reality with a resounding crash. She jerked away from Ethan, causing their little car to sway, and he grabbed for his phone. "Hello?"

Daniel's voice rose through the phone above the crowd and the music. He shouted something she couldn't decipher as Sam's stomach churned. And this time, there was no food to blame.

"We're at the Ferris wheel. We'll meet you by the corn dog stand in about fifteen minutes." Ethan dropped his cell into his shirt pocket, and released a long breath. "Sorry about that."

Sam nodded and forced a smile, but her thoughts were galloping much further ahead. She'd almost kissed Ethan. What was she thinking? It'd be like pairing a goat with a Thoroughbred—impossible. They were on completely different levels of life in status, mindset, goals. Some things just weren't meant to be—even if under the glow of the stars it seemed as if, for a moment, they could.

Sam turned to look out her side of the car as the wheel gently lowered them back to earth.

Chapter Thirteen

The lights and music of the fairgrounds seemed to lose their magic as Ethan and Sam joined Kate and Daniel at the corn dog stand. Earlier Ethan had been contemplating buying a dog, but now his stomach twisted into knots and made food undesirable.

He'd almost kissed Sam. What kind of idiot was he? If he wasn't careful, he'd easily cross the professional line with Sam that he'd been so concerned about Daniel crossing, and then Ethan wouldn't be any better than his womanizing cousin.

Sam joined Kate in line ahead of Ethan, tucking loose strands of hair behind her ears as she peered up at the neon menu. Was she really hungry, or was it all an act? Maybe she hadn't been affected by the near kiss after all. Maybe she hadn't even realized his intentions and Ethan was worrying for nothing.

And maybe all of this country air was getting to him. Ethan groaned. He was losing his mind to a cowgirl with wildflower blue eyes and a quick wit he had yet to find in the usual New York crowd—and rapidly losing his heart to a woman who'd never look twice at him. For once, his money and status wasn't enough, which just made him respect Sam even more. She looked deeper than his wallet, and it figured the one woman who had the maturity and grace to do so was the same one who needed a *real* man in her life—a cattle driver, not a paper pusher. He massaged his temples with his fingers.

"What's wrong? If you don't want a corn dog, we can grab a meat pie instead." Daniel gestured over his shoulder to the row of food booths lining the road.

"It's not the food."

"Ah." A knowing spark lit Daniel's eyes. "I didn't interrupt anything on the Ferris wheel, did I?" He nudged Ethan in the ribs.

"No! I mean, not really. Lower your voice." Ethan whispered, hoping Daniel would follow his cue. "This whole situation is getting sticky, that's all."

"What's sticky?" Kate's red head popped up from giving her order at the window and she stepped out of line with her change.

Ethan swallowed. "Um, the cotton candy."

Kate grinned and pocketed her change as Sam moved to join them, holding a large cup of lemonade.

"How was the roller coaster?" Sam took a sip from the straw.

Ethan frowned. Was she avoiding his eyes? Or was he being paranoid? They really should talk soon, or else working together the rest of his stay at the ranch was going to be more than a little awkward.

He was leaving in two weeks, maybe sooner if his father had his way. His family would eventually get what they needed and go back to New York, slimy contract in hand. To Sam, Ethan would be nothing more than a harsh memory—the man who stole the family farm out from under her and turned a pile of precious earth and memories into concrete and clearance racks. His stomach churned again. Definitely no room for a corn dog with this much guilt taking up space.

"The roller coaster was fun." Kate grinned around her mustard-covered corn dog at Ethan. "Even if your cousin did scream like a girl."

"I did not." Daniel lifted his chin and brushed at the shoulder of his shirt with a fake air of dignity. "I just yelled. Loudly and repeatedly."

"We told you it was fast." Sam laughed.

"How was the Ferris wheel?" Daniel's teasing gaze pierced Ethan until the spark left and all that remained in Daniel's eyes was pointed animosity.

"Great, like I said earlier." Ethan stared back just as intensely, hoping Daniel would detour from the verbal path he was taking. That conversation would lead nowhere productive, and could only further drive a wedge between Ethan and Sam. Or is that what Daniel wanted?

They locked gazes for several moments until Daniel finally blinked, looked away and grinned down at Sam. "Next time you should ride with me." He met Ethan's eyes again in a brief challenge.

Ethan glimpsed Kate's frown. He drew a deep breath. Great. He'd somehow offended Daniel with his back-off vibe regarding Sam, and now his cousin was in it for keeps. Ethan could only hope Sam wouldn't fall for such a tacky, obvious play.

But she seemed oblivious to the tension—and to the fact that Kate's eyes were narrowing to tiny slits. Jealousy? Ethan wished he could bang his head against the giant sign shaped like a corn dog. The children's game *Which of these does not belong?* popped into his mind, and Ethan grimaced. The answer was depressingly easy—none of them. He didn't belong with Sam, Kate didn't belong with Daniel, Sam didn't belong with Daniel or vice versa… Ethan's headache roared and he shut his eyes against the throbbing. So much for a fun night on the town. He'd rather be scooping manure.

"Hey, look, Sam." Kate pointed across the grounds to a tent set up by the ice cream stand. "A mechanical bull. That'd be extra practice for you."

Ethan's eyes widened. Daniel didn't know about Sam's plan to bull-ride. How could Kate have slipped up like that with her best friend's secret? He glanced at Sam. Panic shadowed her expression.

Kate glanced between Sam and Ethan. "What? I told Daniel about Sam's plans when we were in line for the roller coaster. He thought it was great. Really bold."

Sam's face paled. Ethan bit down on his lower lip. *Not good, not good…*

"Hey, it's cool with me." Daniel shrugged, but his gaze held an ulterior motive. "I won't tell anyone."

Kate's brow furrowed in concern. "I figured if Ethan knew, there was no reason for his cousin not to. I'm sorry, Sam."

Sam drew a deep breath and the paper cup in her hand wobbled slightly. "It's okay. No big deal."

But Ethan could tell it wasn't okay. Apparently Sam could see for herself that telling Ethan a secret and confiding the same to Daniel was the difference between trusting a sheep and a wolf. If Daniel passed the info to Jeffrey, he would have not only one-upped Ethan again, he would sabotage the ranch even further—exactly as Jeffrey hoped.

Ethan felt Sam's gaze on him and offered her a smile

he hoped didn't look as forced as it felt. "How about that ride, cowgirl?"

"On a mechanical bull?" Sam laughed, but the worry in her eyes hadn't completely faded. "No, thanks. Lucy could take on that piece of metal in a heartbeat. What's the point?"

"You think riding Lucy is harder than staying on that thing?" Kate pointed to the machine, which whirled in a sharp, tight circle before dumping a thin cowboy on the padded mats below. He stood up and slapped his hat against his leg in disgust before ambling out the open-sided tent.

Sam's lips twisted. "Maybe not."

"Don't tell me you're scared." Daniel's arm landed around Sam's shoulders and she stiffened almost as fast as Ethan did. He fought the impulse to rake his cousin's arm away. Starting a fight would only lead to disaster, and Ethan could only guess whose side his father would take once he heard.

Sam eased away from Daniel's casual touch without prompting and Ethan let out his breath in relief. "You should go for it, Sam. In fact, I'll do it, too."

Daniel's brow rose and he lowered his rejected arm to his side. "In that case, count me in."

"You? On a bull?" Ethan snorted.

Daniel glared. "It's not like it's real. Besides, if you can do it, I can do it."

They squared off and Ethan worked to control the harsh words threatening to fly from his lips. What was Daniel's problem? Why had he suddenly decided to go after Sam? And why bother flirting with Kate if Sam was his goal all along? His cousin had just said at the lodge that he would back off for Ethan's sake. Had Jeffrey anted up the pressure since then?

"You're all crazy. I'll be just fine watching from the sidelines." Kate smirked. "Besides, Sam will beat you both."

"We'll see about that." Daniel winked at Sam again and she quickly looked the other way.

"After you." Ethan gestured for Sam to go ahead of him, then purposefully shouldered past Daniel to fall into step behind her. He might be about to take on his first bull, but he had a feeling the battle with Daniel was just beginning.

Back on a bull again. This time, it was a mixture of faux hair and steel instead of hide and sweat. Still, the nerves in her stomach reminded Sam of what was at stake—not only her dignity, but her ranch. If she couldn't stay on a fake bull, how could she manage a real one in two weeks? No bull, no cash, no stallion, no breeding farm. The equation was painfully simple.

Although according to Daniel and Ethan and the way they kept acting like Neanderthals, one would think the only issue currently at stake was Sam's heart. Any minute now she half expected one of them to grab her ponytail and drag her away as a prize. What was with their sudden testosterone battle? Daniel had ridden the mechanical bull first and fallen after a measly three seconds. One good twist of the machine and he'd slipped onto the mats with a scowl. Ethan had gone next and done better by maybe a full second, but from the look in his eyes, any time longer than Daniel's was enough.

Sam had to ride well—not just for the sake of proving to herself she could actually have a shot at that rodeo prize money, but for the sake of holding her own against two pompous city slickers.

Even if one of them did smell like spicy cologne and had eyes that made Sam's stomach flip like a flapjack on a griddle.

"You ready, little lady?" The older man in jean overalls and a T-shirt working the switchboard control shifted in his metal folding chair, which squeaked in protest under his weight. Sam grasped the padded handle on the bull, took a deep breath and nodded.

With a squeaky groan, the machine sprung to life and whipped Sam to the left. Then to the right. She hung on and fought the urge to grab the horn with her free hand. At least this way if she fell, it'd be on foam and not hard-packed dirt.

But this bull was much feistier than Lucy. Sam's head jerked to the side and she struggled to maintain her balance. The slick rubber wasn't as easy for her legs to grip as they did on the real steer. She wobbled dangerously to one side. *Hang on, hang on.* She couldn't let Ethan or Daniel win.

She glimpsed the figures of her friends—did she consider Ethan and Daniel friends now?—standing to one side of the tent, clapping and yelling. Kate's unmistakable two-fingered whistle split the air and Sam gripped harder with her thighs. "Seven seconds," Kate screamed in encouragement.

The world flew by in a blur of red tent stripes and blue gym mats. Her fingers suddenly slipped and Sam sprawled on the ground in a heap.

"You did it!" Ethan rushed Sam before she could stand and hauled her to her feet. "Nine seconds!" His arms wrapped around her in a tight hug and Sam inhaled his masculine scent. Her arms automatically curled around his neck. Over his shoulder, Kate's eyes widened and her lips parted in shock.

Sam backed slowly away from Ethan's embrace, heat flushing her face. She couldn't believe she'd thrown herself into his arms like that. She really couldn't believe the envy that sprang onto Daniel's face as if he'd suddenly chomped into a lemon.

But most of all, she couldn't believe the impulse to kiss Ethan was back, even stronger than it had been on the Ferris wheel.

Chapter Fourteen

The next morning, Sam practically tiptoed into the barn. Maybe Ethan wasn't up yet. Maybe he'd overslept and wouldn't be helping with the morning chores today.

Maybe he'd forgotten about the way she'd thrown herself into his embrace and hugged him after staying on the bull for the required eight seconds.

Sam's cheeks heated. What a ridiculous victory in the first place. It wasn't like she'd ridden a real bull or accomplished anything other than proving she could linger on a piece of moving steel longer than two greenhorn men. What was worth celebrating about that? It didn't change her circumstances, didn't change the fact that her family's farm was still broke and in danger of moving further into the red every day. No, it didn't change anything—even if Ethan's hug had felt like a tiny piece of home.

Still, the question remained—why was Ethan so excited for her about the riding success when just two days ago he'd been trying to talk Sam out of entering the rodeo? Something was up with Ethan, something strange about his family—and it had nothing to do with Vickie's fashion choices, Jeffrey's absence from activities, or Daniel's flirtation attempts. Maybe Sam was just imagining things because she wanted them to leave so badly.

She drew a tight breath. Was that a past tense "wanted," or present tense? Ethan *had* been a big help to her with the morning chores, leaving Cole available to handle bigger tasks he'd never had the time for. Not to mention having someone to talk to other than the horses made the menial duties more enjoyable. Somehow, Ethan's being at the ranch was becoming less of a hassle and more of a...blessing?

The morning was turning into a brain teaser.

Sam reached for the pitchfork in the barn's supply closet. The wooden stick felt heavy in her hands, and soreness radiated from her shoulder. All those late nights of practicing on Lucy were starting to show, not to mention the core-strengthening exercises Cole was making her do, and her muscles were suffering from it. Would it even matter? Would it be enough?

She shut the door and headed to the first stall. She hated these moments of self-doubt, hated bearing the burden of such pressure. Other women her age at the church were married, some even had kids or were thinking about children. The few single ones left in her class—the last time Sam went, anyway—were satisfied in their careers or pursuing graduate degrees.

Would Sam ever feel free to live her own life?

A figure, shadowed against the morning light streaming into the barn, appeared in the doorway of the stables and Sam hesitated before walking into Wildfire's stall. Ethan. She lifted her hand in a quick wave and slipped under Wildfire's neck to secure his halter. Her fingers fumbled with the familiar buckles and her heart raced. *Calm down. It's just Ethan—the same guy who got on your last nerve just a few days ago.* Technically, nothing had changed. But try telling that to her shaky hands.

Sam jumped as Ethan popped his head over the half stall door. "Good morning."

"Mornin'." She avoided his eyes, hoping the blush had faded from her cheeks by now. She let her hair block his view of her face as she finally managed to buckle the halter on Wildfire.

"Did you practice with Lucy last night? I crashed after we got home from the fair." Ethan's voice, rich and invigorating like morning coffee, warmed Sam's insides.

"No, I took the night off." She spoke into her curtain of brown hair as she clipped the lead rope onto the halter. "One crazy ride was enough for the evening."

"I bet so. Daniel's still asleep. He said he was sore from his ride." Ethan snorted. "Attempted ride, anyway." He opened the stall door for Sam to lead Wildfire out, without her having to ask.

Sam guided the horse into the aisle, unable to resist taking a poke at Ethan's bubble of pride. "You didn't stay on much longer than your cousin."

Ethan shrugged. "Hey, a second longer is a second longer." He grinned.

Sam quickly looked away before her empty stomach could start fluttering again. "Would you mind cleaning Wildfire's stall? I'm going to put him in the pasture and then come back for Piper."

"Sure." Ethan grabbed the pitchfork without complaint and disappeared inside the pen.

Sam slowly led Wildfire toward the stable doors.

Maybe Ethan hadn't noticed how his presence affected her, made her voice falter and heated her stomach like the dead of summer. If she was lucky, she could keep up the indifferent act until these feelings of attraction went away. At best, she and Ethan could be friends until his vacation ended. Anything more was asking for trouble. They were from completely different worlds, and Ethan was leaving hers in two weeks.

The only thing harder than trying to save her family farm would be trying to save it with a broken heart.

Ethan dumped the last wheelbarrow load of manure into the compost pile and headed back into the barn. The last stall was done. Sam had been absent for a good thirty minutes now, but he didn't mind doing the hard work alone. At least that way he didn't have to think about kissing her—or worse, not kissing her—again.

Ethan steered the wheelbarrow into the supply closet. He wasn't sure what brought on that spontaneous hug last night after her ride. Maybe he'd just gotten caught up in the competition and excitement of seeing Sam succeed, watching her achieve a goal he knew was so important to her. The question was, when had Sam's personal goals become so important to *him?*

He shook his head as he shut the closet door. Regardless, she'd felt really good in his arms—like she belonged. That was a dangerous fact to analyze, but right or wrong, it was there, unwilling to be ignored.

He looked up as Sam trudged toward him from the opposite end of the aisle, her expression pinched.

"Would you mind going with me into town? I need to pick up the feed order, and Cole's stuck giving private riding lessons to a guest." Sam stopped several feet away and shoved her fingertips in her jeans pockets. "I might need help loading the bags into the back of the truck. Sometimes if the store is too busy, the workers don't have time."

"No problem. I just finished mucking out the stalls." Ethan gestured toward the rows of pens.

"All of them?" Sam's brows shot upward. "In half an hour? I'm impressed."

Finally. Ethan smiled, hoping his relief didn't show on his face. Who knew hauling manure would be the way into a girl's heart?

Sam's expression softened and she pulled a ring of keys from her pocket. "Ready to go?"

He nodded. "I'm ready if you are." Ethan followed Sam out of the stable and to the parking lot by the main house. *Ready or not.*

Miles of interstate uncurled before them through the front window of the truck like a winding yellow ribbon. Sam kept her booted foot steady on the gas pedal. The trip into town seemed much longer than it had last night heading to the fair, the cab now filled with silence and the heady aroma of Ethan's freshly applied cologne instead of Kate and Daniel's jokes and laughter. Sam preferred the quietness, though awkward at times, to the constant noise and teasing of the evening before. From the contented expression Ethan wore as he gazed out the window, it appeared he felt the same.

Maybe they weren't so entirely different after all.

Sam clicked on her blinker as she eased around a slow-moving sedan in the fast lane. "You'd think they'd stick to the right lane if they insist on going ten under the speed limit."

Ethan laughed. "I'm usually the one going at least ten over."

Sam sent him a sidelong glance.

"Okay, okay, more like fifteen or twenty."

"I thought so, after you way you peeled into the parking lot of the ranch your first day here like you were gearing up for the Indy."

Ethan grinned. "So you were watching me?"

Sam swallowed hard. Busted. She stared at the road, racking her brain for a way to retract the blunder without lying. "How could I not after that dramatic arrival?"

"Now you sound like my dad." The teasing light faded from Ethan's expression.

Sam glanced at the road, then back at Ethan's slight frown. "What do you mean?"

"He thinks all I'm good for is sports cars. Just because they're interesting to me doesn't mean it's all I can do."

An oppressing silence filled the cab, broken only by the loud gush of the air conditioner. Sam reached over and clicked the knob to a lower setting. The whooshing immediately quieted. "I'm sure your dad doesn't actually think that."

"Trust me, he does." Ethan rubbed his hand over his forehead. "But let's not ruin a nice afternoon by talking about my father, okay?"

Sam's hands tightened on the steering wheel. "At least you have a father to argue with."

Ethan's expression contorted and he touched Sam's shoulder. The contact sparked up her arm and her hands shook on the wheel, for a variety of reasons she refused to acknowledge. "I'm sorry." His voice, void of the bitterness it held moments before, lowered with regret. "I wasn't thinking."

Sam inhaled, shrugging her shoulders up so Ethan's hand fell back to his side. "Don't worry about it. But next time you feel like complaining about your father, remember not everyone has that luxury." She exited the highway and turned left toward the feed store.

"Point taken." Ethan ran his hand over his hair, then stared forward, his profile a tight, indiscernible mask. "But you need to remember not everyone's family life is as happy as yours apparently used to be."

Ethan wasn't used to being spoken to so bluntly by a woman—and judging by the shocked expression on Sam's face, she wasn't used to hearing an equal retort, either. But she'd handled it well, pressing her lips together into a tight line as she jammed the truck into Park in front of an aluminum-sided building. Multiple trucks and trailers crowded the small dirt lot, and several people in cowboy hats milled around the front porch.

"They look busy, so I guess you'll have to help me load after all. Ready to work?" Sam's smile, forcibly bright, looked pasted on her face. He had offended her, but she wasn't about to admit it.

Letting her off the hook, Ethan nodded. "Always." He slid out of the cab, ignoring her snort of derision. Sam slammed the door on her side and marched toward the building. Ethan followed her up the rickety front steps, his head barely clearing a crooked, low-hanging sign marked Smithson's Co-Op. A cowboy standing to one side of the porch nodded once as they passed, then spit tobacco into a plastic cup. Ethan inched closer behind Sam to shield her from the cowboy's appreciative backward glance.

Oblivious to her charm, Sam entered the fluorescence-lit shop with a wave to the denim-clad man behind the counter. "Mornin', Harry. I need the usual."

"Howdy there, Sam." Harry's voice boomed across the store as he tossed a pen on the mass of papers covering the counter. He shuffled his bulk to the ancient cash register, which, upon closer inspection, Ethan decided could have easily been the very first register ever made. How did that thing even work? Harry punched in some keys and Sam handed over her company credit card.

"Who's your friend there?" Harry peered at Ethan from beneath bushy eyebrows. Ethan bristled under the inspection. At least he was wearing his tennis shoes today and not loafers—though he had the instinctive feeling Harry could probably spot a city slicker a mile away. Why he felt the need to measure up to this man, Ethan had no idea, but he straightened his shoulders and gave his best smile.

"This is Ethan. His family is visiting our ranch and he offered to give me a hand loading the feed."

"Mighty nice of him." Harry looked suspiciously at Ethan as he zipped the credit card through a separate black machine.

Ethan pretended to study the gum selection at the counter. Was one expected to respond to an indirect, third-person reference? Sam was watching him, so he supposed so. He uttered a quick, "Thanks."

"Good thing, Billy out there is filling a big order for another ranch, and Tom called in sick today." Harry swiped the card a second time with a little frown. "I'm shorthanded as usual."

"No problem, Ethan and I can handle it." Sam smiled, but it faded as Harry zipped the card a third time. "Is there a problem?"

Harry leaned over the counter, his gravelly voice lowering to a whisper that could still be heard across the store. "Your card's been declined."

"What? I just paid— Oh, wait." Sam pulled in her lips and briefly closed her eyes. "Okay. That's fine. Can you bill us instead?"

Harry hesitated, and Sam's gaze turned pleading. "I'd like to, Sam, really I would, but your mother was late on her last bill and I can't afford—"

"Here, borrow mine." Ethan slipped a Visa card from his wallet and slid it to Harry. He elbowed Sam, trying to lighten the mood. "I know you're good for it."

Sam's face flushed scarlet but she didn't object, which spoke pretty highly of her desperation to get the horse feed. She shifted awkwardly beside him as Harry ran the card and handed the paper slip to Ethan to sign. He jotted his signature, glad he'd had the frame of mind to use his personal card instead of the company one, so at least his father wouldn't find out about the impromptu purchase. Jeffrey might be able to eventually understand how Ethan refused to sabotage the ranch, but he'd never understand him helping Sam financially. Ethan refused to let the horses go hungry at the cost of his company's gain.

The amount on the slip jumped out at Ethan as he handed Harry the signed copy. The horse feed wasn't that expensive. How bad off were the Jensons really? He tucked his copy in his jeans pocket before Sam could catch the surprised look on his face.

"You know where it all is, Sam. Help yourself."

Harry gestured to the side door where Ethan could glimpse a loading platform and wheeled carts.

She smiled the same forced grin from before at Harry, lifted her hand in a slight wave and led Ethan to the loading dock.

Outside, Ethan gently caught her arm, turning her around. "Are you okay?"

"Fine." She averted her eyes. "You shouldn't have done that."

Ethan frowned. "Most people would just say thank you." He stepped aside to make room for another cowboy exiting the building and crossed his arms over his chest. Was she so prideful she couldn't accept a little help? A second look at her face proved it wasn't so much pride as it was embarrassment. His defensive guard lowered.

Sam drew in a tight breath. "You're right. Thank you."

"I'm not begging for compliments, Sam." Ethan fought the urge to pull her into his arms and hug away the wounded expression on her face. "Maybe the declined card was a mistake. It happens, you know?"

She turned away, out of his reach. "It wasn't a mistake. Trust me."

"Is your family going to be okay? I know you're riding to win money for the breeding business again, but I'm talking about basics. Food. Bills. Mortgage."

Sam kept walking, snagging one of the discarded metal dollies from beside the building and wheeling it toward the stacked bags of feed. "After your family pays us, we'll be fine."

Ethan froze on the concrete dock, her words hammering his heart like a construction worker on overtime. Sam was counting on their guest payment to cover their upcoming bills and keep the ranch going, all while Ethan's family was intending to buy the property out from under them. Angie Jenson might realize why they were there—or partly, anyway—but Sam didn't have a clue. He'd never even told her his real occupation.

Ethan's palms sweated and he clenched his fists. Sam might think he was some arrogant city slicker or a naive tourist, but he was worse, much worse.

Chapter Fifteen

"Declined?" Kate's eyes widened until her eyebrows practically disappeared into her red hair. She shook her head in sympathy as she readjusted her cross-legged position on the couch. "Sam, I had no idea things were that bad."

"I checked into it when we got home earlier today." Sam closed her eyes, temporarily blocking out the yellow, cheery atmosphere of Kate's cozy renovated farmhouse. If the room was to match Sam's current mood, it'd have to be painted charcoal-gray—with angry red slashes on the walls. "Apparently our business card was maxed out and we're two payments late on top of that. How could my mom not tell me?"

"Maybe she doesn't know." Kate's lips twisted as if even she knew the theory was too far-fetched to be truth.

"My mom has always handled our finances, even when Dad was alive. There's no way she'd forget to make payments. Obviously we can't afford them, and she kept it from me."

"Are you going to confront her about it?"

Sam leaned her head against the soft brown couch, exhaustion pinning her body against the leather. "No. I don't want her to be even more stressed than she already is. Plus she'll just try to bring up selling the ranch again."

"She probably didn't mean to keep it from you, but just didn't catch you before you went to the Co-op."

"Well, I don't know how she thinks we're going to pay the next month's feed supply at this point. Harry didn't seem very open to the idea of billing us." Sam pressed her fingers against her temples. "We're ruining our good name and reputation."

"I seriously doubt that. Everyone in Appleback loved your dad, and your family. Harry just has to watch out for his own company. He knows you'd never stiff him on purpose." Kate tossed a blue striped pillow at Sam. "Cheer up. Tell me about Ethan and Daniel." She grinned.

"What about them?" Sam hugged the little pillow to her chest. "Other than I made a fool of myself in front of Ethan—again. I have to find a way to pay him back for the feed supply. No way am I taking charity from him or anyone else."

"I don't blame you. Paying him back is the right thing to do, even if they can obviously afford that and more."

"No kidding." Sam sighed. "I just don't know why I keep goofing up in front of him. It's supposed to be the other way around. He'd never spent time on a farm, yet he's turning into a regular ranch hand. Go figure." She couldn't even be proud of his improvements because, somehow, buried under all the designer labels and hair gel, Ethan possessed a natural talent for all things ranching. If he ever wanted to start his own farm one day, then he'd have no trouble—with a little help, of course. Every ranch owner needed their own Cole.

"Ethan's a fast learner, huh? What about Daniel?" Kate's eyes lowered and she picked at a loose string on the arm of the couch. "I really am sorry I blurted your secret out like that at the fair. I thought if Ethan knew about the rodeo plans, then Daniel did."

Sam shrugged. "As long as my mom doesn't find out until after the competition, it doesn't matter."

"So you're really going to do it?" Kate kept her eyes averted, and Sam ducked down to catch her gaze.

"You think I shouldn't?" A mixture swirled in Sam's stomach, one part apprehension, two parts bitterness. Was her best friend against her goals now, too? She couldn't do this alone. Cole might be on her side, but even that was mostly because he was as tired of the dude ranch as Sam was and wanted a way out.

Kate finally looked up to meet her eyes. "I think you should do what you feel is right. But I would rather Jenson Farms go under than you get hurt or…" Her voice trailed off but Sam didn't have to wonder where Kate's train of thought headed. Sam's own thoughts chugged toward the exact same place every time she mounted Lucy.

"I know my dad died riding a bull. And the irony of it happening at the same annual rodeo I'm entering isn't lost on me. But I have to do this. For him. For the ranch." Sam bit her lower lip. "For myself."

"Then do it." Kate leaned over and squeezed Sam's arm. "I believe in you."

Sudden emotion pricked Sam's eyes and she swallowed the hard lump rising in her throat. "I'm glad someone does."

They sat in companionable silence, then Kate jumped to her feet. "We can't be mushy without brownies. You want one? I made them this afternoon."

"Sure." Sam joined Kate in the red-accented kitchen and got a plate out of the cabinet. She knew the details of the house as well as Kate did by now, after all the time they'd spent here since Kate's purchase almost two years ago. As happy as Sam was for her friend, she couldn't help the finger of envy that poked her side every now and then. Of course she was glad Kate had her own place, but Sam wanted freedom, too. Not away from Jenson Farms, necessarily, but away from the stress of chores, money, obligation.

In essence, her life.

Kate scooped a giant brownie onto Sam's plate. "Big enough?"

"For now." Sam bit into the chocolate square. "Perfect."

"Speaking of perfect." Kate's eyebrows wiggled as she chomped into her own brownie. "What do you think of Daniel?"

A wedge of brownie lodged in Sam's throat and she bent over double, coughing. Kate pounded her on the back. "I guess that's my answer."

"No," Sam croaked. She took the bottle of water Kate snagged from the fridge door and gulped a mouthful. "Went down the wrong pipe."

"So you don't have a problem with Daniel?" The hope in Kate's eyes made the snack churn in Sam's stomach. "He seems interested in me. I know it's a little far-fetched—he could have any woman he wanted—but I think he's sincere."

Sam brushed at a crumb on her mouth to stall for

time. What could she say? That Daniel seemed like a complete sleazeball? That he came across more focused on money and impressions than anything else? That there was an obvious wedge between him and Ethan that Sam couldn't yet explain? She had no proof to offer other than her instincts. But if Sam warned Kate off Daniel now, she'd look jealous after having just confessed she'd made a fool of herself in front of Ethan. Sam refused to lose the only support she had left.

She raised her brownie to her lips and said the only honest thing she could. "Daniel Ames would be a fool not to like you, Kate." Then she bit into her chocolate dessert before she could add any more truth to her statement.

Ethan couldn't look in the mirror. Every time he did, the image staring back disgusted him. No wonder his father always tried to teach him to keep his personal life and professional life separate. When mixed, they proved combustible.

And someone was about to get burned.

He splashed water on his face, blurring the reflection, and turned away from the bathroom sink. It might be too late already, if his heart had anything to say about it. The first time Sam turned that wildflower-blue gaze on him, he should have known this would happen. How could he have ever thought it'd be okay to keep the truth from her?

His father must be a better teacher than Ethan thought.

Ethan snatched the hand towel from its metal hook. The material snagged a loose piece of paneling on the wall, and he quickly tugged it free. That was the second time that week. He should mention it to Sam to have it fixed before he or the next guests occupying this particular cabin scratched themselves on it.

He quickly wiped his face dry with the torn towel. It wasn't too late. He could go to Sam right now, confess his real profession and why he was on the ranch, tell her he wanted nothing to do with his parents' schemes, and hope she'd forgive him.

But the confession still wouldn't be entirely true. Ethan didn't want to manipulate Sam's family, but how could he please both Sam and his father at the same time? Ethan might be ready to step out from the family business of his own accord, but he was no where near ready to be pushed away—emotionally or financially.

Maybe his father would just claim Daniel as his son instead, and Ethan would finally be replaced in every aspect of his parents' lives. Why not make it official when that's where Jeffrey Ames's loyalties seemed to rest, anyway?

Bitterness coated Ethan's tongue and he reached for his toothbrush, even though he'd already brushed his teeth once that evening. He'd scrub them all night if that meant avoiding lying sleeplessly in bed, contemplating how he'd ever get out of the pit he'd dug for himself. Sure, he could blame his dad for some of the shovelfuls of dirt, maybe Daniel for a few others, but Ethan was a grown man. Despite feeling caged in all his life, he still ultimately made his own choices.

And right now, he had to decide if finally gaining his father's love and respect was worth losing Sam's heart forever.

He could push aside his feelings for Sam, and commit to getting the cheapest price possible on the Jensons' ranch—just as Jeffrey Ames hoped. Only he would go about it honestly, not by means of manipulation. That choice would bring money, the chance for eventual independence from the real estate business, and better yet, it would show his father that Ethan was successful and worthy of respect. And maybe Sam could start over somewhere and be happy.

Or he could be honest with Sam. Tell her the truth and accept the consequences. But that choice would bring only division between her and her mother for the kept secrets, anger at Ethan for being deceitful, and would permanently destroy any chance Ethan had of convincing her he could be worthy of her love.

Ethan left the bathroom and sank on his bed in the cabin. It was early still in the evening, but fatigue clung to the edges of his frayed emotions, coaxing him toward sleep. Daniel's bed remained empty, typical for a Friday night. He was probably at the lodge again. Thankfully, they hadn't spoken much since the fair the night before. Ethan wasn't sure what he would tell his cousin if he broached the subject of the carnival. Encourage Daniel toward Kate in hopes of convincing him to back off the pursuit of Sam? Or just step back and see what would happen naturally?

Ethan flopped back against the bed pillows and closed his eyes, not even bothering to take off his shoes. He was tired of feeling as if his entire life was controlled by his father. Tired of being stuck between choices too hard to make. But most of all, he was tired of his conscience complicating his life.

It'd be so much easier if his moral radar would quit getting in the way. Why couldn't he just be heartless like his dad and Daniel? It was more than simply being attracted to Sam that made him think twice before following Jeffrey's orders. It was the entire way his family ran the business. Underhanded schemes, manipulation, shortcuts. When Ethan first joined the company years ago, he was too young and naive to grasp what was happening behind the scenes, until he and Daniel took over the real estate side of the business. By then, it was easier to keep up the heartless rich guy charade that Daniel naturally mastered than demand answers or ethics from his parents.

But a man could only live off the superficial for so long.

Ethan's eyes opened and slowly adjusted to the dim light of the cabin. Evening shadows fell through the partially open miniblinds, draping his dresser and bedside table in darkness. Night was approaching, and in a few short hours, Sam would be in the paddock practicing on Lucy. He would go watch, be supportive, and try to find a way to keep her safe. It would only be a matter of time before Daniel told Jeffrey about Sam's plans to win the needed money for that stallion. Daniel was probably just waiting for the opportune time that would make him look the best. Ethan never once thought he'd be fighting with his cousin for the same girl.

Then again, he never thought he'd be falling for a cowgirl, either.

Chapter Sixteen

Ethan arrived at the paddock just in time to see Sam slam hard onto the dirt-packed earth. Lucy trotted away, but Sam remained motionless on the ground. "Sam!" Ethan's heart thundered louder than a horse's galloping hooves as he ran toward the pen, a prayer leaving his lips for the first time in he didn't know how long. He scaled the fence, nearly colliding with Cole, who already knelt by Sam. Ethan dropped to the dirt beside him, out of breath. "Is she all right?" *Please, God. She's the one bit of good I still have in my life.*

"I don't know." Barely contained panic masked Cole's face as he gently touched Sam's cheek. "You okay, kid?"

The full moon made her stark features seem even paler against the deep brown of the dirt. Ethan fought the urge to grab Sam and shake her. She had to be okay. Why wasn't she moving? His breath hitched.

"Kid?" Cole's voice wavered.

Sam slowly opened her eyes, then blinked repeatedly. "What happened?"

"You fell off Lucy again." Cole rocked back on his

booted heels, forearms pressed against his jean-clad knees. He lowered his head and inhaled deeply. "You scared us for a second there."

Relief flooded Ethan's senses as Sam struggled to sit up. He gripped her arm to help. Sam winced and reclined back in the dirt. "Maybe I'll just stay here a minute."

The worry returned to Cole's face and he hovered over her once more. "You need a doctor."

"No!" The harsh word shot from Sam's mouth like a bullet from a rifle. "I'm just sore. Nothing's broken."

"Are you sure?" Cole studied the length of Sam's body. "Move your legs."

She complied, somewhat reluctantly, Ethan could see by the frustrated expression on her face.

"Now your arms."

Sam wiggled her arms at both sides.

"Neck."

She rotated it easily around her shoulders.

"Pinky toes."

"What?" Sam sat up, brow pinched. "How could that possibly matt—"

Cole grinned and Ethan let loose the smile he'd been holding once he caught on to Cole's game.

Sam's eyes narrowed at them both. "Very funny." She rubbed her elbows with both hands, smearing dirt up her bare forearms.

Cole shrugged. "Just lightening the mood. But you're sitting now, aren't you?" He stood and offered his hand to pull Sam to her feet.

Ethan stood with them, the residue of fear still weakening his legs. That had been close—too close. Sam was crazy to want to do this. There had to be a different way for her to earn some substantial cash. Either she was clueless as to what that other option was—or another secret lurked that she hadn't told him yet.

"I'm going to put Lucy up for the night." Cole gripped Sam's shoulder. "Holler if you need anything, you hear?" He turned to Ethan without waiting for an answer. "Watch her for me." He then jogged toward the other end of the paddock after Lucy.

"I don't need a nanny." Sam rested her weight against the fence and slid down to a sitting position against the middle rail. She leaned over and braced her head in her hands.

"Good thing, because I'm a horrible babysitter." Ethan inched down beside her, reaching for her shoulder but withdrawing his hand before he could make contact. She deserved better than concocted sympathy. But somehow he knew his feelings were no longer fake. Not if the full-blown panic he'd felt moments ago was any indication. He hesitated, and then rested his hand lightly on the dirty, rolled-up sleeve of her shirt. "Why are you doing this, Sam?"

At his touch, Sam looked up, but her eyes didn't seem quite focused. She stared somewhere over his shoulder, as if privately viewing an invisible shadow far away. Ethan turned but the only thing behind them was open pasture, fields of sage green turned silver in the moonlight.

"My dad died riding a bull."

The words fell from Sam's lips like a buried confession and the weight of their meaning pressed into Ethan's chest. He drew a constricted breath. "When?"

"Two years ago." Sam arched her spine, pressing

both hands into the small of her back. She winced, un-doubtedly sore from her fall. "At the Appleback rodeo."

"The same one you're entering." The brunt of her sit-uation hit Ethan then, clenching his heart like a brutal fist. No wonder she'd bristled at his comment of being trampled the other night. How insensitive could he be?

Ethan's earlier decision to persevere with the pur-suit of the sale, regardless of the consequences to Sam, disintegrated before his eyes. Sam couldn't ride in the rodeo—not because of the potential of winning the prize money and preventing the Ameses from buying her farm—but because in that moment, Ethan knew he couldn't handle losing her. It was too dangerous. See-ing Sam landing in the dirt like that, inches from Lu-cy's horns and hooves, was more than he could handle.

Sam continued on as if she hadn't just verbally and emotionally drop-kicked Ethan in the stomach. "Dad was a big star when I was younger." She smiled, still staring into the distance as if she could still clearly view her father across the pasture. "He used to toss his cowboy hat in the air after each winning ride. It was his trademark. Then he'd point to my mom and me in the stands and wink. He always called me his Rodeo Sweetheart, back when I barrel raced. That's Apple-back's unofficial title for a female competitor who wins their category."

Sam's grin faded and the night breeze tossed a strand of her light hair across her cheeks. Ethan tucked it be-hind her ear.

"Dad quit the circuit for us." Her lips pressed to-gether and tears filled her eyes. "Because it was dan-gerous."

"Then what happened?" Ethan's fingers trailed down

her arm to gently squeeze her hand. Sam clung to his grip, clearly lost in memory. Somehow, painful as it was, Ethan had the feeling Sam needed to share this as much for her own benefit as for his.

"He was invited back for a hometown tribute, here in Appleback where his fame began. The crowd wanted him to ride one more time, show off for them. He did it, even though my mom told him he shouldn't." Sam shuddered. "He was trampled. Spent the last few weeks of his life in a hospital bed surrounded by a bunch of machines, all of them beeping, teasing us with the hope that he'd pull through."

"I'm so sorry." Ethan's words sounded hollow to his own ears, completely useless, but what else could he say? He sat in silence, mourning with her for a man he didn't even know but could safely assume must have been special to have turned out a daughter like Sam. What would it have been like to have such a close relationship with his dad? He couldn't even picture it. In regards to emotion or affection, his father was as good as dead, too. Only pride and power flowed through Jeffrey Ames's veins. Not love.

An empty spot inside Ethan opened then, a fresh wound he'd worked for years to scab over. It ripped apart, bleeding regret into the dry places of his heart. If his own father passed away, would Ethan even miss him? He swallowed hard. He couldn't pursue that thought now, not when Sam was about to make the same mistake her father did. "Don't do it, Sam. Don't ride."

Sam's blue gaze searched his, studying, seeking, full of restrained emotion. Her lips parted to answer, but Ethan pressed on, seizing the last opportunity he might ever get to change her mind. He could hear the desperation in his voice but couldn't restrain it. "Let me help you instead. We can work something out. It wouldn't be charity, I promise. Whatever it takes."

She tilted her head, eyes narrowing in thought. Ethan held his breath. She was considering it. Was there a chance she'd finally listen to reason?

Across the paddock, the chute gate banged open. Ethan jumped. Several yards away, Cole led Lucy from the makeshift stall into the shadows of the field near the barn. Ethan turned back to Sam but the moment was lost, that thoughtful gaze now replaced by a determined sheen.

Sam stood and squared her shoulders. "I have to do this." She crossed the paddock, the rigid line of her back further punctuating her statement, her dirt-covered clothes testimony of her resolve. Then she half turned with a scowl. "With or without your support."

Sam strode away from Ethan, fists clenched, wishing her boots were long enough to kick herself. She couldn't believe she'd almost let him get to her that way. She'd been *that* close to agreeing not to ride in the rodeo—and for what? Because he'd looked at her so pleadingly? Because his eyes held a hint of romanticism she'd only read about in books? She'd never been the type of girl to fall for such a ploy, and the fact that she nearly had scared her more than bull riding.

She yanked open the door to the house and remembered just in time not to clomp up the stairs. She pulled off her boots and tiptoed up the steps to her room, holding her breath as she passed Angie's door. At least Sam had jerked back to her senses with Cole slamming the gate behind Lucy like he did. Otherwise, who knew what she'd have agreed to? *Yes, Ethan, I'll drop out of the rodeo for you. Sure, Ethan, I'll run away with you.* Sam scoffed. Right. Like he'd even offer.

Would you want him to?

Her traitorous thoughts mocked her as Sam locked herself in her room and reached for her pajamas in the top dresser. She didn't know what she wanted anymore. The idea of someone arriving to save the day used to sound like a cop-out, a cheesy notion meant only for helpless females in romance novels and low-budget movies. But now, the notion seemed to carry more relief than annoyance. It'd be nice to have the burden of money fall on more capable shoulders for once. Her own were sunburned, bruised and beyond weary.

A verse she'd memorized as a child in Sunday school came to mind as Sam threw back the covers on her bed. *Come unto me, all ye that labour and are heavy laden, and I will give you rest.*

Rest. What a concept. Some days it felt like Sam wouldn't recognize rest if it jumped up and grabbed her around the neck. She slipped between the cool sheets and buried her head in her pillow, the verse still rolling around in her mind. She wished her family hadn't been forced to stop attending services regularly in order to run the ranch, or maybe she'd have found some comfort for their current circumstances in the fellowship there.

She rolled over onto her back, turning her head away from the glowing alarm clock numbers. *All ye that labour and are heavy laden.* At least she fit the description required for help. With the exception of her mother and maybe Cole, Sam didn't think anyone in the city of Appleback could fulfill the prerequisite better. God could take away her burdens, but she had the sneaking feeling He wanted to help her through them instead.

In between snippets of "heels down" and "chin up," her father had often talked about God. Mini life lessons mixed in with the riding instruction. "God's not a genie, Sam. When you ask Him for something, it better not be selfish."

A nostalgic smile turned Sam's lips. The advice hadn't stopped her for praying every night for a gold buckle in barrel racing, but it sure helped her appreciate it more when she finally earned it. She was the only girl in the competition who told everyone God had helped her win.

A tear slipped from the corner of Sam's eye and trailed into her ear. When her father died, she'd lost that childlike passion for her faith along with the passion for life. She still believed in God, of course, and knew better than to push Him away, too. His comforting arms helped her survive the aftermath of her father's passing, but sometime after that, she'd grown distant, developed the age-old attitude of "God helps those who helps themselves." She set out to help herself, all right, and what had that gotten her? A ranch in the red and a lonely existence.

A weight settled on Sam's chest, pressing her burden even heavier onto her shoulders. She flopped on her side and wiped at her wet cheeks. She really was only a crumbling shell of what she'd once been. Her dad wouldn't have wanted her to stop living just because he did—so why had she?

Maybe this rodeo would be more cathartic than she'd first thought. Not only could she win the money to save the ranch, but she could honor her father's memory.

Maybe then the pain would lessen just a little, and she could finally move on with her life.

Despite Ethan's attempts at persuading her otherwise, Sam had to ride. It was more important than ever. If she didn't, not only would her chances of buying Noble Star disappear, but she feared, so would her very spirit.

Sam closed her eyes, begging sleep to come. To erase the physical memory of landing in the dirt just hours before. To erase the recording of Ethan's coaxing, pleading voice now looping in her head on repeat. But most of all, to erase the imprint of fire his gentle touch on her arm seemed to brand into her skin.

Ethan Ames, handsome or not, was nothing but trouble for a woman with a goal such as hers. Sam had no time to wait around and be rescued, and unless God intervened, she would have to once again save the day herself.

And if one day some prince offered to sweep Sam off her feet, he sure as shootin' better be more of a cowboy than Ethan Ames.

Chapter Seventeen

Ethan clicked his tongue at Wildfire, urging him forward from the stall. The horse grudgingly followed, hay dangling from his thick lips. Regardless of the gelding's voracious appetite, it was time for the Saturday-morning ride, and Sam already had her hands full tacking up the remaining horses in the paddock. Cole had stumbled into the arena minutes earlier with a stuffy nose and fever, so Sam immediately sent him away with strict instructions to take medicine, chug a glass of water and drift back to sleep. It looked like the trail ride was up to Ethan and Sam to handle now. Hopefully the stable hand would be better by tomorrow night to help with the bonfire cookout Sam had been looking forward to for days.

He blinked against the sun as he stepped out of the barn, Wildfire close behind. Ethan's mom was lined up outside with the other guests, along with the honeymoon couple he'd seen at the lodge the other night. Unfortunately, so were Mike and Davy. The father was talking to Angie Jenson—as usual, it seemed—and Davy was attempting to scale the adjacent paddock fence where the stallions grazed, despite his father's repeated protests. Ethan groaned. Figured that the one day they were shorthanded, the terrible twosome decided to show up.

He looped Wildfire's lead rope around the fence post, then his hands stilled over the frayed material. When had he started considering himself part of the staff? He shook his head. Those thoughts would only get him in trouble. Ethan might be participating in chores—and there was no arguing he'd learned a lot over the past week or so—but Sam made it clear that was as far as it went. Would he ever be able to impress her?

And would it ever stop mattering so much whether or not he did?

Across the rail, Sam looked up from saddling Piper and offered a short nod in Ethan's direction. He smiled in return, but she kept her eyes on the task in front of her. Hopefully she was just busy and not holding a grudge against his attempts last night at talking her out of the rodeo. Time would tell if she was mad, that much was certain—with Sam, her feelings were right there on her shirtsleeve along with the tiny red checked pattern.

He should have known she wouldn't have gone for dropping out. But in that one moment in time, he had really thought she might consider it. He just couldn't get comfortable with the idea of Sam risking her life, no matter how worthy the cause.

Ethan secured Wildfire's rope with a quick yank. He wondered what would happen if he bought the Stephenses' coveted stallion for Sam? Called Kate's father, swore him to secrecy, handed over the money—even if it did have to come from his savings—and plopped the horse right there in the paddock, along with the other stallions left over from the Jensons' breeding farm days? She'd never know who did it.

He risked a glance at Sam from the corner of his eye. Yeah, right. Not only would Sam know immediately who'd bought the horse, she'd make Ethan take it back. The only thing firmer than her no-charity rule would be Jeffrey's tone as he threatened Ethan's job—and his place in the family. Talk about the extreme other end of an order. Ethan was supposed to be talking Sam out of entering the rodeo—not offering to make the path easier. *God, a little advice would be greatly appreciated.* Ever since his desperate prayer last night at seeing Sam fall, talking to God had suddenly become easy for the first time in years. Ethan wasn't sure what had changed, but for now, he was rolling with it. It felt good being back on speaking terms.

"Wildfire's ready to be tacked up." Ethan patted the gelding's neck as he ducked underneath to edge closer to Sam. "What can I do next?" At least helping out around the ranch made the guilt that seemed to keep permanent residence in his throat easier to swallow.

Sam straightened from tugging at the saddle's girth strap and brushed a damp strand of hair off her forehead. "If you could saddle Wildfire, I'll bring Diego from the barn. Then we should be ready to ride."

"No problem." Ethan slid the blanket on top of Wildfire's back as Sam hurried toward the stables. He couldn't keep from watching her leave, despite his attempts to focus on the buckles in his hand. Did Sam have any idea how beautiful she was? The girls from his regular group of friends in New York would clamor for their compacts and hairbrushes the second they began to perspire—yet Sam would work up a flat-out sweat in this Texas heat and do nothing other than mop her brow with her shirtsleeve and keep working. That kind of confidence was so much more attractive than the superficial beauty of his old crowd.

Ethan frowned as he straightened the blanket and reached for Wildfire's saddle. Old crowd, as in past tense? This working vacation was messing up his mindset in more ways than one. In a matter of days, he had to go back to New York with his family—to his old life, even if only for a short time while he prepared for his new one. He was getting far too attached to Sam—and to the slower pace of Texas, for that matter. Even the southern accents were growing on him. What would it be like to relocate somewhere with a drawl? Somewhere with grass as far as the eye could see, instead of skyscrapers?

A sudden high-pitched scream split the air, followed by a distressed whinny. Ethan spun around. The trouble-making boy, Davy, had managed to slip inside the stallions' fence and now was trapped between two skittish horses. The terror on the kid's face sprung Ethan into action. He dropped the saddle and bolted toward the paddock.

"Davy!" Mike yelled. His face turned white and he rushed the fence, Angie right behind him.

"Grab him, Mike!"

Sam emerged from the barn, her confused expression a blur as Ethan sped past her. "Come on!"

She immediately sprinted behind him, her booted footsteps thudding in Ethan's wake. Mike had climbed inside the paddock but still couldn't reach his son. One of the stallions reared, clipping Mike's shoulder with his hooves. He crumpled to the ground.

Sam and Ethan reached the fence at the same time. She reached beneath the rails for Mike and grabbed his arms, pulling him away from the danger and into the grass beside the paddock. Angie stooped to help, and Ethan vaulted over the top rail into the pen.

One of the stallions snorted in Ethan's direction and pawed the ground. "Davy, very slowly, come around the horse to my side." He kept his voice even and tried to smile. No doubt the horses were sensing Davy's fear and reacting accordingly. It wouldn't help adding his own anxiety into the mix. Was Mike okay? Hopefully the throng of horses had blocked Davy's view of seeing his dad fall.

Davy, eyes wide and teary, took a half step toward Ethan, but was still boxed in between the disgruntled horses. Ethan nodded. "You're doing good. Keep going."

Then suddenly the brown stallion blocking Davy's path reared up on his hind legs. Ethan snatched Davy's shirt collar and hauled the kid toward the fence before the horse could land. The force slammed them both against the paddock. Better that than falling under the anxious animal's hooves.

Ethan helped Davy scramble back over the rails before quickly doing the same. The stallions tossed their heads, ears pinned flat, but seemed relieved to have the sudden intruders gone from their territory.

Davy flew to his father's side. Mike sat up slowly and groaned. "Daddy, are you okay?"

"Yes, are you?" Mike touched his son's head as if checking for injuries, then pulled him into a tight hug.

"That was a close one." Sam stood from her kneeling position and shoved her hair back from her face with both hands. Relief peppered her expression.

Angie brushed her hands on her jeans and turned an admiring gaze on Ethan. "Well done. The horses really responded to you."

"That's funny. They looked terrified to me." Ethan released the breath he hadn't realized he'd been holding. That *had* been close—too close.

"Red, the bigger of the horses in there, would have had no problem dancing all over you and Davy if he was scared enough to do so." Angie tucked her hair behind her ears. "You calmed him down. Very impressive."

Ethan cleared his throat. "If I had known Red was such a beast, I might not have been so effective." He didn't deserve the attention, he'd just happened to be closest to the situation at the time. It wasn't like he'd jumped from a burning building. He was all too aware of his exceeding lack of superpowers—Jeffrey and Daniel served as a constant reminder of that.

"I just hope a certain young man has learned his lesson." Mike clapped Davy's shoulder as they both slowly stood to their feet. "Isn't that right?"

Davy nodded his agreement and Ethan could barely contain his snort. Hopefully the boy's father would learn a similar lesson in paying attention. If Mike had kept his son corralled instead of flirting with Angie, this wouldn't have happened.

Although Angie didn't seem to mind the attention. She ushered the twosome toward the main house. "We better get some ice on your shoulder, Mike."

"I guess we can get on with the morning ride, then." Sam let out her breath. Her gaze locked with Ethan and he couldn't help smiling at the admiration lingering in her eyes. Maybe he'd finally impressed her after all.

* * *

There just might be more cowboy in Ethan than she originally thought. Sam ambled along on Diego, the warm sun lulling her thoughts far away from the trail ride at hand—and straight toward Ethan riding just a few paces away. She couldn't help being impressed at his rescue of Davy. Ethan hadn't thought twice before rushing into the stallions' pen to save the boy. That showed courage above fear—definite cowboy traits. He'd also had the instinct to stay relaxed and try to calm the horses without further panicking them or Davy. Then, on top of all that, he tried to disregard the praise he'd earned, had even looked a little embarrassed by it. That proved he hadn't done it all for show, but to truly help.

Apparently starched shirts and gold-tipped pens didn't hide character as much as Sam first thought.

She absently brushed a fly from Diego's mane. Sam certainly didn't know any city slickers who would have done what Ethan did back there. It was beginning to look as if she wouldn't be able to use that unofficial label anymore.

She also couldn't keep clinging to the anger that kept her up last night. Despite Ethan's trying to talk her out of the rodeo, it was growing harder and harder to stay mad. He was just looking out for her. Annoying, maybe—but sweet. A far cry from the calloused greenhorn that showed up at the ranch just a few weeks ago. Who knew what soft layer Ethan would reveal next?

Sam urged Diego forward on the trail, his long tail flicking from side to side and tickling the back of her arms. It was actually easier being around Ethan when he played the sarcastic, teasing jerk like when he first arrived, insisting on using her full name and expecting special treatment. This mature, considerate—and masculine—version was far too attractive for Sam's own good.

A few yards ahead, Ethan twisted around in the saddle and glanced back at her, as if reading her thoughts. Sam ducked her head but couldn't keep her traitorous gaze from catching his own once again. He smiled and her stomach shivered, just like last year when she rode the Gravy Train at the fair and began to descend the highest hill.

Sam swallowed hard and looked away. She was falling, all right.

"It's Saturday night. No hot date?" Angie grinned from the loveseat in the den as Sam attempted to climb the stairs to her room. Her mother was always trying to encourage her to have more of a social life.

Sam paused on the bottom step, muscles stiff with fatigue and too much exercise. She should have stretched more before riding Lucy last night—not that any amount of preparation could have softened that particular fall. Plus, the at-home exercises Cole had Sam doing left her abs permanently sore, and all the time she spent in the saddle today hadn't helped. She forced a smile, hoping her mom wouldn't notice her discomfort. "I don't think I've ever had a hot date, Mom." For some reason, the words brought Ethan to the forefront of her mind and Sam shook her head to dislodge them.

"You always did prefer horses over boys." Angie smiled. "A fact that had your father elated. But I want you to be able to go out and enjoy life and not get so bogged down by the farm." She sipped from her oversize mug. "Clara made a fresh pot of coffee before she left for the evening. It's still hot if you want some."

Sam started to say no. After all, it'd be a long day of chores and tourists, and she had only a few hours to sleep before meeting Cole and Lucy again. Reminiscing about the past—boys or her dad—was not at the top of her to-do list. But something hollow and wistful in her mother's expression changed her mind. She sighed. "Sure, why not?"

Sam prepared her coffee and sank onto the couch opposite her mom, nestling back against the cushions. "How's Davy after the near accident this morning?"

"He's fine. Mike is too." Angie gave her a pointed look over the rim of her mug. "They're a little shaken up, but okay."

"Maybe if Mike spent more time watching his son than watching—" The words stuck in Sam's mouth and she quickly swallowed them with her coffee. The hot liquid burning her tongue was more tolerable than the heated expression on her mom's face.

Angie frowned. "Watching what?"

Sam lowered her cup. "You. Mom, don't pretend Mike doesn't follow you around like a lovesick puppy."

"Oh, he does not," Angie scoffed, but something that looked a lot like amusement, even delight, lit her eyes.

"He does, too. He's interested, which is pathetic because he must think you're married." She gestured to the ring on her mother's left finger.

"He knows about your father." Angie's voice softened and she studied the glittering diamond on her hand. "We've talked about it before. He also knows I'm not ready to take this off yet."

Relief filled Sam's stomach and she set her coffee

down, suddenly full. If her mom wasn't ready to take
off the ring, then there was no immediate danger of her
getting serious with another man—especially Mike.
Sam's nose wrinkled. That'd be too many changes at
once. No, one problem at a time. Saving the ranch came
first, then finding love.

For both of them.

"But you know, Sam, one day, we'll have to move
on." Angie's eyes met hers as she leaned over to set her
mug on the coffee table. "Your father wouldn't have
wanted either of us to waste our lives."

He also wouldn't have wanted Mike anywhere near
her mom, but Sam imagined this wasn't the best time to
make such a statement. She nodded, lips pressed tight.

"One day you're going to need a life of your own."
Angie rubbed her hands over her cheeks. "Sometimes I
wonder if I'm putting too much pressure on you, keeping you here to work instead of making your own career, your own path. You just said yourself you don't
even have time to date."

"Mom, no. Don't think that." Sam leaned forward.
"It's my choice. Sometimes I get overwhelmed with
the load we carry, but that's not your fault. You didn't
wish for any of this."

"But I want you to have fun, too." The words came
out a whisper and Angie looked away, fiddling with her
ring. "You know, I hate to push you into something you
don't want, but maybe selling the ranch, starting over
would be good for us. Give both of us a fresh start."

Sam sucked in her breath. "But this is our home. This
is all we have left of Dad."

"That's why I haven't." Angie sighed. "Yet."

"Mom, don't be silly. We'll make it through this.

You're just stressed about our finances. Things will get better soon." Fresh determination to win the rodeo filled Sam's heart and she stood up, arms out to hug her mom. "You'll see."

"I hope you're right, baby," Angie hugged her back, arms tight against her neck. "I hope you're right."

Chapter Eighteen

The bonfire crackled and hissed, orange sparks shooting into the night air for a brief moment of glory before slowly extinguishing on a gust of wind. Ethan held a metal clothes hanger over the flames and rotated the marshmallow dangling from the end. He snuck another look at Sam, laughing on the other side of the stacked wood with Angie and a few other guests. Her face, illuminated by the glow of the flames, shone with happiness as she tilted her head back and laughed.

Ethan's grip on the hanger and his stomach tightened simultaneously. He'd thought she was beautiful before, but when she laughed—wow. He tried to look away but his eyes didn't want to obey. Sam glanced over and met his gaze, and her smile slowly faded from laughter to a private grin, just between the two of them. She whispered something to her mom and then stood and made her way around the bonfire.

His stomach flipped again as Sam settled onto the log bench beside him. He opened his mouth to say hi but his tongue suddenly resembled sawdust. What did

that little smile mean? Did she feel the connection between them, too? Their own personal flame—

"Ethan? Your marshmallow is black."

He jerked his eyes back to the fire and winced. His
once puffy marshmallow now looked like a hardened
ball of charcoal. "Must have gotten distracted." He
lobbed it off into the fire and reached for a new one
from the plastic bag at his feet.

"Distracted by what?" Sam's shoulder brushed his
as she held out her hand for the bag.

Their fingers touched as he handed her the marshmallows and this time he knew there was no hiding the
reaction on either of their faces. He held on to the bag,
refusing to relinquish the small bit of contact. "Sam,
I—"

"Listen up, everyone!" Angie stood by the fire and
clapped her hands.

Ethan jumped, and Sam's hand slipped from his
grasp. She drew a tight breath before turning her eyes
to her mother. Ethan reluctantly did the same. *Great
timing, Mrs. Jenson.*

"We're glad we had such a good turnout for our bonfire tonight. I'm happy you're all enjoying yourselves."
She brushed her hair out of her eyes as a gust of evening wind teased the fire. "If you want another hot dog,
there are leftovers on the card table by the oak tree.
Marshmallows are being passed around now, and extra
hangers are on that line over there. Hurry up and eat,
because the games are about to begin." She smiled before settling back onto the log seat by Mike.

Davy sat beside his father, uncommonly quiet as
he cooked a marshmallow on a hanger. Maybe the incident with the stallions had finally calmed the kid.

Ethan had never wanted children before, and Davy's recent behavior only confirmed that fact. Yet looking at Sam, he couldn't help but wonder if their kids would have her wavy, light-colored hair and blue eyes or his darker looks.

Ethan quickly reined in that thought process. He was moving way too fast, even in his own mind. Sam hadn't been sharing a secret smile earlier, she was laughing at him for burning the marshmallow while staring into space—staring at her. He'd better back off before what was in his heart became too obvious on the outside.

"Your mom looks like she's having a good time." Sam pointed across the camp fire. Vickie sat by Daniel and was trying to trap a marshmallow between two chocolate-covered graham crackers to make a s'more. The marshmallow oozed over the sides onto the plate and she laughed, swiping the excess on Daniel's arm.

"She sure does." Ethan's heart flinched at the easy camaraderie his mom had with his cousin. Once again, he was out of the loop. Some things never changed. What was it about Daniel that his parents preferred? His cutthroat business savvy? His willingness to do what the job took, regardless of the negative consequences to innocent people? Ethan didn't want to be like that—but what if that was the only way to ever earn his parents' affection and respect?

Was it worth it?

"I'm surprised your father isn't here." Sam plucked a marshmallow from the bag and skewered it onto her hanger. "He hasn't participated in many of the ranch activities since you guys got here, though, has he?"

"No, he's not really into country life." The words slipped from Ethan's mouth before he could censor.

Hopefully the night shadows would hide the lies he knew were plastered all over his expression. He turned his face away from the glow of the fire. If he couldn't look at himself in the mirror, no way could Sam see his eyes now. His family's entire cover would be blown in a second flat.

"Then why is he even here? I have to admit, when my mom told me your family was coming and you were big-city VIPs, I wondered about it. I'd have guessed you'd hit up Europe or some exotic beach." Sam held her marshmallow over the fire, directly above where Ethan's burned one had fallen moments ago.

"We usually do." Ethan pressed his lips together and busied himself with another marshmallow. The sticky sweet stuck to his grimy fingers, black ash on white sugar. He dirtied everything he touched. But wasn't that why he was trying to get out of the business—to start a clean life? Yet the notion seemed impossible. There would always be one more lie to tell, one more web to weave before he was completely clear of the past—if he ever could be, with the last name Ames.

"What does your family do, anyway?" Sam bit into her roasted marshmallow, pieces of white crust clinging to her lips. She wiped her mouth with her hand but the sugar stuck there, too.

Ethan handed Sam a napkin from the pile someone had left beside him. The truth stuck in his throat and he coughed. What could he say that wouldn't be incriminating? Developers? Vague but still suspicious. Real estate? Definitely not. That'd be like waving a neon sign over his head. "We, uh...well, we—"

"Game time!" Angie jumped to her feet again, clanging a musical triangle. "We have a spotlight set up over there for horseshoes, and for those of you tired of the mosquitoes, in about thirty minutes there'll be a line-dance demonstration inside the lodge."

The crowd of guests immediately stood and began putting away their trash. Sam hopped up and brushed the dirt from her jeans. "Play horseshoes with me?" The anticipation lighting her eyes only further churned the hot dog in Ethan's stomach. He nodded and forced a smile in return.

Saved by the bell, Western-style.

Sam laughed and tugged the horseshoe from Ethan's hand. "No wonder they're flying over the fence. You're not holding them right." She held the horseshoe up so it resembled a backward C shape. "Grab it here, from the bottom. You want your fingertips to curl under the inside edge."

Ethan took the horseshoe and adjusted his grip. "Like this?"

"Yes, just keep your thumb on the flat side."

Ethan reared back and tossed the curved metal toward the tall pin staked in the ground. It landed at least three feet away. He winced. "I thought this was supposed to be an easy game."

"It can be, if you have any sense of direction or accuracy." Sam grinned.

"Very funny." Ethan shook the second horseshoe at her. "Let me guess. You're probably an expert and can play this blindfolded?"

She grabbed for the horseshoe but he held it just out of her reach. She bumped into his arm and he lifted the metal higher. "You're just afraid I'll show you up." She stretched for it again, jumping on her tiptoes.

"Ethan." Jeffrey Ames's deep voice boomed across the open field. Ethan stumbled backward a step away from Sam, his expression full of guilt as his dad drew closer. "We need to talk."

"Right now?" Ethan smiled, but it didn't quite reach his eyes. "I'm in the middle of a game."

"Right now." Jeffrey turned without acknowledging Sam and stalked up the slight hill toward the lodge, the breeze ruffling the sleeves of his dress shirt. Sam frowned. If Mr. Ames was on vacation, why didn't he participate in anything, or relax in comfortable clothing? If the country life wasn't his thing, as Ethan said, then why even come?

Her growing suspicion about the Ames family doubled and she shot Ethan a curious look. "What's that about?"

Ethan sighed and dropped the horseshoe on the ground. "Must be a business crisis. I'll meet you inside the lodge when we're done talking. I think your mom was right about the mosquitoes." He slapped at his arm as he hurried after Jeffrey.

Sam handed the horseshoe to another guest lining up to play, and started up the grassy incline toward the lodge. She might as well go inside and join the line-dance demonstration, and get her paranoid mind off Ethan and his family's motives. Just because Ethan had yet to tell her what he did for a living didn't mean anything was wrong. He probably just wanted to leave business behind while he was away from the office, and was frustrated because his dad wouldn't let him. That would make sense.

But the logic did nothing to quell the uneasy feeling in her stomach.

* * *

"When were you going to tell me about the girl's plans?" Jeffrey's eyebrows mashed into a thick line, the shadows surrounding the main house drawing harsh planes across his face. Music and laughter drifted from the lodge building next door.

Ethan checked over his shoulder to make sure Sam had continued to the lodge and wasn't within hearing distance. "What do you mean?"

"Don't play innocent with me. Daniel told me about the rodeo and the scheme to win enough money to buy some stallion." Jeffrey scowled. "What have you done to put a stop to this nonsense? She can't win the money, that would ruin everything."

"I know." Ethan rubbed his hands over the length of his face. "I've tried to talk her out of it, but she won't budge. She's determined to do this. It all goes back to her dad and his rodeo career—"

"I don't care if it goes back to Abe Lincoln. You have to stop it. If she wins the money, they might not have to sell the ranch." Jeffrey crossed his arms over his chest, gold cuff links glinting in the moonlight.

"I know, I'm trying—"

"Not hard enough." Jeffrey's eyes narrowed. "You act as if this sale has no benefit to you, no commission earned. What's the problem? I put you on this project, yet Daniel has been much more informative in less time."

Ethan's hands clenched into fists. "That's because you're playing him against me."

Jeffrey tilted his head to one side. "Is that what you think?"

"It's the truth, isn't it? Sending me on an errand just to have him pick up behind me."

Jeffrey glowered. "If you had your head on straight, you wouldn't need someone cleaning your mess. Now get back to that girl and stop her from entering that rodeo."

"Her name is Sam."

"Whatever. I want results, not personal attachment. I've taught you better than that." Jeffrey twisted the ring on his finger. "This ranch will be ours by the time we leave next week. Don't make me add *or else* to that statement."

Jeffrey stalked away before Ethan could reply, narrowly dodging another group of guests heading toward the lodge. Not that Ethan had a lot to say, other than the choice phrases running through his mind that he could never utter to his dad's face. Just because Jeffrey had zero respect for Ethan didn't mean he could be equally cruel back.

Ethan drew a deep breath, then headed for the lodge to meet Sam. Regardless of his dad's intrusion, he was determined to enjoy the rest of the evening with her.

For his own reasons, not his father's.

Chapter Nineteen

Twangy country music and the stomping of boots filled the lodge as Sam made her way inside. The furniture had been shoved against the walls to provide a dance floor, and guests happily twirled and two-stepped around the small space in time to the blaring stereo system. Sam poured herself a soda from the refreshment table in the back, grinning at a young couple who kept stepping on each other's feet. They laughed and teased, and the love radiating between them made Sam wish for something similar.

Longing lingered in Sam's throat after her first gulp of Coke. The conversation last night with her mother had only strengthened the emotions Sam tried to keep dormant. Would she ever have that kind of freedom and happiness? Thoughts of Ethan filled her mind and she quickly chugged the rest of her drink. It didn't matter. She had her priorities straight. Ranch first, love second—if ever.

"Want to dance?" Daniel appeared through the small crowd at Sam's side. "Come on, it'll be fun." He set down her cup and tugged her toward the dance floor before she could protest.

They joined the line of dancers, some with considerably more rhythm than others, and tried to fall into step. "This is my first time at a country dance, believe it or not," Daniel called over the music.

"Imagine that." Sam smiled but wished it were a different Ames man beside her. She slapped the back of each boot then turned a circle beside Daniel. "So are you enjoying your vacation?"

A confused expression crossed Daniel's face, then quickly faded. "Of course. The land is beautiful out here. I don't see much scenery like this in New York City." He winked before doing a slide-slide-step combo.

"You seemed to have hit it off with Kate." Sam tried to keep her voice casual. She wanted to know Daniel's motive for flirting with Kate, even though she figured it was nothing more serious than his flirting with her the same night—despite Kate wishing it to be more. "I know she had fun at the fair."

"I had fun, too." Daniel shrugged. "Gotta love a redhead." He winked again, and Sam wished she could poke something in his eye to keep it open.

"But you're not interested in her?"

The music faded away and a slow song on the CD took its place. Daniel held out his arms and Sam reluctantly allowed him to lead her. If not for trying to intervene on Kate's behalf, she would have made an excuse and fled back to the refreshment table. Even now, Daniel's cold, supersmooth hand on Sam's shoulder made her flinch. What did he do, moisturize every night before bed? Her hands were rougher than his.

"I enjoyed being around Kate." Daniel twirled Sam

in a tight circle and pulled her back in. "But I enjoy being with you, too." A hidden agenda lit his dark eyes and Sam tugged from his grip.

"I should get—"

"Mind if I cut in?" Ethan stood behind Daniel, one hand firmly on his cousin's shoulder.

Relief flooded Sam's veins, and she eagerly moved toward Ethan. Daniel nodded once and stepped aside, but the expression on his face warned he wouldn't forget—or forgive—the interruption.

Ethan didn't seem to care. He gently took Sam in his arms and moved her around the dance floor with much more grace than Daniel had.

"I hope you don't mind. But if we can't finish our game of horseshoes, we can at least talk this way." Ethan smiled and Sam relaxed.

"I don't mind at all." Ethan's light touch on her shoulder proved his hands contained plenty of calluses now, and she smiled back. "What did your dad say? Is everything okay?"

Ethan stiffened beneath her arms, but kept swaying to the song. "Everything's fine. Just business talk."

"What kind of business?"

Ethan frowned. "Let's just enjoy the dance, okay? Talking about work is depressing."

"Do you not like what you do?" Sam tilted her head.

"I don't know." Ethan sighed. "Let's just say it's not what it started out as and leave it at that."

Sam opened her mouth with another question, then slowly pressed her lips together. It wasn't worth picking a fight over.

They kept dancing, the music building to a crescendo of violins and guitars, and she rested her head on Ethan's shoulder. His shirt was soft under her cheek and she closed her eyes, despite every instinct in her body warning her to retreat, to protect her heart, to run away. What was one dance?

The music enveloped them in a warm embrace, and Sam squeezed her eyes shut. It was more than just a dance, and she knew it. It was a temporary escape, a hope for something that could never be. She was falling for one of her dreaded tourists, and falling fast. Even though Ethan had become so much more than the negative labels she'd so quickly branded on him, any chance of a relationship between them was doomed before it began. He was leaving, and she was staying. End of story.

"Samantha." Ethan's voice, low in her ear, jerked Sam from her thoughts.

Her heartbeat quickened but the familiar wave of indignation drowned out the momentary attraction. She stopped moving, forcing Ethan to a standstill. "I can't believe you called me that again."

"No, Sam, I—" Ethan rubbed his hands down his face, then exhaled sharply. His arms fell to his sides in defeat. "Look, I know you hate your name, but you're Samantha to me. You're so much more than tomboy Sam. You put on this front of being hardened, but I see the heart underneath. The soft, caring woman who has such deep love for her family, for honor, for animals. *That's* Samantha." He swallowed, his Adam's apple bobbing in his throat. "That's who I've come to care about more than I ever thought possible."

Sam stared at Ethan, the crowd of dancing guests around them blurring into a mix of swaying colors. Ethan cared about her? As more than a partnership, as more than a means of getting what he wanted by learning the ropes of a dude ranch? Impossible. Yet the thumping sensation in her stomach had nothing to do with the bass of the new song drumming from the speakers.

And everything to do with the man standing in front of her, arms open, heart exposed.

Ethan swallowed again, Sam's silence heavier than the crowd pressing around them. He waited, unwilling to risk more of his heart before she responded. Was she that disgusted with his confession? Or was she afraid to admit the same? He could only hope.

Not that it mattered. He was stirring up a violent nest by even voicing such thoughts. What could come of it other than heartache and conflict? Sam had no idea who his family was or what they did, despite her frequent questioning. He couldn't love her and keep such pertinent information from her, information that would destroy everything she was willingly sacrificing to have.

But he somehow did anyway.

"Samantha?" The name fell from his lips again, and this time her eyes closed in anguish.

"My dad called me Samantha." The pain in her expression slammed against Ethan like a Ferrari crashing into a tree. "No one has since he died."

"I'm so sorry. I didn't know." The hollow words sounded even emptier than he felt inside. He was a complete idiot. No wonder Sam was so defensive over her name. She didn't hate it or try to hide her identity behind a tough exterior—it was sentimental. Something special between her and her late father.

And he'd thrashed it like a horse's hooves galloping over a meadow.

"You couldn't have known." The agony slowly faded from Sam's eyes and she squeezed his hand. "I never told you. I just overreacted when you said it. It's my fault, too."

"You shouldn't have had to tell me. I should have respected your wishes from the start." Ethan laughed self-consciously. "Wow, I'm a real Romeo, aren't I?"

The serious expression returned to Sam's face and she looked over her shoulder. "Let's talk outside."

Ethan noticed the crowd thickening as a few couples meandered inside to escape the night air, and he nodded. "Good idea." He followed Sam outside, away from Davy and Mike still roasting marshmallows and laughing by the fire, and toward a quieter spot by the barn.

A horse's soft whinny broke the stillness of the night and Ethan leaned against the wall of the stables, trying to appear casual. Had Sam guided him here to confess her own feelings? Or to break his heart in private?

She stood in front of him, hands hooked in her front pockets. She looked down before finally meeting his gaze. "I know what you mean."

Hope straightened Ethan's shoulders. "You do?"

"Yes." Sam's eyes darted back to the ground. "But it doesn't matter."

"Why not?" But he knew the reason, knew it as surely as he knew the exact shade of Sam's eyes. The same reason he'd been screaming at himself the entire last week. Some lifestyles weren't meant to blend, theirs being an unfortunately prime example.

"For the same reason it would never work between Daniel and Kate." Sam exhaled loudly, the light of the moon above illuminating the contours of her face. Ethan tried not to fixate on the way the glow highlighted her delicate bone structure. She was even more beautiful by moonlight than by firelight, if that was possible. "We're too different. And you live across the country. And…" Her voice trailed off.

"And?" The word tasted like sawdust in his mouth. Not like they needed another reason but he wanted to hear it from Sam herself.

"And I don't know how much I can trust you."

The words, painfully true, took yet another shot at his heart and Ethan swallowed hard.

She lifted her thin shoulders in a helpless shrug. "We barely know each other. We have different morals, values, dreams."

"But you do feel the same." It came out a statement, not a question, and relief eased the wound on Ethan's hopes as Sam bit her lower lip and nodded.

His stomach tightened. He had to confess, had to tell her all. Regardless of the consequences, he couldn't keep up the charade a moment longer. He touched her arm. "Sam, I really—"

She tugged away, half turning her back to him as she stared up at the sky. "There's also the matter of your dad."

"What about him?" Ethan's hand fell slowly to his side, tingling with rejection.

"I've seen the way you talk to him, talk about him." Sam shook her head. "I know you have issues between you, that much is obvious, but it's not right. I would do anything to have two parents again." Her voice tightened and she sniffed.

Frustration mingled with the momentary dash of

hope and his fist clenched. "You don't know anything about my family."

"And whose fault is that?" Sam's eyes snapped harder than her words.

"Trust me, you don't want to know our problems." Ethan wished he didn't have to know, either. Why couldn't he have been born into a family that valued each other more than money? If riches made people turn out like his father, he would rather drive a beat up car and shop at thrift stores for the rest of his life. He'd gladly trade the designer labels and the sports cars for even a week of unconditional love.

"I can't possibly imagine what kind of issue, business or otherwise, could make you two square off against each other like that. Father and son. It's ridiculous." Sam shook her head, her hair brushing against her cheeks. "Do you know how badly I wish my dad was here to argue with? When you've been in my position, your perspective changes. The trivial goes away, and you realize what's really important in life."

"Did you ever stop to consider that might be exactly what we fight about all the time?" Ethan backed away, his fists tightened into two knots.

"How could I know? Here you are confessing your feelings for me, yet you tell me nothing of your real life back in New York—and you expect me to respond with no hesitation?"

"Feelings you reciprocate."

Sam's mouth opened, and then snapped closed. Ethan tugged her toward him and her breath caught. "Tell me you don't."

She gulped, her eyes fixed on Ethan's lips. He darted

his gaze to her mouth and then back to her eyes. She shook slightly under his grasp. "I can't."

Can't as in wouldn't? Or as in couldn't? It didn't matter. Ethan closed the remaining few inches between them and pressed his lips gingerly against hers. She stiffened in surprise before quickly returning his embrace. The kiss deepened and he cupped his hand at the back of her neck, easing her closer. She pulled away, breathless, and Ethan caught a whiff of wildflowers before she stumbled backward.

"I have to go." She touched her fingers to her lips, periwinkle eyes wide, before turning and slipping away into the shadows of the night.

Ethan collapsed against the barn wall, his heart pounding wildly in his chest. If he knew that was the way to win an argument with Sam, he'd have started a fight days ago.

Chapter Twenty

Sam's eyes fluttered open. She stared at the ceiling in her bedroom as the events of the previous night played in her head. Had it been a dream? She tugged her hand free of the sheets and felt her mouth. No, the kiss had been real. So had the argument, unfortunately.

She sighed as she rolled out of bed and turned off the alarm clock. For once she'd woken before the annoying blare, but the thoughts on repeat in her mind weren't any easier to listen to. Intrigue and regret chased circles around her heart as she dressed for work. Nice as the kiss had been, it didn't change her and Ethan's circumstances. If anything, it made them worse.

Sam pounded down the stairs into the kitchen. Too bad she couldn't leave her thought process behind as easily as her unmade bed. She snagged an apple from the fruit bowl at the counter. Clara stood by the kitchen sink, busy preparing breakfast for the guests. "Morning."

"Good morning." Clara dropped a dollop of biscuit dough on a cookie sheet. "I heard the party last night was a success."

Sam bit into her apple and wiped at her chin as heat flooded her face. "You could say that."

Clara stirred the dough before shaping another biscuit. "Good turnout?"

"Mmm-hmm." Sam chomped another bite, hoping her full mouth would discourage the topic.

But Clara shot a knowing look over her shoulder as she dusted her hands on the apron tied around her waist. "I also heard there was quite a commotion by the barn, around say ten-thirty?"

Sam stopped midchew. The kiss. She forced herself to swallow. "You're not—"

"Oh, goodness, no." Clara winked before grabbing the egg carton from the fridge. "I've never been one to gossip, but I think that other Ames boy doesn't live by the same policy."

Daniel. Sam closed her eyes. If he saw her and Ethan, and was already spreading the word, it wouldn't be long before her mother—

"Sam Jenson, I have a few questions for you." Angie's voice, firm and cold, sounded from the kitchen doorway.

She slowly turned. "I can explain."

"Explain why you were seen making out with a paying guest in public?" Angie crossed her arms over her chest, her brows knitted over narrowed eyes. "When I said I felt badly that you weren't able to date, I didn't mean Ethan Ames."

Indignation exploded in Sam's stomach. "How is that any different from Mike fawning over you? Isn't he a *paying guest,* too?"

Angie's eyes widened and her arms dropped to her sides in surprise. The motion caught Sam's eye and she gasped at what was obviously missing from her mother's finger—her diamond wedding ring. "Mom, your ring—" Sam's voice choked. No. She couldn't be ready to move on that fast. Panic gripped Sam's heart.

Angie's expression softened, and sympathy filled her eyes. "We should finish this discussion outside."

Ethan stared at Daniel across the cabin. "I can't believe you told my dad."

Daniel crossed his arms behind his head as he reclined against the bed pillows. "I call it like I see it, man."

Anger burned in Ethan's gut. "You don't know what you saw." Daniel also didn't know what his telling Jeffrey had done. Or did he? Ethan's father would probably be banging on the door any minute. Ethan swallowed, trying to control his temper, when all he wanted to do was leap across the worn bedspread and strangle his cousin. "You just did this because you're jealous. My dad sent you to try to weasel into Sam's life when I didn't give him any info about the property. You can't handle the fact that Sam's not interested in you."

Daniel's eyes flashed and he sat up straight. "That's not how it seemed when we were dancing."

Ethan jerked forward a step, and Daniel held up both hands with a chuckle.

"What do you think you're going to do, cousin? Less than two weeks on a ranch and you're suddenly so tough?" Daniel stood and faced Ethan head-on. "Just because you can stay on a horse and throw some hay bales around doesn't make you a cowboy. Or even a real man, for that matter."

Ethan's fists balled. "And you think womanizing for your own financial gain makes you a real man?"

"You want to hold up a mirror when you say that next time?"

Ethan's mouth opened, then shut.

Daniel smirked. "Exactly. We're cut from the same cloth, cousin. Whether you like it or not."

No. Ethan refused to believe he could be as cold-hearted as Daniel or Jeffrey. He truly cared about Sam, on a level deeper than Daniel's attraction to her physical appearance alone—if he was even truly attracted. Knowing Daniel, it was only the lure of the chase that appealed. Sam definitely wasn't Daniel's typical target for romance. If Ethan had been able to hide his feelings for Sam from Daniel longer, his cousin might not have seen her as a challenge. He'd learned Daniel's competitive nature over the years—an attribute in business, but a coffin nail in personal relationships. Ethan took a steadying breath. "Look, I don't want to fight."

"No, you don't." Daniel swaggered forward. "I can guarantee that."

Ethan glared back. How could he ever have considered Daniel a friend? Had Ethan's own morals ever been low enough that they used to have things in common?

Daniel grabbed his room key off the nightstand. "I'm out of here, man. Good luck with Sam." He laughed coarsely as he headed for the door. "You'll need it." The door slammed behind him with a solid bang.

Ethan stalked into the bathroom and slammed that door, too, just because he could. He bent and rested his forearms against the cool porcelain sink, rubbing his temples with his fingers. This entire project had become impossible. At this point, how could he please anyone?

Not Jeffrey, unless Ethan betrayed everything he'd finally found good in himself and destroyed the ranch so Angie would accept their insulting offer. That definitely wasn't an option. But he couldn't please Sam, either, especially if she found out why Ethan was really there and where he worked. No wonder she'd been so adamant against a relationship with him, despite the obvious mutual attraction. It was a miracle they were even friends—and by the time this project was over, Ethan would be lucky if she'd stoop low enough to spit on him while passing him on the street.

Unless he got out of it now.

Ethan slowly lifted his head. What would happen if he just cut his ties with the business and abandoned the company? He could confess everything to Sam, beg for her forgiveness, and help find a way to save her farm. He could be her loan, could arrange some form of payment for Noble Star so Sam could bring back the breeding business without having to ride in the rodeo. He could even find himself a place nearby, and live in a cheap apartment until Sam's farm was back in the black and she felt able to pursue a relationship.

Ethan groaned as reality struck a cold punch. Who was he kidding? Sam would never forgive him for the deceit, even if technically he'd been omitting information about his career, and not lying. But it felt the same to his heart, and it would to hers, too. She'd never forgive him.

Ethan's head throbbed. It was a nasty game of timing, and the clock kept striking louder and louder. He felt seconds from doomsday, one way or another. Please his father, and not be able to live with his own conscience? Or please Sam and be guilt free—but alone and broke? He'd still have his family in the first scenario, but how long until his father's love and respect hinged on another unscrupulous business practice? If the target wasn't Sam and her family, it'd just be some other family, somewhere down the line.

He'd never be free of it.

God, what do I do? His headache pounded again in his temples and Ethan reached to open the mirrored medicine cabinet for an aspirin. His sleeve snagged the same piece of loose paneling from the other day and he ripped his arm away, too frustrated to care if his shirt tore. The paneling cracked and Ethan winced. Now the wood splintered from the wall and stuck out even farther than before. Great, just what he needed—to confess to Sam that he'd torn up the cabin's bathroom.

Ethan tried to press the protruding piece back in place, but it refused to stick. He craned his head and peered around the edge. His eyes widened and he swallowed. He'd been in the real estate industry long enough to recognize the splintered, chipped wood that appeared to spread behind the entire wall.

Termites.

It was chicken to pretend to be sick, but nevertheless, Sam sat on the couch in the living room in the dark, save for the sunlight streaming through the closed miniblinds and the glow of the TV flickering images across the carpet. She adjusted the throw blanket over her shoulders and snuggled into the worn fabric of the sofa. Maybe she wasn't pretending after all. Watching the home videos of her father made her stomach churn and her forehead sweat worse than if she had a fever.

She'd dug the videos from the box in her room, something else Angie had put away with Wade's trophies and awards—and now, her wedding ring. Something must have changed in her mother's heart during the bonfire, and maybe it was good she was able to move on—but that didn't mean Sam had to be happy that men like Mike were hanging around. Mike would never be Dad.

No one would ever be Dad.

The conversation with Angie on the back steps left Sam's heart pierced with guilt. She shouldn't have spouted off at her mother like that, no matter how indignant she'd felt. But the kiss with Ethan had happened so fast. It wasn't as if she'd planned it. Besides, the odds of someone seeing them by the barn were low—though apparently not as low as she'd thought if Daniel was busy spreading the word. At least her mom now understood the kiss was an accident, not something they'd planned.

Imagined, dreamed of, yes. But not planned. Still, the thought of running into Ethan or having another argument with her mother left Sam weak and tired. Watching home movies of her father wasn't exactly going to help, but sometimes, it felt good to wallow.

Sam angled the remote at the TV and lowered the volume. Her father, handsome under a cowboy hat, smiled at the camera, which shook under Angie's unpracticed grip. His drawl sounded thicker than Sam remembered as he lifted a child version of Sam onto a black speckled pony. "Boots go here." He pointed to the stirrups and Sam watched herself nervously correct her position.

"Back straight." Wade winked at the camera. "Now smile, darlin'. This is fun."

Sam grinned as the younger version of herself waved and beamed with missing teeth. "Hi, Mama!"

"Be careful, honey." Angie's tense voice sounded from behind the camera. "Wade, watch her."

"I've got her, honey." Wade took the lead rope on the pony's halter and began to walk away. His voice softened. "I'll always have her."

A moment later, the camera shut off with a tilted view of the ground and a beep. Sam clutched the remote with both hands, eyes glued to the white-and-black static scratching across the screen. Her heart cracked again for the hundredth time since her father's death and she didn't try to stop the tear that rolled from the corner of her eye.

What was she doing? She couldn't enter the rodeo, couldn't put herself in the same position as her father had brazenly placed himself. What if something went wrong and Angie had to go through the same pain all over again? Sam swallowed, and the remote fell from her fingers onto the floor. She couldn't risk it, not even for the money. She couldn't put a price tag on her life. There'd been one on Wade Jenson's, and it was labeled fame and glory. She refused to die for the same.

She had too much to live for.

Relief flooded Sam's heart in waves, healing the cracked surface and washing away the crevices of fear. She closed her eyes as more tears dripped off her cheeks. She wouldn't enter the rodeo. There had to be another way to find the money she needed for the breeding business, just like her friends had been trying to convince her. God would provide, wouldn't He? Could she trust that, for once?

Ethan's face filled Sam's mind and her eyes opened

abruptly. She sat up straight and untangled the blanket from her legs. Her thoughts raced with figures and numbers and she nodded slowly. Ethan—the proverbial spur in her side—might be the answer to her prayers after all.

Chapter Twenty-One

Ethan slipped away from his parents' cabin, the screen door banging in his wake. He quickly scaled the stairs toward the main house, hoping to find Sam. He'd snuck in his parents' suite and with a quick tug of a pry bar he'd borrowed from the barn, confirmed the termite damage was in their cabin, too—which meant the little critters likely resided in all of them. They'd need a professional to tell, but it was an obvious problem that wasn't going away.

His heart sank as he mentally compiled the tally sheet for that level of repair. It'd be costly for Sam and her mother, to put it mildly. Talk about bad timing. Here she was risking her life to earn money at the rodeo and this setback would probably take a huge chunk of the winnings—if she even placed in the event. What if she didn't? How would they get by? If the Jensons' credit cards were already maxed, it was safe to assume any savings were also depleted. Maybe their insurance coverage would be enough—if they'd been able to make their payments in light of their current trouble.

He reached the main house and hesitated at the bot-

tom step, one hand grasping the warm staircase railing. Sam had to be inside—she hadn't been at the barn
or saddling up the horses with Cole for the morning
ride. But was Ethan ready to see her? Their kiss still
burned in his memory hotter than the sun now coating his back. He couldn't look at Sam and pretend he
didn't feel what he felt. Not that it was exactly a secret,
after his verbal confession the night before. Still, one
rejection was enough—he couldn't take seeing a second one in her eyes.

Ethan took a step forward, and the stair creaked
under his weight. Sam had a right to know what was
happening to her family's property. This could change
everything for the worse for Sam and Angie financially.
At best, it would be a giant inconvenience. They'd have
to shut the ranch down for weeks if not longer to do the
repairs and construction. That'd be loss of income on
top of the cost of repairs.

He backed off the step onto the ground, his boots
hitting the earth with a thud. Right now, he was the
only one who knew about the damage. It'd be a matter
of time before it was evident, of course—but if he told
Sam and Angie, Jeffrey would find out, as well, when
word spread about the ranch temporarily shutting down.
It'd be the perfect ammo for his dad to barge in, guns
blazing, and convince Angie to sign on the dotted line.
Knowing the extent of the damage, Angie would then
consider Jeffrey's insultingly low offer a good one, not
realizing how little termite damage mattered to a de-
veloper with a bulldozer waiting to level the property
for a strip mall.

A light in the front window of the house clicked off
and Ethan eased away from the house, his heart pound-

ing loudly in his chest. Maybe he should keep quiet about the discovery for now, until his family went back to New York—hopefully *without* the contract in hand. Then he could call Sam and tell her privately so they could take care of the repairs. There'd be less chance of Jeffrey finding out and ruining things for Sam's family that way. Maybe by then he'd have given up on the property and turned his business sights elsewhere.

Ethan turned and headed toward the barn to try to catch the morning riders before they left for the trail.

Sam clutched her handwritten paper with sweaty palms as she hurried down the porch steps. Hopefully Ethan would be back from the morning ride by now and she could pitch her plan. She hadn't talked to him since their kiss at the barn the night before and he was probably wondering where she was and if she was avoiding him. Awkward as it would be to face Ethan, she had to do it—for the ranch. She pushed aside the other, scarier reason hovering in her heart. It didn't matter what she wanted personally with Ethan. She would enlist his help for the sake of her family, for her father's memory—that was it.

She trudged toward the barn, her boots stirring up the dry Texas dust from the grass. Okay, so maybe it was for more than just the ranch or for her dad's honor. But she'd never been the fairy-tale type growing up. As a girl she was more interested in the horses pulling Cinderella's carriage than the princess doll, but something about Ethan sparked the desire to be rescued. Every girl needed a knight at some point in their life—even if hers drove a silver sports car instead of a silver steed.

Sam couldn't help but grin at the thought of Ethan

on a horse in period clothing. Prince or not, he would
help her. He obviously had the finances to do so, and if
the confession of his feelings last night was true, then
he'd want to. Besides, he'd mentioned not too long ago
that he would be willing to help her figure something
out if she'd just avoid the rodeo. He wouldn't have forgotten the offer—would he?

Her stomach twisted with equal parts nerves and
hope, and the paper in her hand bunched under her
tight grip. She'd worked out the figures and how much
she'd be able to give Ethan back monthly until the debt
was paid. It'd take a while, but if the breeding business
boomed again as it should, then it would be worth it.
Ethan might brush off the offer of repayment, but she
couldn't let him. Even if they were dating, she'd insist
on returning the money.

Sam paused on her way to the barn. Dating? Yeah,
right. But the idea draped over her heart like a cozy,
familiar blanket and she took a moment to bask in the
inner warmth. Her and Ethan—ridiculous on all ac-
counts. Yet people made long-distance relationships
work every day. Who was to say they couldn't give it
a try? With Ethan's wealth, he could travel as often as
he wanted.

You don't even know what he does for his money.
Sam shook her head, the fantasy fading to the back
of her mind even as the hope lingered. Attraction or
not, love or not, it would never work. They were too
different. So why was her heart still pounding at the
mere idea? Maybe it was worth at least talking about
with him.

Ethan's muffled voice sounded from inside the stables and Sam picked up her pace, eager to see him.

"I can't believe you would keep something that important from me." Jeffrey Ames's voice boomed from inside the shadows of the barn and Sam instinctively stepped away. She peered around the edge of the door frame. Jeffrey's bulky figure and Ethan's trimmer one was just made visible at the other end of the barn, in front of Wildfire's stall. Ethan held a bridle in one hand as if he'd been in the process of untacking the gelding before talking to his father.

"I just found out this morning," Ethan snapped in response, and Sam winced.

Jeffrey's arms crossed over his middle and he seemed to grow even taller. "You could have found me. Daniel did. Don't you know this changes everything?"

Ethan mumbled something Sam couldn't catch and she leaned closer, ears straining.

Jeffrey's head shook. "She's gotten to you, hasn't she?" The words came out more like a statement than a question. Sam eased back around the white frame. Was she the one he referred to? She had to be. Who else had Ethan met while in Appleback? But why did it matter to Ethan's dad?

Jeffrey continued. "You've forgotten why we're here, Ethan. Why *you* are here. Daniel has once again done your job, and done it well. So you can quit the love act with Sam. It's accomplished nothing." He snorted. "I should just give Daniel all the commission from the sale of this ranch, but your mother would never allow it."

Sam recoiled from the door, dread clenching her throat. She sucked in her breath, and the shadows inside the barn darkened until even the sunlight around her seemed dim. Ethan had been pretending to care for her. The friendship, the chores around the farm, the kiss—all of it was to buy her family's ranch.

Ethan started talking, but Jeffrey interrupted him. "You better get your head out of the clouds and start focusing on what's important. Your business is at stake. I didn't make you head of the real estate division of Ames Development for you to slack off."

The earth tilted toward her and Sam braced her weight against the barn wall. Somewhere behind her, a horse nickered, but it sounded as if from a tunnel. That explained why he'd been so secretive about his job. Ethan had used her. She should have known never to trust him. And after she'd confided in him about her father, and the rodeo—no wonder he tried to talk her out of riding! If she won the prize money, the farm wouldn't need to be sold. Surely her mother didn't know what Ethan and his dad were up to. Angie would never keep something like that from her. They were a team.

Regret rose in Sam's heart. It wasn't exactly team-like of her to keep the secret of the rodeo from her mother. She shoved aside the guilt. Part of her wanted to run to her room and cry, the other part—the survivor part that'd kept her going these years since her dad's death—wanted to storm into the barn and tell Ethan exactly what she thought of him and his manipulative family. Her fists clenched and the carefully prepared finance plan scraped into her palm. The pain jerked her back to reality.

"Dad, listen." Ethan's voice cut through the barn. "Let me explain."

Sam shook her head and she fisted the paper into a ball. Ethan's words weren't directed at her, but it didn't matter. She'd heard plenty. Sam hurled the paper wad at the barn wall as hard as she could and hurried back toward the house, tears blinding her eyes. She wasn't sure what made her the most upset—feeling naive and immature for not seeing the deception coming, or knowing that the ranch might very well be sold out from under her.

She swiped at her tears before throwing open the screen door on the porch. Or maybe the reason for the sob in her throat was because any potential relationship with Ethan was now officially gone.

Chapter Twenty-Two

Ethan slammed his fist into the stall door and winced at the splinters that scraped his knuckles. He kicked the door then leaned forward, resting his palms against the rough wood. His dad left, finally—but not before giving Ethan an earful. How much longer could Ethan put up with this nonsense? He was a grown man, but as long as he stayed under his father's roof—proverbially and literally—he'd never break the vicious cycle of lies and manipulation.

Ethan straightened. Enough was enough. Sam deserved the truth, and he would tell her. He was through with the deception, regardless of the consequences to his checking account, business résumé—and love life. If he had to move clear across the country to find work, so be it—and this time it'd be a career that he wanted for himself, not a job he'd been pressured into by his controlling parents. Too bad the only thing Ethan could picture himself doing was right here in the middle of Texas—about as far from his level of expertise as he could get. But every rancher started out somewhere, didn't they?

As for his love life, well, he'd never win Sam's heart by keeping the truth from her. She might forgive him if he spoke up now. The longer he waited, the faster that door would slam shut and lock.

Footsteps sounded behind him and Ethan turned. Sam strolled across the hay-strewn floor toward him, angry red blotches spotting her neck and cheeks.

"Sam? Are you okay?" He held out his hand toward her but let it fall to his side at her violent glare.

"How dare you?" Her hands shook at her sides and she folded them tightly across her chest. "I heard your conversation with your father."

Ethan's heart landed somewhere near their booted feet. "Sam, let me explain."

"No." She poked his chest with her finger, and he automatically dodged her next attempt. "I'll do the talking. That way you can't lie anymore."

"I never meant to—"

"Deceive me? Manipulate me? Kiss me?" Sam scoffed. "I confided in you, Ethan. I told you about my dad, my dreams for this ranch, my fears of losing it." She squeezed her eyes shut before shooting him another fiery dart of hate. "Fears that have been your goal all along."

Ethan cringed. She was right, but not in the way she thought. "No, Samantha, that's not entirely true. I—"

"Don't call me that." Her voice, low and controlled, shook with audible restraint. "Don't ever call me that again." She poked him harder. "And why don't you take your offer to buy this farm and shove it inside your shiny little sports car on your way back to New York. Because I can assure you, my mother will never sell this place."

"Sam, there's really something you should know." Ethan grabbed her hand and held on, but she wrenched it free of his grasp.

"I know all I need to." Sam turned and strode toward the barn entrance, then paused. "I know I shouldn't have ever trusted you." Her figure, silhouetted by the sun, vanished as she stalked outside into the light.

Ethan collapsed against the stall door and sighed. Wildfire nickered and Ethan rubbed the horse's shaggy neck. "I'm too late, boy. She's made up her mind." Wildfire snorted and Ethan shook his head. "You should know better than me once Sam gets something in her head, that's it." He rubbed his watering eyes and drew a shaky breath. Time to pick up the pieces. It wouldn't be the first time, and unless he left his father's business, it definitely wouldn't be the last.

"I'll be seeing you." Ethan patted Wildfire's nose, then brushed his hands on his jeans as he made his way down the barn aisle.

Sam pulled the ranch truck into Kate's driveway and yanked the key from the ignition. Somehow, Sam had managed to make it through the rest of her chores and avoid Ethan. Not that it'd been all that hard. He'd probably gone back to his cabin to mope—and hopefully pack. She shoved away the pang that accompanied thoughts of Ethan leaving. It'd all been a lie. How could she miss that? Yet the memories refused to let her go.

She climbed from the cab and headed toward the front door. Kate met her on the porch with a sympathetic smile. "You okay? You sounded pretty upset on the phone."

"I will be." Sam lifted her chin and inhaled deeply. "As long as you made more brownies."

"Of course." Kate hesitated in the doorway, then opened her arms. "I think you need a hug more."

Sam allowed Kate's brief embrace, then fell against her friend with a sob. "I trusted him, Kate. I think—I think I even loved him. And now…" Her voice cracked.

Kate squeezed her harder. "Listen, it wasn't your fault. You had no idea." She drew back and ushered Sam inside. "Have you talked to your mom yet?"

"No, I couldn't find her all day." Sam swiped at her eyes as she headed for the kitchen, following the aroma of chocolate. "She's probably somewhere with that Mike guy again." Her stomach grumbled.

Kate plucked a brownie from the pan and put it on a small saucer for Sam. "Have you really thought about all this?"

Sam shrugged, brownie coating her teeth. She swallowed. "As much as I want to think about my mom dating again."

"Not that." Kate leaned her hip against the counter. "I mean Ethan. Yeah, it looks bad, but don't forget all the good things he did."

Yeah, right. Sam snorted and took another bite.

"Seriously." Kate raised her eyebrows. "All his help around the ranch. The dance you said y'all shared at the party. His natural instincts with the horses. It couldn't all be fake."

"Sure it could." But doubt pierced Sam's conviction, and the brownie suddenly tasted like dust. Had she been too hasty in judging Ethan? He had been adamantly trying to tell her something in the barn, but in her anger she'd ranted and raved and never gave him a chance.

The brownie settled like a stone in her stomach and she dropped the remaining bit on her plate.

"Uh-huh." Kate crossed her arms. "Whatever you're thinking, keep heading down that path. I can tell by your eyes you're considering it."

"Why are you so eager for me to give Ethan a chance, anyway? No one in that family seems to have a single redeeming quality."

"But you and Ethan really shared something." Kate pointed her finger as Sam's mouth opened. "Don't try to deny it. No more lies."

No more lies. Sam briefly closed her eyes. If only Ethan could abide by the same rule. Was it too late? Had she been wrong to verbally attack him that way? Maybe she'd overreacted. Her spine stiffened and Sam shook her head. No, she hadn't overreacted. But she could at least hear Ethan's side. Maybe he did know something she should.

But first, she had to talk to her mom about the sale. She deserved to be warned.

"Thanks for the chocolate—and the advice." Sam smiled at her friend. "There's some people I need to find."

"Go." Kate gently shoved Sam toward the door. "And keep me posted."

"You know I will." She headed back for her truck, her heart lighter even if her stomach felt heavier. The only way to fix this mess was the truth—the entire truth, even to her mother about the rodeo.

Sam cranked the key in the starter and backed out of Kate's driveway. No more lies.

Ethan shoved open the cabin door, noted the empty room and slammed it. He couldn't find his parents or

Daniel—not a good sign. It was early evening, and he'd skipped dinner to avoid Sam and to get a head start on his packing. He'd figured his parents would be around after the meal, but he'd already checked their cabin, the entertainment lodge and the barn. Somehow Ethan had to stop his family from offering Angie a low price because of the termite damage. She deserved the truth, just as Sam did. The news was financially devastating, but it didn't merit the underhanded deal his father was sure to try and get away with. If Angie would just take the time to do the proper research, maybe call in some favors from locals, they might be able to swing it—especially with Sam's contribution from the rodeo winnings.

He stepped outside onto the porch, desperate to escape both his thoughts of Sam and the proximity of the open suitcase on his bed. Ethan had to leave, knew this day was coming two weeks ago, but he didn't think it'd be under these negative terms.

Yeah, right. Did you think Sam would give you a going-away party with cake and balloons after you ripped out her heart? Ethan's conscience mocked him. He squeezed the porch railing. He was lying to himself now. Maybe the Ames family manipulation gene was too far buried in his DNA. Maybe it was hopeless to even try to be different. *God, do I even stand a chance?* The breeze rocking the branches of a nearby tree was his only answer.

Across the field, the front door of the main house opened and Jeffrey Ames descended the rickety porch steps, pausing at the bottom to shake Angie Jenson's hand with a big smile. Ethan sucked in his breath, noting the bundle of papers in both his dad's grip and Angie's.

He was too late.

Chapter Twenty-Three

Sam quickly threw on her jeans and the nearest T-shirt by her bed. She couldn't believe she'd slept through her alarm, and on the same morning she wanted to try to find Ethan before starting the morning chores. She wrestled her feet into her boots, hoping it wasn't too late. After leaving Kate's house yesterday afternoon, she'd unsuccessfully tried to hunt down her mother to confess her rodeo plans. Former rodeo plans, anyway—though unless she worked out a deal with Ethan, Sam was financially back at square one.

But Angie had remained MIA and it wasn't until nearly dinnertime Sam remembered her mom said she'd be going into town for the day to talk to a few local banks. Sam had tried Ethan's cabin next, but he and Daniel had been out—or more likely—Ethan was still avoiding her. And rightly so, after the way she'd rail-roaded him. Sam still wasn't sure how they'd get past this bump in their developing relationship—no, make that a giant pothole—but the love gasping in her cracked heart demanded she try.

Even if it was impossible.

Sam thundered down the stairs into the kitchen. Clara looked up from baking, her usual bright smile absent.

"What's wrong?" Sam's stomach pitched and she paused at the foot of the steps.

Clara motioned her head toward an envelope lying on the table. "Jeffrey Ames left this here over an hour ago. Said it was for your mother." She turned back to her dough but peeked at Sam over her shoulder. "I could tell from the bold print through the envelope what was inside. I'm sorry."

Sam trudged toward the thick white envelope lying on the wooden surface, and plucked a thick stack of papers from inside. She picked up the handwritten note with a shaky hand.

Ms. Jenson,
Business matters insisted we return to New York at once. Please find the attached check for our stay. Everything was just as you described it. I'm sorry the recent termite discovery changed our initial offer on your property, but rest assured you are still making the right decision. Please sign and return these sale papers at your earliest convenience.
Sincerely,
Jeffrey Ames
Ames Family Real Estate

Sam's heart skipped, then thudded twice against her chest. Initial offer? Her mother knew who the Ames were this whole time—and accepted a bid to buy the ranch? Sam grabbed the papers, the bold word *CON-*

TRACT taunting her from the first page. Her hands trembled and she dropped the papers back on the table as if they might burn her skin. Betrayed by the man she loved and her own flesh-and-blood mother. Who else was keeping secrets from her? And what termite damage existed on the ranch? Her world rocked on its axis and Sam steadied herself against the table.

"Again, I'm so sorry." Clara's soft voice punctured the thin wall temporarily damming Sam's emotions.

Sam stifled a cry with her hand. "I've got to go." She grabbed the truck keys from the hook and raced out the back door, her mind a spinning blur. Her mom didn't have enough faith in them to get through this tough time financially, didn't believe Sam when she told her it would work out, and now, apparently didn't even trust Sam enough to let her help make a decision as important as selling the family farm. All this time Sam thought she and her mother were a team, when in reality, her mom had only seen Sam as a child.

The door slammed behind Sam as she jogged toward the truck. How dare Ethan! He not only kept the truth about his family's occupation and came to the ranch intending to buy it out from Sam, but he knew that Angie was in on the whole thing and never told her. How foolish Sam must have looked, talking about how close she and her mother were and how she wished Ethan could have that same relationship with his father. Now Ethan was gone, and with him the last remnant of hope that they'd shared something special.

Sam jammed the truck into gear and squealed down the driveway, dirt and gravel mixing into a thick cloud that floated through the open window. She coughed.

Ethan obviously didn't need her, and she refused to need him. Even if the ache in her heart never went away.

She steered the truck toward town and angrily swiped the dust from her face. She'd show them both. She'd save this farm on her own, starting with officially entering the rodeo. She still had time. She'd practice the rest of the week and hope that Cole's training, her exercises, and own sheer determination would be enough to succeed.

A tear tracked down her cheek and Sam brushed it away with her sleeve. She didn't need her family, or Ethan. Riding for her dad's honor and knowing that she'd finally earned the title of Rodeo Sweetheart for him would be all she needed.

That, and maybe a heart transplant when this was all over.

Ethan hated the stiff shirt collar around his neck, hated the phone ringing incessantly in his office, even hated the gleaming, spotless mahogany desk. But most of all, he hated the sick feeling in his stomach that hadn't budged an inch since leaving Appleback, Texas, a week ago.

He slapped the disconnect button on the telephone and dropped into his rolling chair. Usually the supple leather was a comfort, but today the smell only reminded him of the tack at Jenson Farms—soon to be yet another strip mall—and the horses he'd left behind. Who ever thought Ethan Ames, corporate real estate executive to a competitive firm, would miss an animal? Especially one that was three times his size and stank more often than not?

The only thing hurting Ethan's stomach worse than

the new hobbies he'd abandoned was imagining Sam's face when she found the letter his father left with the cook, Clara—and the accompanying paperwork.

"Ethan." Daniel stepped inside Ethan's office, his hands plunged into the crisp pockets of his navy suit. "You gotta snap out of it, man. I told you I was sorry for scooping you with your dad."

"Scooping me?" Ethan stared in disbelief. "You think I'm upset because you told my father about the termites first?"

Daniel shrugged.

"You don't get it. You never have."

"I'm sorry!"

"I know. But that doesn't change anything, does it?" Ethan stood, refusing to give Daniel even an inch of ground. "Innocent people still got hurt. A family ranch still will turn into a mall, and the woman I love—" His voice faltered.

Daniel's eyebrows shot up. "Love? I had no idea it was so serious."

"That's because you never think of anything but your own motivations."

Daniel rocked back on his heels, his brow furrowed.

"Just forget it, okay? It's too late." Ethan rubbed his temples with his fingers, turning his back on his cousin. He didn't particularly want to see the view of the city from his office window, hated the reminder of how much he had and how little Sam did—but it was better than looking at Daniel any longer.

"It's not too late." The whoosh of the air conditioner clicking on almost drowned out Daniel's soft response.

Ethan crossed his arms, his back still turned, eyes focused on the city bustling beneath their high-rise building. "Yes, it is. The deal is done and Sam will never forgive me." *I'll never forgive myself.*

"It's not done until Angie mails her signed paperwork in." Daniel's footsteps shuffled across the thick carpet, and Ethan's back straightened at the truth in his cousin's words. "It's not too late—if you can get to Appleback and convince Angie why she shouldn't take the offer after all."

Ethan spun around, grabbing Daniel's arms with both hands. "Why would you even suggest this? You already have my dad's favor and the corner office." His eyes narrowed. "What else is left to take? You've won."

Daniel stared back into Ethan's eyes. "I don't blame you for not trusting me. I've jerked you around as much as anyone else has in this business." His gaze flickered over Ethan's shoulder, then back. "But you're different, man. You don't want any of this. This isn't your world anymore." He offered a little shrug. "So why don't you go back and save the world you do want?"

Ethan's heart blasted his chest in full force, and he shook Daniel slightly. His cousin might be unpredictable and not the trustworthiest, but he did have a point—a great point. "Do I have your word you won't tell my father?"

Daniel checked his watch. "You've got a four-hour head start. Some of us still have to do what it takes to make it in this business, and that means not suffering the wrath of Jeffrey Ames."

Ethan clapped his cousin's shoulder and abruptly released him. He'd take what he could get. He reached over and grabbed his leather briefcase from under his desk and hurried for the door. Daniel remained in the center of the room, and Ethan paused briefly in the frame. "Thanks, cuz."

Daniel grinned. "Go get 'em, cowboy."

Ethan left the office before Daniel could change his mind. But three steps down the plush hall, he knew there was one more step he had to take—in the opposite direction from the elevator. He turned on his heel and pushed open the heavy glass door to his father's office.

Jeffrey Ames looked up with a start from his desk. "Ever heard of knocking?"

Ethan crossed his arms over his pounding heart. "I'm leaving."

"Fine. Bring me a coffee when you get back. And see if Daniel wants anything." Jeffrey continued marking on paperwork with his pen. "Make mine nonfat this time."

"No, Dad. You don't understand. I'm leaving the company—for good." Ethan widened his stance, prepared for the verbal blows about to fly.

Jeffrey's pen lowered and he finally looked up. "What's that?"

"I'm done, Dad. Enough is enough. Let's be honest— I'm not what you want for this company, and believe me, this company isn't what I want."

Jeffrey stood, his imposing figure seemingly towering above Ethan even though their height difference was only an inch or two. Ethan lifted his chin, refusing to back down. This decision should have been made months ago, maybe even longer, and he would stand his ground.

Even if his knees shook a little.

"Are you insulting my life's work?" A growl formed in the back of Jeffrey's throat.

"I won't, though trust me, it's not from lack of material." Ethan shoved his hands in his pockets, hoping the move made him look more casual than he felt. "Daniel is better suited for this job, Dad. Always has been, and you've never had a problem pointing that out. So don't even pretend to be upset. You replaced me a long time ago."

Jeffrey harrumphed as he settled back into his chair. "That may be, but what do you think you're going to do? With no money or prospects—"

"I've got money."

Jeffrey's eyebrows bunched but he remained silent.

"I've been preparing for this day, and it's here. So, I'll be in touch." Or not. Ethan would make that call later. After Jeffrey found out what Ethan was truly leaving to do in Appleback, he'd probably be denied access to his family for a long time. As much as that thought stung, it was the only choice. Ethan refused to sacrifice his morals, ethics and character for his shady father one more time. God would provide for Ethan, would surely bless his obedience for doing the right thing.

And if Ethan still struggled financially, well, then at least he would be on the same page with Sam.

"I won't stop you." Jeffrey shrugged, picking up his pen once again. "Good luck with whatever you choose to attempt. You'll need it."

Yet another dig at his capabilities, but this time, the barb didn't pierce as deep. *Thank you, God.* Ethan gave his father a brief nod before striding down the hall to the elevator, peace making his steps lighter—until grim reality settled on his shoulders. He'd just walked away from the only security he'd ever known, and a future with Sam was iffy at best.

But like it or not, Sam's prince was riding in to save

the day. Ethan checked the time on his cell phone as the elevator doors opened with a ding, and grimaced.

Even if he might be a little late.

Chapter Twenty-Four

The arena buzzed with the sound of excited chatter, stomping hooves and cracking lariats. Horses snorted and bulls pawed the ground, cloaking the worn bleachers and fence rails with a fine layer of dust. Sam clapped her hands against her leather chaps, more of a nervous release than an attempt to rid them of dirt.

"Don't worry, Sam, you look great." Kate smiled. "And you're going to do great."

"Thanks." Sam tried to return it but the effort made her nauseous. Too bad her appearance couldn't be her top concern of the moment. She shook out her hands, wishing the adrenaline had a release from her tense body.

"You okay, kid?" Cole gripped Sam's shoulder with one hand, his eyes boring into hers. "You don't have to do this."

"If you know me at all, then you already know my response to that." Sam adjusted the white paper number on the front of her vest. Seven—her dad's number. Hopefully the number would apply to her father's successful career instead of his tragic last ride. She gulped.

No point in thinking of that right now. She had a job to do—distractions would only get her hurt.

Or worse.

"All right, then." Cole squeezed Sam's arm and turned her toward the chutes. "Go line up. They'll be calling your number in a bit."

"I'm going to get some lemonade. You want a drink before you ride?" Kate gestured toward the snack booth set up on the far side of the bleachers.

Sam shook her head. "No, thanks. My stomach can't handle it." She managed a slight wave at Kate before turning to join the line of riders—all male. She straightened to her full height, refusing to let them intimidate her. Sam was competing against them, yes, but more than that—she was competing against herself. Her throbbing left shoulder testified to that, as did her sore back and tight quad muscles. She resisted the urge to rub the cramp forming in her calf. Maybe practicing the majority of the night on Lucy wasn't the best idea. Then again, a full night's sleep wasn't much ammo against the thousand-plus pound animal in the chute, either.

The bull nearest Sam huffed, and the fluorescent arena lights glinted off the giant ring in his nose. Sudden panic gripped Sam in a vise and she clutched Cole's sleeve with both hands. "Am I crazy?"

Cole pried his shirt from her grip. "You just said you made your decision. So quit acting like a greenhorn."

"I know." Sam swallowed. "But it's a crazy decision."

"An inexperienced female bull rider competing in the same rodeo her father used to? Nothing but crazy." Cole's voice softened. "But you can do it. You're ready."

"I practiced on a steer, Cole. A *steer*." Sam's voice trembled and she couldn't tear her gaze away from the bulls waiting their turn—for revenge. She shook her head to clear it. "4-H kids ride steers. Those giant animals in those chutes are the real deal. I might as well have been practicing on a dairy cow."

"That's not true, and you know it. Quit spurring on your fear." Cole shoved his cowboy hat away from his eyes and held Sam's gaze. "The same concepts apply to both steer and bull riding. Grip with your legs, keep your upper body loose, and counterbalance by leaning the opposite direction of the buck." He tapped the top of Sam's hat. "The rest is up here."

Sam nodded slowly. She could do this. She *would* do this—for her dad. Her mother might not believe in her, but Sam would prove her wrong. She'd avoided Angie the majority of the week, throwing herself into her chores and her training. Sam couldn't look at her mom without the fury of the secret sale boiling in her stomach—right beside the guilt of her own kept secrets she tried to ignore.

She'd prove Ethan wrong, too. Just remembering his betrayal sent a spark of anger trailing Sam's spine. It also made her heart pound painfully in her chest, but she wouldn't think about that right now. The love still residing within would catch up to her mind's resolve soon enough. In the meantime, there were bigger issues to conquer. Her eyes narrowed. "I'm ready."

She had to win. Losing would only earn Sam a permanent job at the dude ranch and the title of laughingstock among the male competitors—not to mention a likely ride in an ambulance. She forced back a shudder. *Focus, focus.*

"Up next, number thirteen, George Daniels." The announcer's drawl boomed over the loudspeaker with a burst of static. "On deck, contestants number four and seven."

"That's you." Cole nudged Sam toward the chutes. "Eyes on the target, kid. You can do it. I'll be there in a few to help you mount."

Sam's boots—and previous burst of self confidence—felt connected to someone else as she shuffled her way toward the line of riders. *God, help me. I don't want to make the same mistake Dad did.*

Ethan thrust a handful of bills into the taxi driver's hand and jumped from the cab. There'd been no time to arrange a car rental from the airport. He slammed the door and raced up the walk to the main house. *Please let them be inside, please let them be inside.* The prayer echoed in rhythm to his pounding heart as he banged on the front door. He waited, then knocked again.

Clara opened the door, a spatula in one hand and a firm wrinkle nestled between her drawn eyebrows. "Can I help you?" Attitude radiated from her apron-covered body and Ethan took a step back.

"I'm looking for Samantha—I mean, Sam, and Angie. Are they here?" He craned his head to look over Clara's shoulder, but she pulled the door halfway shut.

"I believe that's none of your concern." Her arms crossed over her chest and Ethan took another step away.

"It's important. Please." He heard the panic in his voice and cleared his throat. "I can't let her— It's urgent. Trust me."

"Can't let her what?" Clara's hand holding the spatula lowered and the frown on her face eased.

Ethan ran a hand over his hair and huffed an impatient breath. "I can't let her sell the ranch to my father's company."

"Your father's company? I thought it was yours, too."

"Not since I left a few hours ago to come warn Angie and Sam about his intentions."

Clara's lips twitched to the side. "Well, why didn't you say so in the first place? You better stop her quick. Angie signed the papers and just left for the post office to mail them. Never seen a body so discouraged. But she was taking 'em anyway."

"She's already gone? Where's the post office?" Ethan's hands balled into fists. He couldn't have come this far to be too late. Maybe he could fly back to the office in New York and catch the letters in the mail before they reached his father—assuming he would even be allowed back on the premises after this move he pulled.

"You can still catch Ms. Jenson. The post office is only a mile or two away. Take one of the horses." Clara pointed to the barn. "Looks like Wildfire is still saddled from the afternoon ride. I know Cole won't mind if you borrow him, he's not here anyway."

Ethan stopped on his trek down the stairs. "Where is he?" Cole never left the ranch except for supplies, not even when he was sick last weekend.

Clara glanced over her shoulder, then back down at Ethan. "You didn't hear this from me, but Cole and Sam are at some rodeo in town. I don't know what they're up to, but I know they have secrets. Big ones."

Ethan's heart jump-started with a jerk. The rodeo. That was tonight? His head swam and he gripped the staircase railing. Sam was going to ride—and he wouldn't be there. What if she got hurt? He squeezed his eyes shut as panic racked his senses.

He couldn't be in two places at once. Stop Angie from mailing the contract, or stop Sam from making a huge—and potentially deadly—mistake?

Sam's breath came in tight gasps. The cowboy on her right nudged her with his shoulder. "You okay there?"

She forced a smile and squeezed the rail with both hands. The dirt ground under her feet felt as sure as quicksand. "Fine." *Just perfect. I'm about to die the same way my father did.* Terror gripped her with two hands and she struggled against the panic clawing at her lungs.

"Good luck." The cowboy, number four, tipped his hat to her and moved up in line to take his turn.

Sam couldn't help but stare as he easily scaled the chute and settled on the bull's broad back. He made it look so easy. She squeezed her eyes shut. *You can do this, you can do this. Oh, no I can't!* Was the farm worth it? Worth her life? If she died, there would be no breeding business to enjoy again. No more horseback riding. No more campfires and trail rides and long talks with Kate.

No more kisses with Ethan.

Her heart skipped a beat and Sam opened her eyes. Dust flew as a bell dinged and cowboy number four charged into the arena. She stared unseeing as a dozen memories with Ethan flickered before her. His taut arm muscles as he lifted bale after bale of hay into the bed of her truck. The expression of content he wore while ambling beside her on a trail ride. His dark chocolate gaze daring her to hate him. Oh, how she'd tried. But Ethan's true character overcame the prejudiced, city-slicker label she'd stuck on him at his arrival, and he quickly became a real cowboy in her eyes.

If he hadn't betrayed her, she'd have easily entertained ideas of him being the one.

A buzzer sounded and jerked Sam from her thoughts. She swallowed as contestant number four slipped from the bull and jogged to the chute. The horned beast galloped toward the clown attendants waiting for him, and they quickly corralled the animal at the other end of the arena.

She was next. It would take several minutes to ready the next bull, so she had five, eight minutes tops to stall.

Or escape.

Sam rubbed slick palms down her jeans. *Just breathe.* She inhaled deeply but the anxiety refused to let go. *God, if I'm making a mistake, stop me!*

"Sam!"

Sam's eyes widened at the familiar voice calling to her from the stands. She turned just in time to see Ethan and her mother running to her through the crowd, pushing past a man in a black hat and nearly knocking over a young girl with braided pigtails.

Ethan reached Sam first, grabbing her shoulders with both hands. He panted, trying to catch his breath. "You can't—please don't—" He squeezed her arms and tried again. "Don't hate me."

Tears crowded Sam's eyes and she blinked rapidly against the threatening torrent. "Why not?" Her heart screamed a thousand reasons why not and she begged them to shut up. Ethan had betrayed her, had kissed her as if he meant it and pretended to like her. To love her. All for the sake of a real estate sale.

But could he really have pretended that realistically?

"Why not?" Ethan's voice pleaded over the sudden applause from the stands behind them. "Because I'm here." His eyes searched hers and Sam turned away. But her hands shook for reasons completely outside her pending bull ride, and she couldn't deny it another minute. She opened her mouth, still unsure what to say, but her mom interrupted.

"Sam, don't do this." Angie brushed messy hair from her eyes and futilely tried to push the loose strands into her ponytail. "I should have told you about Jeffrey's offer. But I wanted to make the best decision for us, and knew that you would influence me toward keeping the property. Sometimes you're too strong for your own good. I wanted you to be able to get on with your life." She let out her breath. "But I had no idea how much the breeding farm really meant to you until Ethan talked to me on the way here."

"What choice do we have? If I don't ride, you're going to sell." Sam's voice caught in her throat and a few of the tears pressing against her lids slipped free. "You might still sell anyway."

"No, she's not. Or rather, she shouldn't." Ethan reached toward Sam, then let his hand fall to his side. Her fingers burned just imagining the contact and she squeezed her hand into a protective fist. Ethan continued, turning to Angie. "My dad can't be trusted. The highway is being relocated near your ranch. If he buys your property, it's being turned into a strip mall. He lied about his intentions in order to offer a lower price. I've known that, but thought if I could just play his game long enough, I could escape it all. But there's no escaping his level of lying and manipulation." He exhaled slowly. "I just thought if I held in there a little longer and stayed on the inside, I could protect you, Sam. I'm sorry for deceiving you. I never meant to."

"I know." The words left her lips before she could fully process and Sam blinked in surprise.

"You do?" Ethan's head dipped toward hers.

She nodded and wiped at her eyes. "I do." The truth filled her heart in sweet relief. She knew Ethan couldn't hurt her that badly, not after all they'd been through together. The doubts scratched the surface but deep down, Sam knew better. The overheard conversation and anger at Angie over selling the ranch had pushed Sam over the edge. If she'd just thought long enough about Ethan's true character, the man he'd been slowly revealing himself to be these past couple weeks, she would have seen it was a mistake.

Ethan reached again for Sam's hand. And slowly, carefully, she threaded her fingers through his.

Chapter Twenty-Five

Ethan's heart raced at the gentle contact with Sam. He swallowed against the knot rising in his throat. "Do you forgive me? I did lie to you—at first because I was doing my job. But then to protect you. But I'm done, Sam. No more manipulation. No more false pretenses. It's just me." His hands shook and he squeezed her fingers, hoping she couldn't feel the desperation in his touch. "Hopefully that's enough."

"Oh, I think it's plenty." Sam smiled up at him and his stomach pitched like he was riding a roller coaster—or maybe a bull. Her lips parted slightly and he automatically leaned closer.

Angie cleared her throat. Sam winced. "Sorry, Mom."

"You don't have to apologize." Angie gestured toward the arena. "But I believe they just called your number. Your dad's number." Her eyes darkened with emotion.

Sam shook her head at Angie's drawn expression. "I can't do this to you, Mom. I thought I could, but I can't. It's not worth it. Even if we lose the farm."

Angie crossed her arms. "I don't want to accept Mr. Ames's offer, especially if he's turning our beloved property into a mall. But with this termite issue, I'm not sure how the ranch will survive otherwise."

"Unless I ride." Sam's eyes shut briefly and she sighed.

"I have an alternative plan." Ethan tugged at Sam's hand to get her attention. His next statement would either seal their relationship or ruin it for good. But he had to try. He couldn't stand by and let the Jenson farm go to ruins when he had the means to stop it. "Look, I'm buying Noble Star for your ranch, and that's that. You can think of it as a business investment or pay me back however and whenever you want, but I'm doing it." *Or maybe you'll marry me in the next six months and the stallion will become mine along with your heart.* He smiled, hoping Sam couldn't read his eyes. Too soon for the M word—but not for long.

Sam's mouth opened and Ethan gently tapped her chin to close it. "And that's that."

"Ethan, I can't let you do this." Angie touched Ethan's shoulder, stepping closer as a family carrying popcorn shouldered past them toward the stadium seats. "It's too much."

"You don't realize all you two have done for me." Ethan slipped his arm around Sam's waist, glad the pressing crowd gave him reason to lean closer to speak. "You Jenson women showed me how a family is supposed to operate. Without that inspiration, I might never have gotten the guts to quit my father's business and try life on my own. So consider this my gift back to you." The purchase would negatively affect his savings account, but at the moment, he could think of no worthier cause. He'd figure it out—get a real job or even two. Whatever it took.

Angie's eyes filled with tears and she nodded slowly. "I can do that. Sam, can you?"

Ethan tucked a lock of Sam's hair behind her ear and she studied his expression before nodding slowly. "I think so. But we *will* pay you back."

His heart swelled with the reality of what she was entrusting him with, and he smiled in relief. But there was a catch. "I wasn't finished." He cupped Sam's chin in his hand and held her gaze. "I want you to ride."

"What?" Sam's eyes widened. "I thought that was the whole point of your offer—to keep me from riding. It's all you've wanted since you got here—for various reasons." She rolled her eyes.

"The main reason was because I was worried about you." Ethan drew his hand from her face. "But I know you, Sam. If you don't do everything in your power to meet your goals, you'll never be happy—and you'll end up resenting me for buying Noble Star, even if you pay me back. You'll always wonder what if."

"And what if I win?" Her eyebrows quirked into a question mark.

"Then the prize money will go to the ranch and the cost of repairs for the termites and whatever else you need." Ethan gestured toward the arena and the bulls waiting in the chutes. "It's your choice. I support you regardless."

"But, Mom…" Sam's voice trailed off and she cast an anxious expression at Angie. "I can't. You'd never forgive me."

"If it's important to you, then do it." Angie's voice,

soft and firm, barely rose about the noise of the spectators and announcer.

"Are you sure?" Sam's cheeks flushed.

"Make your father proud, honey. He'd want this." Angie turned Sam toward the chutes. "You've worked so hard to get here. If you want to do this, we'll be in the stands cheering you on."

Sam stumbled toward the pen, looking over her shoulder only once before giving a determined nod. Her gaze lingered on Ethan, then with shoulders shoved back, she marched toward the bulls.

Angie gripped Ethan's arm with white knuckles. "I hope I'm not making a mistake."

Sam really hoped she wasn't making a mistake. She quickly made her way toward the pen, half hoping she was too late and her call was over. But the other cowboys by the pen motioned for her to hurry.

"Just in time." Cole appeared to her right and guided her to the chute. He hoisted her onto the fence. "Where've you been?"

She swung one leg over the rail. "Ethan and Mom are here."

Cole's lips twisted. "Good. But don't get distracted." He gave her a final boost.

Sam gasped as she settled on the bull's wide, leathery haunches. *Too fast, too fast.* She couldn't catch her breath, couldn't think. Couldn't process. Her legs gripped both sides of the bull automatically and Cole helped her wind her hand around the rope.

"Hang on tight." He cinched the cord tighter. "How's that feel?"

Sam wiggled her gloved fingers beneath the rope.

"Secure." Right. Like there was anything secure about what she was going to do.

A cowboy hanging on the fence nearby squinted at Sam beneath his hat. "You ever done this before?"

Sam managed to shake her head once before two other riders to her left laughed. "Good luck, darlin'." One nudged his friend with his elbow and shook his head.

"Shut it or beat it." Cole gave the group a menacing glare and they quickly snapped their mouths closed and looked the other direction.

"And now, contestant number seven, Samantha Jenson." The announcer's drawl rang through the arena and a hush blanketed the crowd. Sam sucked in her breath. She must have accidentally scrawled her full name on the sign-up form. Now the entire arena knew she was the only female contestant of the night. Could she really pull this off?

"Focus." Cole's voice brought her back to the present, away from memories of her dad and away from Ethan and Angie sitting exactly six rows up in the bleachers.

"Looks like we've got a potential Rodeo Sweetheart here tonight." The announcer chuckled. "Good luck, honey!"

"Why does everyone keep saying that?" Sam gritted her teeth.

Cole flashed a white smile and dropped backward off the fence. "Good luck." He tipped his hat at her and nodded to the chute attendants.

The buzzer sounded, the gate opened, and Sam bit back a scream. She squeezed with both legs until her leg muscles felt numb. The bull rocked forward, wild and out of control. Sam struggled to keep her eyes open.

She tried to focus on the giant beast's head, so she could predict which way to lean. *Just like on Lucy.* No, who she was kidding? This bull was bigger, meaner, and faster—not to mention more likely to chase her when she fell off. Sam forced the thought from her mind. *Hang on, hang on.*

The seconds ticked by but felt like months. Dirt stirred by the bull's hooves slapped her face. Her body ached but adrenaline drowned out the cry of her muscles. Somewhere behind her, Cole's voice rang through the noise and cries of the spectators, and she focused on his encouragement. Then Ethan's cry rose above the crowd. "You can do it, Sam!" She clung to his words as she twisted left, then right.

"Two seconds left!"

Sam wasn't sure who yelled those inspiring words but she clenched her teeth and found a deeper level of strength. Two seconds. She could do this. Not for her dad, not for the ranch, but for herself.

The bull gave a final buck just as the buzzer sounded. Sam's arm dropped like a limp noodle from her death grip on the rope and she slipped from the animal's broad back. *Run, run!* But she collapsed to the ground, her legs unable to support her, as the bull pounded the earth. Dirt crowded her vision and she coughed, curling into a protective ball. A flash of red and yellow to her left proved the rodeo clowns were doing their job, and within seconds the bull was at the other end of the arena.

Sam struggled to her knees. *It's over, it's over.* The chant echoed in her mind but all she could hear was the roar of the spectators, on their feet and applauding. Cole jogged to her side and helped her stand. "Samantha! Samantha!" The crowd cheered and stamped in rhythm.

Tears pressed Sam's eyes as she smiled at Ethan, who was clapping so hard she thought he might sprain his arm. Tears poured down her mom's face, and matching ones slipped down Sam's cheeks as Ethan, Kate and Angie began making their way down the bleachers toward the arena. She'd done it. But there was one last thing to do.

She tugged off her dusty cowboy hat and threw it high above her head. It spiraled into the air in a blurry, tan arch. *This one's for you, Dad.*

Ethan met her at the side of the pen. Sam scooped up her discarded hat before climbing over to join him. She dropped into his arms. He squeezed her in a tight embrace and then stepped back to meet her gaze. "You were amazing."

"I was terrified." Sam laughed and her throat felt raw. She'd done it. Now it was a matter of waiting for her score. But she was already a winner—even if it felt at the moment she had spaghetti noodles for arms.

Ethan's hands rested on her waist and she forgot the ache in her muscles. "By the way, did I tell you I was leaving the real estate business?"

Sam shrugged. "I sort of figured that when you said you left your father's company to come warn us about him."

"Well, I forgot to mention there's one more sale I still have to make."

Sam frowned. "What do you mean?"

"You know that vacant property down the street from Kate? One hundred acres, small catfish pond, three-bedroom ranch house?"

Sam nodded. "It's been for sale for months."

"Not for very much longer." Ethan grinned.

Sam's eyes widened. "You mean—"

Ethan cut her off with a kiss, which she gladly returned. She wound her arms around his neck and breathed in his spicy cologne.

Angie and Kate joined them by the pen, and Sam reluctantly ended the kiss. Angie looped her arm around Sam's shoulders and squeezed. "They're about to announce the winners." The relief dripping from her voice nestled in Sam's heart and she hugged her mother back. It was over. No matter what happened from here, they were going to be okay.

"You did so good!" Kate squealed and joined the group hug around Sam. "Just don't do that again anytime soon, okay? I think I was just as nervous as you were." She clutched her stomach.

Cole stepped up beside them, and elbowed Sam's ribs. "It's in the bag, kid. That bull was mean."

"Now you tell me." But even sarcasm couldn't dampen the joy bubbling in Sam's heart. The farm still needed the money, but even if Sam didn't place, she'd found what she was looking for. Peace. Contentment. Happiness.

And Ethan. She looked up at him and smiled, then realized she'd been tuning out the announcer.

"Contestant number thirteen, George Daniels, eighty-nine out of a possible one hundred points."

Sam winced. That was a great score. Her nails dug into Ethan's shirtsleeve and Angie's arm tightened around Sam.

"Dennis Montgomery, contestant four, seventy-two!"

Cole sucked in his breath. "You should be next."

The announcer paused as papers shuffled over the loudspeaker. "And finally, contestant number seven, Samantha Jenson, with a score of eighty-eight. Congratulations to our winner, George!"

"Second place!" Cole ruffled Sam's hair. "Not bad, kid. There's a cash prize for that."

"Sam, I can't believe it." Angie grabbed her into a hug. "Your father would be so proud! I'm so proud."

Sam hugged her, then pulled back. "I want the farm to have all the money." She reached over and took Ethan's hand. "Use it for whatever we need the most, Mom. If we need to keep running the dude ranch, it's fine by me."

"Are you sure?" A puzzled frown tightened Angie's brows. "But the breeding business—"

"Sam, it's your dream." Kate's head tilted to one side. "It's what you've worked for this whole time."

"I'm sure. If it hadn't been for our family's new venture into dude ranching, I've have never met Ethan." Sam grinned at Cole. "But if you do keep the dude ranch, you have to hire Cole some extra help." She winked and Cole laughed.

Angie nodded. "We'll figure out all the details later. With your prize winnings, we have options now." She brushed a tear from Sam's cheek. "Go get your check, baby. We'll meet you at the truck." She motioned for Cole and Kate to follow her, leaving Sam alone with Ethan—or as alone as they could be in a crowded arena.

"I'm so proud of you, Samantha." He winced. "I'm sorry, I've got to quit calling you that."

"No, I want you to." She reached up and touched his cheek. "At first I was riding for money. Then for my dad. But I realized something while I was out there on that bull. Mainly, that I was crazy." She shuddered and laughed. "But secondly, that this was for me all along. I needed to make peace with the past. Mom finally moved on from Dad's death. But I couldn't do that without proving to myself what I was capable of."

He smoothed her hair. "You're the strongest woman I know."

"I realize now that being strong outwardly wasn't being strong emotionally. Like my mom said, sometimes I'm so strong that I live in denial. I had to accept my dad's death—not drive myself crazy trying to prove myself to him or to his memory. I finally feel like I've made him proud. Not because I rode a bull, but because I realized it's okay to move on, to live like he would have wanted me to." She smiled. "So call me Samantha. I think my dad would like that."

"I can do that." Ethan wrapped his arms around Sam and she snuggled against him with a sigh. "Exhausting day."

"No kidding." She laughed hoarsely.

"Looks like you didn't win the title of Rodeo Sweetheart after all."

"Titles are overrated." Sam mumbled into his shirt, inhaling the crisp aroma of laundry detergent mixed with the familiar scent of horses and leather.

"You'll always be my sweetheart," Ethan whispered into her hair, and she shivered.

"Promise?"

"Isn't a real cowboy as good as his word?" Ethan smiled.

Sam grinned back. "I don't see a real cowboy around here."

Ethan stiffened in protest. "Hey, I've made some real progress—"

"You didn't let me finish."

He quirked an eyebrow.

Sam tightened her grip around him and rose up on tiptoe to meet him face-to-face. "I only see the one man capable of lassoing my heart." She pressed her lips against his before Ethan could argue.

But from the way he kissed her back, she knew he wouldn't have anyway.

* * * * *

Questions for Discussion

1. Sam's family ranch is everything to her. Have you ever been particularly attached to a house or piece of land before? Why?

2. One of the reasons Sam is so anxious to make her family home what it used to be is because of her father. Have you ever tried to do something in honor of a lost loved one? What was it?

3. In the story, Sam feels that she can't talk openly with her mother, Angie, about her plans to bull ride because she feels her mom would disagree and talk her out of her goal. Have you ever had to keep a secret in order to do what you felt was the right thing?

4. When Sam first met Ethan, she labeled him a "city slicker" and a "greenhorn tourist." Have you ever judged someone prematurely before meeting them? Why?

5. Ethan was immediately attracted to Sam because she was so different from the type of girls he was used to seeing in New York. Do you believe opposites attract as a rule or as an exception?

6. Ethan's family was at the ranch under false pretences. After Ethan got to know Sam, he wanted to share his secret with her. Why did he feel he couldn't yet?

7. Jeffrey Ames only cared about wealth and status, even at the sacrifice of his own son. Do you know anyone who has allowed the greed of the world to overcome them in this way? How do you handle being around such people?

8. Sam and Ethan were an unlikely match—seemingly polar opposites. But what did Sam and Ethan have in common?

9. Sam was willing to put her very life on the line in a dangerous attempt to meet her goals. Have you ever been so passionate about something that you risked your life to succeed? How did the situation turn out? Would you do it again?

10. Sam's best friend, Kate, was a stable force in Sam's chaotic life. What friends have you had over the years that were there for you in a crisis?

11. In the story, Sam rode a mechanical bull at the town fair. Have you ever ridden a mechanical bull? What was your experience like?

12. Sam is very comfortable around horses, having spent her entire life on them and around them. Do you enjoy horseback riding? When was the first time you ever rode a horse?

13. Ethan was willing to put the comfort of his wealthy lifestyle aside when he fell in love with Sam. Have you ever had to change careers or lifestyles in order to be with your spouse or significant other?

14. When Ethan revealed his father's plans for the Jenson ranch, Sam knew she had misinterpreted Ethan's intentions. Have you ever been in a misunderstanding with someone that hurt you, only to find out you had misunderstood them? How did you get past the hurt?

15. When Sam rides in the rodeo at the end, she tosses her hat in a tribute to her father. Have you ever made a public gesture in honor of a loved one in your life? Tell us about it.

WE HOPE YOU ENJOYED THESE TWO LOVE INSPIRED® BOOKS.

If you were **inspired** by these **uplifting**, **heartwarming** romances, be sure to look for all six Love Inspired® books every month.

Love Inspired ®

Save $1.00

on the purchase of any
Love Inspired® book.

Available wherever books are sold, including
most bookstores, supermarkets, drugstores
and discount stores.

Save $1.00

on the purchase of any Love Inspired® book.

Coupon valid until July 31, 2018.
Redeemable at participating retail outlets in the U.S. and Canada only.
Limit one coupon per customer.

Canadian Retailers: Harlequin Enterprises Limited will pay the face value of this coupon plus 10.25¢ if submitted by customer for this product only. Any other use constitutes fraud. Coupon is nonassignable. Void if taxed, prohibited or restricted by law. Consumer must pay any government taxes. Void if copied. Inmar Promotional Services ("IPS") customers submit coupons and proof of sales to Harlequin Enterprises Limited, PO Box 31000, Scarborough, ON M1R 0E7, Canada. Non-IPS retailer—for reimbursement submit coupons and proof of sales directly to Harlequin Enterprises Limited, Retail Marketing Department, 225 Duncan Mill Rd., Don Mills, ON M3B 3K9, Canada.

U.S. Retailers: Harlequin Enterprises Limited will pay the face value of this coupon plus 8¢ if submitted by customer for this product only. Any other use constitutes fraud. Coupon is nonassignable. Void if taxed, prohibited or restricted by law. Consumer must pay any government taxes. Void if copied. For reimbursement submit coupons and proof of sales directly to Harlequin Enterprises, Ltd 482, NCH Marketing Services, P.O. Box 880001, El Paso, TX 88588-0001, U.S.A. Cash value 1/100 cents.

52615199

5 65373 00076 2 (8100)0 12313

® and ™ are trademarks owned and used by the trademark owner and/or its licensee.

© 2018 Harlequin Enterprises Limited

LICOUP0318

HARLEQUIN®

Save $1.00

on the purchase of any

Harlequin® series book.

Available wherever books are sold, including
most bookstores, supermarkets, drugstores
and discount stores.

Save $1.00

on the purchase of any Harlequin® series book.

Coupon valid until July 31, 2018.
Redeemable at participating retail outlets in the U.S. and Canada only.
Limit one coupon per customer.

52615203

Canadian Retailers: Harlequin Enterprises Limited will pay the face value of this coupon plus 10.25¢ if submitted by customer for this product only. Any other use constitutes fraud. Coupon is nonassignable. Void if taxed, prohibited or restricted by law. Consumer must pay any government taxes. Void if copied. Inmar Promotional Services ("IPS") customers submit coupons and proof of sales to Harlequin Enterprises Limited, PO Box 31000, Scarborough, ON M1R 0E7, Canada. Non-IPS retailer—for reimbursement submit coupons and proof of sales directly to Harlequin Enterprises Limited, Retail Marketing Department, 225 Duncan Mill Rd., Don Mills, ON M3B 3K9, Canada.

U.S. Retailers: Harlequin Enterprises Limited will pay the face value of this coupon plus 8¢ if submitted by customer for this product only. Any other use constitutes fraud. Coupon is nonassignable. Void if taxed, prohibited or restricted by law. Consumer must pay any government taxes. Void if copied. For reimbursement submit coupons and proof of sales directly to Harlequin Enterprises, Ltd 482, NCH Marketing Services, P.O. Box 880001, El Paso, TX 88588-0001, U.S.A. Cash value 1/100 cents.

5 65373 00076 2   (8100)0 12314

® and ™ are trademarks owned and used by the trademark owner and/or its licensee.

© 2018 Harlequin Enterprises Limited

HSCOUP0318

Get 2 Free Books,
Plus 2 Free Gifts —
just for trying the Reader Service!

YES! Please send me 2 FREE Love Inspired® Romance novels and my 2 FREE mystery gifts (gifts are worth about $10 retail). After receiving them, if I don't wish to receive any more books, I can return the shipping statement marked "cancel." If I don't cancel, I will receive 6 brand-new novels every month and be billed just $5.24 for the regular-print edition or $5.74 each for the larger-print edition in the U.S., or $5.74 each for the regular-print edition or $6.24 each for the larger-print edition in Canada. That's a saving of at least 13% off the cover price. It's quite a bargain! Shipping and handling is just 50¢ per book in the U.S. and 75¢ per book in Canada.* I understand that accepting the 2 free books and gifts places me under no obligation to buy anything. I can always return a shipment and cancel at any time. The free books and gifts are mine to keep no matter what I decide.

Please check one:

☐ Love Inspired Romance Regular-Print
(105/305 IDN GLWW)

☐ Love Inspired Romance Larger-Print
(122/322 IDN GLWW)

Name   (PLEASE PRINT)

Address   Apt. #

City   State/Province   Zip/Postal Code

Signature (if under 18, a parent or guardian must sign)

Mail to the **Reader Service:**
IN U.S.A.: P.O. Box 1341, Buffalo, NY 14240-8531
IN CANADA: P.O. Box 603, Fort Erie, Ontario L2A 5X3

Want to try two free books from another line?
Call 1-800-873-8635 today or visit www.ReaderService.com.

*Terms and prices subject to change without notice. Prices do not include applicable taxes. Sales tax applicable in N.Y. Canadian residents will be charged applicable taxes. Offer not valid in Quebec. This offer is limited to one order per household. Books received may not be as shown. Not valid for current subscribers to Love Inspired Romance books. All orders subject to approval. Credit or debit balances in a customer's account(s) may be offset by any other outstanding balance owed by or to the customer. Please allow 4 to 6 weeks for delivery. Offer available while quantities last.

Your Privacy—The Reader Service is committed to protecting your privacy. Our Privacy Policy is available online at www.ReaderService.com or upon request from the Reader Service.

We make a portion of our mailing list available to reputable third parties that offer products we believe may interest you. If you prefer that we not exchange your name with third parties, or if you wish to clarify or modify your communication preferences, please visit us at www.ReaderService.com/consumerschoice or write to us at Reader Service Preference Service, P.O. Box 9062, Buffalo, NY 14240-9062. Include your complete name and address.

LI17R2

Love Inspired®

Inspirational Romance to Warm Your Heart and Soul

Join our social communities to connect with other readers who share your love!

Sign up for the Love Inspired newsletter at **www.LoveInspired.com** to be the first to find out about upcoming titles, special promotions and exclusive content.

CONNECT WITH US AT:

Harlequin.com/Community

 Facebook.com/LoveInspiredBooks

Twitter.com/LoveInspiredBks

LISOCIAL2017

LOVE
Harlequin
romance?

Join our Harlequin community to share your thoughts and connect with other romance readers!

Be the first to find out about promotions, news, and exclusive content!

Sign up for the Harlequin e-newsletter and download a free book from any series at

www.TryHarlequin.com

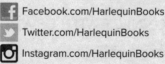
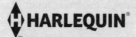